A
Mersey Duet

Anne Baker trained as a nurse at Birkenhead General Hospital, but after her marriage went to live in Libya and then in Nigeria. She eventually returned to her native Birkenhead where she worked as a Health Visitor for over ten years. She now lives with her husband on a ninety-acre sheep farm in North Wales. Her previous novels, *Like Father, Like Daughter, Paradise Parade, Legacy of Sins, Nobody's Child, Merseyside Girls* and *Moonlight on the Mersey*, are also available from Headline.

A
Mersey Duet

Anne Baker

HEADLINE

First published in 1996
by HEADLINE BOOK PUBLISHING

First published in paperback in 1997
by HEADLINE BOOK PUBLISHING

12

ISBN 0 7472 5320 X

Typeset at The Spartan Press Ltd,
Lymington, Hants
Printed in England by Clays Ltd, St Ives plc

HEADLINE BOOK PUBLISHING
A division of Hodder Headline PLC
338 Euston Road
London NW1 3BH

Book One
1912–1925

CHAPTER ONE

Christmas Eve 1912

'Time, gentlemen, please.'

Cassie Gripper, proprietor of the Railway Hotel, had to shout to make herself heard above the strains of 'Good King Wenceslas' coming from the public bar. It felt like Christmas now, the holly leaves she'd laid along the shelves adding to the festive atmosphere.

'Time, gentlemen.'

She pushed her thick brown fringe back from her forehead, feeling hot and excited. Many of her customers had already finished work. Everybody was in high good humour, but she had to bring this hectic lunchtime session to an end.

Reluctantly empty glasses were being put down. 'Merry Christmas,' customers were shouting as they moved towards the door. 'Happy Yuletide.'

One old man patted her arm on his way to the door. 'A grandmother at last, eh? That'll please you, missus.' The place was emptying now.

'What did John have? A son to carry on here?'

Cassie laughed. 'I'll be carrying on here. Got plenty of years in me yet.'

'Course you have, missus.'

'It was a girl, six and a half pounds.'

'We'll be back to wet the baby's head. Haven't done her justice yet.'

'You don't look old enough to be a grandmother.'

Cassie grimaced. Fifty was more than old enough, and she was afraid she looked every day of it. It was all the late nights she'd had.

'You're in your prime, lass. Merry Christmas to you.'

She managed to close the front door at last. The Railway Hotel served the small cluster of streets huddling between Birkenhead's main railway lines. There were plenty of thirsty throats because nearby were several big industrial concerns caught between the tracks too.

Usually Cassie was tired by this time of day and in need of a hot dinner. She made casseroles with jacket potatoes, food that would cook without supervision. Then she and the boys would rest before they had to open again at six.

But not today, though the bar had been filled to bursting and they'd been short-handed without John. She was delaying dinner for another hour or so. The boys wouldn't mind nibbling on what they could find until then.

John, her eldest son, had come to work this morning saying that his wife was in labour and the midwife had pushed him out. Later, one of his neighbours had popped in with a message that Elsa had given birth to a baby girl. She'd sent John home, he hadn't been doing much anyway. Just smiling round at everybody from up in some seventh heaven.

Cassie felt she'd roller-coasted through the rest of the session with the other two. She'd made up her mind that this was going to be the best Christmas ever, because the pub would be closing down after Boxing Day until New Year's Eve. The brewery was coming in to redecorate and give the place a face-lift. It would be a rare break for them all. Cassie had been looking forward to this holiday for months. The boys too.

Bernard, her third and youngest son, was planning to take advantage of it by getting married. It meant he could take a honeymoon trip to London. Cassie thought he was too young at nineteen to be even thinking of marriage, but there was no talking him out of it.

'Vereena's old enough,' he'd smiled. 'And I don't want her to get tired of waiting for me.'

'You've only known her a few months!'

The bride-to-be was a school teacher, which had impressed them all, but like all women in the professions, she'd be forced to give it up on marriage. Cassie wasn't sure what to make of her.

'Cash up for me, Bernie,' she called now. 'I'm going round to our John's. Can't wait to see the new arrival.'

It was a happy coincidence that John's wife had had her baby today. It was a few weeks early.

Paul, her middle son, was already putting his coat on. 'I'm going down to the market, Mam, to get a turkey for tomorrow.'

'About twelve pounds if you can. No more than fifteen or I won't get it in the oven.'

They were good-looking boys, all of them. Light-brown hair like their father's, well set up and strong. But of the three, Bernie had the handsomest hazel eyes and the most engaging smile.

Cassie gathered up her long skirts and ran upstairs. Her brown hair was working loose from her bun, but she hadn't time to redo it now. She combed her fringe, then tucked in a few stray ends, pleased to see hardly any grey visible, before skewering her hatpins through her big feathered hat.

As she flicked a powder puff over her nose, she could see her brown eyes dancing with excitement in the mirror. Her cheeks needed no rouge today. As she reddened her lips, they kept breaking into smiles. A little paint was expected of ladies in her position.

She snatched up the gifts she'd wrapped yesterday. A nightshift in white wool flannel for Elsa, all frills and furbelows. She'd sewn it herself, as well as the two nightgowns for the baby. She'd managed to cut a few binders, too, from the left-over bits of cloth. For John, she'd bought cigarettes. Then there were the curtains she'd made for their scullery, because as yet they hadn't got round to fixing the house up properly.

Cassie walked briskly down the street, looking forward to seeing her daughter-in-law, shy Elsa Ingram, holding her first-born. She didn't look strong enough for child-bearing but she'd managed it, and quickly too. Couldn't wait to see her new granddaughter. She felt on top of the world, though it was one of those dark, dull days that looked as though it wouldn't reach full daylight.

Right outside the little house John had rented, close against the gas works in Elizabeth Place, two bicycles were propped up by their pedals against the pavement. One would belong to the midwife; it had a guard made of strings over the back wheel to prevent her skirts being caught in it. As she knocked on the door, she wondered who owned the other. There was a large carrier in front, but it was too smart to belong to a tradesman.

John was taking his time coming to the door. At last it opened six inches.

'Yes?' The midwife, her face tight with tension, stared at her suspiciously. Cassie felt deflated. She'd expected to see John's face, wreathed with smiles.

'Can I come in?' She was pressing against the door, juggling with her parcels.

'Well, it's not . . .'

Cassie felt a trickle of unease. 'Is something the matter? I'm the new grandmother.'

Grudgingly, then, the door opened wide enough for her to step inside.

'I'm Sister Jones.' Her plump face was kindly. She looked young and efficient. 'It was twins.' Her voice was flat.

Cassie drew in a sharp breath. This was the first time

there'd been any mention of twins, though she knew they ran in Elsa's family.

'The second baby? It's all right?' She was very much afraid it was not.

'Yes, another girl. Just over five pounds. Not so big as the first, but she's doing fine.'

Cassie stood stock still. 'It's Elsa then?'

'You'd better wait here.' They were in the tiny living room. The bedroom above was reached by the stairs in the corner.

'I'll tell them you've come. The doctor's here. I had to send for him.'

Cassie's heart was thumping as she perched on the edge of a chair and listened to the low voices and the creak of the floorboards overhead.

After an ominous few minutes John came down. A very changed John since he'd left the pub. His straight brown hair was standing up from his forehead, his grey eyes were dazed and clouded with tears.

'Oh, Mam!' He came straight into her arms, seeking the comfort she'd given him as a child. He was clinging to her, and she could feel his body shaking with anguished sobs.

'What's happening, love?' Cassie felt sick with horror. She hadn't seen John cry since he was nine years old. 'Elsa's had a bad time with the second twin?'

He sniffed. 'She's bleeding terribly. They can't stop it.'

'They will,' Cassie soothed.

'No, Mam, you don't understand. Elsa's fading . . .'

'Fading? You don't mean . . .?' She knew from John's shocked face that he did. She was stunned. 'That's terrible!'

'I'm going back . . . Can't leave her.'

Cassie sank back against the chair, her mouth dry. It was all so sudden, she couldn't believe it. Elsa was so young. There must be some mistake, some hope.

Outside in the street there were carol singers. She could hear the faint strains of 'Away in a Manger'.

She couldn't sit and listen to that. It was choking her. She went out to the scullery and put the kettle on to make tea.

Moments later there was another knock on the front door. Cassie went to answer it, ready to get rid of callers. It was the last thing they needed now.

But it was Elsa's parents, Harold and Mildred Ingram, who owned the shop opposite the pub. Mildred took off her hat as soon as the door closed behind her. Her hair was losing its colour, no longer fair nor yet grey. She wore it twisted into prim earphones. Her eyes were red and tear-stained behind her glasses. Cassie knew she wouldn't have to tell them the terrible news.

Harold patted her on the shoulder. Mildred clasped her in a silent hug. It wasn't what they usually did.

Cassie believed they considered themselves to be a bit above her. She thought of Harold as an ambitious man. Mildred owned a fur tippet and bragged about dealing in antiques, though most of their stock was household junk. They felt that what they did was socially superior to running the pub.

But they were neighbours as well as in-laws, and this was a trouble shared. In the streets between the railway lines, neighbours supported each other when there was trouble.

'How is she? John sent a message.'

Cassie shook her head. She had a reputation for being outspoken, even forthright, but she couldn't bring herself to talk of Elsa now. From the bottom of the stairs, she called up to John, announcing their arrival.

'You'd better come up,' he answered. Their footsteps echoed through the thin drugget on the stairs. Cassie followed on tiptoe. She heard Mildred's sudden intake of breath. Seeing Elsa brought home to her just how bad she was.

The foot of the double bed had been raised on two chairs. Elsa lay without pillows, flat and lifeless. Her face was putty-white, her flyaway blonde curls were darkened with sweat. She hardly seemed to be breathing. John slid back on to the chair beside her bed and took her hand in his.

The doctor, a serious expression on his middle-aged face, moved so that Mildred could sit stiffly on the other side, gripping the bed itself.

'Elsa,' John whispered. 'Your mam's here to see you.'

Her eyelids fluttered up for a moment and her sunken eyes looked into her husband's. She managed a half-smile for him. Then she moaned and her eyes closed again.

'Elsa.' Her mother reached across the bed for her other hand. 'We've come to see your babies.'

There was no response this time. Mildred was trying again, a note of desperation in her voice. 'Elsa?'

'She's losing consciousness,' the doctor murmured.

Cassie was appalled, horrified that this could happen so swiftly.

John Gripper couldn't believe that the still figure on the bed was Elsa. Yesterday she'd been wrapping gifts.

He'd come home from the pub today in high spirits. He knew the baby had been born. He'd expected to find Elsa sitting up nursing her, relaxed and smiling now her ordeal was over. Instead, a fraught midwife had sent him running to fetch the doctor, with a message to come as soon as he could. He was needed urgently.

Nothing as bad as this had happened to him in all his twenty-seven years. It was a nightmare. Sister Jones had tried to keep him away from his wife.

'Better if you wait downstairs,' she'd said. 'Where you won't be in the way.'

But he wasn't having that. He had to be with Elsa. He'd told them he was staying, and that was that.

John had never seen so much blood. It was everywhere. The raw scent of it caught in his throat. Sister Jones was using a bowl to scoop it from the mattress to a jug. That brought home to him just how dangerous this was for Elsa. There surely couldn't be much left in her veins.

He'd lit a fire in the bedroom grate this morning, and the small room was stiflingly hot. He watched the doctor and the midwife take turns to rub Elsa's abdomen. He could feel their tension like a solid wall. He sensed they were struggling with growing panic that they wouldn't be able to stop the bleeding. A pool was collecting again around Elsa's thighs.

'You've got to save her,' he told them.

'We're doing our best.'

It was a long time before they let him close enough to hold her hand.

'How do you feel, Elsa love?' he whispered.

From far away, her voice came. 'I don't know.'

It couldn't be happening, not here in their own bedroom where he'd always felt so safe. Not with Elsa's navy serge dress over the back of a chair with her favourite brooch, a blue butterfly wing set in silver, still spearing the collar.

They were all round her bed, his mother and Elsa's parents. It felt unreal, he was quite detached from them. Elsa was sinking fast now, even he could see that.

'Help her!' he shouted at the doctor, when he realised they'd given up working on Elsa. 'You've got to help her.'

'She's very peaceful,' the doctor answered from the foot of the bed. John wanted to rail at him. He wanted to see Elsa her old happy self, not at peace like this. He felt despair. What would he do without her? All he'd ever wanted, all his plans for the future, were bound up with her.

'Don't go,' he implored her. She gave no sign that she heard. 'Don't leave me, Elsa.'

Impossible now to see whether she was breathing or not. He thought not, but then she gave a gentle sigh.

'Is that it?' He felt bewildered.

The doctor was listening for a heartbeat, feeling her pulse. 'I'm sorry,' he said.

It had come so heartbreakingly quickly. John was shattered. He knew Mildred was crying too.

Sister Jones moved closer and pulled the sheet up over Elsa's face. 'She's gone to heaven now,' she told him gently.

John snatched it back. 'She doesn't want to go to heaven. She wants to stay here with me and the babies.' He was angry with them. They hadn't done enough to save her.

He knew that his mother's arms were trying to draw him downstairs, away from Elsa. He couldn't leave her, not yet. He insisted on staying where he was for a little longer, nursing her hand between both of his.

Cassie couldn't watch any more. She rushed down to make tea for them all and found the scullery filled with steam. She'd forgotten she'd put the kettle on earlier. She was setting out cups and saucers, when she found the midwife behind her.

'How much milk is there in the house? These babies will have to be fed.'

They could find only the jugful Cassie had put out for the tea.

'Can you run round to the dairy right away? Before it closes? It's Christmas . . .'

Cassie paused for a moment appalled. These babies would have to be artificially fed, and who was going to take care of them? John would never be able to manage.

Sister said: 'I've got some teats and feeding bottles at home. I'll fetch them and show you how to make up the feeds. I won't be long.'

11

Cassie found two large jugs in a cupboard, rinsed them with boiled water as the midwife had advised and set off down the street at a brisk trot. The dairy was on the point of closing but two pints were found for her. If they needed more before it reopened after the holiday, the girl told her it would be available from the farm in Rock Ferry.

Feeling hot and harassed, she returned in time to see the doctor pedalling away on his bicycle. She found a shocked and emotionally charged group crowding the tiny living room. The tea had gone cold, but she drank it thirstily.

'A terrible tragedy,' Harold Ingram kept saying. Cassie knew he'd been very fond of his only daughter. Elsa had been just twenty years old. 'Poor girl, she saw nothing of life.'

'Only ten months married,' Mildred mourned. 'If only the babies hadn't come so quickly.' She was looking at John's bent head, as though blaming him for that. 'Before even one year of marriage was out.'

After that, they didn't know what to say to each other. They sipped their tea in silence.

Sister Jones had come back. She'd shown them how to scald the bottles and make up feeds by diluting the milk and adding sugar. Two patent baby feeding bottles, complete with rubber teats, were ready and waiting. She'd gone upstairs to check on the babies again. Now, in the back bedroom, one baby was whimpering intermittently.

Cassie said awkwardly: 'Ought we to go up and see to them? Or will she?'

There was a sudden full-blown cry of hunger from the other twin. She said more firmly: 'Sister isn't going to stay for ever. I think I'd better go up.'

Mildred jerked from her chair. 'I'll see to one.' She shot upstairs ahead of Cassie and went through to the back bedroom.

Until now, Cassie hadn't even been in this room. Yet when she'd knocked on the front door, the only thought in her head had been to see the baby. That seemed years ago, but in reality it was a scant few hours.

Sister Jones had just finished changing one of them. 'She's lovely,' she told them, and put her in Mildred's arms.

The other twin was wailing for attention. Cassie went over to the old-fashioned cot. The babies had been lying top and tail, it was plenty big enough. All her sons had slept in it in their turn. John had gone up to the pub's attic to fetch it and Elsa had been delighted to have it.

'This is the first-born.' The midwife was beside her, lifting the infant out. 'She's quite a lot bigger. A bonnier baby all round. They're not identical twins.'

Cassie held out her arms for the baby. She stroked a soft cheek with her finger. Round blue eyes stared up at her. She was enthralled with her grandchild. It almost hurt to see the perfection of the tiny fingers and the soft blonde down covering her head.

Maternal love was tugging at her heart. She turned to Mildred. 'Isn't she absolutely beautiful?'

Mildred was staring down at the baby she was holding, her eyes hard and cold. She was choking on the words: 'Is this the twin nobody knew about?'

'Not until she made her presence known.' The midwife was defensive. 'She was born two hours after the other.'

'How can that happen? That nobody knew about her?' Cassie wanted to know.

'It was the way they were lying, one behind the other. I could hear only one heartbeat. The doctor too. It happens sometimes. Undiagnosed twins.'

Mildred was stiffening. 'And that's why our poor Elsa . . .?'

'No!'

'It cost our Elsa her life.'

13

'It wasn't the baby's fault. Your daughter had a bad bleed. It was nobody's fault.' The midwife's voile cap crackled with starch. 'We couldn't stop it. That was the problem.'

Mildred dropped the infant back at the bottom of the cot, a look of distaste on her face.

'Let me see that one.' She was taking the infant from Cassie's arms before she realised what was happening.

'This one's more like our Elsa.' Mildred looked up with a wan smile. 'Just like she was at this age. The spitting image.'

Cassie picked up the other twin and felt a rush of pity. Mildred was trying to blame this tiny child for her mother's death. She was a skinny baby, over-red and with a thin, wizened face which she was screwing up to cry. Not nearly so pretty as the first-born.

'Take them downstairs and feed them,' the nurse suggested. 'It might comfort the father to see them.'

Cassie was filled with foreboding as she followed Mildred down to the living room. How was John going to look after these babies and earn a living for them? Two would have been a heavy burden for Elsa, even though she'd been young and had a husband to support her.

The tragedy had given him an insoluble problem. It wasn't as if she could help much, with the pub to run. The future that had seemed so rosy earlier in the day now looked bleak. John was slumped in a chair, the picture of misery.

'I don't know how our John's going to manage,' she said to Mildred in the scullery as they collected the feeding bottles.

'Well, of course I'll help.' Mildred was nursing the first twin as though she'd never give her up. Back in the living room she lowered herself on to a chair, hugging the baby closer.

'We'd like to take one and bring her up, wouldn't we, Harold?'

'Well . . . Yes, I suppose we could.'

'She'll take Elsa's place. Well, of course no baby could do that, but you know what I mean.'

Cassie's mind was a riot of emotions as she watched Mildred tentatively push the teat into the infant's mouth. The child latched on to it and was sucking hard within seconds. Mildred looked up and smiled with satisfaction.

'What do you say, John?'

He looked round at them numbly, without speaking.

'It's the only way you'll cope,' Mildred added. He still didn't answer.

'Leave it for now, Mildred, you're rushing things,' Harold advised. His wife started on another tack.

'Elsa told me that if she had a girl, you'd decided to call her Lucy.'

John nodded.

'A fine name. Lucinda on the birth certificate, of course. Elsa Lucinda, I think. To be known as Lucy.' Lucy was still sucking vigorously. 'What will you call the other?'

John pushed his hair back from his forehead. 'I don't know.'

Cassie could see that she'd have to help John with this tiny twin. Long ago, she'd chosen the name Patricia for her own child, but sons were what she'd had. She'd like to name this infant Patricia, Pat for every day, but now was not the moment to say anything. John mustn't be faced with any decisions just yet.

Mildred said: 'Please, John, let me have this one to bring up. You'll be able to pop in and see her just as often as you want. It's only over the road.'

Cassie's spirits sank even further. 'John can't think straight right now,' she said. 'His mind isn't working as it should. Give him time to think it over.'

The twin she held didn't seem to know what sucking was. The milk in her bottle was hardly going down at all. Cassie felt inept at bottle-feeding.

As she saw it, John had no choice about giving up Lucy to the Ingrams. He wouldn't survive if he tried to stay here with both babies. He should count himself lucky that Lucy was going to her mother's old home, where she'd be loved and well cared for.

Neither did he have any choice about giving up this house. Much too early to talk about that, too, but she'd get him to come back home to the pub, it was the only way they'd be able to manage. Together, as a family, they could cope with one baby. Somehow they'd do it.

Trust Mildred to take the baby that would be the least trouble. The little mite in her arms was snuffling and pushing the teat out of her mouth. She was going to need more patience. Cassie hoped that she and John would have it.

CHAPTER TWO

The lamplighter had already lit the streetlights when Cassie walked the short distance home to the Railway Hotel in Cambridge Place.

A little way to the east were the multiple lines of the main-line railway companies, bringing passengers and goods into Birkenhead Woodside. Two hundred yards south of the pub, the Mersey Railway line branched away from the others to run into Central Station. It then went underground and under the Mersey to Liverpool.

Caught in this triangle between the rail tracks were a few streets of houses and all manner of industrial buildings. The biggest concern was the gasworks, with its brightly lit offices, tall chimneys and great black tanks. The air was sulphurous with its smell.

The railways had their workshops here, and their turntables and engine and carriage sheds. All had been built during Victoria's reign, and were blackened with soot and smuts from the great steam engines that raced past. Lights were kept burning all night here; shunting never stopped, nor did the roar from the furnace at the gasworks.

Cassie had to tell her other two sons what had happened to Elsa. She watched their festive smiles fade and knew that the last thing they were going to have now was a good Christmas.

'Bernie, please put your wedding off for a few months,' she pleaded. It had been arranged for the day after Boxing Day. 'We're none of us in the mood for it now.'

17

She had given her permission for the marriage very reluctantly, and only after a lot of cajoling from him. She hoped that if it could be postponed for a while, he would get over his infatuation and it would be permanently off.

Freda Tarrant, the bride's mother, didn't think much of the match either and proved to be an unexpected source of support. She'd been a widow for many years and ran a boarding house to support herself and her daughter. Cassie was surprised to find that she enjoyed her company. They seemed to have a lot in common, apart from their intractable children.

Bernie and Vereena insisted on going ahead with their plans. Many of their wedding guests came straight from Elsa's funeral. Cassie found it a joyless occasion.

John was locked in terrible grief and having the pub closed only gave him more time to think. The one good thing about it was that they had time to get used to the new baby.

It was a long time since she'd handled any baby, and Cassie hardly knew where to begin. It took up so much of her time and energy she didn't know how she'd be able to run the pub as well.

The following weeks were drab. When it came to giving up the house, John said: 'Everything about the place reminds me of Elsa. The baby and me – we'll be better off at the pub. Easier to cope.'

Cassie patted his arm. 'I wouldn't want you to be on your own. No life at all for you.'

Now that Bernie was married and had moved out, it meant that John could have a room to himself. He brought the old cot home again and Cassie had it put up in her room. She reckoned she could cope better with the wakeful nights than John could.

She found it very hard to start with, and while she struggled to get Patsy to feed, Mildred reported that Lucy ate and slept well and was very little trouble.

John did his share of feeding and nappy-changing, and all three of the boys would take Patsy out in their old pram if she sent them on errands to the shops.

Eventually, Patsy settled into a routine and started to gain weight. The biggest problem then was that they had to leave her alone upstairs during opening hours. When her own boys were small, Cassie had had a girl living in to help. Cassie usually served in the private bar, which was directly under her bedroom, and she left all the doors open so that she would hear Patsy if she cried.

If there were four of them serving, usually she or John could be spared to see to the child. And even if there were only three on, and were busy, there was usually some woman she knew sitting in the bar who was willing to take her port and lemon upstairs to give the babe a bottle.

The boys had to run the public bar, which was usually busier than the private, and serve at the jug and bottle as well – the hatch where children knocked when they were sent to buy beer for their fathers.

When Patsy caught croup and was ill, Vereena's mother and the neighbours in Cambridge Place rallied round to help. Alice Smedley, the lamplighter's wife next door, Sara Donovan, wife of the general grocer on the corner, and Freda Tarrant took turns to sit with her in the evenings.

Next to the pub on the other side was a newspaper shop. The owners were the only people in the street to stay aloof. From them, Cassie felt the chill of enmity. If Orlando Parry could make trouble for her, he would.

He complained both to her and to the police about the bad behaviour of her customers; about their loud singing, bad language and general rowdiness, and about the children hanging about outside at night.

At closing time, she had to get everybody out promptly. She knew that if she gave him the slightest chance, he'd report her for being open after hours. She had nothing to

19

thank Orlando Parry for, and even less reason to think well of his wife. A long time ago, Gladys had been employed as a barmaid at the Railway Hotel.

Cassie tried to stop her mind sliding back through the years. It still brought a stab of hurt. Paul had been four years old and a real handful; John had been eight. She'd been pregnant with Bernie, in the final weeks. She was feeling exhausted by the late nights and the long hours she spent standing behind the bar.

She'd managed to work right to the end of her pregnancy with the older two, but now, suddenly, she decided she'd have to get a barmaid to stand in for her for a few weeks.

Cassie had had her name over the pub door from the beginning, though after she'd married, Alfred, her husband, had done much of the work. They'd run the pub between them apart from a woman who cleaned and a barman who came in on Friday and Saturday nights. In those days there was work for all who wanted it and getting a reliable barmaid on the spur of the moment wasn't easy.

Alfred had taken Gladys on while Cassie had been upstairs resting. As soon as she'd set eyes on her, she'd known Gladys was quite the wrong type; straight off a Welsh farm, too young and too naïve for the job. Gladys had been a pretty girl in those days, buxom and fresh-faced. She should have known she'd caught Alfie's eye, but she'd trusted him when she shouldn't have.

Alfred had been like Bernie was now. A handsome, well-set-up fellow, with a smile that could light up the bar. The sort ladies went for. That was why she'd always served in the private bar herself. Not many women drank in the public, only drunken sluts who were not likely to attract him.

Cassie knew she'd handled the whole thing badly. It wasn't as though she hadn't had her suspicions for some time. After closing time, there was no mistaking the sounds that drifted up from the private bar; Gladys's giggles, the scuffling, Alfred's hearty laugh. Then there was the length of time it took them to cash up and lock up for the night, as well as Alfred's over-innocent manner and a sudden reduction in his demands for what he called his bit of slap and tickle.

Bernie had been five days old. They'd both slept through the early hours of the night. Closing time often brought noisy farewells, banging doors and the rasp of iron-heeled boots on the pavement. It had woken them both.

Still drowsy, she'd taken Bernie into her bed to give him a feed. She'd heard the rattle of coins as Alfred cashed up. She knew Gladys would be drying the tankards and glasses, putting them away, wiping down the bars. They were talking and laughing together.

At last Bernie was satiated with milk. He was in his cot settling back to sleep. The pub had now been closed for some time, and Cassie expected every moment that Alfie would come up to bed. There was no point in her going to sleep until he did, because he'd only wake her again.

The talking downstairs had stopped but she could hear an occasional scuffle. She knew that Gladys was still there.

She couldn't pretend she wasn't suspicious about what they were doing all this time. It was the half-suppressed grunting that made her get out of bed again and creep downstairs. The gaslights in the pub had been turned off but there was a glow from the streetlamps outside.

Really she'd known exactly what they were doing, she just didn't want to believe it. She loved Alfie and trusted him. She'd just been delivered of his child.

She felt sickened and betrayed as she watched Gladys pulling down and straightening her skirts. Cassie had turned to the night's takings on the bar and paid her off there and then.

'Don't ever come in here again,' were the only words she spoke to her.

Alfie was hopping about trying to get his trousers on. 'Don't bother making yourself decent for me,' she'd told him. 'You won't be coming to my bed tonight.'

She'd felt the sharp sting of tears and rushed back upstairs before they saw them washing down her face. Childbirth was an emotional time for her, even when things were going well.

She'd turned the key in her bedroom door and pulled the blankets over her ears by the time Alfie had come up and was pleading to be let in. He'd had to lift Paul into his brother's bed and sleep there, not only for that night but for several weeks afterwards. Cassie had got over it eventually, she'd had to. For Catholic women like her, even lapsed ones, marriage was for life, but she'd never felt quite the same about her husband after that.

Gladys Jones had never been able to bring herself to look Cassie in the face again. Cassie wished she hadn't been able to bring herself to marry Orlando Parry and move in next door either. By that time, Alfie had been ill with TB. She'd nursed him in the back bedroom for over a year, done the best she could for him, but he'd died at the age of thirty-six.

Taking care of Patsy became harder as she grew older, because she was sleeping less and less during the day. John had to ask Bernie's wife to keep an eye on the child then, and Vereena, being what she was, had to be paid for it. When Mildred Ingram heard that, she offered to have Patsy over to play with Lucy for three morning sessions a week.

'She can have dinner with us too,' she said. 'Only right the girls should see more of each other. They are twins, after all.'

There was much more to-ing and fro-ing across the road between the junk shop and the pub. But Cassie could feel rivalry growing between her and Mildred. Each loved the child they cared for and felt she was making better progress than her twin.

'Lucy's cut her first tooth,' Mildred reported proudly, knowing that Patsy's gums were still bare. Lucy was stronger, she crawled and walked first too. 'They don't seem like twins at all.'

'She started with the stronger child,' Cassie told John indignantly when she was back in the rooms over the Railway Hotel. 'Lucy ought to be doing better. Something the matter if she weren't.'

Cassie was very conscious that there was another reason why they didn't appear to be twins. She ran up little dresses for Patsy on her sewing machine, buying remnants of cloth in the market. She'd always enjoyed sewing. Lucy was always beautifully turned out. Mildred went over to Liverpool and bought her clothes from the big shops.

'She pays for dressing,' Mildred smiled. By that, she meant that Lucy's good looks were enhanced by the lovely clothes she was able to buy her. Lucy was the prettier of the two anyway, and was sturdy and bonny, while Patsy remained fragile and skinny.

Cassie felt better when she was able to say to Mildred: 'I think our Patsy's quicker with words. She's going to talk first.'

Whenever she sat down, the child would climb up on her knee and throw her arms round her grandmother's neck. She did the same with her father, too.

'Patsy's a more loving child,' Cassie beamed at John. 'I wouldn't swap her for anyone now.'

'Ah well,' he replied awkwardly. 'We see more of her, don't we?'

The twins were almost two when the Great War started. Recruiting campaigns started too. Posters were appearing all over town telling young men that England needed them. Cassie was scared when she heard that men were joining up in droves.

'I can't run this place on my own,' she told her sons. 'At least one of you will have to stay and help me.' They decided between them that it should be John, though Vereena didn't want Bernie to go either.

Paul went off straight away to fight for his country and was killed at Ypres the following year. Cassie felt terrible about that. He'd been dead for two weeks by the time she was notified and that made it even harder for her to bear. She couldn't stop herself thinking of his strong young limbs lying twisted and broken in the mud. It was such a brutal waste of a young life. She'd had high hopes of what Paul might achieve. He'd been the most able of her three sons.

His name was published in the lists of those killed in action, and that meant many of her customers offered their sympathy. It was months before she could stop her eyes flooding with tears at any mention of his name.

Vereena persuaded Bernie to stay home for a time, but appeals to young men to join up continued, and white feathers were sent to those who did not. Eventually, Bernie went. They'd all been very fearful for his safety.

Cassie hadn't foreseen the shortages that war would bring. Often the pub sold out of beer and she was able to close early. It made running it easier, though less profitable. When the armistice was signed at Versailles and the war was over, Cassie counted herself lucky to have lost only one son. She knew many families who had lost them all. Bernie told her that signing up was the worst decision he'd ever made, but at least he'd survived to tell the tale.

He and Vereena found a house to rent in Thomas Street, which was nearby and still within the triangle of streets between the railway tracks. Cassie thought it a friendly district, and when Bernie came back to work at the Railway Hotel, she was confident that life would settle back to normal.

24

The twins were growing up, and she had her circle of friends. She particularly enjoyed the nights when Sara Donovan from the corner grocery shop came into the private for a drink and a laugh. Alice Smedley from next door came in quite often too.

The years began to pass more quickly. Every few days, early in the morning before opening time, Cassie went down to the market to buy food. Today John had come with her to help carry it home. Patsy was swinging on her hand.

Back in Cambridge Place, Cassie paused in front of Ingram's shop to survey the contents of the window, and said in surprise:

'Used to be just rubbish, pots and pans, old chairs, that sort of stuff.' Now there were cut-glass decanters and mahogany tea caddies.

'Harold Ingram's doing very well for himself.' There was a touch of envy in John's voice. 'Wouldn't have given tuppence for his chance of going upmarket like this. Not a year or two back.'

Cassie shook her head, making the feathers on her hat flutter. 'I would, Harold's got plenty of drive. He's ambitious and a hard worker too.'

The shop had been repainted, and was easily the smartest in the street. In gold letters on scarlet, the sign now read 'Mersey Antiques'. Cassie had thought of her own family as the most go-ahead in business round here.

'Mildred likes posh things, but she won't have done much to bring this about. Likes to be seen out shopping wearing her fur tippet.'

Harold had seen them looking in his window, and was coming out to have a word. He was wearing striped trousers and a good black jacket and looked more prosperous too.

'Hello, John.' His hand went down to fondle Patsy's pale hair. 'How you're growing, little one.'

'Is Lucy in, Grandpa?'

He called up the stairs for her, then nodded in Cassie's direction. 'Nice set of cut-glass decanters there. Bohemian.'

'Can't afford fancy stuff like that,' she retorted.

Lucy came out. 'Hello, Dadda.'

She watched John bend to give his other daughter a formal kiss. Lucy was eyeing Patsy uneasily, saying nothing.

Patsy tugged at Cassie's hand. 'Can Lucy come and play with me?'

Cassie knew she wouldn't. She hated to see Patsy's feelings hurt like this, but what could she say? 'Yes, love, if she'd like to.'

Lucy stepped backwards. 'I'm helping my nanna,' she said primly. 'I can't just now.'

Cassie knew how Patsy felt about Lucy. She'd heard her holding imaginary conversations with her twin, playing make-believe games. She was always saying how Lucy thought this or wanted that. Often she asked: 'Can Lucy come and live with us?' It made Cassie feel for Patsy from the bottom of her heart.

She wouldn't change her granddaughter for anyone now. She was a sweet-natured and loving child, the daughter she'd wanted but never had. She squeezed her hand affectionately. 'I'd like you to help me get the dinner on, pet. You're quite busy too.'

Seeing the seven-year-old twins side by side, Cassie couldn't help but notice that Lucy was a good inch taller and broader than her sister. There was no denying she was the prettier of the two.

Suddenly Harold was looking her straight in the eyes. 'You've heard about the factory?'

Adjoining Ingram's shop was a gaunt building with wire grilles over the windows. It had long housed a small factory turning out flock mattresses. That business, too, was prospering in the post-war years.

26

'I've heard they're moving to larger premises,' she said. 'Building a new factory down Price Street.'

Harold leaned forward, smirking at her. 'Have you heard what's happening to this place?'

'What is?' John wanted to know.

'I've bought it.'

Cassie felt stunned. 'What you going to make in there? Not mattresses?'

'I'm going to turn it into a saleroom. Hold auctions. Alternate Fridays, to start. Perhaps have an additional monthly sale for the better stuff.'

'My goodness, Harold! You are going up in the world.'

'What about the shop?' John asked. 'You're keeping it?'

'For the time being. See how things go.'

Cassie knew that things were continuing to go well for the Ingrams. Within two years, she heard that Harold had bought two more shops through which to sell his antiques, one in West Kirkby and one in central Liverpool.

'That's where the best antique shops are,' John mused.

'His business is helping us in the pub,' Cassie admitted. 'We get more trade on auction days. I wonder, now he's got the other shops, if he'll keep this one on too?'

John saw more of the Ingrams than she did. 'It's going to be turned into an office where people wanting to put goods and chattels into his sales can hand them in, and where those buying at auction can pay.'

'That'll please Mildred.'

On Sundays, John often took Patsy over for tea with the Ingrams. They invited Cassie too, but she seldom went. It upset her to see all the expensive toys Lucy was given, and the way Lucy refused to let Patsy play with any of them.

'You mustn't be envious of what Lucy has,' Cassie had said slowly one day when they'd gone home. It hurt that she couldn't provide Patsy with the same things. She knew it hurt John too.

'I'm not envious, Gran,' Patsy had said. 'I want Lucy to have the best of everything.'

'But you want dresses and toys like her?'

'Ye-es, but what I really want is for her to like me better than anybody else. Be my best friend. She's my twin. Twins should be best friends.'

That made Cassie gather her up in a hug. She understood, then, that what Patsy really wanted was love.

'I like you better than anybody else, Patsy. I love you, always have. And I do believe Dadda feels the same about you.'

She saw Patsy's smile of pleasure. Then it wavered. 'I want Lucy to like me best too,' she breathed.

'She will one day,' Cassie comforted. It didn't surprise her that the twins had never bonded. Not the way things had been for them. It did surprise her that Patsy wanted it so badly.

Cassie knew that Mildred liked her to go up to her flat above the shop. She would beam at her through her glasses, trying to make her feel envious as she showed off her new gas stove or electric iron. Their rooms were continually being smartened up.

Cassie could remember when there'd been a stag with huge antlers and a moth-eaten head hanging on the living-room wall. And Harold had once told her that as a child his bedroom had been furnished with an alabaster bust of Julius Caesar on a marble pedestal.

The Ingrams used to furnish their living quarters with the goods that passed through their business. Mildred told her they were things they liked so much they couldn't bear to part with them. Cassie believed they were things they'd expected to sell and found they could not.

'But it's a little palace now,' she said to John. For herself, she was not envious; she could manage without modern gadgets and fine curtains. But she wanted what money could buy for her family. Particularly what money could buy for Patsy.

She'd always felt a rivalry between herself and Mildred, and now the balance of power was changing, and not in her favour.

Cassie told the Ingrams that she had a friend of her own she wanted to visit, and that Sunday was the only day she could do that in comfort.

She preferred Vereena's mother's company to Mildred's, and had continued to see her regularly. The years were being very unkind to Freda Tarrant. She had contracted a severe form of rheumatism and was often in pain.

Cassie offered sympathy and tried not to notice her swollen joints and wasting muscles. Freda was younger than she was, but she held herself stiffly, and with her sparse white hair like a dandelion seed head, she looked much older. They drank cup after cup of tea and had long discussions about their children.

'The trouble with Vereena,' Freda would say, 'lies with her father. A weak man, really.'

'The trouble with my lads too,' Cassie agreed. 'Work isn't in their blood. And they don't use their brains either.

'But the real trouble with Vereena is that you've over-indulged her. Given her everything she wanted, and she can't understand now why she can't go on having it.'

'We all like to give our children the best we can.'

'You've spoiled her. Been too generous.'

One Sunday night, Cassie was late getting home from Freda's. John had already seen Patsy into bed and had made a pot of tea.

'Guess what Mildred's just told me?' He was frowning.

'What?' Cassie didn't like guessing.

'They're looking for a house in Oxton.'

This was momentous news. 'Moving out from over the shop?'

'And they've taken on a manager to run the saleroom. He's going to live in their place when they go.'

Cassie felt another stab of envy. 'Mildred's always wanted a house. I thought they might move soon. With two shops and the saleroom they don't have to live round here.'

'I'd rather they weren't going,' John said slowly. 'Not that I wish them ill, but . . .'

'He's growing rich and we aren't?'

'I want them to stay here, where I can see Lucy any time I want. Patsy's always hankering after her company. I want Lucy to know us, to spend time with us. I feel the Ingrams are breaking up my family.'

'Have you told Harold?'

'He said: "We won't lose touch. Of course we won't. You must both come to tea every Sunday just the same."' John was exasperated.

'Lucy's going to grow up with much more of this world's goods than our Patsy,' Cassie sighed.

'They won't be like twins at all. Not close. I wish I could get Lucy back.'

'Now they're older, they'd be company for each other. Better for them too.'

'I can't do it, though.' He looked downcast. 'You know I can't. The Ingrams were too clever for me. They foresaw the time might come when I'd want her back. I signed formal adoption papers for our Lucy, didn't I? When she was a baby. She's Lucy Ingram officially.'

Cassie fumed about the Ingrams for the rest of the evening. She felt they were pulling steadily away, and that they'd take Lucy with them.

CHAPTER THREE

26 August 1925

Patsy Gripper was in a huff. Her grandma had taken her to Duckworth's in Grange Road this morning to buy her a new pair of shoes. Up to now, she'd only ever had boots that laced up over the ankle; made of strong black leather with steel tips on the soles and heels. They were so strong she never wore them out, but as her feet grew she needed a larger size.

Lucy never wore boots, only shoes, and this year Gran had promised that she too might have shoes. She'd been looking forward to getting them.

'I want button-over straps, like Lucy's,' she'd been telling Gran for days.

'You saw what Lucy was wearing on Sunday,' she'd said to Dadda. 'Weren't they smart?'

'Very pretty,' he'd agreed. 'But patent leather isn't hard-wearing.'

That should have warned her, because this morning when they reached the shop, Gran wouldn't listen.

'For you and Lucy it can't be the same. Not ever. I'm sorry, love, but you need shoes to keep you warm and dry. It'll be winter before we know it.'

'Winter's coming for Lucy too,' she'd told her mutinously.

'Lucy only wears those shoes indoors. They're party shoes. You need them for school, we can't afford party shoes as well.'

31

Patsy looked down at her feet. She'd ended up with a substantial pair of black leather lace-ups. Not at all what she'd had in mind. On this fine, sunny morning, they felt hot and heavy.

As a treat, Gran had let her wear them immediately and have her old boots parcelled up in the box. Patsy knew by the time she walked home that they were almost as heavy as her boots.

Since she was a baby, Gran had been telling her: 'Your dad and me could never have managed twins, Patsy. Not two babies, not with the pub. We chose to keep you, and sent Lucy off with Nanna Ingram.' Not for the first time, Patsy wondered if Lucy had had the better of the bargain.

She followed Gran through the main door of the Railway Hotel. Above it was printed in gold letters: 'Cassandra Agatha Gripper. Licensed to sell wines, beers and spirits.' Patsy was forbidden to use this door if she was on her own. Gran called Dadda up from the cellar to see the new shoes.

'Shoes at last, eh, Patsy?' he'd grinned.

'Not the sort I wanted,' she'd grumbled, stamping them. 'The nearest thing to boots.'

'There's many that has to go without,' he'd said gently. 'You've seen barefoot children outside here. In the cold, too.'

She had. That made her feel ungrateful.

'Come on, love, you said you weren't envious of what Lucy had.'

She'd said that, too, but it wasn't always true.

'Cheer up, Patsy.' She felt Gran ruffle her hair. 'We'll go upstairs and you can make us a nice cup of tea.' Gran thought that in allowing her to do that, she was giving her another treat.

'I'll have a cup too,' Dadda told her. 'I'll be up in five minutes.'

Feeling contrite, Patsy watched as Gran's barrel-shaped figure filled the narrow staircase leading to their living quarters. Gran wore black lace-ups too, with black wool stockings. The skirts of her copious petticoats flapped round her ankles as she climbed slowly. She was always breathless by the time she reached the top.

Patsy skimmed up after her; flashed to the back kitchen to fill the kettle, poked up the fire in the range and put it to boil. Carefully, then, she set out two cups and saucers and Dadda's big mug.

'We'll have ginger biscuits with it,' Gran allowed. That was another treat. Gran had collapsed into an armchair near the range, her face red with the heat of the day. The stairs were creaking now under Dadda's tread. He came and slumped on a chair, yawning and rubbing his eyes.

'Can't get going this morning. It's a real hot one.'

Gran stirred, pursing her lips. 'It doesn't have to be like this for you, John. You're dragging your feet now. You've done your best for the twins, no one can say you haven't.'

'Give over, Mam,' he said, rubbing his eyes even more.

Patsy found Dadda looking sideways at her, but Gran was not the sort to take notice when she was told to give over.

'It's time you found yourself another wife. There's plenty would jump at the chance. You don't have to think the best is over. You're barely forty.'

Patsy could feel his embarrassment as she lifted the brown teapot to pour. It was so heavy it shook slightly, and she knew she'd overfilled it. Tea spilled into both saucers and made a pool on the oilcloth that covered the table.

She wailed in dismay. 'Just look at the mess I'm making. I can't do anything right.'

While Dadda smiled sympathetically, Gran's belly laugh rumbled out. Patsy felt her plump arms enfold her in a hug.

'Course you can, love. You're just out of sorts this morning. Not her day, is it, John?'

Gran was rarely out of sorts. She barked at people and had strong opinions about everything, but she was jolly too. The deepest lines on her face were laugh lines.

'When you're grown up, you'll be able to do anything, Patsy. The women in our family always could. It's in the blood. Inborn, bred into you. Just give yourself time to learn.'

'You're always saying that.' Patsy wasn't sure whether Gran really meant it. All the stuff about things being bred into people was Gran's hobbyhorse.

She also knew that Gran thought her small for her twelve years. Too pale, too thin and too quiet.

'Patsy's very like her mother. Same fair hair and blue eyes. Same delicate features. I just hope she'll end up stronger.'

Patsy had heard it all before many times. It sent her to the mirror to see what her mother had looked like. She saw a serious child with straight fairish hair drawn back from her face with a big bow of ribbon on top of her head. She knew that nobody's mother ever looked like that.

Gran was very forthright, and Patsy understood that everything depended on whether she took after her mother and the Ingrams, or whether she'd be lucky enough to be like Gran's side of the family.

Her grandmother took a noisy mouthful of tea. 'You could manage a pub like this if you wanted to. My mother did it before me. I've done it for more than forty years. I can teach you how to follow on after me.'

Dadda smiled at her over his cup. His eyes said that Gran had a bee in her bonnet about what women could do, and that he, being a man, had already been discounted.

Patsy knew that Gran was a Lynch, and it was the Lynch women who were strong. Gran didn't think much of the Grippers because Alfred Gripper had died of tuberculosis when he was thirty-six and had left her with three young sons to bring up.

The sash window in the kitchen-living room was already open top and bottom because of the heat. They all heard the clatter of horses' hooves and the creak of the dray as it came down the street.

'Is that the brewery?' Dadda asked, already getting to his feet. Patsy leaned out over the sill to look.

'Yes, Dadda.' She heard him take another swig of tea before clattering back down the stairs.

She was watching the bright-red dray being positioned against the pavement. The two draymen, with their long aprons flapping round their boot tops, were letting down the ramp at the back. The brewery was making its weekly delivery of beer.

From up here she couldn't make out the gold lettering along the side of the dray but she'd seen it often enough to know that it read: 'Birkenhead Brewery Company Limited. Brewers, Bottlers, Wine and Spirit Merchants.'

'Lovely horses,' Patsy murmured. They always brought a boy with them to hold them.

'Shire horses,' Gran told her. 'Course, the brewery's got lorries too now. They say that sooner or later the horses will have to go.'

The huge wooden barrels banded with iron were being rolled from the back of the dray to the pavement. The draymen were using iron hooks on long handles to control the speed and direction of the barrels, so that they ended up exactly where they wanted them.

Below, on the pavement, Dadda was lifting the metal plate that led down to the cellar. She could see the bald spot showing through his light-brown hair.

'They're here early today,' Gran said, pouring more tea for herself.

Patsy leaned further out until she could see the ramp

going down to their cellar. The first great barrel rolled on its way down. Then a second and a third.

She could hear Dadda laughing down below at some joke, and the draymen were both doubling up. Suddenly, the hilarity turned to cries of consternation. Above the screeching and the rumbling, she heard someone swearing.

She felt the crash shake the foundations of the building. Alarmed, she asked: 'What was that?'

Gran was suddenly beside her, leaning further out. Below, the men were shouting and waving their arms about. Patsy was filled with horror.

Then Gran was gone. Despite her bulk she was hurtling downstairs. With her heart in her throat, Patsy flew down behind her, afraid that something dreadful had happened to Dadda.

She couldn't look at him when she got down. Somehow a barrel had broken free of the hooks that controlled its descent. Dadda looked like a rag doll, pinned to the wall behind it.

She could feel panic in the air. The draymen seemed to be rushing about, but she saw that they were using their hooks to swing the weight of the barrel off Dadda. He slid to the floor, limp and white.

'Is he dead?' Patsy felt a scream fluttering in her throat.

'No,' Gran said firmly. It was she who took charge then.

'Get the cellar door off its hinges,' she ordered the men. 'Use that as a stretcher. We've got to get him to hospital, and the sooner the better.'

They had it off its hinges and were carefully lifting Dadda on. Patsy was surprised how little time it took. Gran seemed cool as she told them what she wanted.

'Up the stairs and on to the dray.'

That took longer. Dadda was heavy, and they had to get a man from the street to hold his shoulders on the door as they manoeuvred the improvised stretcher round the bend in the narrow cellar stairs.

By the time Dadda was out on the pavement, he'd come round and was shouting with pain. A small crowd was collecting.

'What's the matter with you all?' Gran yelled at them. 'Come on, give a hand, can't you? Let's lift him on the cart.'

Every man there rushed to help lift the burden. 'So sorry, Mrs Gripper,' they were saying. 'Poor old John.'

Gran said: 'Come on, straight to the Borough Hospital. It's no more than a mile or so up the road.'

The boy was sent back to the brewery to tell them about the accident. The senior drayman wanted his mate to stay with the beer barrels they were leaving on the pavement.

Gran objected. 'It'll take two of you to lift him off the cart and carry him in. He's too heavy for me.'

'The hospital has porters . . .'

'Come on. Takes time to find porters. It might make all the difference to our John.'

'Brewery orders. Never leave . . .'

'Nobody can move them barrels. Much too heavy.'

'They'll have a good try if they know they're full, missus.'

'I'll come and lift John for you, Mrs Gripper.' It was Robert Parry who stepped forward, a freckle-faced youth, the son of the newsagent next door to the pub.

For Patsy, there was no mistaking the additional shock on Gran's face. All Cambridge Place knew that she and the Parrys didn't speak to each other and hadn't done for years. She'd heard Gran say disparagingly of Robert: 'Thin as a beanpole. Needs fattening up, poor lad.'

But all the Parry family were out on the pavement, as were most of their neighbours. This had the makings of a disaster for the Grippers. There was sympathy on all their faces. Even the Parrys wanted to rally round. Patsy saw Gran look towards Mersey Antiques. She'd have preferred Grandpa's help.

Alice Smedley, Gran's friend, came and put an arm round Patsy's shoulders. She heard her urge: 'Let him help you, Cassie.'

Gran took a deep breath and said: 'Thanks, lad. I'll be glad of a hand.'

'Get yourself up then, let's go.' The head drayman was satisfied now that he could leave a man behind. But getting Gran up on the cart involved the help of several men.

She shouted to those staying behind: 'Keep an eye on the pub for me, will you?' The drayman was already closing the door.

'Patsy!' she shouted again. 'Run a message for me. Go and tell Uncle Bernie what's happened. Got to have somebody here by opening time.'

Patsy watched the two great horses move off. She heard Dadda shout again with pain as the cart jolted forwards.

Patsy didn't like going to Uncle Bernie's house because she wasn't fond of Auntie Vee, but she ran as fast as she could now. They lived just round the corner, in Thomas Street, in a small terraced house of smoke-blackened brick.

All the front doors here opened straight off the pavement. Each house had one bay window in the living room. Auntie Vee mourned the fact that their bedroom above did not have one too.

'Not posh enough for Vereena,' Gran had sniffed. 'Lucky to have her own house, I'd say.'

Uncle Bernie still came to work at the Railway Hotel, though it was no secret he'd tried to get other jobs.

'Work?' Gran could be scathing. 'Bernie doesn't know the meaning of the word. Both my boys work here, but your dadda does eighty per cent of it.' Dadda was Gran's favourite.

'I blame *her*, of course.' Patsy knew she meant Auntie Vee.

Patsy blamed Auntie Vee for almost everything that went wrong in her world, too. She hoped against hope that she wouldn't be in now, but it was Vereena who came to the front door.

'What do you want?' she asked irritably. Auntie Vee was never nice to anybody. 'I'm just going out.'

Patsy tried to suppress a shiver of fear. When she'd been younger, Auntie Vee had looked after her during opening hours. She'd borne the brunt of her bad moods then and had often received a vicious swipe. Patsy had gone crying to Dadda.

'Were you being naughty, love?'

'Auntie Vee said I was,' she'd sniffed.

'Then the answer,' he'd told her gently, 'is to be a good girl. Do what Vereena tells you. Then she won't spank you.'

She'd also told Gran, with much the same outcome. The end came when Vereena had been walloping her in her bedroom and Cassie had heard her screams from the private bar. She'd come rushing upstairs and gathered her into a comforting hug.

'There, love, don't cry.' She'd rocked her in her arms.

Patsy had choked out: 'Auntie Vee doesn't like me, she's always smacking me. I'm not that naughty.'

'We won't let her look after you any more,' Cassie had crooned. 'There's no call for this. Vereena's got a terrible temper.'

'I'm old enough to stay by myself.' And from then on she had.

She'd been trying to tell them that Auntie Vee was cruel and vicious, but they hadn't believed her because Vereena didn't look that sort. She was attractive and quite passionate about clothes. Today she looked very smart, in a loose pink dress with the belt dropped to the level of her hips. It had a flat, wide collar and a velvet tie in deeper pink. Patsy thought it heavenly.

'Skimpy dresses,' Gran called them. 'Only a brazen hussy would show her knees like that.'

'Vereena's got good legs,' Bernie had smirked proudly.

'And doesn't mind how much of them she shows,' Gran retorted. 'She thinks she's the cat's whiskers, with her skirts up to her armpits.'

But Patsy knew that Vereena's clothes were the height of fashion. She was wearing a deep-pink cloche that covered all her dark hair except for a kiss curl on each cheek. She had flesh-coloured rayon stockings and, most desirable of all, high-heeled button-strap shoes of stone-coloured leather.

Patsy blurted out: 'Dadda's been hurt. Gran's taken him to hospital. She wants Uncle Bernie to be sure to come early. He'll have to open up by himself.'

Auntie Vee's dark eyes burned down at her. 'I hope she won't expect him to work tonight?'

'She will.' Patsy burst into tears. 'Dadda won't be able to.'

'You'd better come in. Can't blubber on the doorstep. What'll the neighbours think?'

Patsy stumbled up one step into their living room. Uncle Bernie smiled up at her. He looked a bit like Dadda, but was more handsome, less serious and eight years younger. He was balanced on the edge of a dining chair playing his banjo.

'What's happened to our John?'

Patsy told them about the accident. Without saying anything, Bernie began to pick out the tune of 'Campdown Races'. Slowly at first, each note true and sweet. Then at a more bouncy pace, going faster and faster until the music was racing along.

Patsy felt her spirits lift. Uncle Bernie could certainly play. She was tapping her foot in time to his music. Gran said that Bernie had asked for a banjo for his sixteenth birthday. She'd bought him a second-hand one and he'd taught himself to play. When he'd married Vereena, who played both the accordion and the piano, she'd suggested he have lessons. Since then, he'd improved enormously.

Gran had been very scathing about Vereena's latest idea. She'd formed a troupe of players calling themselves the Dixie Minstrels.

'I'm going to manage them,' Patsy had heard Vereena tell Gran. 'I know people in the business. They're helping me get bookings, I've got one or two already.'

'We're really good, Patsy.' Uncle Bernie was always talking about the band when he came to the pub.

'We've got six banjo players, and four have been playing professionally for years. There's another who plays the mandolin, and with Vereena, there's three accordionists. We black our faces and sing Dixieland songs, "Swanee River" and that sort of thing. It's a way of getting out of the pub trade. My best bet. I'm pinning my hopes on it.'

Once, they came to play outside the pub for practice, passing a hat round between the tunes. Gran wouldn't let them come inside; she said there'd be no room for customers if they filled the public bar.

Patsy hung out of her bedroom window so as not to miss a note. Afterwards she'd told Gran that they were the most wonderful band she'd ever heard.

'You haven't heard any other,' Gran said dismissively. 'They think they're aiming for the moon, but they'll be paid no more than a pittance. This is a good, steady business. It won't earn our Bernie a fortune, but he won't starve either. He needs to keep his feet on the ground or he'll come a cropper.'

Bernie finished 'Campdown Races' with a flourish, and said: 'I knew I was on this dinnertime. I'll come early to open up.'

'But he won't be able to take John's place tonight,' Vereena said firmly.

'Gran will want him to.'

Bernie said: 'She knows I can't. The Minstrels are playing at the Floral Hall all week. Friday and Saturday are the big nights.'

'We're doing well,' Vereena smirked. 'The audiences love us.'

'Would it matter if there was one banjo less?' Patsy asked.

'There's no question of that.' Vereena folded her arms determinedly across her flat chest. 'Of course Bernie must play with us for the rest of the week. He can't let the band down.'

It was on the tip of Patsy's tongue to say that Gran would feel he was letting her down if he wasn't at the pub.

Vereena turned on her husband then. 'This is your big chance. You've worked hard for it. You can't let it go. Your mother won't expect you to.'

Patsy swallowed hard. 'She won't be able to manage. Not on her own.'

'Your gran thinks she can manage anything.' Vereena looked at Bernie and smirked again. 'Of course she'll manage. She'll have to.'

That made Patsy fearful. 'You will come and open up this morning?'

'I said I would, didn't I?' And Bernie started to play 'My Little Grey Home in the West'.

Patsy walked home slowly. She'd seen the concern on Gran's face, heard the whispers of the crowd that had gathered to see Dadda carried out to the dray. He'd looked bad, sounded bad too, groaning and crying out with pain. She was worried. She knew Gran couldn't manage the pub without him.

She turned the corner into Cambridge Place. Donovan's grocery shop was on the corner; the pub was a few doors further up. The crowd had dispersed. The drayman was leaning against a barrel smoking a cigarette and enjoying the sun. The metal cover over the cellar was back in place.

Gran had told her that the Railway Hotel had originally been a private house and dated back, like all the others in the street, to 1844. It had first become a beer house in 1868, and her family, the Lynches, had been running it ever since.

Upstairs, there were old sash windows and walls of uneven brick. Downstairs had been revamped by the brewery before the Great War. Shiny brown tiles rose from pavement to first-floor height. The windows were set high and were of frosted glass. Not ordinary frosted glass but specially made with the words 'Birkenhead Brewery Ales' in a semicircle, and ornate ribbons and wreaths looping below them.

Above the windows was a cornice with faded gold letters that read: 'Birkenhead Brewery Company's Ales'. And beneath it, in even larger letters: 'The Railway Hotel'. Patsy went in through the side door and straight upstairs. She was strictly forbidden to be downstairs once the pub was open.

'If you're caught downstairs, I'd lose my licence,' Gran had said. 'And then what would we all do?'

'We'd all starve to death,' Dadda had agreed.

'But I wish I could . . .'

'Not until you're eighteen.' And that was final.

Because she was excluded from the pub premises and Gran and Dadda were in the pub eight hours a day, Patsy often felt lonely upstairs by herself.

Gran always said when she went down in the evening: 'Be undressed and in bed by eight o'clock and either Dadda or I will come up and tuck you in. Be a good girl and see you are.'

When she first put out her light, Patsy would hear the board creaking as it swung on rusting chains below her bedroom window. The pub's name was emblazoned here too, in faded gold letters.

It seemed that there was fun to be had down in the pub every night, and a party atmosphere seemed to develop on Friday and Saturday nights when people had just been paid. As the night hours drew on, Patsy would hear laughter and animated talk. Sometimes, towards closing time, the laughter would become raucous and there would be singing.

Quite often she'd hear Gran's rather quavery voice joining in. They mostly sang old wartime songs like 'It's a Long Way to Tipperary'. But the modern 'Yes, We Have No Bananas', was a regular favourite too.

Patsy went upstairs to the living room. It was dominated by an old-fashioned kitchen range. Their kettle swung on a hook over the fire, saucepans could simmer on the trivet, and meals were cooked in the oven alongside.

The fire was almost out. Taking the coal scuttle, she ran down to the yard at the back to refill it. She thought of the yard as a dismal place; as well as the coal shed there was a clothes line, and a smelly lavatory for pub customers. The gate to the back entry had been walled up.

Usually Dadda fetched the coal; the long pull upstairs was beyond Gran's strength. Patsy knew that Dadda wouldn't be able to manage it either now. She wondered what was happening to him.

She had to use more paper and sticks to relight the range. It was time to get their dinner on. They always ate it very late, after the pub had closed for the afternoon. Gran had bought three sheeps' hearts while they were out shopping this morning.

She prepared them as she'd seen Gran do, peeled some potatoes to go round them, and put a roasting pan in the

44

oven with some dripping. She knew that the dripping should be hot before she put the hearts in, but the fire had gone too low. She put the hearts in anyway, afraid they wouldn't be ready by dinnertime. She wasn't hungry, but Gran always was.

The tea she'd made earlier was still on the table, hardly touched in the cups. She took them to the back kitchen and washed up. Then she tidied the newspapers piled on the treadle sewing machine under the window.

She wished Gran was back. The whole building seemed still and quiet. She wished Uncle Bernie would come. Gran was a stickler for opening on time.

She heard him then. The front door was being hooked open. He was whistling 'Campdown Races' to himself. Soon there was the tramp of footsteps and the familar murmur of voices downstairs. She was pushing some red coals under the oven when she heard the clop of horses' hoofs and the rattle of wheels outside in the street. She rushed to the window.

The dray was coming back. Rob was sitting up in front with the driver. She hadn't expected to see Dadda, but there was no sign of Gran either. That made her feel sick with panic. She went hurtling downstairs to find out what was keeping her.

CHAPTER FOUR

By the time Patsy reached the pavement, Robert Parry and the drayman were lifting the cellar door off the cart.

'What's happened to Gran?'

Rob jumped down to talk to her. 'She's waiting to see the doctor.'

'Dadda's not . . .?'

'No. Don't be afraid, it's not that bad.'

'His bones are broken, they must be.'

'I don't know, Patsy. We carried him into the hospital and a doctor came to see him. I'd done all I could so I came back on the cart.' She knew he wouldn't feel at ease with Gran. He'd hardly ever spoken to her.

'I didn't want to elbow in,' he said awkwardly. 'He's getting the best attention, that's all I can tell you.'

'Gran'll know more when she comes?'

'Yes, she said to tell you she'd be back as soon as she could.'

Patsy shivered, though she was standing in the full sun.

'Are you by yourself up there?' His brown eyes went up to the kitchen window.

She nodded. 'I'm used to that.'

He put a hand on her shoulder and said gently, 'Come to our house. You don't want to be alone at a time like this.'

Pasty was surprised at that, and reluctant to go. Her family thought of the Parrys as ogres. Yet Rob was comforting. She allowed herself to be steered into the shop next door. She'd never been inside before; Gran had forbidden it. If she had money for sweets, she spent it in Donovan's.

She couldn't help but gasp aloud at the wonderful array of confectionery. There were jars lined up on shelves all round the shop, and open boxes of gobstoppers and liquorice bootlaces on the counter, a much better selection than Donovan's ever had.

And the smell of newsprint was lovely. She'd caught that outside as she went past. There were comics and chocolate bars and bottles of ginger beer, too.

Rob's parents were both in the shop. She knew them by sight, of course, but she'd never spoken to either of them. They looked stiff and unbending and hardly seemed to know what to say to her.

'They're teetotallers and Welsh chapelgoers,' Gran had explained. 'They don't like lapsed Catholics who keep a pub like ours. We aren't their sort. His mother's a bitter woman. Years younger than me, though you'd never think it.'

'A terrible thing,' Rob's father spoke at last, 'to see your dad carried off like that.'

Patsy found their comfort hard to bear. Rob was ushering her into the dark living room behind the shop.

'You mustn't worry. He could be home again, pulling pints, in no time,' he told her.

'He's badly hurt,' Patsy choked.

'You don't know yet.' Orlando Parry was a large man with thick auburn hair just beginning to show the first signs of grey. There was a benign and kindly look about him. 'I mean, look at our Robert.'

Patsy stared up at Robert. He had auburn hair too. It was growing darker now but once it had been very carroty. She could remember when his face had been covered with freckles; now they were much fewer. His brown eyes were large like his father's, too.

'I had an accident when I was your age,' he told her. 'Don't you remember?' She didn't. Gran didn't talk much about the Parrys.

'It was my own fault, I was knocked down by a charabanc at Woodside. Not looking where I was going.'

'Jaywalking,' his father added. 'He broke his leg. Better now, of course, but never been really right since.'

'Dad! It is.'

'Your mother's saved your dinner for you.' He went back to the shop door and called: 'Gladys? Is there enough of that scouse for Patsy to have some?'

Patsy felt him easing her into a seat at the table. 'You'll have a bite to eat?'

She tried to refuse.

'You'll feel better if you do.'

Rob had shared the scouse between two plates by the time his mother came. She was a faded, mouse-like woman in her fifties. Her hair was already white.

'I think there might be, dear,' Gladys said. Her face was heavily lined and she had a permanently worried look. She backed into the shop again.

Patsy wasn't hungry. She watched Rob eating with relish. 'You don't limp.'

'Not at all.'

'All the same, it stops him doing what he wants.' His father was setting out cups and saucers.

'Does it?' Patsy felt alarmed. Would Dadda be able to do what he wanted after this? Would he be able to work in the pub again?

'No, I don't let it stop me,' Rob insisted. 'I do exactly what I want.'

'Can't pass a medical, that's the problem.' His father tried to smile.

'Twice I thought I'd got an apprenticeship – to do engineering,' he admitted.

'He'd made up his mind it was what he wanted, you see.

49

They said his leg wasn't as strong as it should be. They didn't think he could do the long hours. Of course, engineering can be heavy work.'

'It's heavy in the shop sometimes,' Rob said. 'Around Christmas. On my feet from morning to night.'

'That doesn't bother you?' Patsy asked.

'No, it doesn't.' But his grimace showed that perhaps it did.

'The doctors said a desk job would suit him better.'

'But it's getting one.' Rob was mopping up the last of his gravy with bread.

'He's going to night school.'

'Got to get my school certificate.' His smile was lopsided. 'Next year I'll do it.'

'He's determined.'

'I have to be. Won't stand a chance otherwise.'

'What'll you do?'

'A clerk,' his father said.

'Dad, the shop sounds busy.' They all stopped to listen. It did. 'Mam will be needing you.'

As he went out, his father added: 'I've made a pot of tea. It'll be brewed now.'

There were two iced buns on the table, fresh from Donovan's. Patsy saw trays of them being delivered to their shop every morning. Rob pushed one towards her.

'Not clerking. I'm getting more ambitious.' He grinned at her. 'Perhaps I could be an estate agent or an accountant.'

'What about this shop? Isn't there enough work here?' Patsy knew that many businesses were handed down through the family.

'There's plenty of work all right. Not enough in the profit margin, though, not for all of us. I need to get a job. Anything to tide me over until I can try for a desk job. I'm a dead weight on them here. I've tried, Patsy, but it isn't easy. There's too many out of work now.'

She could hear his parents out in the shop, serving customers with cigarettes and pop and newspapers. She was finishing her second cup of tea when Rob's mother put her head round the living-room door again.

'Your gran's back. I've just seen her get off the bus.'

Patsy was on her feet in an instant. 'Thank you for my dinner, Mrs Parry, you've been very kind. You too, Rob.'

Both pub doors stood wide open on this hot day. Patsy went in through the side door. Gran and Bernie were out on the stairs leading up to their private quarters. Bernie was looking mutinous.

'How's Dadda?' Patsy wanted to know.

'He'll be all right, love.' Gran put an arm across her shoulders. 'Crushed ribs, several broken. They tell me he's lucky one of them didn't pierce his lung. He's got a broken arm, but it's his left one, and it's a miracle the only other bone broken is a small one in his foot. He's badly bruised too, of course, but he'll get over it.'

Patsy was almost crying with relief. 'Can he talk?'

'Yes, he sends his love. Said you mustn't worry.' She felt Gran's arm urge her upwards. 'Put the kettle on for me, Patsy. I must have a cup of tea.' Patsy went up three stairs, then stopped.

'Bernie, you've got to stay,' Gran was saying. 'You know I can't see to everything on my own.'

Only now did Patsy realise they'd been having a row. Bernie's face was white with determination. Gran closed the door to the private bar so they wouldn't be heard.

'No sense of responsibility. You never have had. Playing in Vereena's band! I suppose you think you'll make a fortune that way?'

'Ma, I told you a month ago I couldn't work evenings this week. You know what it means to us. You'll have to get someone else.'

51

'Who else can I get?' Gran's hands were shaking. 'I need help now. I can't go looking for people. Would it matter if Vereena had one banjo less in her band?'

'I don't want to be left out.' Bernie's face was aghast. 'It's doing well. I could lose my chance.'

Patsy felt sick. She hated to hear anyone fighting with Gran. 'What about—'

Gran turned on her angrily. 'Upstairs, miss. I'll be up in a minute.'

Patsy climbed another two stairs and sat down. 'What about Rob Parry? He'll come and help you. He'd like to.'

'He's not old enough.'

'He's turned eighteen.'

'How do you know?'

'I asked him. His father made me stay for dinner. He was asking how old I was.'

'You went round there? To that shop? I told you not to have anything to do with the Parrys.' Gran was angry.

'I haven't been near till today, and you took Rob with you to the hospital. I just asked him where you were and what had happened to Dadda.'

'Rob would do.' Bernie put his oar in. 'He'd be all right.'

'He knows nothing about bar work. You'd say anyone was all right to get you off the hook.'

Patsy took a deep breath. 'He serves in the shop. He takes money . . . He needs a job, Gran.'

'Not in this pub. They wouldn't let him.'

'He's desperate for a job, I'm sure he is.'

Gran looked defeated. 'It would have to be our John who copped it,' she complained.

'You let Rob go with you to help with Dadda.'

'I suppose he's better than nobody. See if he'll come round. Right away, mind. I need him now.'

Patsy rushed back to the paper shop. Rob was straightening the newspapers on the counter.

She burst out: 'Gran wants to know if you'd work for her. She needs somebody to take Dadda's place right away.'

Both his parents were in the shop though there were no customers at that moment. They stared at her open-mouthed. If she'd thrown a bomb it would have had much the same effect.

'No.' His father recovered first. 'You can't work in that pub.'

'Definitely not.' His mother's face had gone chalk-white.

'Why not?' Rob demanded, turning on them. 'I'll be able to help you. Haven't I tried and tried to get a job? Any job? It's honest work that's offered.'

Patsy felt their tension. It was more oppressive than thunder. She knew she was opening a rift between them but didn't understand why. She seemed to be cutting Rob away from his parents.

He said quietly: 'I'm going to see about it. Come on, Patsy.'

As he padded along the pavement beside her, he added: 'Don't say anything about that to your Gran. I'll be glad to have the job.'

Patsy pushed him into the private bar and hung about the doorway listening. She could hear Bernie serving in the public.

'I've got to have somebody here right away,' Gran was telling him. But she wasn't looking him in the eye. Wasn't at ease with him, either.

'I can start now, this minute.' She could see Rob's face alight with anticipation.

'I wish you knew something about cellar work.'

'I'll do my best, Mrs Gripper. I'm quick to learn.'

'Right. I'll pay you the same as I pay our Bernie. It's temporary, mind, just till John's well again. I've got to have somebody.' Patsy heard her give a great gusting sigh.

'Your mother doesn't mind you coming here?'

'Why should she? I need work.'

'I'll have to write down the prices of everything. Different here from in the public. Here, put this apron on, there's more customers coming in.'

Patsy stepped backwards as she saw Gran turning round. She spotted her.

'Upstairs, young lady, and make me that tea. I'll send Robert up in five minutes to fetch it.'

Patsy went up slowly, wondering what had happened between Gran and the family at the paper shop. It was very strange: they'd ignored each other for years, and neither side wanted Rob to work here. She liked him and was glad she'd been able to help him. He'd been kind to her.

Once the tea had been made, she felt restless upstairs by herself. Below in the pub, the voices became more animated as time went on.

What else could she do to help Gran? She looked round. In front of the kitchen range, an impossible mound of washing was airing on the rack above her head. Gran's strange garments dangled low. She was very fussy about airing clothes, but everything was bone-dry. Some had already been ironed.

Patsy let the pulley down. Gran had petticoats galore and wore a various number according to the weather. There were both cotton and flannel ones in the wash from last week, and three pairs of well-darned black stockings.

She took them to Gran's bedroom and put them away in her already over-stuffed chest of drawers. She did the same with Dadda's combinations and shirts.

She folded her own things, a nightie, vest, knickers and liberty bodice, and took them to her bedroom. She hated the liberty bodices Gran made for her on the treadle sewing machine. Made from remnants bought in the market, they were quilted for added warmth and as thick and strong as a man's waistcoat.

Only this morning, she'd pushed one made of scarlet flannel under her mattress where Gran wouldn't see it. It was too hot to wear now. She'd seen Lucy's liberty bodices, all white and bought ready-made, of thinner material. When she'd asked Gran for some like that, Gran had been scornful.

'There's no warmth in them. Just flannelette. No good at all. You need real wool flannel.'

Patsy banked up the fire again though the room was already hot. The dinner was not cooking as fast as it should and Gran was always hungry. She started to set the table with two places. It seemed odd not to be setting one for Dadda.

Robert Parry felt dazed by the sudden change. He'd never been inside any pub before. According to his father, public houses were the haunt of thieves and sinners and fallen women. Places where decent men didn't go.

To step over the threshold made his heart race. He'd defied his parents to be here. For the first time ever, he'd gone directly against their wishes. Dad would be angry and his mother upset. The pub felt like forbidden territory.

He tried telling himself that working here was not so very different from serving in the shop. Except that he didn't know where anything was kept, or anything at all about alcohol. He'd tasted beer once when he went out with a school friend, but nothing else. The variety of alcoholic drinks amazed him. Cigarettes he understood; luckily, for they seemed to sell more here than in the shop.

'Two pints of stout and a port and lemon.' He was immediately at a loss.

Beside him, Cassie said quietly: 'Draught stout ... watch me. Now you draw the second pint. That's right. The port is over here. This is the glass for a measure of port. Lemonade over there.'

Cassie was making price lists for him and sticking them up, one in each bar and one beside the jug and bottle.

He had to keep his mind on what he was doing, check every price he charged. Back in the shop everything was as familiar as breathing.

'What's bitter?' he asked Cassie; he'd never heard of it.

'A sort of beer.'

'Is there more than one sort?' That raised a real laugh.

'His dad's teetotal,' Cassie told the customer with a wide smile. 'I should have known that'd give him problems.'

'I bet his mother remembers what bitter is.' That raised another laugh.

'Long memories round here,' Cassie whispered to him by way of explanation.

Rob swallowed hard. 'My mother?' They'd got that wrong; she thought the Devil dwelt in every pub. And what was so funny?

'Another gin and it.'

What on earth was 'it'? He must stop thinking about his family and concentrate on the job.

Next door in the paper shop, Gladys Parry had to force herself to look up at a truculent customer.

'You're short-changing me,' he complained. 'It was half a crown I gave you, not two bob.'

She'd put it in the till, whatever it was, but she was almost certain he'd handed her a two-shilling piece. Some tried it on but she couldn't argue. This sort of thing made her feel sick.

'Sorry.' She handed him another sixpence and felt the tears starting again.

'Go and have a rest,' Orlando said when the customer had gone. 'We aren't busy. I can manage.'

Gladys made for the kitchen, feeling for her hankie. 'I'll see about making some tea.'

Lando was such a good man, an honest, God-fearing man. He'd been a wonderful husband. She didn't deserve him, and that made things worse.

The nightmare was going on and on. She'd thought that when she was married, everybody would forget, that they'd be able to have a normal family life. But they never had.

Lando was hard-working, a good businessman, but because of her, they were poor. She'd brought him nothing but trouble.

He came to the living-room door. 'Don't be cross with Rob.' She could see the length of the shop behind him, devoid of customers.

'He knows how I feel about that pub. He shouldn't have gone against our wishes.'

'He's desperate to get a job. Anything at all. He feels he's a burden on us. Wants to help.'

Gladys knew it was ridiculous to blame Lando, but she couldn't help it. 'You shouldn't have encouraged him. You told him to go to the hospital with Cassie Gripper.'

'To help with John.'

'If you hadn't done that . . .'

'We should put out a helping hand to those in trouble,' he said gently.

'But not work in that pub. Not our Rob. She wouldn't have offered him the job if you hadn't pushed him forward.'

'Come on, Gladys. Rob's almost a grown man, he has to learn to stand on his own feet. If we've brought him up properly we won't need to protect him now.'

'You said that pub corrupts everybody.'

'I said drink did that. I hope Robert won't drink even if he works there.'

Lando had never tasted alcohol in his life; he looked upon all pubs as iniquitous places. Gladys knew he'd thought of her as an innocent sinner he must save. He always wanted to help those in trouble. That was his way.

He'd stood by her. He'd kept his part of the bargain. She ought to be grateful to him. She was, of course, but by the time Lando had proposed her life was already ruined.

'You've got to stop our Rob. Before it's too late.' She could see he wasn't going to.

'It may not be for long, Gladys.'

'He'll get in with that crowd. They'll pull him down.'

She was glad when the shop bell pinged and he'd had to go. Lando was too well-meaning. He didn't believe anybody was totally bad.

When at last she could close the pub, Cassie climbed wearily up to the kitchen. It had been one of the worst mornings of her life. The emotional shock of seeing John unconscious in the cellar and taking him to hospital had drained her.

She relied heavily on John to run the pub, and with him out of action and Bernie refusing to give more help, she'd been forced into making an instant decision to take on Rob Parry. Him of all people!

She was ready to bet his mother was dead against him working here, and it could lead to more trouble from the paper shop. They were paranoid about the liquor trade. Cassie found it hard to cope with bitterness and bad feelings. She wanted everybody to have a good time and enjoy themselves.

When she saw Patsy dishing up a meal she felt her head swim with relief. She hadn't given a thought to dinner until this moment. Patsy had tidied the kitchen as well.

'You're a good girl, Patsy. At least I can rely on you.' She was her one comfort today, the one person she could be proud of. Patsy was growing up a lovely girl. She had a sweet and generous nature and it showed on her face. She was growing prettier.

'I don't know, Gran, I don't think I've cooked them properly.'

She could see the child was upset that everything wasn't perfect, and that upset her too. She wasn't entirely in control of her emotions today. But she mustn't give way and weep, that would only make it harder to carry on tonight.

She fondled Patsy's soft pale hair. It was her usual gesture of love and support. She tried to eat, if only to show appreciation of what Patsy had done, but the potatoes were hard and the hearts half raw. She wasn't hungry anyway. After a morning like she'd had, the last thing she wanted was food.

'What else do we have there? A bit of bread and cheese?'

'I'm sorry, Gran. I wanted it all to be nice for you.'

'You've done wonders, love, but all I want is a cup of tea. It's you I'm thinking of.'

'Mrs Parry gave me dinner at the paper shop. I'm not hungry.'

'Then we'll put the hearts in the oven again tomorrow. There'll be plenty for us two.'

Cassie almost drank the teapot dry. She could feel herself dozing off before she'd finished her last cup.

'Don't let me sleep beyond five, Patsy. I'll need to pull myself round before opening time.'

But when she settled back in her chair, sleep wouldn't come. She felt bone-weary and yet beyond sleep. She rested with her eyes closed, worrying about John and listening to Patsy turning the pages of her book.

Already she regretted taking on Rob Parry. Alice Smedley from next door would have run down to Conway Street to see if that lad who'd come asking last month still wanted the job.

Cassie didn't want to think of the Parrys. In particular she didn't want to think of Gladys. The memory of what she'd done with Alfie was too painful. She'd felt betrayed by both of them.

And then Gladys had been brazen enough to come and live next door. Cassie had expected the worst, but she didn't think anything had gone on after she'd married Orlando.

Still, retribution had come to both of them. Gladys had borne a handicapped daughter, and Alfie had caught TB and been dead for well over a quarter of a century. It all ought to have been forgotten by now, but it wasn't.

She heard the hammering on the main door and Patsy running down to answer it. It was five o'clock. She was suddenly stiff with dread that somebody was bringing bad news about John.

Then she heard a woman's voice call, 'Cooee!' It sounded like Vereena. She got up and went to the window to look down on the top of Vereena's pink cloche. She couldn't remember when her daughter-in-law had last come to the pub. She was wide awake and upright in her chair by the time Patsy brought her upstairs.

'I've come to tell you Bernie isn't coming. Not tonight.'

There was an air of defiant confrontation about Vereena. Her dark eyes were burning feverishly.

'I didn't expect him to stay and work,' Cassie said coldly.

Vereena always made sure nobody did her down. 'He said you told him—'

'I asked him to come at half past five for half an hour. Just to explain things to the new boy I've had to take on. Cellar work and that. He said he would.'

'The band is playing tonight.' Vereena spoke slowly, as though explaining to a dim-witted child. 'He told you ages ago that he couldn't work evenings all this week. We thought you'd fixed up a replacement for him.'

'I have.'

Patsy knew she'd arranged for Agnes to come in as temporary barmaid for the week. She'd worked here for odd weeks before and wore thick glossy lipstick that ran into the wrinkles round her mouth.

'I've even got somebody to stand in for our John. You have heard he's had a bad accident? That he's in hospital?'

'Yes, of course.'

'I don't expect Bernie to work tonight, just for half an hour. We were too busy at lunchtime to explain anything to the new lad. And by the time we were closing, he'd had enough. Couldn't have taken much in by then. I asked him to come back half an hour early tonight.'

'You can't expect Bernie to come. He'd be rushed getting to New Brighton.'

'I thought the show didn't start till half seven?'

'It doesn't. But I'd be worried in case he was late, and we might want a run-through some of the numbers first. We all need to be relaxed and in the right frame of mind. He can't come rushing round here at the last moment.'

'I didn't think I was asking too much.' Cassie was drawing herself up to her full height.

'Well, I think you are. You know what this chance means to us.'

'It'll come to nothing, you'll see. It's all pie in the sky.'

Vereena gasped with indignation. Cassie went on bitterly: 'You'll be paid a pittance anyway. Far more sensible for you to come and give a hand here when we have a crisis like this. I suppose you can add up well enough to give change?'

'Of course I can, but I don't care for the pub trade.'

'You should, it's kept you for the last twelve years.'

Usually Cassie tried to avoid pitched battles with her daughter-in-law, but Vereena goaded her from time to time.

'I'd really prefer that my husband didn't have to work in a pub either.' Vereena was projecting a long-felt hate. 'Specially a low drinking den like the Railway Hotel. Hotel indeed!' She sniggered behind her hand.

Patsy piped up: 'I wish I was eighteen and could help you, Gran.'

Vereena turned on her: 'I'd stay well clear of it, if I were you. It's a filthy trade. I hate the stench of stale beer, and the drunkenness. Aren't you afraid of drunks?'

Cassie could see Patsy shrinking back. 'No need to be afraid,' she maintained. 'Firm handling is what they need. You'd soon learn how to deal with them.'

'Some parents drink every penny they earn instead of spending it on food and clothes for their children. They go barefoot while their fathers drink. It's disgusting because it's the children who suffer. I know, I used to be a teacher, remember?'

Cassie had heard too much about Vereena's teaching career, and how, like all women in the professions, she'd been required to give it up on marriage. She'd also heard her say that with hindsight it had been a great mistake. Cassie knew that Bernie was not turning out to be as good a provider as Vereena had expected.

'I know you're giving him big ideas. Telling him he's too good to work in his own family's business.' She was snorting with indignation. 'You're too big for your boots. Your mother's spoiled you, making you think that you're better than the rest of us. What was she thinking of?'

'I thought she was your friend,' Vereena said coldly.

'Somebody has to be friendly towards her,' Cassie returned with fury. 'Poor woman, I don't know how you can leave her on her own in that state.'

Cassie thought Vereena neglected Freda, only going near her when she wanted something for herself. 'Bernie ought to do more for her. Like getting her coals in.'

'Bernie reckons he's knocking himself out for everybody. He doesn't have a lot of energy. It's the awful trade he's in. I keep telling him he can do better.'

Cassie felt an urge to slap her. 'Isn't he good enough for you now?'

'You don't pay him enough. We can't live on it.'

'You can't manage money, Vereena, that's your trouble.

He gets the same rate as our John. We're none of us living in luxury.'

'That's what I mean.'

Vereena was showing her streak of selfishness. She felt that the world owed her and Bernie a living, and it had better be a good one.

'You couldn't marry him fast enough. Like greased lightning you were, rushing him to the altar. And him nothing but a child.'

Vereena was four years older than Bernie, and didn't like to be reminded of the fact. She turned on her heel without another word and clattered off downstairs.

Later on that night, Gran was huffing from climbing upstairs.

'What a terrible day it's been. Get yourself to bed, love.' She bent to kiss Patsy's cheek. 'I wish I could turn in too. I'm whacked.'

Patsy sat on the edge of the bed to unlace her new shoes. She was surprised now that she'd been so upset by them. All right, she'd prefer to have shoes with straps, but at least they were shoes and not boots.

It had taken today to show her what her real problems were. She wished she could put the clock back and have shoes as her only worry. Without Dadda, everything seemed less secure.

And Gran having that terrible row with Vereena. It had been like a battle of the Titans.

CHAPTER FIVE

By the time the Railway Hotel was ready to close that night, Gladys Parry knew she'd worked herself up to fever pitch.

'Come to bed,' Orlando had yawned an hour back. 'You must be tired.'

'No, I'll wait up for Rob.'

'No need. He's taken a key.'

'You go up.' She knew he had to open the shop again at six in the morning. The hours they worked were the very opposite to those worked at the pub.

'Don't say anything to upset him.'

'No, I'll have a pot of tea made ready.' But Rob had hardly got inside the door before she started.

'Don't you dare touch a drop of liquor over there.' Gladys put his tea in front of him.

'Don't worry about me, Mam. I'll be all right.' She'd thought the same years ago. It made her more fearful for him. 'I'm not going to come to a sticky end.'

That brought a flash of anger. 'Are you saying that's what I did? Is that what you mean?'

'I didn't mean anything. I'm tired, not thinking properly.' Rob looked contrite. Gladys could feel the tears prickling again.

'I don't want you to make a friend of Cassie Gripper or that girl Patsy. They're no good. I'd much rather you stayed out of their clutches.'

'Mam.' His gentle manner made him seem very like his

father. 'Cassie's been patient and kind and friendly to me. This isn't easy for either of us. I'll come to no harm over there, I promise you, and it's a job. As for Patsy, she's a brave little thing. Got her head screwed on the right way, that one.'

'I'm glad somebody has in that place. That Bernie needs a kick up the backside, and I hear John isn't much better.'

'I'm going up to bed. Aren't you coming up too?'

Gladys stood up with a sigh. 'I'll just rinse these cups first.' The last thing she felt like was sleep. Her mind was on fire. Not many men would have married a woman in her condition, pregnant with another man's child, as Orlando had.

All right, his wife had died the year before in childbirth, and his baby too. He'd needed a wife badly. Having to open the shop at six every morning for the papers and stay open till eight at night was impossibly hard if there was nobody to light a fire and make a meal in the back, or to give a hand in the shop when it was busy.

'You were very young, Gladys. He gave you drink so you didn't know what you were doing.'

She hadn't liked the gin Alfred had given her. It burned like firewater and had made her feel very strange, as well as sick. She hadn't touched a drop since.

'I blame the man. He took advantage of you.'

Orlando had been right about that. Alfred Gripper had been a handsome man with a charm he could turn on. She'd found him attractive. He'd known how to make a girl feel like a queen. Betty, the Saturday barmaid, had warned her to be careful, that he was hot stuff.

She'd been just seventeen – she'd lied to him about her age – and too innocent by far. He'd helped her get a job at the Lighterman's Arms after Cassie had thrown her out of next door. He'd given her a good reference then.

'It doesn't have to be the end for us,' he'd said. 'You won't be able to come to the old Railway again, but we can meet somewhere else. How'd you like to go to a variety show at the Argyle one night?'

And she'd been fool enough to agree. He'd turned her head with the beads and brooches and scent he'd given her. The show had been wonderful; she'd loved every minute of that. But what had happened afterwards had shown her what Alfred Gripper was really like.

As they'd come out into the night, he'd pulled her arm through his. 'Where are we going to do it, then?' he'd asked.

'Do what?'

He'd laughed and tried to kiss her. She'd turned her face away. 'Not now. What'll everybody think?'

'They won't think nothing of a kiss. How about a drink?'

'No thanks.' He'd already had a couple at the theatre bar. She'd felt buoyed up with the excitement of the show, but she was tired and wanted to get to bed now.

'You want to show your gratitude, don't you, Gladys? Can we go to your room?'

For the first time, she'd realised what he was on about. She'd thought that since he couldn't take her back to the Railway Hotel, she was safe from that. She hadn't liked it anyway, it made her feel cheap and guilt-ridden.

'No, the landlady's always about. She won't let you in.'

'You owe it to me,' he'd laughed. 'We'll find somewhere. It'll have to be a knee-trembler.' She thought he was leading her towards the Railway Hotel.

'No!' She'd hung back. 'I can't go there. What about Cassie?'

'The railway yard's the place. Easy enough to get in from Elizabeth Place. Nobody much about at this time of night.' In the dark shadow of some mammoth shed, he undid her coat.

She could still taste the terror she'd felt that they'd be caught. She'd heard that if you were, you could be taken to a police station and classed as a common prostitute.

'It's quite safe,' he'd soothed. 'You can't get pregnant if we do it standing up.' She'd been fool enough to believe that too.

As Gladys dried the tea cups she started to cry again. It had been her own fault, even if Orlando told her otherwise. She'd known from the start that Alfred Gripper was married. She still crawled with horror when she thought of the awful day when she'd finally realised why she was sick every morning.

What was she going to do? She didn't know anybody here in Birkenhead except Alfred Gripper.

She'd left home against her parents' wishes. She couldn't possibly go back; her father would thrash her. It would be a terrible disgrace for him, a deacon at the chapel. In the village in Wales where she'd been brought up, things like that couldn't be kept quiet.

Alfred Gripper hadn't wanted to know when she told him.

'How do I know it's mine?' he'd leered at her. 'How do I know you really are in the family way? You don't look it. You could be making trouble for me and Cassie.'

She'd burst into tears. She'd thought she was being abandoned to her fate and she'd no idea where to turn next.

'All right.' Alfred had given her his handkerchief at that. 'Don't take on so. There's ways of getting rid of it.'

'You've got to help me.'

There were some things she hadn't admitted even to Orlando. Things best never said to anyone. She'd never told him that she'd done everything she could to rid herself of the baby.

Alfie had suggested lots of gin and hot mustard baths. He'd provided the gin himself and sent her to the bathhouse opposite Central Station. It failed to do the trick. He'd suggested Epsom salts and she'd consumed vast quantities, but that had not had the desired effect either.

'I've heard of a shop,' he said. 'A shilling's worth of pennyroyal or bitter apple is what you want.' He'd given her the shilling, and steered her towards a shop selling surgical supplies. She'd tried first one and then the other, and they'd made her feel so sick she couldn't work.

'I hear that lead's the thing,' he'd said after that. 'But it leaves a tell-tale blue line on the gums.' That had terrified her. Everybody would know.

'There's other stuff. Ergot and rye. Go back to that shop and ask what else they have. He's got everything there.' He'd given her five shillings. Almost dying with shame, she'd gone back.

They'd sold her all manner of pills, one sort after another, and she'd swallowed them all; pink ones and green ones and some horrible brown medicine. They all made her feel sick or light-headed, or gave her cramps in her gut. She was frightened that none of them would work. Every different pill bought renewed hope, only to be dashed.

Finally, the man in the shop told her to come round to his back door after tea with five pounds. That his wife was a midwife who could ensure a miscarriage.

Alfred had complained at the cost, but he'd given her the money and, shaking with terror, she'd gone. But even surgical interference had done no more than provoke a slight bleed.

She had to go back yet again. 'There's no budging this one,' the woman had said. 'He's a real tough laddie, hanging on by his fingernails. But I'll have him out. I'll have another go on Tuesday for you, and I'll do it for a pound this time, seeing it's a repeat.'

But there hadn't been a second go. She'd told Orlando by then and he'd offered marriage. That had seemed the ideal way out of her problem. Her tough baby boy would be born and grow up as a member of a proper family.

Gladys dried the cups and put them back in the

cupboard. They'd all been mistaken: it wasn't a boy and it wasn't a way out at all.

When baby Dilys was born she was a pathetic, puny little girl, and she'd never been right. There were problems with her heart, with her hearing and with her sight. It had taken Gladys a few months to realise just how much mischief she'd done to her own child by swallowing all those pills and potions. Just thinking of it now brought a hot rush of vomit up her throat.

Dilys wasn't right in the head, couldn't talk, couldn't walk until she was four. And Gladys had deliberately swallowed them, meaning to kill the child. But she hadn't done that; she'd only damaged her. Handicapped her, and handicapped her whole family.

Gladys had been afraid she'd go mad herself, living next door to the Railway Hotel and seeing Alfred Gripper go past their door. He never came in and neither did Cassie, but she knew he was there. He knew Dilys was his child.

She'd never told Orlando what she'd done. She never could. She couldn't bear him to think so ill of her. He accepted Dilys as a burden he must support. He told Gladys that the best thing for them all was to have another child as soon as she felt strong enough.

'The next one will be perfect, you'll see,' he'd said. And Robert was, but he couldn't take away the pain of Dilys.

She'd found it exhausting coping with a handicapped child as well as a new baby. Orlando had found a home over in Liverpool that would take Dilys in. But they'd had to pay for her keep, and that had proved to be a heavy financial burden.

Gladys knew it had soured everything for her. She was a wreck, a ghost of the woman she'd once been. She couldn't throw off the guilt for what she'd done to her unborn child. Or the guilt for what she'd done to Lando and Rob. She was keeping them poor. They were working to keep Dilys in that home.

Once she'd heard Rob ask his father why they didn't bring her back to live with them, and it made her wonder just how much Orlando understood.

'Dilys is better where she is,' he'd said. 'She's being looked after properly there.'

'I suppose, with the shop, and all of us working in it, it wouldn't be easy?'

'It's not just that. Your mother feels enough guilt without seeing Dilys day in and day out. Having to do things for her that an ordinary child could do for herself. It's a question of how much your mother could stand. I decided this way was better for us all.'

The next morning, Patsy saw Gran at the living-room window, looking across the street at the Mersey Antiques saleroom. It was run by a manager now, a Mr Solly, an elderly man with a lot of grey hair. He lived in the rooms over the shop.

'Grandpa Ingram's car is there.' Patsy knew he was always there on auction days, but he also came two or three times a week to collect the takings and see how Mr Solly was getting on.

She studied the bull-nosed Morris parked at the kerb. This morning, she could also see him through the big shop window, a portly figure, dressed in a dark pinstriped suit. The sun was catching the gold watch chain that stretched across his waistcoat.

'Run across and tell your grandpa what's happened. He'll be expecting you and your dad to tea on Sunday. Tell him you won't be able to come.'

Patsy felt a little shy of her grandfather, and would have liked Gran to come too. Usually when she spoke to him she had Dadda's hand to clutch.

'Go on with you,' Gran urged. Patsy obeyed slowly, dragging her feet as she went down the stairs.

When she went into the shop, Grandpa was sitting on

Mr Solly's chair behind the counter, his balding head bent over a ledger. Old Mr Solly was very deferential, ignoring the high stool. He didn't sit down in his employer's presence.

Patsy waited in front of the counter, studying Grandpa's bowler hat that was upturned on it. It felt like waiting to be served at Donovan's shop. Grandpa looked up. She thought it odd he should have such bushy eyebrows and a droopy moustache when he had so little hair on top.

'Hello, little one.' That was his name for her. She didn't like it. Lucy had always been bigger. It seemed to reduce her further.

'It's Dadda,' she whispered. 'He had a terrible accident yesterday.'

He closed his ledger. 'What sort of an accident?'

Patsy let it all come out then, about how bad Dadda had looked lying on the cellar door. About how he'd been taken to hospital on the brewery dray. About his fractured arm and ribs.

'And how is he this morning?'

Patsy shook her head numbly, fighting back the tears. 'Don't know.'

'There, there ... We can find out, can't we?'

There was a telephone on the wall. Patsy watched through her veil of tears as he wound the handle to get the operator.

'Do you know which ward he's on?'

'Ward Two,' she sniffed.

She watched while he talked into the instrument. Uncle Bernie thought they ought to have a phone at the pub.

Grandpa looked up and smiled. 'The sister says he's had a good night's sleep and he's brighter this morning. That's good news, isn't it?'

Patsy smiled.

'He'll be all right. Might take a bit of time, but he'll get over it. Don't you worry, little one. Now then, what shall I tell Lucy and your nanna? That Granny Gripper will bring you to tea, or you'll be coming by yourself?'

Patsy shook her head. 'Gran and me will be going to see Dadda at the hospital. Sunday afternoon is visiting time.'

'Of course.'

'We can't get there for evening visiting, you see.'

Patsy could hear him jingling the coins in his trouser pocket. It was a familiar sound.

'Here, Patsy.' A sixpence was pressed into her hand. 'Get yourself some sweeties.' It was what he always said. Grandpa was very generous.

'I'll take some to Dadda,' she flashed gratefully. 'Or get him some cigarettes. He likes those better.'

As she crossed the road back to the Railway Hotel, her eyes fastened on the blue enamel letters emblazoned across the window of the paper shop. 'Park Drive, 10 for 4d., 5 for 2d. Plain or tipped.'

She decided she'd consult Gran first. Usually she was allowed to spend only a halfpenny on sweets, and the rest went into her money box, to be transferred later to her account in the Post Office.

'You must have something against a rainy day,' Gran insisted when she asked her. 'You never know when you'll need it. Mustn't fritter it away.'

'But cigarettes for Dadda?'

'We sell them here. I'll take him a packet. No need to go near the paper shop.'

Harold Ingram watched her go and shook his head. He knew that her brown dress must have been made by Cassie; it was less than a success. It made him feel guilty to see her like this. He knew Patsy was not getting the advantages he was giving Lucy, and they were both Elsa's daughters, after all. He sighed, seeking excuses for himself.

It was only recently that his business had grown and he was able to provide more comfort for his family. To start with, he couldn't have afforded to spend on Patsy too.

Once they'd moved to the house, the next thing he and Mildred considered important was a decent education for Lucy. They'd taken her away from the council school and sent her to the high school. Already her speech was more middle-class.

He knew he ought to have done the same for Patsy, but the thought of two lots of school fees had been daunting at that time. Then there was the practical difficulty of getting Patsy to and from the high school every day. He'd have had to ferry her around himself.

He should have done it when she reached the age of eleven. By then she'd have been old enough to go on the bus.

He knew he hadn't treated Patsy fairly. He'd fobbed her off with an occasional sixpence and watched her face light up with pleasure. He went home that evening and took Lucy on his knee to tell her about her father's accident.

'He'll be all right. It'll just take time,' he reassured her. 'But he won't be bringing Patsy for tea on Sunday.'

'Serious for Cassie.' Mildred pushed her glasses further up her large nose. 'He won't be able to work in the pub for a while.'

'What about our picnic?' Lucy asked. Harold had promised her that if Sunday was a fine day, he'd drive them all out to New Brighton for a picnic on the beach. 'We'll still be going, won't we?'

'I think we ought to go to the hospital to see your dadda instead. He'll expect it.'

'Oh no!' Lucy said, pulling a face. 'You promised a picnic.'

'I don't like hospitals,' Mildred said.

'Neither do I,' Lucy added.

'You're quick to pick up on what your nanna says. You've never set foot in one.'

Harold sighed. He knew that Mildred wasn't over-keen on Lucy having a lot of contact with the Grippers. And Lucy said openly that she didn't like going to the pub; it smelled of sour beer, it was a rough place. Both he and Mildred were afraid that Patsy was growing up in the wrong mould.

'The Grippers are a bit common.' Mildred mouthed the words in case Lucy heard. 'Cassie wearing all that paint and powder at her age.'

Harold had heard she wasn't above kicking up her heels in the pub and singing with the drunks. John was a bit of a rough diamond too. He couldn't help it, of course, he'd been brought up that way. Mildred had never been able to understand what Elsa had seen in him.

And there was this wall between them always: Elsa's wedding in February and her funeral the following Christmas. Getting her pregnant with such indecent haste. It was hard not to blame John for what had happened to their only daughter.

Patsy loved Sundays because the pub didn't open. She helped Gran in the kitchen all morning, pot-roasting a joint of mutton for dinner, and baking apple pies and cakes. Gran made enough to keep them going for days. Today she seemed on edge. There would be no Dadda to tuck into Sunday dinner.

'I don't know how I'll manage without him.'

'You've got Rob. How's he getting on?'

'A bit slow.'

'Won't he do?'

'He'll have to do. He's all there is.' Gran straightened up from the range, her cheeks red from the fire.

'Aye, lass, he's doing all right. Just needs to get used to it. That takes time. He's not likely to be much help with drunks. Too young and slight. And then there's the cellar work. There's no relying on our Bernie these days.'

After dinner was eaten and cleared away, Patsy got herself ready to go to the hospital. She changed into a pink cotton dress that had once belonged to Lucy. Because she was smaller and slighter, she could wear Lucy's dresses when her twin had grown out of them. It took Gran much longer to get ready. Patsy went to Gran's room to watch her. She always wore black.

'Everybody thinks I've got a whole wardrobe of clothes,' she told Patsy proudly, 'and here's me with only three frocks.'

She'd made them all from the same pattern: full of skirt, tight of waist, long sleeves and a plain round neckline. One of silk for best, cut lower in the neck and two of serge for everyday. Gran was changing into the silk.

'In a pub, you can't let yourself get dowdy.'

'What will you wear with it?' Patsy ran her hands over the collection of gold chains, lockets and pendants, strings of beads, amethysts and pearls.

Cassie pulled open a drawer to reveal scarves, jabots and bows; loose collars, large and small, lacy and plain, satin and silk, in every colour.

'This, I think.' Gran carefully fastened a lacy white jabot round her neck.

'You look very smart.' Patsy gave her a hug.

It was a treat to ride up to the hospital on the bus. Gran didn't like walking much these days. They were early and had to wait.

Patsy rushed up the ward the moment the doors were opened to allow visitors in. Her father was smiling up at her from his pillows. She threw her arms round him in such a hug of love she saw him wince. 'How are you, Dadda?'

'Go easy, love, that hurts.' But he was smiling, pleased to see her. 'I'm bruised all over.'

Patsy kissed him again, relieved to find he was able to talk to her. He had his arm in plaster and then in a sling.

Lucy came walking sedately up the ward twenty minutes later, holding firmly on to Harold Ingram's hand. She looked cross. Her kiss was cool and formal.

'Only two at a bed at a time, please.'

Sister stood watching them, arms akimbo. 'How old are you?' She fixed Patsy with an eagle stare.

'Fourteen,' Gran answered before she could. Nobody under that age was allowed in. 'They're both fourteen. Twins.'

Patsy felt very nervous. They wouldn't be thirteen until Christmas; she was afraid Gran's fib would be found out. Lucy smiled at the nurse, full of confidence.

Grandpa said: 'We'll leave them with John for ten minutes, shall we, Cassie? That's what he'll like best. We'll wait outside.'

As Patsy watched them walk away, Dadda was asking: 'How are you, Lucy?'

'We were going to go on a picnic. Gramps promised if it was a nice day, and it's lovely and sunny. We were all going to go together. Nanna said we could take a raised pork pie.'

'That would have been a real treat. I'm sorry I've missed it.'

'You've made me miss it too,' she complained.

'Your nanna will make it up to you, I'm sure.'

Patsy thought Dadda sounded weary. She said to Lucy: 'Nanna's very kind to you. Grandpa too.'

'He's kind to you too,' Lucy said crossly. 'I call him Gramps, not Grandpa. It makes him sound more mine.'

'He's very generous to all of us,' Dadda told them, 'whatever we call him.'

Patsy nodded; her grandparents always gave her lovely presents, and every Christmas Eve they provided a big party with a conjuror, to celebrate their birthday.

77

Lucy invited all her friends. Patsy felt she knew them too because she met them at every party Nanna gave. There was Colin, who wore owlish spectacles and lived next door on one side, and Ruth with a long pigtail, who lived further down the road.

Lucy had a best friend who was in the same class at school. Patsy didn't care much for Madge. She and Lucy always had their heads together, giggling at something she didn't understand. Patsy felt that Madge pushed her out, and that was hurtful because she wanted Lucy to belong to her.

Nanna always asked her if she wanted to bring a friend with her, but she didn't have any friends of her own. Anyway, Nanna wouldn't like the children she knew, she'd say they didn't behave properly.

Patsy thought the time dragged when Grandpa and Gran came back and she and Lucy were dispatched to sit outside.

'There's not that much the matter with Dadda.' Lucy frowned.

'I was afraid too. That he'd be much worse. I didn't think he'd be able to talk to us like this.'

'Such a lot of fuss about nothing.' Lucy swung her legs, watching Patsy warily.

'Oh no, it was a terrible accident. I thought he'd been killed.'

'You would.'

Dadda was always telling her that she was like Lucy. Perhaps she was. There was a family resemblance, but no more than sisters usually had. They had similar features, but Lucy's were more refined. The same colour hair – almost; Lucy's had brighter blonde streaks. Her eyes were violet, not plain blue. She always had smarter clothes. Patsy had to admit it, Lucy was prettier. Except when she was frowning heavily, as she was right now.

'I wish we were more alike,' Patsy said. She desperately

wanted to look more like Lucy, be dressed more like Lucy, live the sort of life Lucy did. But she wanted to do it with Dadda and Gran, not move to Caerns Road where the Ingrams lived. When she went there she had to stop herself looking round at Lucy's belongings, wondering how long it would be before she'd be finished with them and give them to her.

Patsy sighed. 'Everybody knows twins belong together.' That they should be specially close and share everything. A twin should never be lonely. It bothered Patsy, this distance between them. She wanted to close the gap, but didn't know how. It wasn't good to feel uneasy with a twin sister.

The most hurtful thing was that as far as Lucy was concerned, she didn't care if they were strangers.

At last Grandpa came out and took Lucy off, leaving Patsy to go back to join Gran at Dadda's bed.

CHAPTER SIX

When visiting time was over, the crowd thronged out of the hospital.

'We'll go to see Freda,' Gran said as they stood in line to get a bus back into town. 'She'll be expecting me.'

Patsy was used to going to the big old house in Kendal Street and felt quite at home there. More at home than she was at Caerns Road with Lucy and the Ingrams. As a small child, she'd often been left with Auntie Freda during opening hours.

Like her daughter, Freda had once been a schoolmistress, and had about the house lots of toys, jigsaw puzzles and children's books. She'd taught Patsy to read before she started school. Patsy couldn't understand why Vereena had turned out such an unpleasant person.

'She doesn't take after her mother,' Gran had told her. 'But then Bernie doesn't take after me.'

Recently, Gran had started sending Patsy round during opening hours with a piece of apple pie or a cold slice from the Sunday joint. Kendal Street was only a short walk from the Railway Hotel.

Patsy knew that Freda rarely went out. She couldn't get upstairs either, or even answer the front door easily. She suffered from rheumatoid arthritis. Because of this, they always went in the back way, up the entry and through the yard. Gran knocked on the back door, opened it and stepped inside, calling: 'Hello, Freda? Anyone at home?'

Once, Freda had run this place as a boarding house. She

81

often spoke of the well-known artistes playing at the Hippodrome, the Argyle Theatre and the New Theatre Royal who had stayed with her. But Gran had told Patsy that the bread and butter of her business had come from the long-term boarding of telegraph boys who worked at the General Post Office down the road.

'Hello, Freda?'

It was only when Patsy crowded round Gran's bulk in the sitting-room doorway that she realised that Freda already had visitors. She could feel tension crackling between them.

Uncle Bernie was sitting in an armchair by the window. Vereena, wearing her pink cloche again, was standing with her back to them and was even more angry than when Patsy had last seen her at the Railway Hotel.

'You mean it will go to the bank when you die?' There was incredulity in her voice. 'What about me?'

Patsy could see stark anguish in Freda's dark eyes; pain in every line of her old face.

'I didn't know what else to do. I've got to live.' Her misshapen fingers were clawing at her fluffy white hair; she was distraught. 'I gave you my capital to start your dress shop.'

'I wish you wouldn't keep dragging that up.'

'Normally I make a point of never mentioning it. I know you can't bear to be reminded. But you're asking why I need money. I gave you all I had.'

'All right, the shop went bust. I couldn't help it. Having it in a side street was a mistake.'

'Mother's here,' Bernie put in awkwardly. Vereena swung round to face them. Patsy was shocked at the hate in her dark eyes as they met Gran's.

'We'd better go.' Bernie was embarrassed. He took Vereena's arm.

'No point in staying. This is getting us nowhere.'

Her mother said bitterly: 'If you're that desperate to

have money when I die, there's always life assurance. Take out a policy on my life. That's the only pay-out you'll get now.'

When the front door slammed behind them, Freda dropped her head in her hands.

'I had to do it,' she said. 'I had to get money from somewhere, what with medical expenses and Betty to pay and everything.'

Patsy knew that Betty came in for three or four hours each morning, to clean and to cook Freda a hot meal. She watched Gran put an arm round her shaking shoulders to ask: 'What have you done?'

'Assigned this house to the bank. They've fixed it so I get income now.'

'Where will you live?'

'Here. As long as I keep paying the interest on what they've given me, there'll be no problem. It's sort of mortgaged to the bank again. Vereena's cross because I won't be leaving it to her.'

'Don't you worry about Vereena,' Gran said grimly. 'Patsy, how about putting the kettle on?'

She got up immediately. She could see Freda trying to pull herself together.

'There's cold sausages, and some cake. Open a tin of pineapple chunks too, Patsy.'

Patsy liked having tea here. The food was very different from what Gran provided. In the kitchen she set the trolley that Freda used for all her meals now. She found little packets of bought cake to put out on plates. She could hear the two friends talking as she worked.

'I know you've done your best for her and Bernie.'

'I really have. I wish they'd come and live here with me. It would solve . . .'

'You spoiled Vereena as a child. Too much of her own way.'

'"I'd rather stay in my own house, Mam," she said.

When there's all those rooms upstairs and they know I can't get up there. Surely it would feel like their own place after a week or so?'

'She's afraid you'll ask her to help you.'

'Oh, I know what's she afraid of,' Freda sighed. 'Of course, I'm getting worse. She's afraid I'll get to the stage when I can't do anything for myself and she'll have to help.'

'She's a selfish girl.'

'"I've got my own life to lead," she said.'

'You'll get precious little sympathy from her.'

'It doesn't matter how much I give her, she always wants more.'

Patsy was discovering that it wasn't just her and Gran who couldn't get on with Vereena; her own mother couldn't either.

'Wouldn't hurt her to lift a hand here once in a while. Nor Bernie either. They're both very self-centred. Deserve each other really.'

'It can be very lonely, here on my own.'

Gran came into the kitchen to cut bread and butter, and check that Patsy was doing things right. Together they pushed the rattling trolley into what had always been Freda's private sitting room.

As she ate, Patsy looked round. It was a very comfortable room. She couldn't understand why Auntie Freda considered herself poor. She had a carpet square and lovely mahogany furniture, and there were chintz covers on the three-piece suite.

Freda was a frail old lady who moved stiffly and slowly when she moved at all. She sat on an upright chair because she no longer had the strength to pull herself up from the more comfortable settee. She was even having difficulty holding her tea cup in her knotted fingers.

Patsy knew that Gran felt sorry for her friend. That was one reason why she was visiting more and more often. They were both fond of her.

'Poor Freda. The doctor can't do much for her,' Gran said, huffing as they walked home. 'Not a lot to look forward to, has she? Likely to get worse, and no help at all from her only daughter.'

For Patsy, Sunday evenings were the high point of the week. After tea, when they got home, Gran and Dadda usually did some stocktaking down in the pub, so that Gran could re-order what would be needed for the coming week.

Because the pub was closed, Patsy was allowed to go down with them to help. Being on what was normally forbidden territory was a real treat.

She said: 'I'll count the bottles for you today, Gran.'

Usually that was Dadda's job. Her task was to put polish on the little oak tables in the private bar and try to obliterate the white circles made by long-forgotten drinks.

'I don't know what I'd do without you, Patsy. Come on, we might as well get stuck in. We'll start with the cleaning.'

Though the pub had been closed all day, the air remained blue with tobacco smoke. The whole place smelled different from upstairs.

'That's the disinfectant in the lavvy,' Gran told her, but it wasn't just that. It smelled exciting. Something of the jolly atmosphere hung around with the smoke.

Patsy thought the private bar must have been very smart when it had been freshly done up. Now there were cigarette burns in the brown Rexine upholstery covering the long bench under the window, and the mirrors advertising Birkenhead Brewery Ales were becoming mottled.

Patsy heard the first indication that a train was coming. The railway lines were so close that it made the glasses vibrate on the shelves. They were beginning to tinkle, softly to start with but growing louder until the roar of an express drowned the sound out. As the rumble receded, the glasses could be heard tinkling prettily again until they settled down. On weekdays, it happened every few minutes.

With the big broom, Patsy swept the brown lino in the private. It was cracked and wearing into holes now. She swept on, straight through the lobby and into the public bar. Here, sawdust covered the oak boards so there was much more to sweep up. The spittoons in the corners had to be washed out under the tap in the yard.

Gran threw down clean sawdust. 'Got to be careful when you do it, love, not to get this stuff into the spittoons. Put fresh sand in them.'

Patsy never tired of hearing Gran tell the story of how a customer had thrown a cigarette butt into a spittoon and started a fire.

'Your Uncle Bernie's fault, that was. Threw sawdust everywhere. In the spittoons as well; couldn't be bothered getting the sand.'

'But the customers put the fire out, didn't they?'

'Tipped their beer on it,' Gran grumbled.

'It wasn't good for business?'

'I had to give them refills on the house, didn't I? And rogues that they were, they tipped their dregs into the spittoon and expected me to give them a free pint. Long after the fire had gone out, too.'

No seats of any kind were provided in the public. But beer cost less here. Patsy thought it a heady place. Sometimes, when they were singing at night, she crept halfway down the stairs to peep.

The gaslight hissed and flickered on the pewter mugs that hung across the front of the bar. It was Dadda's job to scour them with silver sand once a week.

'They'll do for now,' Gran said, putting out clean towels over the great pump handles that siphoned up beer. Back in the private, Gran opened her books on the bar, and Patsy counted the bottles for her. So many of port and sherry, so many of spirits, so many of lemonade and soda water.

When Gran was satisfied they'd done what was needed, she poured herself a port and lemon.

'Get yourself a glass, love.' This was the weekly ritual. Patsy put a tumbler on the bar and Gran emptied the rest of her lemonade into it. They took their glasses up to the living room. Gran brought out more ledgers, opened them up and spread them across the table.

'Now then, we'll do our sums. Have you got your pencil and paper? We'll each do them, and if we get the same answer, I'll be sure it's right.'

Patsy loved it. 'This is much more fun than doing sums at school.'

'These are real sums, that's why.'

'Not just made-up ones for me to practise on, like at school.'

'That's right. I'm teaching you how to keep the accounts. This is real-life business.'

'Can I write in your books? I'll be just as neat as you.'

'Come on then, you've got to start sometime. This is my cash book. Write in this week's transactions. Here are the bills.' Patsy pulled the bottle of ink nearer and took Gran's pen.

'Why do we do this, Patsy?'

'You have to, so you know how much is being sold in the pub.'

'Yes, then I can work out how much profit we make.'

Patsy thought everything about the pub was wonderful. She couldn't wait to be eighteen so that she too could enjoy herself down there every night.

'Wait for me,' Bernie said, as he and Vereena started to walk home. 'What's the hurry?'

Vereena paused. She'd been stepping out furiously. It had come like a kick in the stomach to find that her mother had assigned her house to the bank. She'd been relying on inheriting it when Freda died.

'She has no right!'

'But you don't even like your mother's house.'

'I could have sold it and bought one we did like. Just think, we'd have had no rent to pay ever after. She shouldn't have done it.'

'But she said she—'

'Wouldn't you feel cheated?'

'I'm not expecting anything. My ma hasn't got much, and what she's got she'll leave to John. He's her favourite.'

'She shouldn't have favourites,' Vereena fulminated. 'I know she doesn't like me. She did her best to stop us getting married.'

'She thought I was too young. It wasn't that she didn't like you. She was impressed that you were a teacher.'

'I wish she'd stop going round to my mother's. What does she want round there all the time? She puts her up to doing these things.'

Bernie took her arm. 'There's a way round it. You heard what your mother said. Why don't you take a policy out on her life? At least you'd get something when she pops off.'

'That's just her way of being bitchy. She knows we can't afford to pay for that every month.'

'She can't last much longer, surely? She's quite poorly.'

'Nobody dies of arthritis.'

'She's over seventy.'

'She's seventy-two but she'll go on till she's ninety. You'll see.'

'You could persuade her to pay the premiums. She feels guilty because you won't get her house. You could see that.'

'She kept it from me until it was all cut and dried.'

'She doesn't like to think she's doing you down. You can get round her.'

Vereena slowed her pace further. Her fingers teased her kiss curl back into place against her cheek. 'Do you think so?'

'Take her a bit of fish round. She likes that. Soften her up a bit. She'll do anything for you.'

Vereena didn't feel confident about that.

'It's worth a try. You don't want to be cheated.'

Vereena's dark eyes jerked up to her husband. This wasn't the first time she'd been cheated. Not by a long chalk. Bernie had cheated her. Time itself had cheated her. It had thickened her figure, put lines round her eyes, made her look older than her thirty-six years.

But the years had been kind to Bernie. He was more handsome now than he'd been when she'd married him. Time had filled him out, broadened his shoulders, made him look more a man of the world, though a man of the world was the last thing he was. Thirteen years of marriage had shown her that.

Bernard Gripper was weak; he always swam with the current. He left every decision to her. She knew now that she'd thrown herself away on him. She'd been a schoolmistress; if she'd stayed single, she could have had a career of her own, been independent, had money enough by now.

She'd met him, all those years ago, when she'd been returning from Liverpool by ferry, carrying a new dress she'd bought in Bunny's. She'd looked up to find Bernie beside her, leaning over the boat's rail, handsome and with a delightful smile. He'd amused her with his chat. She'd thought him charming. He'd offered to carry her parcels as he'd walked her home, though she'd meant to catch a bus at Woodside.

Years later, Bernie had had the nerve to tell her that he'd fancied her and had deliberately set out to bed her.

She'd never have married him if she'd known that. Or the lengths to which he was prepared to go.

'Haven't you heard?' he'd laughed in his easy-going way. 'All's fair in love and war.'

He'd told her he was in his last year at Liverpool University, reading architecture. He went on and on about his ambitions, about what he was going to achieve. She'd been stupid enough to believe him. He'd lied about his age, too.

Bernie had rushed her into passion and into sex. She should have had more sense than to think he was her big chance in life. She shouldn't have given in as she had. If she'd known he was a nineteen-year-old barman she'd have run a mile. He'd never have got near her. It was too late by the time she found out. She was pregnant.

'Why did you tell me such lies?' she'd screamed. She'd been hysterical.

He'd shrugged. 'I like a bit of skirt, and sometimes I have to shoot a line to get it.'

That had been a terrible moment in her life. The worst. That she'd fallen for a trick like that.

'We'll get married,' he'd said. 'I'll do the right thing by you. I still fancy you, Vee.'

By then she wasn't sure whether she fancied him or not. He was good company and very presentable to look at, but she didn't much like what she saw beneath.

'Do think carefully about marrying him,' her mother had said seriously, when her wedding plans were being made.

'I know you love him, but just think of the future. All that studying to become a teacher, and you're going to throw it away after working for just a few months. What is the hurry?'

Vereena had been unable to tell her. She'd been terrified of telling anybody. Marriage had seemed the only answer. Her one stroke of good fortune had come too late. She'd had a miscarriage, but by then she'd been on her honeymoon. Nobody here at home ever knew about the pregnancy, that was the only good thing.

She knew that if she'd had the miscarriage before she was married, she would not have gone through with it. And it had put her right off having children.

'I thought you loved them,' Cassie had said. 'Thought you and Bernie would have made me a grandma again before now,'

'We can't afford it,' she'd retorted. 'Not on what Bernie earns. I'm glad he doesn't want a family.'

For herself, the thought of getting pregnant again was totally abhorrent. She took steps to guard against it. Life was cheating her all the time. She ought to be used to it. Bernie was weak. It didn't help to know she must rely on herself and pull Bernie along with her. He'd turned out to be a bit of a layabout.

'You ought to run your own business,' her mother had said. 'You could do that. It's no good relying on Bernie. You must know that by now.'

Vereena hated to think that her mother saw through him too. If she wanted a decent living she'd have to earn it herself.

'This boarding house is getting too much for me,' Freda had said. 'Why don't you come and live here and take it over? It seems the obvious way out for you.'

Vereena had been brought up in the boarding house. Her father had been a bank manager, but he'd died when she was twelve, and after that her mother had had to support them. She knew the drudgery boarders brought. All the cooking and cleaning. They'd done breakfasts and evening meals too.

'The fortunate thing about it is that it's near enough for Bernie to live here and still work at the pub.'

Vereena knew she couldn't face that again. 'Not the boarding house, Mam.'

'You know the trade. And I'd be here to guide you.'

'No, Mam,' she'd said firmly. She wasn't going to land herself in any other situations she didn't like. She was getting a raw deal from life as it was. The last thing she needed was to be at the beck and call of lodgers.

But another sort of business? Everybody told her she had marvellous dress sense. She loved clothes. She loved shops that sold them. Vereena made up her mind to follow her own inclinations. What she really would enjoy was to open a dress shop.

She'd had another raw deal over that. She'd taken a lease on a shop in a side street because it was cheaper. She knew now that she should have gone to the high street or not at all. Her shop had gone bust, giving her another bad time.

And Cassie Gripper had rubbed that in. 'You and Bernie never showed much interest. Clothes, yes, but not in running the business side. I wanted to help. I tried to tell you what you needed to do, but you wouldn't listen. That was the trouble.'

'D'you know what surprised me?' Bernie asked now, taking out his key to unlock their front door. 'Your mother asking us to go and live with her again. Do you think we should?'

'No.' Vereena went straight to the kitchen to fill the kettle. 'Do you want some tea?'

'It would save paying rent here, and it's not as though she's still running the business.'

Vereena flopped down on the settee. Her mother had persuaded her to go back once. It had been another of her terrible mistakes.

'There's all those empty rooms upstairs. She wouldn't bother us, she can't get up the stairs any more.'

'No, Bernie, she'd be shouting for me to come down. She'd have me waiting on her hand and foot. I know what she's like. Nothing will persuade me to go back again. Last time I did that, Mam gave me a rotten time.'

Bernie put a cup of tea in her hand, then, lifting his guitar, started softly picking out the notes of 'It's a Long Way to Tipperary'.

'That was years ago, in the war. Things are very different now.'

It would have been about 1917. Vereena saw herself tossing the *Daily Post and Mercury* away from her. The news from France was of ferocious fighting in slime and mud and sleet. It sickened her to read of the endless, mindless slaughter.

She'd had to steel herself to look at the list of deaths, printed within a black border. She was half expecting to see Bernie's name amongst them. She didn't think she'd ever see him again, so many were being killed.

She'd read of the courage and strength and dogged determination of the British Tommies fighting at Passchendaele. They were not qualities she associated with Bernie. He wouldn't be coping with any of it.

The war was having a disastrous effect on her own life. At twenty-eight, she felt that her youth was ebbing away. Already she could see the first signs of crow's-feet beginning round her dark eyes, and there were lines developing across her forehead.

The day after she'd noticed them, Vereena had the front of her dark hair styled into a fringe. She kept the back long enough to put up into a loose bun. She enjoyed men friends and liked to get out and about, yet here she was living alone and having no fun at all.

As Bernie's wife, the British Army paid her the standard allotment from his pay as a private soldier, but she couldn't manage on it. Vereena found it wasn't enough to allow her to go on renting the house they'd lived in since their marriage.

'It would be sensible to come back home,' her mother had said. 'You can give me a hand if you like. I'll pay you pocket money and you can have your keep free. Then you can save Bernie's allotment. Build up a nice little nest egg. No point in paying out rent on a house for yourself.'

Vereena hadn't wanted to live with so many fifteen-year-old telegraph boys. Their heavy red bikes propped up outside the house were a constant reminder of their presence. But eventually she'd had to go.

Vereena found she had to share a bedroom with her mother and was expected to help with all the chores that taking in boarders brought. Her mother employed a woman to do the heavy work, but it left them more than enough to get through.

'Come and help serve breakfast,' Freda was always calling up to her. Or it was to help serve an evening meal to a dozen cheeky boys, and the fact that they did shift work meant the house was never free of them.

'Could you just run a cloth round the bathroom, Vereena?' or 'There's the bedrooms to sweep out,' or 'Count the laundry and make out a list, would you?'

To Vereena it seemed there was no end to what her mother required of her, and she'd forgotten just how impatient Freda could get. Every time she sat down for five minutes, her mother would come bustling in.

'For heaven's sake, Vereena, can't you hear the milk-man knocking at the door?' or 'Surely it wouldn't be too much for you to put out clean towels?'

Occasionally, Freda lost her temper. 'Vereena, I asked you to slip out for an extra loaf, and you've been gone four hours. You knew I needed it straight away. I had to ask Billy to go when he came in.'

'And why not? It wouldn't hurt him. He's been sitting about all day at the Post Office.'

'But you said you'd like a little walk.'

Vereena felt the gorge rising in her throat. She wanted to enjoy life, while her mother was happy wearing herself out polishing and cleaning.

'You're turning me into a drudge. You expect me to

work all the hours God sends, and it's not as though you pay me much.'

She saw her mother's cheeks flush with anger. 'With your keep, you're more expensive than Mrs Potts. It's more trouble to get you off your backside to do little jobs than it is to do them myself. You're bone idle, that's your trouble.'

Vereena had had only three exciting weeks since she'd been here. Last summer, a handsome baritone who sang romantic ballads in the halls under the name of Henry Hammond had lodged with them for a week. The piano on which Vereena had learned to play as a child was still in the front room. When he asked her to accompany him as he practised, she thoroughly enjoyed it.

She'd called him Henry, because it suited him better than his real name of Sydney Pratt. To have his big, appreciative eyes looking at her over his song sheets had stirred responses within her. He followed the movement of her hips as she tried to walk in her new hobble skirt, and stared at her legs. She felt alive again. He was a man who appreciated women and knew how to give them a good time.

Henry had played two shows nightly at the Argyle Theatre. He'd arranged with the doorman to let her in to see the show as often as she wanted without having to pay sixpence for a seat.

Her mother didn't approve of the music hall. She thought ladies shouldn't go alone. She didn't consider it as safe as the cinema, where audiences sat mute in the dark.

Music-hall audiences joined in the choruses of well-known songs. They stamped their feet to martial music. They could make the Argyle echo like a drum. Every night they booed and catcalled a quavery soprano, but for Henry they always clapped appreciatively. Vereena basked in their praise of him.

Henry told her that when he was able to command a personal accompanist, the job would be hers. At the moment, his accompaniment was provided by the pianist in the orchestra, and they varied greatly from theatre to theatre. Many set their own pace and it wasn't always to his choice.

Vereena was in the audience the night the pianist at the Argyle had a problem with his digestion. Henry said he'd eaten too well of Mersey winkles.

He'd come to her seat and asked her to play for him, and because she'd practised with him at home, it had gone like clockwork. Nobody would have known she wasn't a professional. She'd felt like dancing on air.

She'd stayed in the orchestra pit for the rest of the night, playing through the programme as well as she could. There had been missiles thrown at the quavery soprano and a juggler; apple cores and matchboxes and darts fashioned from the programme. Many fell short of their target and into the orchestra pit.

The conductor said she'd done magnificently, and the manager had paid her two shillings for her trouble. She went to the theatre the following night, and was disappointed to find that the pianist's bowels had recovered sufficiently to allow him to stay in the pit throughout the performance.

Henry had been booked to play the following weeks at the Lyric Theatre in Everton Valley and the Tivoli in New Brighton. He moved his lodgings over to Liverpool but came back within two days. 'I can't bear to be parted from you,' he told her.

So Vereena was usually in his bed when she should have been helping with breakfasts for the telegraph boys. She'd made no secret of the fact that she was married. It didn't seem to matter to Henry; he told her many times that he loved her.

As she washed up and dusted, she found herself

fantasising about what would happen when Henry had to move on to his next booking in Grimsby. Vereena felt quite dreamy as she imagined him holding her close and kissing her.

'Come away with me,' he'd whisper in his throaty baritone. 'What I really want is to make you my wife. We'll just have to pretend you are until we hear definitely that something's happened to Bernie.'

Just to think of it made her heart beat faster. She made up her mind that she'd go with him. Life with Henry would be exciting. She'd earn her living on the stage with him. She'd be his accompanist, and perhaps after a month or so, she'd be asked to play a solo too.

She thought of the posters outside theatres advertising their turn. 'Henry Hammond with his glamorous accompanist Vereena Gripper.' No, not Gripper. She'd call herself Vereena Valhalla, perhaps, or something romantic like that. She started getting her clothes ready.

As his third week drew to an end, she waited for Henry to ask her. On his last night in Kendal Street, she was driven to broach the subject herself.

'Come with me?' His eyes were no longer warmly appreciative. She could see horror in them. 'I told you I lived in Grimsby? I'll be at home, not in lodgings.'

Vereena had laughed. 'I can stay in lodgings for a few nights. To give you time to introduce me to your family. My being married already, well, it might be embarrassing. They can get used to the idea gradually.'

'I'm married too,' he'd said, and his face had been as hard as a stone wall. 'There's no question of you coming.'

'You didn't tell me.' Vereena couldn't get her breath.

'You didn't ask. I've also got two children, and my wife's shortly expecting our third. Of course you can't come with me.'

Vereena felt she'd been kicked. 'You said you loved me.'

'I thought you understood how it was with us – just a fling.'

She wasn't going to let him see how hurt she was. She took herself off to the bathroom, locked herself in and took a long, hot bath. She had her cry and washed away her tears, ignoring frequent attempts from the telegraph boys to use the room. She slid into her bed in her mother's room and never spoke to Henry again.

'Aren't you coming to Woodside to see me off?' he'd had the nerve to ask as he stood with his suitcase in the hall. Vereena ignored him, preferring for once to chop carrots in the kitchen.

It had taken her a long time to get over Henry, and even longer to accept that the humdrum routine of her life was not going to change.

She hated the telegraph boys in their blue serge tunics and trousers piped with red braid. Their pillbox hats made them look like monkeys, and they were always causing trouble between her and her mother.

Life had become so awful that Vereena had gone down to the General Post Office in Argyle Street and asked for a job herself. It was just about the handiest place to work, as it was only a few hundred yards from Kendal Street.

She'd been lucky enough to be taken on as a counter clerk, and although it was no great shakes as a job, it was better than being at her mother's beck and call all day. Also, she was working with people of her own age.

Vereena continued to live at home because it was easier to sit down to ready-cooked meals than it would be to fend for herself. Her mother had said that if she did a few jobs at the weekend she wouldn't have to pay for her keep, but of course she was expected to help with the washing-up every evening, and there was no end to the other chores her mother wanted done.

At work, she'd been pleasantly surprised when she'd been introduced to her supervisor. Alec Jepson had eyes that followed her everywhere. His touch on her arm could make her heart turn over. He was popular with all the girls.

'Vereena?' Her mother came to the door of the bedroom they shared.

'I'll be down in a minute,' she replied. She felt she was entitled to ten minutes' rest when she came home from her day's work. Mother seemed to think she should leap straight into dishing up dinner for others.

'Those boys are saying—'

'I said I'll be down, Mother,' she repeated testily.

'They're laughing about you and your supervisor, Mr Jepson.' Her mother's voice had risen half an octave. 'Sniggering behind their hands about the scandalous way you're carrying on with him, at the Post Office, in front of them all. Him a married man, too. Where were you last night until after midnight?'

Vereena sat up slowly on her bed. She'd been out with Alec, of course. He was nothing important, just a bit of fun on the side. She'd learned her lesson from Henry Hammond. It was no good getting too involved. Don't take men friends too seriously.

'They're gossiping about you. A married woman, with her husband away, fighting for his country. What are you thinking about?'

Vereena came out of her reverie to find that Bernie was still picking over the same piece of music. Her tea had gone cold.

'I don't suppose it matters where we live now.' His radiant smile lit up his face. 'You've got everything stitched up this time. The Dixie Minstrels are going over big.'

Vereena felt mollified. 'I'm thrilled we're booked for another week on Llandudno pier.'

'Things are going to change for us, Vee. You'll see. We'll soon be in the money.'

CHAPTER SEVEN

Cassie kept pausing to think of Freda. She could see her condition deteriorating. When she'd last visited her on Sunday she'd seemed low in spirits, even despondent. Cassie was worried about her.

Poor Freda, if anybody had drawn the short straw in life it was her. After teaching for many years, she'd married a bank manager, only to be widowed within a few short years. Her husband had carried enough life assurance for her to buy a bigger house and set up her business.

Then, just when she was making a success of it, her doctor had told her that the pain and stiffness in her joints was likely to get worse and leave her increasingly incapacitated. She'd struggled on to support Vereena through college, and now the ungrateful girl wouldn't lift a finger to help her.

Cassie decided to call round and see Freda the following day. She went up the yard and let herself in as she usually did, calling out to her as she went through her kitchen. When she reached the sitting room she pulled up with a jerk. She'd never seen her friend look so dejected.

As soon as Freda saw her, she began mopping at her eyes with her handkerchief, trying to hide her distress. It cut Cassie to the quick.

'Freda! I was afraid you were feeling low on Sunday. I should have come sooner. Vereena upset you. Is it what she was saying?'

Freda blew her nose and shook her fluffy white head.

101

'I'm old and I'm lonely and I'm ill. They'd put me to sleep if I was a dog.'

'Don't talk like that.'

'If the pain gets any worse I'd rather do it. I'd rather die.'

'No you wouldn't. You're feeling down now, but you'll get over it.'

'What good am I to anybody?'

'You're a good friend. You've done a lot for me and Patsy in the past.'

'In the past, that's right. Can't any more.'

'We love coming round to see you, and we haven't forgotten all the help you've given us. We're very fond of you, Freda.' Cassie heard her sniff again. 'You're here too much on your own, that's your trouble. You need to get out and see more people.'

'How can I, the way I am?'

'I've told you before, you ought to get yourself a wheelchair. I know you've been too proud up till now, but the time has come.'

Cassie pulled her chair closer to her friend. 'You can't manage on sticks any longer. Let me make enquiries about wheelchairs, find out what's available. You've got such big rooms here you'd get round all right inside. Just look at the width of the doors.'

'I don't know ... I mean, how could I get out by myself? I'd be scared to try.'

'I could push you round to the Railway Hotel. It'd do you good to have a drink and a singsong in the private.'

'I don't think that's my sort of thing, Cassie.' Her smile wobbled, but she'd perked up.

Cassie said, 'You'd be better if it was. I'm going to find out about wheelchairs, and I'm going to get our Patsy to run round here every evening when we open up.'

'She comes often enough as it is. I don't want to be a bother to her. She's only a child.'

'You won't be, she likes to come. She remembers how you taught her to read. You still lend her books.'

'I can manage by myself.'

'It won't hurt for her to come round. She can make you a cup of tea, see to the fire, that sort of thing.'

'Betty does—'

'I know she leaves something ready for your tea. But Patsy can talk to you. She loves to help. See you let her.'

Patsy was delighted when she heard that Dadda would be coming home from hospital at last. He'd been kept in over three weeks.

For days Gran had been saying: 'We'll have to get a taxi to bring him home.' But then Grandpa came across the road to say there was no need for that, he'd fetch him in his car. When Patsy came home from school Dadda was sitting upstairs with his feet on a stool. His arm was still in plaster, but otherwise he seemed the same old Dadda.

'Don't throw yourself at him,' Gran said. 'His arm's still sore.'

He grinned at her as she kissed him decorously. 'Lovely to have you home again, Dadda.'

She heard Gran say that the doctors had told her it would be a long time before he was fit to work again. But Dadda was downstairs in the bar the next day.

'Don't overdo things,' Gran had pleaded. 'Don't tire yourself out.'

'You're the one that looks tired out, Mam. Has Bernie done much to help?'

'You know Bernie. I've had Agnes in every night. And Rob, the lad from the paper shop, is shaping up well. I can manage, John. I don't want you to exhaust yourself.'

'Don't worry, I won't.'

Over the next year, Cassie was relieved to find John gradually regaining his strength and taking over all his old jobs in the pub.

Things had changed because she'd taken on more help. She'd had to, to survive without him. Bernie was wanting to do fewer and fewer hours.

Agnes they could rely on. She was a good-natured, raddled woman of fifty who had worked at the Lighterman's Arms for years. She was coming in full-time now.

Rob Parry did much of the cellar work and was popular in the bar, but he made no secret of the fact that he was aiming for better things than bar work. He was doing what she'd hoped her boys would do, making a real effort to improve himself.

Cassie had passed her sixty-third birthday, and no longer had the energy to do all the work she used to. John understood that. When things were quiet, he would say: 'Go upstairs and have a rest, Mam. There's no need for you to be on your feet eight hours a day now.'

'Go on,' Agnes urged. 'You should be taking things easy.'

'There's plenty to do upstairs. Dinner to see to, and the ironing.' Cassie knew as she climbed the stairs that what she really wanted was for John to become the licensee. Last time she'd renewed her licence, the brewery had seemed to hint that perhaps it was getting too much for her.

When he went into the public bar to start work on Saturday night, Rob Parry had to smile at the new notice Cassie had propped against the cash register.

'God we trust. For other customers, our terms are strictly cash.'

He'd heard men pleading for 'one on the slate', and he understood Cassie's problem, but it wasn't the sort of witticism his parents would appreciate. They were staunch members of the Welsh Free Chapel on Claughton Road.

Tonight, however, the notice seemed unnecessary. The gasworks had paid a half-yearly bonus to its workers, and a nearby shirt factory had closed for its week's annual holiday. The early evening was busier ⸻

were raised and animated, there was a lot of laug⸻

nine o'clock both bars were packed and he heard the first

quavering notes of voices raised in song.

By ten, it was 'Yes, We Have No Bananas', over and over, and he could hear Cassie's voice leading the chorus. A tidal wave of enjoyment seemed to be washing through the pub. Rob felt buoyed up by it, though the customers kept clamouring to be served and he didn't get a moment's rest.

It was a warm, sultry night. As closing time approached, the air was blue with tobacco smoke and the level of noisy banter rose until the atmosphere seemed electric.

Suddenly, all the good humour was gone. In a corner of the public bar, a couple of dockers could be heard arguing. Others joined in, voices rose again, effing and blinding. Then a spark of anger flashed across the room, and in no time at all, fists were being raised.

John shot from behind the bar to separate the combatants, but customers were taking sides. He ejected several burly men.

'Time, gentlemen!' he was shouting.

'Yer five minutes early, gaffer. What yer thinking of?' The customer turned to Rob. 'Here, give us another pint.'

'No, we're closing,' John said firmly. 'Clock's slow. Time, gentlemen.'

The mood was aggressive. The bar felt like a tinderbox as tension mounted. Insults were being shouted by angry voices. Rob sidestepped as a pewter mug came crashing across the bar.

'Get Ma down here,' he heard John hiss. There were drops of perspiration standing up on his forehead. Cassie had gone upstairs, but she must have been aware of what was happening because she came bustling down to clear both bars. Rob was conscious of Patsy huddling on the stairs, buttoning her coat over her nightdress.

was scared; things were turning nasty. He could hear the fight continuing on the pavement outside. Then above the roar of the angry crowd came the crack of splintering glass.

He shot outside to find that his father's shop window had been shattered by a mass of brawling bodies. As a child he'd heard drunks being turned out on the street at closing time. Sometimes they'd fought beneath his bedroom window, but never quite like this.

His father came shooting through the door like a wild bull. Rob had never seen him so angry. His neck was red above his flannelette nightshirt, his eyes flashed fire and his voice rang with authority, the same way it did in chapel.

'Stop this, all of you! Have you taken leave of your senses? It's like animals you are. You're grown men, all of you. Why can't you behave decently?'

One by one they stood back. Fists were lowered. Slowly and self-consciously, those knocked to the ground stood up, pushing the broken glass out of their way with their boots.

Rob could see his mother's head coming round the shop door, a heavy pink sleeping net over her hair. But his father had caught sight of Cassie.

'Cassie Gripper, it's a disorderly house you keep. It shouldn't be allowed. There's no peace living next door.'

'I'm sorry,' Cassie panted. Rob had never seen her so harassed. 'I don't know what sparked that off.'

'Letting your customers brawl on the street, breaking up my property. It isn't safe for decent people to live near you. A dreadful noise all night. How do you expect your neighbours to sleep?'

Rob knew that most of the neighbours had been in the pub themselves.

'The police can settle this. I want them here. Complain I will, we can't go on like this. Rob, go and fetch them.'

Rob hesitated, feeling caught between parent and employer and not wanting to fall foul of either.

'Wait a minute,' Cassie said, holding up her arms in a gesture of placation. 'I'll pay to have your window mended.'

'Cassie Gripper, you're only saying that because you know they'll take away your licence. I want the police here. I know my rights.'

Rob gasped: 'Better if I board the window up for you. Before anything gets stolen.'

He felt he had to get away. This was terrible; it was widening the rift between the paper shop and the pub when he'd hoped to close it.

He went through to the yard behind the shop where he knew there were pieces of wood that had been used for this purpose on a previous occasion. He knew that his father had sent somebody else for the police. The crowd was melting away like ice in the sun.

Rob was carrying the nails and the sweeping brush through to the front when he heard his mouse-like mother turn on Cassie. Shock and anger had given her courage.

'It's take away your licence they will. You're always bragging you can control anything, Cassie Gripper; that you can prevent trouble from drunks. Now look what you've let them do.'

'I'm sorry. Terribly sorry. This time it got out of hand.'

'It's keep pushing the ale down their throats you do. It's good for your own profit, isn't it? Not a thought for what it does to them.' Gladys's face was working with fury.

'You take every penny men earn, instead of letting them spend it on their children. They go barefoot while their fathers drink.'

His mother was always on about this, and Rob had seen it for himself. He'd known many who wore shoes to school but in order to make them last, went barefoot when they played in the street. Particularly in warm weather such as they were having now.

He knew that the children he served with beer for their fathers in the jug and bottle were often hungry and in rags. He knew that others hung around outside the main door night after night while their parents drank within. He could see Patsy shrinking back into the pub doorway.

'A family man should be spending his wages on food and clothes and a decent place to live. Not on drink.'

'Hold on a minute, Gladys.' Cassie's voice was louder, rising with her temper. 'I'm not responsible for the way any man spends his wages.'

'Get them so drunk you do, they don't know what they're doing. Some go home and beat their wives.'

'You can't blame me for that!'

'I do,' Gladys retorted. 'I know what goes on in that pub. It's an evil trade. Disgusting because it's the wives and children who suffer.'

'If people are short of food and clothes it's not the fault of the pub trade.' Cassie's voice was strident. 'Men are daft if they drink their wages when their kids are starving. They say they aren't being paid enough. Aren't they all talking of going on strike? You can't blame me for every ill in the world.'

'It's a terrible trade. You play on people's weaknesses. Let them drink themselves silly you do.'

Rob saw Cassie's face change. She was furious now and determined to get the better of his mother.

'Is that what happened to you, Gladys, you drank yourself silly? You didn't even realise you were breaking up my marriage? Was it just a bit of fun for you – seducing my husband?'

Rob could see his father's mouth opening in horror. Instantly he was trying to steer Gladys indoors.

'I don't know how you have the nerve to live next door to me. Every time I see you, I'm reminded that your Dilys was my Alfie's child. Surely you can't believe I don't know? Everybody round here knows that.

'Your Dilys was a cuckoo in the nest, wasn't she? No wonder you don't want her home with you.'

Cassie gave a snort of disgust.

'So I don't like your holier-than-thou attitude, Gladys Jones. There's things you've done that I never would.'

Rob had hardly dared breathe throughout the exchange. He'd known there was more to Dilys's birth than he was being told, but in his wildest moments he'd never have thought of this. Not Mam!

Yet he couldn't doubt it was the truth. That showed in Dad's protective attitude, and the shock and shame on his mother's face.

She was still shouting: 'A filthy trade, disgusting ...' but his father had urged her inside at last. The door banged behind them.

Rob took a deep, shuddering breath. Now he knew exactly what it was that had caused the rift between his family and the Grippers. His gut was twisting in agony.

As Cassie ushered her family back inside the pub, Patsy's frightened eyes levelled with his. He guessed she hadn't known before either.

He lifted the first board into position across the shop window and began to nail it in place, bringing the hammer down with all his might. It released some of the tension that was knotting him.

After tonight everybody would know. Those who had forgotten would have been reminded. Bitterness would have been renewed on both sides. He wondered if it would be possible for him to go on working at the pub. Whether Cassie would want him to.

He thought of Dilys, the poor handicapped sister he hardly knew because she'd never lived at home. He'd been aware that the cost of her care was the cause of his family's straitened circumstances.

Now, for the first time, he understood how much his mother was to blame and just what his father had done to help her.

Rob was hammering the last piece of wood home when he heard a policeman's heavy tread on the pavement behind him.

'You've had a bit of trouble here tonight?' he was asking.

Rob could see his notebook and pencil coming out, and said: 'I'll get my father.'

Orlando was just coming downstairs. 'I've got your mother back to bed,' he whispered. 'Warm some milk for her and make sure she takes two of her sleeping tablets.'

When he took the milk up a few minutes later, Rob couldn't stay with his mother. Her anguish was obvious. Her eyes were red and swollen, her face wet with tears she still couldn't control. It made him realise how deeply ashamed she felt at the public airing of her past sins.

'He's a good man, a religious man,' she sobbed. 'Nobody but a saint would have done what he's done for me. How can you work for that wicked woman? She didn't have to bring it all up again.'

He made his escape as soon as he could. He couldn't tell her that she'd goaded Cassie into a public slanging match. That Cassie appeared to be the innocent party, the one still in control of her life, still caring for others, while Gladys was fast becoming a nervous wreck.

He went down to the living room. The policeman was sitting at the table, his notebook in front of him. Orlando's face was white and set. Rob felt wary, afraid that this was to be vengeance on Cassie. But his father's tone was not vindictive. He'd calmed down now.

'Tell me,' the policeman said, 'the names of those who were fighting in the Railway Hotel next door.'

Again Rob felt cut in two.

'Do you know them? They're mostly local men who drink there.'

Rob knew them. He had to support his father in this. He dictated a list of names and addresses.

* * *

110

In the rooms over the pub, Cassie lay back on her chair with her apron over her face. She could feel herself shaking. The fire in the kitchen range had gone out, but Patsy was poking newspaper and sticks under the kettle to make a blaze. She just had to have a cup of tea.

John and Agnes were downstairs, silently cashing up for the night. When at last John came wearily up to join them, she said: 'You should be thinking of having your name over the door. The time's come.'

'No.' He shook his head. 'No, Mam.'

'I couldn't cope with another night like this one. I'm past it.'

'It was awful,' he agreed. 'Takings are up, though.'

'My licence might be taken away. You know what the police are like.'

'You'll be all right.' John took a noisy gulp at the tea Patsy had poured for him. 'You cope better than I could.'

'Next year, when it comes up for renewal, I want you to do it. Now, while I'm still here to help you.'

John put down his mug. 'I'd have the books and the ordering to do. I'd never get it right.'

'Course you would. Anyway, Patsy can do the books. Look, Patsy, it's high time you were in bed. Off you go now.'

As Patsy kissed them both and went, Cassie said: 'She's doing the books now.'

'But I'd never be able to. I'd have to rely on her.'

Cassie sighed. She'd tried to teach him how to keep the accounts, heaven knows she had. Why was it always the women in her family who took the responsibility; the women who had the energy and the brains? The men never did make much of themselves.

She took a deep breath. 'John, I can't do the cellar work. It's too heavy for me, always has been. But I didn't let that stop me.'

111

'You know what needs to be done in the cellar, Mam. That's the difference. No, I'll leave the pub for Patsy. She's your best bet as the next licensee.'

'She's not fourteen yet,' Cassie snorted. 'I can't keep going till she's old enough. Have some sense. I don't know what's the matter with you men.'

But John was shaking his head wearily. They were all too upset by what had happened to make any decisions tonight.

As Cassie got ready for bed, she knew she was pleased with the way Patsy was shaping up. She could see herself in her granddaughter. Patsy would try her hand at anything. She didn't know the meaning of the word can't. Not like her father.

Patsy had been keeping the books for almost a year now. Cassie kept an eye on what she was doing, of course, but the girl didn't make many mistakes. And when she did, she usually managed to sort them out.

Shortly after breakfast the next morning, John went downstairs to see who was knocking on their door. Cassie was somewhat taken aback to be called down to speak to a policeman in the private bar. 'You stay too,' she told her son.

Cassie was fearful for her licence. She'd known of other publicans who had had theirs withdrawn after similar problems. Neither did she want to name names. It was no good expecting her customers to remain loyal and drink in her pub if she landed them in trouble.

'I understand there was fighting here last night,' the policeman said.

'I didn't see who broke the paper shop window,' she replied. 'I serve here in the private bar. There was no trouble in here.'

'But in the public bar? You must have heard fighting break out?'

'Five minutes before we closed there was an argument

there. I'm not prepared to say any more, and I certainly don't want to give any evidence in court.'

'Then can I ask your son? You were in the bar—'

'Not him either,' Cassie broke in. 'He was busy serving. Why don't you ask one of the other customers?'

'Madam, you must co-operate if you want to keep your licence.'

'Nobody's complaining about what went on in here. The fighting was outside.'

'There've been complaints about the noise coming from here.'

'That'll be the paper shop too. Blowing things up because of their window. You ask the other side,' Cassie told him. 'Or across the road. I bet nobody else will say we was noisy.' She felt confident of that; most had been in here last night.

She was worried that Rob Parry wouldn't turn up for work this morning and she'd have to start looking for somebody else. But ten minutes before opening time he was facing her across the bar.

'Do I still have a job here?' He was biting his lip. She could see he was as anxious and upset about what had happened as she was. She swept round the counter and gave him a hug.

'Course you have! It all happened years ago, for God's sake! I was dreading having to look for someone else. Thank goodness you've got your feet on the ground.'

She polished the glasses in the private after that and felt better. All she had to do now was to persuade John to take the licence when it came up for renewal. She was determined that he would, but first she had to give him time to get over this.

Book Two
1926

CHAPTER EIGHT

Cassie knew that Freda was definitely getting worse. Patsy was going over every evening. She stayed for an hour and made sure Freda had everything she needed. She was doing what Vereena should. Cassie believed it was Patsy who'd kept Freda going over the dark days of last winter, and was pleased Patsy wanted to do it.

Freda had had her wheelchair for several months now. The first time she'd ventured outdoors in it, both Cassie and Patsy had gone with her. Cassie had noticed that Patsy was catching Lucy up in height. She was growing stronger too. She'd encouraged her to push Freda about in her wheelchair, and found she could manage it better than Cassie could herself. Patsy had more strength.

'Let her take you shopping, Freda,' she'd said. 'You'd like that, wouldn't you?'

As the weeks went on, Patsy started taking Freda up Grange Road on fine Saturday mornings, and sometimes to the outdoor market.

But now Freda was so stiff she could hardly move in the mornings. Cassie thought her case pitiful and wished she could do more to help.

'What is there for me to look forward to?' Freda mourned. 'It takes me all morning to get myself out of bed and into my clothes. I can feel myself going downhill. I wish I had the guts to end it, put myself out of my misery.'

'Don't you say anything like that to our Patsy,' Cassie

117

warned her. 'She'll be more upset than I am to hear you talking like this.'

Cassie still thought that the best thing to jolly her out of her moods of despair would be a session in the private. But Freda resisted it. 'I've never been one to go to pubs.'

'Too toffee-nosed,' Cassie sniffed. 'Too posh, too middle-class.' Even now, she was surprised they'd become such good friends.

'There's three steep steps up to your door.'

'Two doors and three steps up to both, Freda.'

'It would take two men to lift my wheelchair in and out.'

'There's always plenty around to do it.'

'But how safe would it be? When they've had a few pints of ale?'

Cassie knew she'd never persuade her. Even when she'd been able to visit, she'd always come when the pub was closed. She'd accept an occasional drink, but only upstairs in the kitchen.

Sometimes, when they had a quiet night, Cassie would take a bottle of port round to Freda's house and have a drink with her there. After a couple of glasses, Freda would let her hair down and they'd have a good gossip. The shortcomings of their respective children was a favourite topic. But after all the years she'd known her, it came as a surprise to hear Freda say:

'I can't blame Vereena too much. She wasn't my husband's child. I had her six years before I was married.'

The word formed itself on Cassie's tongue but Freda said it for her.

'Illegitimate. Such a terrible disgrace for me. Vereena was looking through my drawers and found her birth certificate, I tried to try and explain . . . We never got on well after that.'

'That's no reason—'

'She loved Alan. It upset her. She went round telling everybody I was her stepmother. That he'd been married before and her real mother had died.'

'That must have been hurtful.'

'I think she convinced herself it was true. Alan's mother was alive in those days, and after he died, we were talking about his will. About how much Alan had left me. I was trying to make up my mind whether to try to get back into teaching or start a boarding house.

'Vereena suddenly broke in. "How much has he left me? I've as much right to it as you. More right really."'

'I hope you told her . . .'

'I said Alan knew I'd always look after her interests and that I'd make sure she had her share.'

'How old was she then?'

'Twelve. Not much younger than Patsy is now.'

'A nasty piece of knitting, even then.'

'She was always headstrong, determined to get her own way.'

'Like marrying our Bernie.'

'They seem to be getting on all right. Better than I ever thought they would.'

'Bernie swings with the tide. He's happy to go in whatever direction Vereena pushes him, so naturally they get on well. We don't see much of him in the pub any more.'

'But he hasn't another job?'

'Only Vereena's band.'

'Lunchtimes though? He comes then?'

'He said he'd come every lunchtime, but there's often some reason he can't. It doesn't matter to me now I've got Agnes.'

'All the same . . . I wish he had a full-time job.'

'Don't we all. But you know what men are like. Won't take any responsibility. At least, not in my family.'

Cassie poured them each another drink. 'Different for you, your husband was a bank manager.'

'Didn't have much energy for anything else, though. Expected to be waited on hand and foot once he came home.'

'But you had a live-in maid to do it. If I'd had a man who could afford to give me that, I wouldn't complain. Certainly not.' Cassie felt she'd had to work hard all her life.

'You said you had a girl to look after your children when they were small.'

'A fourteen-year-old. Didn't get much work out of her. Kept the boys company, looked after them, that's about all.'

'Your Bernie was round here again last night. And Vereena, of course. After Patsy went home.'

'What did they want?' Cassie asked suspiciously. 'Money?'

'Bernie needs a new banjo and the band needs new costumes. They say it's doing very well. They've had a lot of engagements.'

'They're exaggerating. Over Christmas they did well, but nothing then until this Easter. Though they've got a few bookings for the summer. End-of-pier shows mostly.'

'Vereena talks as though it's going to make their fortune. They've got some new numbers, all they need are new costumes and they'll take off.'

'Wish I had their optimism,' Cassie retorted. 'They were just the same over that dress shop.'

'I said I'd think about it.'

'Think about what? You've been very generous to them, and where has it got you?'

'Vereena says I've got a whole house full of furniture that's never used. Why not sell some?'

'Sell your lovely furniture? Cheek, I'd call that.'

'It'll be hers one day but she reckons she needs it now. Just a little push and the band will earn real money. Bernie thinks it would be a good investment.'

'He would. Tell them to work for it. If we wanted money, that's what we had to do. That band will never earn more than peanuts. I'd have given Vereena a job in the pub if she'd wanted it. She'd earn more from me.'

'Vereena wouldn't work in a pub!'

'You're as bad as she is, Freda. You've given her big ideas.'

'I was thinking I could sell that davenport.'

'That little desk thing?' Cassie turned to look at it.

'Could you help me sell it?'

'Don't do it,' Cassie advised. 'It's a pretty little thing. Looks lovely there. Useful.'

'Cassie, you know I can hardly hold a pen these days. What use is it to me now?'

'Something from upstairs? You don't want to part with that. It's too nice.'

'What's upstairs isn't worth anything. Vereena might as well have the money if she wants it that bad.'

'If you didn't have to pay Betty to do what Vereena should be doing, you'd have plenty of money for everything.'

'Yes, well Betty has asked for a week off. She wants to go and see her auntie in London. Vereena says she'll stand in for her.'

'So she should. She does little enough. Rather sit at home with our Bernie.'

'Since she's going to come, I thought I should—'

'You let her twist you round her finger. Just think what you've done for her already. You've even taken out that insurance. Think of yourself for a change.'

'Cassie! Can you help me sell it?'

'Well, I can ask Harold Ingram for you. He'll give you a fair price. You're daft, Freda.'

'I know I am. I've spent most of my life providing for Vereena. Can't get out of the way of thinking that I should. Not now.'

Cassie sighed. She felt much the same way about her sons.

'Time they all learned to stand on their own feet,' she grunted.

The following evening, as usual, Patsy went round to Freda's just after six o'clock. She banked up her fire and carried in another scuttleful of coal. Freda felt the cold very much.

'Makes me stiffen up even more,' she told Patsy as the girl filled two hot-water bottles for her bed. Then she made a cup of tea for them both.

'Anything else I can do, Auntie Freda?'

'I've been trying to empty the drawers of this davenport. Will you help me put these things away?' Patsy was on her feet in an instant.

'Put these papers in the drawer in my bedside table, will you? And these can go in that drawer in the Pembroke table over there.' Patsy did as she was asked.

'All this torn paper you can put out in the bin. And on your way back through the kitchen bring the beeswax and a couple of soft cloths.

'Then there's these things here. Would you like them?'

Patsy felt a quiver of delight. 'Yes please.'

'It's little enough for what you do for me.'

'There's such a lot.' Patsy turned over a cameo brooch and a fountain pen.

'I don't think they're worth much.'

'Lovely red ribbon, and these pencils . . .'

'I'm very grateful. I don't know what I'd do without you, Patsy. I'd never manage now.' Freda sighed, and a gnarled hand settled over Patsy's own.

'I like to do it,' she told Freda. 'I'd rather come round here than stay upstairs in the pub by myself.'

The gnarled hand patted hers some more, and Patsy thought Freda's eyes looked quite watery. She was gulping: 'Your grandfather's coming round to buy the davenport.'

'Then I'll polish it to make it look its best. What a strange little desk. It's so narrow the drawers are round the side.'

Patsy carefully took four drawers out and wiped them free of dust. 'Now the other side.'

'No, those are just false knobs, to make both sides look the same.'

Patsy pulled on one and laughed. 'Of course, it's only wide enough for one set of drawers.'

'Twenty-two inches. Lift the lid. There are more inside.'

'Tiny ones, aren't they sweet? I've never seen anything like this before.' Patsy was intrigued.

'There's more to it than you think. It's got a secret. Here, let me show you. You have to pull out this bottom piece of beading.'

Patsy watched as the knotted fingers failed to put enough pressure in the right place. Frustrated, Freda gave up.

'You'll have to do it. Put your fingers underneath, just here, and slide the catches back.'

Patsy did as she was bid and a flap dropped down, showing a shelf that ran the width of the fitted interior.

'Nobody would find that if they didn't know it was here.' She laughed with pleasure as she pushed the duster into the corners.

'Then to close it, just lift the flap and push the beading back until it clicks. There, everything's hidden again.'

'There doesn't seem to be space for it, and the beading runs all the way round.' Patsy was fascinated.

'Desks often have secret drawers.' Freda smiled. 'But they're less common in davenports.'

Patsy polished it inside and out, enthralled with it.

'Is it old?'

'Yes, very.'

'Is it valuable?'

'I think it could be.'

'Grandpa knows all about things like this.'

When Patsy arrived home from school the next day, Gran said:

'I've been over the road to see your grandpa. He says he'll come with you at six o'clock tonight to see Freda's davenport.'

Harold Ingram was waiting outside his saleroom when Patsy went out, rubbing his hands with his usual genial good humour. He was a dapper-looking man in his pin-stripe suit.

'Hello, little one. You're coming with me to Mrs Tarrant's, then?'

'Yes, Grandpa. Are you going to buy her davenport?'

'Perhaps.'

'I polished it for her yesterday.'

He was opening the passenger door of his car for her. 'Come on, we'll drive round there.'

Patsy felt a surge of delight. She'd ridden in his car twice before, when Grandpa had brought her and Dadda home from his house. She considered it a great treat.

'I'll have to go straight home afterwards. I don't want to be late for my dinner.'

The journey was too short for Patsy. They left the car in the road and walked down the back entry. She led him in through the kitchen to Freda's sitting room.

Freda didn't seem as bright as she'd been the night before. Patsy had to tell her twice that she'd brought her grandpa to see the davenport. Then Freda waved one gnarled hand towards it.

'Show it to him, Patsy. There's a good girl.'

'This is it, Grandpa.' She opened it up.

'Very nice. A George IV mahogany davenport. Hinged

leather-lined writing slope with fitted interior.' He closed it again and stood back. 'Drawers down one side, dummy drawer handles on the other.'

Patsy set about making up the fire and putting the kettle on to boil.

'Very nice quality, Mrs Tarrant. How long have you had it?'

It took Freda a long time to rouse herself. 'Must be thirty years. It was a present from my husband.'

'Will you take eighty pounds for it?'

'Is that what it's worth?'

'That's a good price.'

She sighed. 'Yes, then I will.'

'Anything else you want to sell?' Harold Ingram was looking round. 'That's a nice Pembroke table you have there.'

Freda was shaking her white fluffy head.

'Just the davenport, then? You'll take a cheque?'

'Yes, that's fine.'

'I'd like to take it in my car now, but better not. Might scratch it and that would be a shame. I'll send my van round to collect it. It won't be tomorrow, though. Early next week. Is that all right?'

On Sunday afternoon, John was still dozing in his chair when Cassie said: 'Come on, Patsy, we'll walk round to Freda's.'

She knew as soon as she stepped inside the house that something was wrong. In the sitting room she found Freda lying on her settee, shivering under a blanket. The grate was full of grey ash. It was a mild day in early spring, but it was colder inside the house than out, and Freda felt the cold.

'What's happened?' Cassie demanded. 'I suppose Vereena didn't come this morning?' She felt very cross with her daughter-in-law. 'After she'd promised to stand in for Betty!'

Patsy began raking out the grate to set a fire.

'I don't suppose you've had any dinner?'

Freda didn't answer. She was trying to pull herself up the settee. Cassie went to help her. 'Well, did you?'

'Bread and cheese. I can get as far as the kitchen.'

'I'll get the kettle on.'

Freda looked very depressed. There were deep furrows on her brow. Her dark eyes looked leaden. Cassie had never seen her look this bad before. She tried to jolly her out of it.

'You sold your davenport, I hear? Got a good price for it.'

'Yes,' Freda grunted. There was misery in her voice.

'Harold said to tell you he'd send the van for it on Tuesday morning. Shall we put it out in the hall now? So it's ready?'

'Yes.'

'Come on, Patsy, give me a hand to move it.'

She turned back to Freda. 'They won't need to disturb you now, if you're having a nap or something. But I'll remind Vereena to be here on Tuesday morning.'

Freda was listless and staring straight ahead.

'Come on, Freda,' she cajoled. 'We're here now. We'll soon make you a cup of tea and have a fire going.'

She sent Patsy home to ask John to cut a couple of slices off the joint of beef they'd had for dinner. There was nothing much to eat at Freda's house.

'Bring some of that rice pudding we had, and cut half of that sponge cake I made.'

Patsy said: 'There's cake here, Gran. Freda and I bought it on Saturday while we were out.'

'Didn't you get any meat? What were you thinking of?'

'Yes, we bought chuck steak for today. Vereena was here, she said she'd take it home and make a casserole with it.'

'I'd tan Vereena's hide for her, I would. Leaving her mother without any dinner.'

But though they made a meal for her, Freda had no appetite and pushed the food about her plate.

'I don't feel well,' she said. 'The pain is awful.'

She looked really dejected. Cassie decided she must see her into bed before they left.

'I'm glad you didn't come alone tonight,' she said to Patsy when they'd let themselves out. 'She seems very low again. I think we should walk round to the doctor's and leave a message. Ask him to visit her tomorrow morning. She's not at all well.'

Every time Cassie thought of what Vereena had done, she could feel herself getting hot under her collar. Early on Monday morning, she went round to the house in Thomas Street.

Bernie looked a bit bleary-eyed when he let her in. Vereena was wearing a pretty candlewick dressing gown over her nightdress. They were sitting at their living-room table tucking into a breakfast of eggs and bacon.

'Your mother's worse and no thanks to you,' Cassie announced without ceremony. 'I think you'd better get round and see to her. She had no dinner yesterday.'

Instantly, Vereena was bristling and defensive. 'She did have dinner. I took her a hotpot round.'

'There was no sign of any hotpot when I got there,' Cassie told her. 'She said she'd had bread and cheese.'

'I put it in the oven, ready for her to warm up.'

'Did you tell her? She said you hadn't been.'

'I told her on Saturday dinnertime I would. I cooked her a chop then—'

'But when you took it round on Sunday, you must have seen her?'

'She was asleep. I didn't want to wake her.'

'For God's sake, Vereena! What time was that?'

'In the morning, early.'

'But you said you'd stay, get her breakfast and see to

her. You didn't light her fire either, and you know what that does for her aches and pains.'

'I wasn't well myself yesterday, was I, Bernie?'

'But I bet you were out on Saturday night?'

'I felt all right then. I was playing in the band.'

'Having a fine old time, I've no doubt.' She caught Vereena's glance of pure hatred.

'And what stopped *you* going round to light a fire for her, Bernie?' He laid down his knife and fork. 'Did you have a hangover too?'

'Not a hangover,' he said indignantly.

'Sounds like that band's too much for you to cope with. At the very least, you could have let me know. I'd have sent Patsy round to see to things.'

'I'm sorry,' Vereena was saying. 'I didn't realise . . .'

Cassie swung back to her. 'Of course you did! You can't be that stupid. Letting her down when you know she can't manage by herself. After you promised to do it. Your own mother, too.'

Cassie gripped the back of a chair. She hadn't meant to fly at them like this, but she couldn't help herself.

Bernie said: 'If you must know, Mam, we had to go to Rhyl on Sunday. We heard some other act had cancelled on Saturday night.'

Vereena added: 'We've got a booking there for Thursday, Friday and Saturday next week. Then we had to book lodgings for all of us. We can't come home at that hour of the night only to travel back the next day.'

With pent-up frustration, Cassie said: 'Vereena, you've got your mother to see to.'

Vereena rounded on her with the fury of a tiger. 'Everything falls on my shoulders. I never have a minute to myself. Not only do I play in the band, I have to make all the arrangements, as well as look after Mother.'

'She'll find some girl to go in and see to her,' Bernie said easily.

'And I suppose you think that's all right? A perfect stranger going in to your mother?'

'Betty was a perfect stranger when she started; now she loves having her. I meant to come round and tell you, but I was tired out. I've had a whole week of late nights.'

'Wait till you've had a lifetime of them, like me,' Cassie snorted. 'You're feeling strong enough to go round this morning and do something for her? Yes, you can't be feeling too bad, not if you can tuck into a breakfast like that.'

'Of course I'll go.'

'About tomorrow . . .'

'I'll go then, too,' Vereena snapped. 'I wish you'd mind your own business.'

'You ought to be ashamed of yourselves. Both of you.'

Still breathing fire, she felt for the door, slamming it as she went out. All day, she alternately fumed about Vereena and worried about Freda.

These days, she and John didn't eat dinner until Patsy came home from school and could have it with them. Afterwards, while they were opening up again, Patsy ran round to Freda's.

Cassie was listening for her step on the stairs as she returned, and went up to ask how Freda was.

'Much the same.' Patsy was frowning. 'Didn't want to talk at all. Said the pain was still bad.'

'Did Vereena go round?'

'Yes, she'd lit the fire and made her a dinner. Freda hadn't eaten much of it. There was cold ham put out for her tea, but she hadn't touched that.'

'What about the doctor? Has he been?'

'Yes, this afternoon. He left a bottle of pills for her. Painkillers, she said they were. I made her take a couple.'

'You're a good girl, Patsy. You'd make two of Vereena any day.'

* * *

129

On Tuesday morning, Vereena was still grumbling to Bernie. 'I wish you'd stop your mother poking her nose into my affairs. She's always round at Mam's.'

'She's her friend,' Bernie said mildly from behind a newspaper.

'I wish she'd leave her to me. There's no reason why Mam can't get up and do a bit for herself. Your mother encourages her to sit back in that wheelchair and be waited on. How do we know she's in such pain? I think she could be playing on our sympathy. She hardly spoke to me yesterday. Never even said thank you.'

Bernie lowered his newspaper. 'You'll have Ma on your back if you don't go again this morning.'

'I have to, don't I? Otherwise she won't want to part with the money she's promised. From that davenport.'

'Ma said to tell you she's sold it to Harold Ingram. He's going to collect it.'

Vereena was late setting out. When she let herself into the house in Kendal Street with her front door key, it didn't please her to see the davenport waiting in the hall. There seemed little hope of getting the money out of her mother until that had gone.

'Mother?'

There was no answer. In front of the hall mirror, she eased off her new straw hat with the big floppy rose that came against her cheek. She fluffed up her dark hair and wondered if she should have her bob cut into a shingle.

'Mother?'

The house seemed very still. She went to the kitchen and tied an apron over her new art deco print dress. The last thing she needed was to get dirty marks on it.

'Mother?'

She put her head round the sitting-room door, expecting to see her in her wheelchair. The room was empty and in semi-darkness. Usually her mother was up by this time. The clock on the mantelpiece told her it was ten thirty.

Her spirits sank. If Mam wasn't up, she might ask for help to dress. She didn't want to start that sort of thing.

'Mother?'

The bedroom door was slightly ajar. She pushed it further. The curtains were still drawn, but there was just enough light to see the thin figure under the old gold eiderdown.

Vereena was bristling with impatience as she flung open the curtains. She'd never be finished here at this rate.

'Mother?'

When she turned round, the figure on the bed hadn't moved. Her heart was suddenly in her throat; she could hear it pounding like an engine. She was gripped by fear.

Her mother's eyes were open, staring straight at her but seeing nothing. Her face was slacker than she'd ever seen it before.

Vereena moistened her lips and whispered: 'Mother?'

Very slowly, then, she edged nearer the bed. Put out a shaking hand to touch the grey forehead. She snatched it back, drawing in a long, shaky breath. She was dead then. Really dead. She wasn't imagining it.

CHAPTER NINE

Her mother was dead! Vereena was shaking. She groped her way back to the window and stood staring out at the familiar street. She told herself it was just shock. She'd be all right in a few minutes.

It was just her rotten luck that she should be the one to walk in and find her mother like this. She was still jittery; it was so unexpected. But it solved a few problems. It wasn't as though Mam was getting any pleasure from life. She'd been a misery for years.

Now, at least, what her mother owned would be hers. She wouldn't have to come cap in hand for every penny she needed.

Vereena had never seen a dead person before. Curiosity made her take another look, but she held on to the back of a chair for support. Her mother was dreadfully still. Her mouth had sagged open. Her teeth were in a tumbler by her bed, and beside it was another glass that had held water. And a pillbox open and empty.

'Christ! What have you done?'

Vereena jerked forward as the blood rushed to her head, pounding in her ears. She was sweating with panic. She'd been assuming that her mother's life had drawn naturally to an end.

By the glass was a note. She picked it up with trembling fingers. It was difficult to read, the writing spidery and uneven, every letter showing the painful effort it had taken her mother to write.

133

I can't go on any longer. I can't bear the awful pain, or the loneliness, or knowing it will get worse.

There's nothing more the doctor can do for me. I know it's wrong to end my life, but I'm a burden to everyone and have been for years.

I haven't the strength to struggle on. I'd rather die.

Her mother had signed it with her full name, Winifred Mary Tarrant.

Vereena stared down at the note, feeling sick. Oh God! Mam had committed suicide. She found it hard to believe she'd done such a thing. She'd never hinted she might, and besides, she'd gone out of her way to make sure she had income enough to live on. It was only last year she'd done the deal with the bank.

It was a good job she'd had the nous to persuade Mam to take out life assurance. At least she wouldn't lose out on everything. Another awful thought came thudding into her mind, making her crumple the note in her fingers. Hadn't she read somewhere that life policies were not paid out for suicides?

There was the bitter taste of gall on her tongue. She'd seen the policy that she'd persuaded her mother to take out, but not read it through. Perhaps . . .?

She snatched open the drawer in her mother's bedside cabinet. It was full of handkerchiefs, and at the back she kept her jewellery. Where had she seen her put that policy?

In the davenport. Vereena was shooting off to the sitting room when she saw it standing in the hall. She threw herself at it, jerking open the drawers, trying to remember which one she'd seen her mother put it in. They were all empty. She flung open the writing slope to get at the drawers inside, but they too had all been cleared out in readiness for its sale. She touched the beading that hid the secret hiding place and the shelf fell open. That too was empty.

As she remembered the drawers, they'd always been stuffed with letters and photographs and all sorts of odds and ends. Everything had been moved somewhere else. She rushed to the sitting room and started searching.

She found the policy in the drawer of her mother's Pembroke table. Only one premium had been paid and it was still in force. Renewal date was still three months off. The small print was dancing before her eyes. She had to make herself sit down and concentrate before she found what she was looking for.

A wave of fury swept over her. She'd known she was right about that. Death by suicide was excluded. It made the policy null and void. It was worthless. After all the trouble she'd gone to to get her mother to take it out!

'Damn you.' Tears of rage were blinding her. She went back to the bedroom. 'Damn you,' she said at the still figure on the bed.

Her mother had done her down. Never a thought for anybody's interests but her own. Why did she have to be so blatant about killing herself? If she'd just got on with it, nobody would have been any the wiser. Vereena pushed the policy down the neck of her dress.

Could she hide the fact that her mother had taken her own life? She could destroy her note. Nobody need know about that.

She saw her mother's calf handbag on a chair. She rummaged for her purse, pocketed a few pound notes. The bag was stuffed with letters and papers. She was looking at a cheque for eighty pounds!

So her mother had already been paid for the davenport. Vereena wondered if she'd be able to pay the cheque into her own account. She turned it over. No, she didn't think so. It was made out to Winifred Mary Tarrant.

Still, she could pay it into her mother's account, and eventually it would be hers, but there was no way she could get her hands on this money in time to buy new outfits for the band. They needed them now.

Vereena sat down, covered her face with her hands and tried to think. Her mother had other valuables here. If she took a few things now, while she had the chance, she could sell them and raise money that way.

The drawer in the bedside table was still open. She felt for the ring boxes at the back, flicked one open. Her mother's engagement ring was an emerald circled with diamonds. Far better than the crystal Bernie had given her.

Where was her own handbag? She found it and started pushing things in. Another ring, a few brooches and a necklace. Her mother's gold watch. The little silver clock from her bedside table.

In the sitting room she took a pair of miniatures off the wall. Her mother had thought highly of them. They left marks on the wallpaper, but so what? It wasn't as though she was stealing them, they were hers now.

Suddenly she froze. Was that the doorbell? She'd been so carried away with rage she had to stop and listen to see if it came again. It did. She was struggling then to fasten her handbag. It was too full. She flung it on the floor behind an armchair, in case she had to ask somebody in.

As she hurried to answer the door, she saw the crumpled suicide note lying in the open davenport. She grabbed it but had nowhere to hide it on her person. She mustn't go to the door with it in her hand. She pushed it into the secret drawer, pressed the beading until it clicked home and closed the writing slope.

When she got the door open, she told herself she needn't have panicked. It was only her mother's coalman on the step.

'I put two hundredweight in, love. Standing order. Couldn't make anyone hear round the back. That'll be seven bob.'

'Thank you. We'll pay next time.' Vereena was closing the door.

'It's cash on the nail. Boss's orders, and he's very strict. Where's Betty then? She always has the money ready.'

'She's away on holiday.'

'Is it in that green vase there? That's where Betty usually keeps it.'

Vereena took the vase down from the hall windowsill. There was a ten-shilling note inside; she handed it over.

'That's it. You'll soon get the hang of how they do things here.'

She was waiting for him to count out change from his leather bag when she saw a van pull in to the kerb behind the coal cart. It read 'Mersey Antiques' on the side. The driver was getting down. Harold Ingram was with him and crossing the pavement to speak to her.

The coalman was pressing coins into her hand. 'How is Mrs Tarrant?'

Without thought, Vereena said: 'She's fine.'

'Better then, is she? Very glad to hear it.'

'Hello, Vereena,' Harold said. 'I've come to collect the davenport.'

She'd guessed what he was coming for the moment she'd seen him. She was running with sweat. Why had she pushed that suicide note under the false beading? Blindly she stepped backwards to let them in. She knew she was panicking. She could feel the strength ebbing from her legs.

'Good, you've got it out ready for us. Very nice condition. A lovely piece. You must have grown up with it?'

'Yes.'

He was opening the lid, flicking open the drawers. Vereena held her breath, closed her eyes. His fingers didn't go near the secret drawer, but he touched everything else.

'Cassie told me to ask how your mother was. Did I hear you say she was better?'

Vereena's mouth was horribly dry. 'Yes.' How could she admit that her mother was dead and she'd done nothing about it?

'I understood she was very poorly.'

'She's much better.' How could she stop him taking the davenport? 'Asleep at the moment, though,' she added hastily, in case he should ask to see her.

'Right, we'll get on then.' He signalled to the driver to lift the other side.

'You're not taking it now?'

'Yes, that's what we've come for. I've got a couple of men off sick. Such a nuisance having to come out with the van myself.'

Vereena was almost choking with gall as she watched them tie a grey blanket round the davenport and lift it into the van. What if someone else found that suicide note? She should never have put it in the davenport. She couldn't think properly; her mind felt full of wool. What was she going to do now?

She ought to go for Dr Westley, let him know her mother had died. But she'd just told Harold Ingram she was much better!

What a fool she was! She should have burst into tears and thrown herself against his shoulder. If she'd done that right away, Harold would have forgotten his davenport and gone round for the doctor. She could have retrieved that note and burned it while he was away. She sat down for five minutes in the cool of the sitting room to still her quaking. She felt flustered, but she had to think this out.

She'd go out and buy a small piece of fish. Pretend it was for her mother's dinner. A walk in the fresh air would steady her nerves, give her time to pull herself together. She felt as though she was falling apart. She couldn't stop shaking.

She could say that her mother was alive when she'd first come round, but that she'd found her dead when she got back with the fish. She'd go straight round to the doctor after that.

Cassie felt she'd been tossing and turning for half the night. Patsy had told her that the doctor had left Freda a new box of pills, and that fact kept going round in her mind. She was very uneasy about it.

Once, when Freda had been telling her she meant to end her life, and she'd been trying to jolly her out of it, she'd said:

'It's not all that easy to move into the next world, you know, Freda. What're you planning to do? Put your head in the gas oven?'

'Don't think I haven't given it plenty of thought.' There was vehemence in Freda's voice. 'Pills would be the best way. Sometimes I take four when the doctor says two.'

'You take a double dose?'

'I have to, two doesn't take the pain away any more. I think if I took a whole boxful I'd get a lovely feeling. I'd just drift away and never wake up.'

'You're talking daft. And don't you be trying it. You're a worry to me, you know. How many pills have you got here now?'

She'd opened the box and been relieved to find there were only six. That was some time ago, and Freda had picked up for a few months. But she'd been very low last Sunday, and now she had a full box of pills again.

Perhaps Cassie should have said something to the doctor? But Freda wouldn't like her doing that, telling tales behind her back. The trouble was, she couldn't be sure Freda meant what she said.

The next morning, Cassie found she'd run out of sugar, and was heading down the road to Donovan's when she saw Harold Ingram.

'I'm going down to Mrs Tarrant's house this morning to collect that davenport. There will be somebody with her?'

'Her daughter should be. You know Vereena?'

'Your Bernie's wife?'

'Yes. Ask her how her mother is, will you?'

She watched him climb into his Ford T van with the words 'Mersey Antiques' emblazoned along both sides. After that she set out for the market to get some shin beef to make a stew for their dinner. She liked going to the market; she'd look at the stalls selling cloth and see if they had any flannel shirting. John needed a couple of new shirts.

As she was coming down Jackson Street on the way home, she saw Harold Ingram again. He was loading a dining table and chairs from a house and having trouble fitting them all in his van.

'How was Freda then, did you ask?'

'She's fine. Much better.'

Cassie paused, surprised. 'Are you sure? She was pretty bad. I had to send for the doctor for her.'

'Well, that's what Vereena said.'

Her first feeling was one of relief, but she found it hard to believe. The very nature of Freda's illness meant she couldn't be fine. Cassie hesitated, swapping her shopping bag from one arm to the other. This was such a sudden change from what Patsy had told her last night.

She had the feeling that something was very wrong. She went on more slowly. By the time she reached the pub, she knew she wouldn't rest until she'd made sure Freda really was all right.

John was coming up from the cellar. She pushed her shopping bag at him and said: 'I'm just slipping round to Freda's. I won't be long.'

If all was well she needn't stay. Perhaps she should put some of those pills out of Freda's reach. She really was half afraid she'd take the lot, as she'd threatened.

She went down the back entry and in through Freda's kitchen as she usually did.

'Freda?' She raised her voice. 'Anyone at home?' The silence surprised her.

'Vereena?' She should be here too.

Cassie looked in the sitting room and found nobody there. It made her cluck with impatience to see the cold, empty grate again. What was Vereena thinking of? She knew her mother needed a fire. The house felt quite bleak.

She knocked on the bedroom door, not knowing whether Freda was dressing. Some mornings that could take her hours. 'Freda?'

There was still total silence, so she opened the door.

What she saw made her gasp with horror. She held tight to the doorknob. She knew immediately that Freda was dead. It was a few moments before she dared move. Then she crept closer and touched her. She was cold. She saw the empty pillbox. She had to sit down.

Poor Freda!

Cassie was struggling with a pall of guilt. She'd known how Freda felt. This was her fault. She'd guessed that Freda wouldn't be saying those things to anyone else. She should have done more to stop her.

She couldn't sit looking at her friend. She pulled herself awkwardly to her feet and stumbled out. When she'd closed the bedroom door, she had to lean against it to stop her head swimming. This was dreadful.

Had Vereena gone round to tell the doctor? Or had she gone upstairs somewhere?

'Vereena?' she called. There was no guessing what Vereena might do. Why had she told Harold Ingram that her mother was much better when in fact she was dead? She didn't understand the girl at all.

She hadn't the strength to climb up two flights of stairs and go trailing round the seven bedrooms. She didn't think Vereena was here now. Better if she made sure the doctor knew what had happened.

She went as fast as she could to the doctor's house. His front door was open; she went in and spoke to his wife, who acted as receptionist.

'Yes, we do know about Mrs Tarrant. Her daughter's been in. The doctor's just finishing morning surgery now. He'll come round straight away.'

Cassie walked slowly back down the street, relieved that Vereena had done what was necessary. Perhaps Harold had got things wrong.

She would have liked to go home, but if the doctor was coming to Freda's straight away, perhaps she ought to go back and wait for him. Unless he knew the back door was open, he wouldn't get in.

If Vereena was back, she needn't stay.

Vereena knew she was in a cold sweat. She could see her fingers quivering like an old woman's. The walk down to the fish shop had not calmed her as much as she hoped. She'd done most of the things she'd decided had to be done; she had to brace herself now to face the doctor.

She was still in a lather about losing her mother's suicide note. Why hadn't she just opened the drawer while Harold Ingram was there and taken it out? He wouldn't have thought twice about it if she had. She just hadn't been quick enough.

The best thing to do about it now was to go into the saleroom and look for the davenport. She'd retrieve the note when no one was looking. Then she'd go home and burn it. She wouldn't feel safe until she knew it had been destroyed.

She was terrified of what she'd already done. She'd tampered with the evidence. But she'd wanted that note out of sight and she mustn't lose her nerve now.

There was another important decision she had to make,

and make quickly before the doctor came. She got up and went to her mother's bedroom for the third time. She was still dithering about what to do about that empty pillbox. Twice she'd removed it and put it back again.

If she left it there beside her mother, then note or no note, suicide would still be the first thought that would come into the doctor's mind. He would know when he'd prescribed the pills for her and exactly how many. The empty box was a complete giveaway.

But if she removed it, and the doctor still thought her death had not occurred naturally . . .?

Vereena had read that these days, in suspicious circumstances, the contents of body organs could be analysed to prove the cause of death. Then, with no evidence of suicide, she was afraid it might look like murder.

The very thought of being accused of murder was terrifying, but she had to risk that or write off the insurance money. Her mind was on fire; she couldn't decide what to do. The piece of cod she'd bought was on a plate in front of her on the kitchen table, smelling the place out.

Dr Westley was an old man, old-fashioned in his ways. He should have retired years ago. He'd been looking after both of them for over thirty years, and he'd come so often to her mother that they knew each other well. Vereena thought he would be the last person to question the cause of her mother's death. Just as long as nothing pointed obviously to suicide. Surely he'd be glad to see her mother put out of her pain?

Vereena's head was spinning; her mind had been going round and round this for too long. Dr Westley would be here any minute. She had to make up her mind now.

She rushed back to snatch up the empty pillbox and lid. The water tumbler! She grabbed that too, in case it suggested medication to the doctor. Her heart was thudding again, and she daren't look at her mother. She tiptoed out of the room and closed the door, telling herself she'd done the right thing.

She found a box of matches and set fire to the cardboard pillbox in the sitting-room grate. She washed up the tumbler and put it back on the kitchen shelf. When she went back to the grate, the flames had died out but there was a heap of warped and fragile ash, still recognisably pillbox-shaped.

Vereena went to the front window and looked down the road. There was nobody coming just yet. When the ash had cooled a little she gathered it up on her palm and took it out to the back yard. Crumbling it to dust, she opened her fingers and blew on it, scattering it. The morning breeze tumbled it more. It was invisible on the dusty concrete of the yard.

At that moment, she heard somebody pushing open the back gate. It was another shock to find her mother-in-law's stout figure coming in. Vereena never welcomed Cassie's presence, but at this moment she just couldn't cope with anyone, let alone her. She wanted to scream at her to go away. Too much depended on what the doctor said, and what she said to him. She needed to keep her mind clear.

Also, she had to tell Cassie that Freda was dead. She opened her mouth to do so; she had her story about that clear in her mind.

'I'm sorry about your poor mother,' Cassie said before she'd got a word out. There was something strange about the way Cassie was looking at her.

This was totally unexpected. How did she know? Vereena no longer felt in control. She burst into tears and retreated to the kitchen to slump on a chair.

Cassie followed her in. Vereena wondered if she was seeing suspicion on Cassie's face. She couldn't stop herself shaking.

'It must have come as an awful shock to you,' Cassie

said. 'Shall I make some tea?' She was filling the kettle when the front door bell rang.

'That'll be the doctor now,' she said, bustling up the hall to the front door. That frightened Vereena even more. How did she know? She followed her, half blinded with panic and tears.

Dr Westley was wiping his feet on the doormat as he always did before coming up the hall.

'Vereena, don't upset yourself,' he said, patting her shoulder, his grey eyes full of sympathy. 'I know, when it comes, it's a terrible shock.'

'In here,' she sniffed, leading them all into the bedroom.

Vereena had to support herself against the dressing table. She felt dizzy, her head was whirling as she stole a glance at the bedside table. There was a row of medicine bottles and a couple of other pillboxes. She couldn't bring herself to look at the body.

Slowly, the doctor got out his stethoscope and turned back the bedclothes.

Cassie's voice was thick. 'All those pills you gave her the other day. It was too easy for her.'

Vereena held her breath; the room swam round her. Cassie was giving her away!

Cassie went on: 'I blame myself. It makes me feel guilty. I shouldn't have . . .'

Vereena felt the fog lift from her mind. For the first time that morning, she saw her opportunity.

'You shouldn't have done it, Cassie. I told you it was wrong. You should never have made my mother swallow all those tablets. You killed her.'

Dr Westley had straightened up to look from her to Cassie. His Adam's apple moved slowly.

'I didn't,' Cassie gasped. 'Don't tell such lies.'

But he was opening the boxes on the bedside table. There was one of ointment and two more of aspirins and laxatives.

145

'Last Friday,' he said, and Vereena could see no sign of sympathy in his eyes now, 'I left her some new pills. To take away the pain and help her sleep. Are they here?'

'Those are the ones I'm talking about,' Cassie told him. 'She's swallowed them all; she threatened to do it.'

'The ones you forced down her,' Vereena added viciously. 'She wouldn't take them of her own free will, I know she wouldn't. You used them to kill her.'

She burst into noisy tears again. It was a nervous reaction but it also meant she didn't have to say any more.

She heard the doctor saying something about being unable to sign the death certificate under the circumstances, and he'd better get the police in.

'Even if Mrs Tarrant asked you, it's against the law to help her do it.' He looked at Cassie, his face very serious.

Vereena felt her world had turned upside down. She and her mother-in-law were invited down to the police station. A polite request, but she knew there was no way they could avoid going.

'We need to get a clear picture of what really happened,' they were told.

All the way there, Cassie wouldn't leave her alone.

'What are you playing at?' she kept asking. 'Why are you telling these lies? Why did you tell Harold Ingram that your mother was much better? You knew she was dead. She was stone-cold. Must have died in the night.'

Vereena found it very upsetting. She didn't know how to answer, and police ears were listening. She was glad that Cassie was taken off somewhere else as soon as they arrived. She couldn't trust herself not to scratch her eyes out. It looked as though her mother-in-law had ruined all her plans.

It was Cassie's fault they were here at all. Every time she thought of how she'd come barging in at the wrong moment her blood boiled. Even so, if she hadn't opened

146

her mouth so loud, Vereena was sure she'd have got away with it.

Old Dr Westley was not the sort to think fast. He'd have signed the death certificate and she'd have got her money, no questions asked. As it was, the questions went on and on, the same ones over and over.

But Vereena had her story worked out and she stuck to it. She'd gone to her mother's house to help her. She'd been alive when she'd arrived. She'd spoken to her.

'What was her state of mind?' she was asked.

That flummoxed her. Cassie would be saying she was depressed and in pain. So would everybody else who had seen her recently. She could hardly say she was cheerful and in good spirits, or why had she left her in bed so late in the morning?

She'd had to say: 'She was in pain, not well. Feeling a bit low.' Though she knew that would make it sound more like suicide.

It was only after that that she was told her mother would be taken to the morgue, and that a post-mortem would have to be performed. Vereena knew then that there was no way the fact that she'd taken all those pills could be hidden.

She'd lost. Cassie had defeated her. Vereena dissolved in to tears again. She was upset and still shaky, but it was all right to be upset, she'd just lost her mother, hadn't she?

After what seemed like hours and hours, they told her that Bernie had been summoned to the station and she could go home with him. Half an hour later, she was led out to the desk and found Bernie waiting for her. She thought he looked ill and somewhat dazed, not his normal self at all.

'I blame your mother for all this,' she complained, as he took her arm and together they stumbled out into the street. She'd been boiling with fury about Cassie all day, and now she had a thundering headache. 'At it again.'

'They didn't tell you,' he said. 'Left it to me. Thought it would be better.'

'Have they charged her with murder?' She hadn't asked what was happening to Cassie. 'I wouldn't be surprised from what she was saying.'

'No.' His face was stony, uptight. He was striding out.

'What then?'

'Ma collapsed under questioning. They took her to the Borough Hospital but she died.'

Vereena jerked him to a halt. 'Died?'

'A heart attack.'

Vereena felt the blood surging to her head. Nobody could blame her for that!

Everything would have worked out as she'd wanted it if Cassie Gripper hadn't charged in at the wrong moment. Cassie would be alive now, and Vereena would have the insurance. But as usual her mother-in-law had had to come poking her nose in. She was an interfering old busybody. It served her right.

'It's all her own fault,' she told Bernie, and he agreed. But she didn't tell him the full story. It wouldn't do for him to know everything.

All the same, Vereena felt floored, aghast with the horror of it all. She didn't dare think about the suicide note.

Later that week, on viewing day, she went into Mersey Antiques' saleroom to look for the davenport. It wasn't there. She went over to their shop in Liverpool to see if it was on sale there, but there was no sign of it. It was a real bind having to go to the shop in West Kirby. It shocked her to find that the davenport wasn't there either. It looked as though it had disappeared off the face of the earth.

But perhaps the suicide note would never turn up? The secret flap that let down was hard to spot. The new owner might never find it. If he did, given average luck, he wouldn't know who Winifred Mary Tarrant was.

If it came to the worst and the police questioned her about it, she'd swear she'd never seen it before, and that it must have been Cassie who put it there.

Cassie Gripper had never liked her. Well, she'd not come out on top this time.

CHAPTER TEN

23 May 1926

Patsy came home from school at four o'clock, and pulled up with surprise when she read the notice on the pub door: 'Closed until further notice'.

She'd never, ever known such a thing happen before. Was it some sort of a joke? She looked on the main door and the same notice was there. It was Dadda's writing. With her heart hammering, she raced upstairs to find him. He was stretched out in his usual armchair, looking totally defeated.

'Dadda!'

He pulled himself to his feet then and put his arms round her in a hug. It only increased her anxiety.

'What's happened? Where's Gran?'

'It's terrible, Patsy. You'll have to be brave. Your gran's had a heart attack. They took her to the Borough Hospital, but she died this afternoon.'

Patsy held her breath. Moments passed; she heard the coals collapse in the range because they'd burned away. Outside, a train rushed past. It was worse than anything else she could imagine. Gran was the centre of their lives.

'Why?' Patsy demanded. 'Why Gran?'

Her father started to tell her something of what had happened, haltingly and with some confusion.

'And Auntie Freda's dead too?' Patsy felt appalled. 'On the same day?'

The room was spinning round her, the flowers on the print curtains a blur of pink and purple. Cold fingers were running up her spine but she could feel sweat breaking out on her forehead. She thought she was going to be sick.

'There's just the two of us now,' Dadda whispered.

'What are we going to do?'

'I don't know. I don't know how we'll manage without her.'

Patsy felt as if the bottom had dropped out of her world. Nothing could ever be the same again. Through her own shock and horror she had to pity Dadda. He was totally distraught. Without Gran, it seemed he couldn't function. The fire was almost out, no preparations had been made for dinner. It was Patsy who re-lit the range, boiled the kettle and found them something to eat.

'It's the women in our family who have the get-up-and-go,' Gran had said, and now, for the first time, Patsy could see what she meant.

The rooms above the pub seemed empty without her. Silent, too, without her gutsy laugh and strident opinions. Dadda looked devastated, sagging back in his armchair, unable to pull himself together to do anything.

Later that evening, Alice Smedley from next door came round to say how sorry she was to hear about Gran. She brought them a cake she'd baked. Sara Donovan from the grocer's on the corner was hot on her heels with a big box of tea and sugar and other staple groceries.

'To tide you over,' she said, 'till you get on your feet again.'

Patsy started to make tea for them all, but Alice took over. It was better for Dadda that they had company tonight.

Rob Parry came upstairs to the kitchen to say how shocked he was to hear about Cassie. He carried coal up from the yard and backed up the kitchen range for them.

'My father told me to say how sorry he is,' he said awkwardly. 'And to offer his help.'

Patsy watched her father pursing his lips. He'd see that as sympathy from the enemy. It didn't help that three customers had been charged with unruly behaviour after breaking Parry's window.

'Do you need help with the funeral arrangements, Mr Gripper?' Rob asked.

'Funeral arrangements?' Patsy could see from Dadda's face that he hadn't given them a thought.

'You'll need to get things fixed up. My father is related to Edward Tomkins – d'you know his funeral parlour? They're second cousins or something. Dad says he'll treat you properly.'

'There's two funerals.' John raised himself from his torpor. 'I ought to go round to our Bernie's and see what they're doing for Freda Tarrant.'

'Dad says he'll come round and see you, if you want that. He'd like to help.'

'Yes please,' Patsy told him firmly.

Now, because the pub would normally be open, they heard men thumping on the door and shouting up to ask what was going on.

Rob wrote out new notices: 'Due to the sudden death of the proprietor Mrs Cassandra Gripper, this hotel will be closed until further notice.'

'That should stop the shouting,' he said, 'out of respect for your gran.' And it did.

'I don't know what the brewery's going to say.' Dadda shook his head. 'I'll have to go down there tomorrow and let them know.'

'You should go to school as usual,' Alice advised Patsy.

'I want to stay with Dadda.'

'It'll take your mind off things if you go to school,' Sara told her.

Patsy felt bereft. 'It's the twenty-fourth tomorrow, Empire Day. A half-day holiday anyway.'

'Go in the morning then. Better if you do.'

Rob asked: 'Are you having the usual show?'

'Yes, we've been practising for weeks.'

'Are you still doing the colonies pageant?' Sara wanted to know. 'I remember my girls doing that years ago. Bet you did it at school, John.'

'What's that?'

'I told you, Dadda. Every colony is represented by a member of the class. The person who is New Zealand carries a toy lamb to show its produce. Another is India, with a bowl of curry powder and a length of cotton cloth, and so on.'

Dadda said: 'I remember the whole school marching round the yard behind the Union Jack, singing "Land of Hope and Glory".'

'We're doing that and "Rule Britannia",' Patsy said. 'I'm to be dressed up as Britannia, and I'm going to recite a poem about England's greatness.'

'Then you'll have to go,' Sara insisted. 'You can't let the the others down.'

Patsy's lip quivered. 'Gran was coming to see me do it. Everybody will have their parents there.' Her father wouldn't meet her gaze, but she knew he had other things he had to do. 'Or somebody . . .'

'What about me?' Rob asked awkwardly. 'Not the same as having your Gran there, of course, but I'll clap loudly for you. I'd like to come and see it all again.'

'Yes, you go and watch,' Alice urged. 'The best thing.'

'Thank you,' Patsy said, feeling comforted. She managed a half-smile.

'Not so long since I was in it myself.' Rob's gaze wavered sympathetically.

The next morning, Patsy got out of bed, lit the fire and reheated the porridge she'd made last night. It was what Gran always did. It helped to be busy, and to know she was useful to Dadda.

He was only just getting out of bed when it was time for

her to leave for school. She could see he hadn't slept much; he looked weary and despondent. To see him like that made Patsy feel worse, and she left reluctantly. As she drew nearer the school she could hear the children playing in the school yard and knew she was in good time.

On this very different day, the children seemed noisier at their play. Spirits were soaring in holiday mood. Patsy didn't feel like joining in. She was in the top class now, and would be leaving at Christmas when she'd had her fourteenth birthday.

She stood alone near the railings, waiting for the whistle to blow and school to start. She knew there would be a final rehearsal before parents and visitors came to see the pageant at eleven o'clock.

Many of the children came from the streets between the railway tracks. They'd already heard about Gran and were not as kind to her as the adults had been last night.

'Is your Gran really dead?'

'What did she die of?'

'Who's going to look after you now?'

'My dad wants to know when your pub'll open again.'

'Mine said shutting it down was a damn nuisance and shouldn't be allowed.'

A boy called Tommy Dale from her class came up and stood, feet apart, in front of her. He was a bully. 'Your gran's a murderer,' he taunted.

Patsy shivered in the light spring breeze. 'Course she isn't,' she said.

'She killed her friend, Mrs Tarrant. Did you know her? That's what everybody's saying.'

Patsy felt appalled. She rounded on him. 'She did not. They were best friends, she wouldn't want to hurt her.'

'She did then, my dad says so,' he hissed. The taunts continued.

'They must have fallen out.'

'The police caught her.'

'She'd have hung for it if she hadn't died.'

Patsy clung to the cold railings in horror. It all added up. Last night she'd felt it at home: Dadda's stunned disbelief, and the two deaths on the same day. That had seemed incredible when he'd told her.

Dadda had changed, the whole atmosphere at home had changed. So many people coming round with gifts, and talking in whispers. There must be more to Gran's death than she'd been told. It wasn't just a heart attack. And nobody was saying what Auntie Freda had died of.

The whistle blew at last, and the children formed up in lines in the yard. The taunts stopped. They marched into school, a class at a time.

Her teacher had heard the news about Gran, and after taking the register, she said how sorry she was. It made Patsy squirm because she said it in front of the whole class. She probably knew all the things they were saying about Gran. It made Patsy feel worse; she just wanted to be left alone.

There was a mad scramble then to fold back the partitions between the classrooms and turn the desks and chairs to face one end. The school piano was pushed close to the open door.

They had prayers and then the rehearsal began. Patsy made a horrible hash of her poem, forgetting her lines and drying up. Her teacher kept making her start again from the beginning. It took four attempts before she managed to recite it all through.

She was dreading break time, afraid there'd be more taunts in the yard about Gran, but they didn't come. Nobody took any notice of her.

Back inside, the teachers swathed cloth over her dress and gave her a prong and a shield to make her look as Britannia does on pennies and ha'pennies. Parents and visitors were thronging into the school yard. Patsy tried to pick Rob out in the crowd but couldn't see him.

Around her, she could feel the excitement mounting. At last they started circling the yard behind the Union Jack and the percussion band. It almost drowned out the sound of the piano.

They sang a song from each region of the United Kingdom, starting with 'Jerusalem' and 'Land of our Fathers'.

By the time the colonies pageant was starting, she was able to pick out Rob's red head. He gave her a little wave but Patsy couldn't relax. She kept saying her poem silently over and over, afraid she'd disgrace herself when her turn came.

But she got through it without stumbling, and heard Rob leading the applause. The show ended with the announcement of a half-holiday, and everybody sang 'God Save the King'.

Patsy was glad it was all over. She had to give her props back to her teacher before she could leave. Rob was waiting for her at the gate.

'You were great as Britannia,' he said, his brown eyes shining with enthusiasm. Suddenly it was all too much for her, and Patsy burst into tears.

'Hey.' She felt an arm go round her shoulders. He was pulling her shaking body against his as they walked along. 'What's the matter? You were fine.'

She tried to tell him how she felt now she'd lost two of the people she knew best: Gran, who had been a mother to her and had taught her sums, and Auntie Freda, who had taught her to read.

'There's only Dadda left,' she said. 'What would I do if something happened to him?'

'I'd look after you.'

'Would you?'

Rob was smiling down at her. There was a tenderness about his mouth. 'Of course. But nothing's going to happen to your father, and you have other grandparents. You wouldn't be alone.'

'It's very strange them dying on the same day,' she whispered. 'I can't get over that. And they're saying at school that Gran murdered Freda.'

She saw the outrage on his face, felt his arm tighten round her shoulders.

'Nonsense, your gran wouldn't have hurt a fly. You know that.'

'Dadda's acting very strange. He seems sort of bewildered. There's something very wrong. It's bad enough that Gran's had a heart attack and died, but it's as though there's worse.'

'Your gran couldn't do enough for people, and Freda Tarrant was her friend. You know how much she did for her. She sent you there every night to make sure she was all right.'

'Then why was Gran at the police station? I don't understand that.'

'Neither do I, Patsy,' he said. 'But I know your gran wouldn't have hurt anybody.'

'It must mean something bad happened.'

'Ask your dad when you get home. He'll know.'

'He should have told me last night.' She could feel the tears stinging her eyes again.

'He's upset too, Patsy. Shocked. He couldn't talk about it last night, but he will if he knows you're worried. Don't you listen to those rotten kids at school.'

Patsy drew in a great shuddering breath. 'But nothing can bring Gran back. What are we going to do now?'

'You'll have to be patient and see what happens.' Rob escorted her to the pub door. 'Let's see if your dad's back.'

There was an Austin Seven parked outside. Patsy knew that it belonged to the man from the brewery. As soon as they started to climb the stairs, they could see Dadda in the private with him.

'I'd better make myself scarce,' Rob whispered. 'Your

158

dad won't want me around just now. Don't forget, ask him about the police station when you get a chance. I'm sure he'll set your mind at rest about that.'

When Rob had gone, Patsy sat on the stairs to listen. She gathered from what was being said that Gran's death was going to bring more changes than she'd first supposed.

She'd known all along that Dadda didn't want his name above the door. Now she heard him telling the man from the brewery.

'We'll have to open up again tomorrow, Mr Gripper. If you're sure you don't want to do it, we'll have to put in a manager.'

Dadda was mumbling something.

'We've a man called Jack Dawson, do you know him? I'll bring him round and introduce him. Of course, he'll be on a month's trial, but after that, if all goes well, he'll want to move into the living accommodation upstairs. You do understand that goes to the manager?'

Patsy was stiff with apprehension. Move out of their home? The very thought was upsetting. She couldn't imagine living anywhere else. And what about Dadda's job?

'Yes, of course, better for the new man if you stay. You'll know more about it than he will to start. Yes, we'll want you to carry on.'

Patsy was still sitting there, numb with worry, when Alice Smedley came through the door.

'Hello, love, I've made a pan of lob scouse for your dinners. I lit your fire earlier on. Put this in the oven to keep warm till your dad's ready.'

Patsy took the pan upstairs and did as she was told. She felt frightened. How would they find somewhere else to live? Dadda hardly knew what he was doing. She started to set the table for dinner. It bothered her, too, that they were suddenly very dependent on the neighbours.

When Dad came up he was leaden with hopelessness. Neither of them managed to eat much. Patsy worried about adding to his burden, but she had to get it off her chest.

'They're saying at school that Gran murdered Auntie Freda.'

She heard Dadda snatch at his breath. Again she was enfolded in comforting arms, but she didn't want comfort, she wanted the truth. She pushed him away, growing more fearful.

'Dad, I don't understand about Auntie Freda. Why did she die? And what was Gran doing at the police station? Something very strange must have been going on.'

She could see fear in his eyes too. 'Course she didn't kill Freda. But Vereena says she did, and she was there.'

'Vereena was with them?' Her heart was suddenly hammering away again.

'She was taking Betty's place, you know that.'

'She's telling lies.'

'We don't know that, love.'

Patsy felt sure of her facts. 'If someone killed Freda, it must have been her.'

'Patsy, we don't know what happened.'

'I'm almost sure ... I was closer to Gran and closer to Auntie Freda, I know what was going on there better than anybody. I'm telling you, Dadda, Vereena must ...'

He was covering his face with his hands. 'It's all a nightmare.'

'Let's go round and see her. Find out what really happened.'

'I was there this morning.'

'But you didn't ask her about this, did you?'

'No. Don't make any more trouble, Patsy. We can't accuse Vereena. It would only cause another row and more bad feeling all round.'

Patsy felt hot with anger. 'This is Vereena's fault, I

know it. I know her better than you do, Dadda. We can't let her get away with this.'

'Please don't, not ...' He was weeping, and she'd never seen Dadda cry before. She hugged him. 'Don't do anything. I can't take any more of this.'

She felt mutinous. 'I can't believe Gran would do such a thing.'

Her father sighed. 'Neither can I. Don't make more fuss, Patsy. Please.'

Harold Ingram had a sinking feeling in his stomach. He couldn't keep his mind on the takings of his saleroom this morning.

As soon as he'd arrived, Mr Solly had told him that Cassie Gripper had had a heart attack and died in the police station. He still felt cold with shock. He must be the only person who hadn't heard last night; he couldn't get over it. He'd spoken to her so recently and she'd seemed so full of life. He'd been across the road to knock on the pub door three times already, but it seemed that nobody was at home.

'They are there,' Mrs Solly told him when she brought him a cup of tea. If the pub had been open, he'd have had a brandy to pull himself together.

'Is John all right?'

'Must have come as a terrible shock. I boiled a piece of ham for them last night and took it across first thing. He seemed dazed, poor lad. Didn't look as though he knew whether he was coming or going.'

That made Harold feel worse. He should have done more for Patsy than he had. Now she and John had been catapulted into a crisis. He had to do something to help them now or he'd never stop feeling guilty. He was restless, and since he couldn't talk to John, he went home to discuss it with Mildred.

'John's got no stamina, never has had,' Mildred sniffed.

'He'd never have amounted to much if our Elsa had lived. And the other son goes his own way. Cassie never could do anything with him.'

'So what can we do? I'd like to get Patsy into school with Lucy.'

Mildred pulled a face. 'Patsy hasn't had a sheltered upbringing, living in that pub, left on her own every night. She'll have seen the seedy side of life. They're a tough lot round there.'

'Cassie could stand up to them.'

'We heard her throwing the drunks out often enough, when we lived opposite. Swearing at them, too. A rough lot. That's why I wanted to get Lucy away. She's a real little lady now.'

'But what about Patsy? She's our Elsa's child too.'

'I'd like to have her here,' Mildred said. 'Look after her properly.'

'You're sure?'

'She's our own flesh and blood. It's only fair.'

'Good, that's how I feel.'

Mildred said: 'The high school will soon civilise her. You can afford two lots of school fees now?'

'Of course. I'll get in touch with the headmistress, go and see her.'

After a heavy lunch of pork chops, Harold drove back to Cambridge Place and knocked again on the door of the pub. Patsy came running down to let him in.

'How are you, little one?' He followed her up to the kitchen and found they were just finishing their meal. What remained in the pan looked good. Better than he'd have expected John to make.

It was a long time since he'd been up here. He'd forgotten how shabby it was. It looked dire. He kept his arm round Patsy's shoulders.

'I've just heard about Cassie,' he said. 'I'm so sorry. She was a good sort. We'll all miss her.'

Neither of them answered. He sat on a lumpy armchair by the old-fashioned range.

'What're all these rumours I'm hearing? That she killed Freda Tarrant? Lot of nonsense, is it?'

'Yes,' Patsy said. Harold saw the warning look her father gave her. 'She wouldn't, Freda was her friend. It's all a pack of lies, I know she wouldn't.'

Harold pursed his lips. He'd heard what the neighbours were saying in his saleroom. 'No smoke without fire. We'll know for sure after the inquest.'

Perhaps it was just as well Cassie hadn't lasted long enough to be charged. Much worse if they'd had to watch her being tried and then sent to the gallows. A most awful scandal for them. Odd that he'd met Freda Tarrant so recently, been in her house too.

'Freda was so ill,' he said slowly. 'If she asked Cassie to help her die, then it was a very brave thing for her to do.'

John had his head in his hands. His bald spot was growing bigger. 'It's against the law,' he grunted.

Both he and Patsy looked agonised. Harold tried to change tack. 'How can I help? The funeral?'

'Next Saturday, ten o'clock.'

It surprised him to find John so quick off the mark. He said sympathetically, 'You'll need to make a few changes now, John.' He knew he'd have to approach his son-in-law carefully about offering Patsy a proper home. 'You won't find it easy to look after yourself, never mind a young girl.'

It wasn't natural for a man to do much about the house, and anyway, he'd have the pub to see to.

'We've got to move out,' Patsy said, her face stark. 'Look for somewhere else to live.'

John started to talk at last. Harold couldn't believe he'd refused the chance of being the licensee here. Such a thing had never occurred to him, but it should have. As Mildred said, John had no go about him. He would have managed, when it came to doing the job. Of course he would. He wasn't stupid.

'I told them I'd rather stay as a barman.' John wiped his face in a helpless gesture. 'Even though it means I have to start looking for somewhere else to live.'

Harold stood up. He'd expected John to stay on at the pub; now that it seemed he wouldn't be, he needed to think again.

'I want you both to come round to our house for tea tonight. You might as well if the pub isn't opening. Do you good to get out of this place for a bit. We ought to talk things over. Make plans for yourself and Patsy.'

John said nothing.

That same afternoon, Harold Ingram went to see Lucy's headmistress to ask for a school place for Patsy.

'For Lucy's twin sister?' Tall and thin, the headmistress sat the other side of a polished desk.

Harold tried to explain something of the circumstances that had parted the twins.

'What school is she attending now?' The woman looked to be an academic; he could see books in Latin and Greek on her shelves.

'Hemingford Street council school.' Harold saw her expression harden.

'I don't think it's feasible for her to change to a school like this.'

Harold straightened up in dismay. 'She's doing well where she is. She's thought to be the brighter of the twins.'

'It isn't a question of being bright. Patsy is now thirteen and a half. She's missed the beginning of the senior school course, more than two years. It's a question of what grounding she's had in the subjects we teach. The sciences, for instance, and mathematics. She'd have to have a modern language and preferably Latin too.'

Harold shook his head.

'At a council school, Patsy will have been given a grounding in the three Rs, with perhaps scripture, sewing and a little cookery. Am I right?'

He was very much afraid she was.

'We pride ourselves on our academic achievements. She'd find it impossible to cope here now. It doesn't matter how bright she is.'

Harold knew by the look on her face that she didn't think Lucy was brilliant. 'She'd never find her feet. It would be a demoralising experience for her.'

He felt taken aback; he hadn't realised he'd left it too late. 'Is there no way now?'

'Perhaps if you found her a private tutor, in two or three years she might be able to catch up. Then if she passed the school certificate, I'd welcome her into our sixth form.'

It left Harold feeling thwarted and irritable that his plans for Patsy could not go ahead. He'd spent too much time thinking of his business and not enough about her.

He drove home trying to console himself. Both he and Mildred had left school at fourteen and they'd done all right. He'd done better than many he knew. Patsy would be fine, if she took after him.

He'd been brought up in the flat over the shop in Cambridge Place. It was known generally as the junk shop then; his father had traded in house clearance and general bric-à-brac from the closing years of the last century. He hadn't achieved much but he'd lived in eternal hope, like a gold prospector who expects one day to turn up a huge nugget to make his fortune.

Harold had been brought up on stories of goods making fifty times what was expected. He remembered being told of a picture of immense value being found in a pub where nobody knew its worth.

Much of the rubbish his father collected, he'd passed on to rag-and-bone men for a few pence. The rest was mostly sold through the shop. Any decent piece that came his way, he took to an antique dealer.

Harold had seen straight away that a better profit could be made on higher-class goods. He'd started going further afield to buy, aiming for top quality. Once he'd bought the van, he'd been able to go to country house sales.

The weekly auctions had proved profitable. Everything changed hands. It wasn't just the stock he bought in; private clients brought in goods which he sold on commission. Because he found that antique dealers were attending his auctions and buying up much of his stock, he'd opened up the other two retail shops.

Later, he'd added premises where he restored old furniture, and now he was about to start a new venture. He hoped it was going to be the most profitable of them all. He was going to make good-quality copies of popular antiques.

Harold felt he could be proud of what he was achieving.

CHAPTER ELEVEN

Patsy sat with Dadda on the top of the bus going up to
Caerns Road. When they got off, she hung on to his arm.
All the houses here were very grand and set back in large
gardens.

The Ingrams' house had a monkey puzzle tree in the
front. Patsy admired it but Nanna was always talking of
having it cut down. She thought it stopped the light getting
to her windows.

The front door seemed as wide as that of a church.
There was stained glass set in the lobby door, and the hall
smelled of beeswax and was bigger than the living room
over the pub.

There were not as many bedrooms as in Auntie Freda's
house, but it was very much grander, with lovely Turkish
carpets and antique furniture everywhere. Most impressive of all, they had a cook-general called Mrs Judd, who
let them in. Patsy knew that Dadda found the place
intimidating.

'There you are, Patsy.' Mildred met them in the hall,
wearing a dark wool dress and a triple row of pearls. She
supervised the removal of Patsy's shoes as well as her hat
and coat. As usual, she was given a pair of Lucy's slippers
to wear.

Mildred's glasses were thicker but she still wore her
hair, which was nearly white now, twisted into prim
earphones. Two inches of straight hairpin protruded from
one of them.

Patsy stood on tiptoe to kiss Grandpa. His eyebrows were growing bushier, his droopy moustache felt like wire against her lips. Lucy came downstairs to greet them.

'Lucy, why haven't you changed?' Nanna asked. Patsy thought she looked very smart in her school uniform.

'Take Patsy up to see your room.' Mildred's voice seemed artificially bright. 'There are things Gramps and I want to discuss with your dadda.'

Patsy wanted to hear what was being said. She knew it was about their future. Being sent upstairs with Lucy was much the same as being excluded from all the excitement of the pub.

'Can't I stay with Dadda?' she asked.

Nanna's hand was firmly on her back. 'Run along now, dear. You want to play with Lucy, don't you?' Reluctantly, she followed Lucy upstairs.

'Gran's died,' she said miserably as they went up. 'Isn't it awful?'

'Yes, Nanna told me. All this is about what's going to happen to you and Dadda.'

Patsy was riveted. 'Do you know? Have they said?'

'No.'

It hurt that her sister wasn't more upset. She wanted Lucy to give her a hug and say she was sorry about Gran, that she'd miss her.

'Look, I've had my study redecorated. I chose the wallpaper. Isn't it lovely?'

Patsy looked round. It used to be known as Lucy's playroom, but the big toy box filled with golliwogs, teddy bears and building bricks had gone. So had the doll's pram and cot. Only her magnificent doll's house and two handsome china dolls remained. A small desk and more bookcases had been added.

'It's beautiful,' she said, trying to throw off the gloom she felt and share some of Lucy's pleasure. 'You are lucky to have a room like this for yourself.'

Lucy's school satchel was on her desk. She tipped the contents out. 'I do my homework here. I've got algebra and history tonight. Most girls have to do it in their bedrooms.'

'I don't get any homework.'

'Why not?'

'Nobody does in my school.'

'Then you'll all grow up stupid,' Lucy said contemptuously.

Patsy flicked through Lucy's algebra book and found it incomprehensible. Lucy must be right; that made her feel worse.

'I want to change into my new dress. I've got a new hat and coat too. Come on, I'll show them to you.'

Patsy followed Lucy to her bedroom. It was twice the size of hers, with filmy curtains as well as thick ones at the window. Patsy found she was looking through the top branches of the monkey puzzle tree. The house across the road was almost hidden behind green foliage.

Lucy was spreading her new clothes across her bed. Patsy thought they were as fashionable as Vereena's. She started to undress, stepping out of her black gymslip and leaving it on the floor. Patsy found a hanger and put it back in her bulging wardrobe. She fingered the smart black blazer and black and white tie.

'Don't bother about those, they're just my school uniform,' Lucy told her. 'How do you like this?'

She was twirling in front of her looking-glass, admiring her new red dress. Suddenly she tired of it. 'Let's go down. It's boring up here on our own, and anyway, I'm hungry.'

'Can we?'

She crept downstairs behind Lucy, half expecting that they would be sent back. A frowning Nanna met them at the sitting-room door.

'There you are, I was just coming to call you down to

169

tea. Lucy dear!' She sounded quite brusque. 'Red is not suitable. You're in mourning for your grandmother. You'll have to have black too, Patsy.'

'Let her be,' Grandpa said, leading them into the dining room. 'We want our tea now, and there's only family here.'

As they sat down, Patsy noticed that the atmosphere had cooled. Grandpa was buzzing with impatience, Nanna bristling with ill-humour, and Dadda was more upset than he had been when they arrived.

At each place setting was a plate of luscious ham. Spread out on the white starched cloth were salad and crusty bread, a bowl of fruit and cream, and seed cake. Patsy thought it impressive, considering it wasn't even Sunday. The salad bowl started to circulate.

'Perhaps we'd better put it to her?' Mildred suggested coldly. 'I don't want her to think that she isn't welcome here. I want to do my duty.'

Patsy met Dadda's tired grey eyes. They were swimming with misery. He looked out of his depth.

Grandpa said: 'We've asked your father, Patsy, if he would be willing to let you come and live here with us.'

Patsy couldn't get her breath. It wasn't at all what she'd been expecting. It knocked her sideways.

'Your twin sister is here. We think it would be better for you to be with us too. Now that Granny Gripper ... Well, there's nobody to look after you now. And it's not right for a young girl like you to be left by yourself every evening. You need a proper home, a settled home.'

Patsy felt that every eye was on her. They were waiting. She couldn't speak, couldn't even swallow the ham in her mouth.

'Well, what do you say? Would you like that?' Nanna pressed. Dadda wouldn't even look in her direction now.

'What about Dadda?' she choked. 'Will he come here too?'

'No,' Mildred said. 'Just you.'

Grandpa said gently: 'It would take the responsibility off his shoulders. Give him less to worry about.'

Patsy felt as if the silence was going on for ever. She made herself look Grandpa in the eye.

'I'd rather stay with Dadda. He needs me. He won't like being on his own.'

She heard her father's sigh of relief. 'That settles it then.' He lifted his eyes from his plate and smiled at her. 'We're staying together. I was afraid you might want to come here.'

'No.' She was ready to weep again, but there was joy in it. Dadda loved her as much as she loved him. She could see that even he was tearful.

'I've nobody but you now, Patsy.' His voice shook.

She swallowed hard. 'It's very kind of you to offer, Grandpa. But Dadda and I—'

'But who is going to look after you?' Mildred seemed outraged.

'I can look after us both,' Patsy said. 'I can cook and clean. Gran showed me how.'

She knew now why the atmosphere had chilled. Dadda had already refused their offer. They were angry with him.

'All we need is to find a house to rent. Somewhere close,' she added.

Harold sighed heavily. 'Perhaps I can help you there. Did you know Solly is about to retire? He's moving down to London to live with his daughter. The flat across the road, over the saleroom, will be empty soon.'

'Will it?' Patsy reached impulsively across the corner of the table to clasp his hand. 'That would be just the thing. We wouldn't have to move away. Do say we can have it, Grandpa.'

'Well, it's not that straightforward. I'm looking for somebody to run the saleroom instead of Solly. What about it, John? Would you like to take on the job as well?'

171

'I don't know anything about auctioning stuff.' There was panic in his voice.

She could feel Grandpa trying to curb his impatience. He took a deep breath. 'Solly can show you what's to be done. It wouldn't be beyond you.'

Dadda was shaking his head in dismay.

'Basically, all you'd have to do is be there to take in the articles people hand in to be auctioned. You'd have to catalogue them, and arrange for the catalogue to be printed. And on the day of the sale you'd have to collect payment before the goods can be taken away.'

'There's a lot of paperwork?'

'Well, yes, there has to be book-keeping.'

John was shaking his head. 'I couldn't do paperwork.'

'I could do that for you, Grandpa.' Patsy tugged on his arm.

'Don't be silly, dear,' Mildred said. Lucy was staring at her as though she'd gone out of her mind.

'I've been doing the books at the pub for Gran for over a year. Haven't I, Dadda? I know I can do what you want. All you'd have to do is show me.'

Grandpa turned to her and laughed. 'The little one takes after Cassie, that's for sure. Or is it our Elsa? Thank goodness . . .'

Patsy guessed that what he'd started to say was: 'Thank goodness she doesn't take after her father.'

Dadda said mildly: 'You have to go to school, Patsy. You can't leave until Christmas.'

'And I have to find a manager,' Grandpa said. 'I have to have the shop open all day, and it's often late closing on sales days.'

Patsy put down her knife and fork. 'Grandpa, I've just had an idea. What about Robert Parry? He's been cellar-man at the pub since Dadda had his accident.'

'That's not the sort of person I want.' Grandpa was showing impatience again.

'Yes, he is,' Patsy insisted. 'He's just filling in at the pub till he can get a proper job. He's got his school certificate, and he's studying book-keeping at night school. That's why he has Monday and Wednesday nights off. And he lives next door to the pub.'

'He's a good lad,' John said slowly. 'He'll be able to do cataloguing and anything else you want.'

'And if he gets the job, he'll not want to move into your place and Dadda and I can have it,' Patsy gulped.

'We'll have to see,' Grandpa said slowly.

Her father spoke up. 'You won't find anybody more reliable.'

'I'll have to talk to him. See what I think.'

'He's a very nice person,' Patsy urged. 'You'll like him too, I'm sure.'

'There's something else I should tell you about.' Grandpa helped himself to more bread and butter. 'It's a new venture for me, and I'm quite excited about it.

'You know I've had a small workroom for restoring antique furniture? Well, the lease was up and I've taken new premises, a much bigger building. I'm going to start making new furniture as well. It'll be a small factory making replica antiques. High-class stuff.'

'Just tables and chairs to start with,' Mildred added enthusiastically.

'Most people prefer their furniture to look new and smart. Yet they admire the classical styles.'

'I'm sure it will be a great success, Harold,' Mildred said. 'Like everything else you do.'

'A factory?' John looked brighter. 'You'll have jobs going there?'

'I'm taking on men now.'

'Would there be something I could do?'

Grandpa was frowning. 'I need cabinet-makers mostly, a French-polisher, and later on perhaps upholsterers. But a few unskilled men, yes.'

'I think I could manage a job like that.'

'John, you're capable of more than that. You'd have done better to become licensee; it's a trade you know. You should go back to the brewery, tell them you were upset about your mother, and now you've thought it over—'

'No.' He was shaking his head. 'I don't want that. I'd be happy as barman, but a factory ... What time would work finish?'

'Six in the evening. Eight till six.'

'Then I wouldn't have to leave Patsy alone. I could be at home every night.'

All the way back on the bus, Patsy held John's hand, telling herself that she and Dadda were closer than they'd ever been. She needed him, she was glad they'd agreed to stay together.

Vereena felt sick with dread. It was the first time she'd ever attended a coroner's court and she knew she'd be called on to give evidence.

To talk publicly about it was bad enough, but she also knew she must stick to her original story, and what she was going to say was not entirely true. The time of her mother's death, for instance. So much depended on the outcome that she'd hardly slept since it happened.

Vereena leaned forward on the hard wooden seat, gripping it with both hands, finding it hard to sit still.

Beside her, Bernie was chatting to John as though he hadn't a care in the world. Compared with her he hadn't. She hadn't told him that her story was at variance with the facts.

She hadn't expected Patsy Gripper to be here. Would she be giving evidence too? She was afraid of what Patsy might know; she'd been closer to Cassie and her mother than anybody else.

Vereena kept telling herself that Patsy was only a child,

but it didn't help. Her stomach had turned over when she'd seen her and John getting out of Harold Ingram's car outside.

Bernie had paused for a word with them. And when she'd looked at her watch to make sure they weren't going to be late, she'd seen Patsy's eyes hone in on it.

It heightened her sense of insecurity to know that Patsy had noticed she was wearing her mother's engagement ring and gold watch. What had possessed her to put them on today? Though it was none of Patsy's business what she did with them.

There was something about Patsy's knowing blue eyes that gave her the creeps. They were wary but full of suspicion. She was so afraid that Patsy knew. She might have got rid of Cassie, but her granddaughter was another pain in the neck.

She could hear Patsy and her Ingram relatives whispering together now. Cassie's family had turned out in force, and so had many of their neighbours. Vereena stifled a shiver. She felt icy.

At last the proceedings began. She held tightly to Bernie's arm until she was called on to give evidence about what had happened that day.

She could feel her heart racing and didn't dare look round at the familiar faces. She didn't want to see accusation on them.

She'd been over and over her story in her mind, and she stuck to it. Her mother had been alive when she'd first gone to her house that morning. She'd found her dead when she'd returned from doing some shopping. She was deliberately vague about the time. When she'd first spoken to the police, she'd inferred it was all much earlier than it had been. She hadn't noticed any pillbox or evidence that her mother had taken any pills. She sat down, still shaking, to hear the rest of the proceedings.

The post-mortem on Mrs Winifred Mary Tarrant had

found that her stomach contained a large amount of barbiturates. Death was due to a massive overdose of amylobarbitone sodium. This had been prescribed by her doctor over the last twelve months for intractable pain and insomnia. A new supply had been provided two days earlier.

There was no evidence as to how or why the barbiturates had been administered in such quantity. The coroner's verdict was suicide. There was mention that she might have been assisted.

Vereena was sure Cassie Gripper had been suspected of that, but now there was nobody to be charged. She felt weak with relief when it was over, that nothing terrible was going to happen to her.

But one thing was certain: the insurance company would not pay out on that policy. She felt very bitter and angry about that. After all she'd done to prevent her mother's suicide coming to light, after all the worry and nervous energy she'd put into it, her plans had come to naught.

What she needed to do now was put it all behind her. Forget about it. Hold her head high and show the family, particularly Patsy, that she wasn't afraid, and that she had nothing to be ashamed of.

There were other ways of getting money, she mustn't forget that. She was glad that the Mersey Minstrels were playing tonight. She'd been undecided whether to accept the engagement or not. It was not the sort she sought: a church hall in Liverpool.

Patsy was huddled in Gran's old armchair in front of the kitchen range. She'd had butterflies in her stomach for days. She'd tried to talk to Dadda about what Vereena had done, but he wouldn't listen. Tried to tell Grandpa, but he'd said Freda's inquest would tell them if anyone was to blame. But it hadn't.

At the inquest, she'd sat only a few yards from Vereena, listening to the evidence she was giving. It was all lies. She knew enough of what had gone on in that house to be quite certain of that.

She'd never liked Vereena, had always been a little frightened of her. Vereena was capable of terrible things that changed for ever the lives of everyone round her. Patsy was afraid that if she wasn't stopped now, she'd go on doing that. Hurting the people around her. Dadda, for instance, he'd be putty in Vereena's hands.

When she heard Rob Parry coming up with a second scuttleful of coal for the range, she said: 'This is all Vereena's fault. I'd like to make her pay for what she's done. Screw her neck.'

She couldn't hold it back any longer; the words were tumbling out. Rob sank down on the edge of Dadda's chair and listened carefully.

'They told us that Gran must have had a problem with her heart for some years, and that the fatal heart attack could have come at any time. But it's Vereena's fault she had it then. I wish Gran had never gone near Freda's that morning.'

'We can all wish that.' Rob's face was serious. 'Cassie must have felt terribly stressed. Freda's unexpected death, then to be taken to the police station.'

'I want to shout it from the roof tops, let everyone know what Vereena's like. I blame her. She tells lies. She's wicked.'

He was making sympathetic sounds. 'Patsy, you've no proof. And you're so young, no one will believe you.'

'Dadda doesn't,' she sniffed. 'But Vereena's bad. I'm afraid she'll do it again.'

'How can she?' He got up to perch on the arm of her chair then, and put an arm across her shoulder. 'Your Gran's dead, and so is Freda. Vereena can't do them any more harm. Better put it behind you. It's over and done with.'

'She could hurt others. She'd do me down if she could. I can see it in her eyes.'

'She won't do anything,' he soothed. 'Poor Patsy, you're feeling terrible now. It's understandable. You've just lost the ones you loved.'

'I feel desperate about this.' She could feel the tears prickling her eyes again. 'So alone.'

'There's me. You need never be alone. If there's anything you want me to do . . .'

Patsy sighed, though she felt comforted. 'I want justice. I wish there was some way to prove that Gran was innocent of all this.'

'What Cassie did or didn't do hardly matters now.'

'But it does,' she insisted. 'She wouldn't want you to think she'd harmed Freda. She didn't, I know she didn't. She did all she could to keep her alive.' But even Rob didn't seem convinced.

'I wish Gran was here to tell her side of the story.' She'd have let it all come flooding out in her usual forthright way. Patsy was almost sure about what had happened, but not absolutely certain. It remained a nasty mystery she could see no way of clearing up, and added a black cloud that wouldn't go away.

Patsy felt stiff and cold throughout Gran's funeral the following day. She kept hoping she'd wake up and find it was all a horrible nightmare.

Nanna had bought her a completely black outfit. For the first time ever, she and Lucy were dressed alike. The whole district seemed to have turned out for Cassie. The church was full because so many had known and liked her.

But the person who stood out from the crowd was Vereena. It didn't seem to matter which way Patsy looked, Vereena was in front of her. She seemed more confident today, in a hat of shiny black feathers.

Many of the mourners came back to the rooms above the pub afterwards. Alice Smedley had made sandwiches and Sara Donovan had provided meat pies. Vereena reached the teapot before Patsy did and poured out with a proprietorial air. Patsy watched her jealously as she chatted up Harold and Mildred. Putting on airs.

'Poor Mother-in-law.' Her eyes were dry but she fluttered a black-edged handkerchief round them. 'Such a shock for us all.'

For Patsy, knowing that she'd have to go through Auntie Freda's funeral the following day made it seem worse.

The Railway Hotel had reopened with Jack Dawson in charge. Patsy thought her father was upset by his decision to give up the licence. He'd been reluctant to go down and start work. He told her it seemed all wrong.

For Patsy, left alone to sort and pack their belongings upstairs, the sounds drifting up were familiar.

Grandpa had told her to tell Rob to go across to the saleroom at twelve o'clock, so that he could talk to him about the job. She knew that Rob had asked for an hour off to do it.

She kept a watch at the window, waiting to see him cross the road, willing him not to be late. She could see Grandpa's car outside, so knew he was there ready to interview him.

Patsy was sure Grandpa would like Rob. But it was five minutes to twelve, it was time he was there. Then she saw him, wearing his best Sunday suit of grey flannel, with his dark-reddish hair newly brushed and damped down. He'd been home to change. She hadn't thought of that.

She saw Grandpa meet him at the door and shake hands, and then they moved out of sight. She was too high up here to see much of what went on in the office.

Patsy felt as much on tenterhooks as if she was having

the interview herself. She wanted Rob to get the job for his sake, but also for her own. It would suit them all very well. Three-quarters of an hour dragged by. Patsy could wait no longer and went downstairs. At street level she still couldn't see either of them. Mr Solly was sitting behind the counter attending to a client.

She took a turn down to Donovan's shop window. Usually she drooled over the iced buns and jam tarts. Today she had other things on her mind, but Sara Donovan was beckoning her in, putting two buns and two tarts into a paper bag and handing it to her.

'For your tea. For you and your Dadda,' she smiled.

Patsy was moved by her kindness and hoped they wouldn't have to move away from this street. She was on her way back when she saw Rob striding towards her, grinning from ear to ear.

'I've got the job!'

His brown eyes shone with elation. 'What can I say? You're my fairy godmother. You wave your wand and you find me a job. I can't believe my luck.'

He threw his arms round her in a hug, sweeping her off her feet.

'Mind my buns,' she said.

'Come with me.' He was towing her into the paper shop. His mother was serving.

'I've got the job, Mam,' he announced. 'I'm thrilled. It's exactly the sort I was looking for.'

'It's not really a desk job, dear.' Gladys avoided looking at Patsy, but for once, she was all smiles.

'Not manual labour, either,' one of the waiting customers said. They were all taking an interest.

'But you'll have to lift furniture about.' Gladys frowned. 'Stands to reason.'

'There's a couple of handymen to do that. They go out with the van as well. I'm going to manage the saleroom. Keep the books and everything.'

'It sounds a good job.'

'Better than I expected, to start.' Rob couldn't stop smiling. 'I want to buy you a box of chocolates, Patsy. You deserve it, you put my name forward for this. Which one would you like?'

'You don't have to.' Patsy hung back. 'We're friends . . .'

'More than that,' Rob smiled, reaching up to the top shelf. 'The biggest box then, to say thank you.'

Patsy saw Gladys's face go white, but she was trying to smile. His father came in from the room at the back to add his congratulations. 'And it's the second job she's found for you.'

'There's something in it for me and Dad too,' Patsy tried to explain. 'We want the rooms over the shop.'

'I'll have to change and go back to the pub.' Rob swept his red hair away from his face. 'I'm going to give a week's notice. That'll give me two weeks with Mr Solly before he retires. Just think, I won't have to work every evening from now on.' He sighed with contentment at the thought.

'You had two nights off every week,' Patsy reminded him.

'To go to night school. I'll still be doing that. On my first free evening we'll go to the pictures. What d'you say, Patsy?'

Patsy felt the first stirrings of pleasure. 'Lovely.' That was a very rare treat because of the hours her family had always worked.

Rob's eyes smiled down into hers.

Patsy went straight over to see Grandpa to thank him, still holding her chocolates and buns. 'You like him, Grandpa?'

'I think he'll suit me.' Grandpa was rubbing his hands in a genial manner, a sure sign he was pleased. 'A nice lad. He seems very keen.'

'And we can move into the rooms here? Rob doesn't want them, he'll still live at home.'

'Yes,' he said. 'You can move in when Mr and Mrs Solly leave.'

Mr Solly wanted her to go upstairs and see the rooms straight away. He called to his wife to show her round. Patsy went eagerly.

Grandpa had been brought up in this flat. He and Nanna had modernised it before they'd left, making a separate kitchen, installing a brown soapstone sink and the latest black gas stove standing on four slim legs.

The rooms were lighter and brighter than those over the pub. There would be a bedroom each for her and Dadda, a living room and a proper bathroom. The Sollys were very house-proud and were always painting and papering.

'Can I bring my father to look round?' she asked Mrs Solly. She hoped it would make him feel better too.

Dadda seemed to be locked in grief. He'd always been mild and even-tempered, but recently he was being torn apart with sudden bursts of rage. She'd been very upset after one of these, and told Rob how worried she was.

He'd taken her hands in his, his brown eyes full of sympathy.

'Your father can't see his way forward. Your gran died so suddenly, and the rumours and suspicion make it hard to bear. It's turned everything upside down for him and brought changes he didn't foresee. He's not angry at you, but at what's happening to him. It'll take him time to settle down.'

Patsy hoped that now their future was settled, she and Dadda would get back on an even keel. Rob had been wonderful to her; she felt very close to him.

Rob had been shocked at Cassie's death, but now it seemed he was to benefit from the changes it was bringing. He'd enjoyed working at the Railway Hotel, but felt it was high time to move on. The place wasn't the same without Cassie, and the new manager was making big changes. He felt buoyed up because he'd got what he'd been aiming for.

When the pub closed that night and he went home, Rob was surprised to find both his parents waiting up for him. Usually he ate a lonely supper, something cold his mother left between two plates on the living-room table. Tonight they were sitting with him, drinking tea.

'We're delighted about your new job.' His father sounded elated. 'You've succeeded.'

'Dad, I'm over the moon. It's going to be very interesting. I'll be my own boss in that saleroom, have a bit of responsibility.'

'I'm just thankful you're leaving that pub,' his mother told him wearily.

She'd taken to her bed for three weeks the night the shop window had been broken. They'd told customers who asked after her that she had flu, but she hadn't served in the shop since.

'It's preying on her mind.' His father was very worried. 'She can't put it behind her.'

Rob was concerned about his father too. He was getting over-tired; he needed the help Gladys had given. These days she hovered behind the living-room door, listening to what customers were saying, convinced they were talking about her and the terrible sin she'd committed.

Rob had started getting up early on alternate mornings to open up the shop and mark up the paper rounds, so that his father could have a lie-in.

'I'll be glad to get back to normal mealtimes.' He cut into his slice of gala pie. 'Pub hours play havoc with meals.'

'It was a terrible job,' his mother added. 'The pub itself . . .'

'It served its purpose.' Rob beamed. 'It let me earn my keep.'

'You've been very generous. Helping towards . . .'

'I wanted to, Mam. And Mr Ingram said the pub was good experience for me.'

'Well, he would say that. The Grippers are related to him.'

'It seems Cassie had spoken of me. She'd told him I was doing a good job and she didn't want to lose me. He said that was the best sort of reference anybody could have.'

'You're well out of there, before you come to harm.'

'Away from the demon drink, you mean?' Rob smiled at them both. He'd come to see them as somewhat bigoted about alcohol. He knew they feared it.

His father jumped on him. 'You didn't drink with them?'

His smile widened into a grin. 'Not enough to do me any harm, Dad.'

'You mean you tried it?'

'I needed to know what it was I was selling, didn't I?'

Gladys's face was twisting with anguish. 'I told you those Grippers would be a bad influence.'

'No, Mam, Cassie was kind, she'd never hurt anybody. John is very gentle.' Rob had to stop himself saying any more. In some part, he knew he was to blame for his mother's state. He'd gone against her wishes by working there at all.

'You got too involved with them. That's what I was afraid of. You're still too involved with Patsy. You make far too much fuss of her.'

'I wouldn't have this new job if it wasn't for her. I wanted to show my gratitude. What's wrong with that?'

'You're overdoing it. Did you see the way she was looking at you? You're putting ideas into her head. I wouldn't like to think you'll end up by marrying the likes of her.'

'Don't be daft, Mam.' Rob laughed outright. 'Patsy's not fourteen yet.'

'You seem very close.'

'I see a lot of her, I like her, but she's more like a little sister than anything else.' Rob saw his mother wince, and knew he should never have said the word 'sister'.

'I'm talking about what she thinks,' his mother flared. 'It's plain from her face she doesn't look upon you as a brother.'

Book Three
1927–1932

CHAPTER TWELVE

Patsy found that Rob was as good as his word. As soon as he started work at the saleroom he asked her to go to the pictures.

'Rudolph Valentino's on this week in *Blood and Sand*. Do you like him?'

'Never seen him. But Lucy has, she says he's lovely.'

Rob dug her playfully in the ribs. 'They say he really captivates the ladies.'

The intimate darkness of the picture palace heightened all Patsy's senses. She thought Rudolph Valentino very romantic, but he was just a celluloid hero.

She had her real-life hero here beside her. He was an attractive, broad-shouldered young man with dark-auburn hair, already working for his living with his career planned out. She noticed that other girls, older than herself, turned to look at him.

More than five years her senior, he already seemed to have adult wisdom. He could explain what was worrying Dadda and advise her on things she knew nothing about. He treated her as though she was adult, too. She had no other friends near her own age. Her time had been spent with elderly people like Gran and Freda. She was more at ease with Grandpa than she was with Lucy.

Robert Parry was quite different, her first real friend. She enjoyed his company and felt very attached to him. She didn't need Rudolph Valentino.

The day came when the Sollys moved out. Grandpa

sent his two handymen to help move their furniture across the road. Even with Dadda and Rob helping, it took all one Saturday afternoon. Patsy worked hard to get the rooms straight and the beds made up. John had given in his notice at the pub and had started work at Grandpa's new furniture factory.

'It's all hand-finished by master craftsmen. Very high-quality replicas. They use burr walnut, yew and mahogany.'

'But cheaper than the real thing?' Rob wanted to know.

'You won't be able to afford it,' John told him. 'We make copies of Georgian and Regency stuff and chairs after the style of Chippendale and Hepplewhite.' It seemed that even Dadda was taking an interest in antiques now.

Patsy felt she was settling down to a different life. It was as though she'd suddenly grown up. She often thought of the old days when Gran and Dadda had looked after her at the pub. Now she felt she was looking after her father.

Sometimes she had a meal ready for him when he came home from work, sometimes they prepared it together. She thought that for her, life was becoming more interesting.

She saw more of Rob. He was working downstairs in the saleroom every day. When she wasn't at school, she was down there talking to him.

'I couldn't have found a more interesting job,' he told her. 'The more I find out about antiques, the more they fascinate me.'

'There's an awful lot to learn.'

'Your grandpa's teaching me. I have to be able to recognise what's what so I can sort out the best pieces to go to the retail shops, and keep the best of the rest for the monthly sale. What's left is ordinary household stuff, and that's auctioned off weekly.'

To start with, Rob needed help with the cataloguing, which had to be exactly right. Patsy discovered that Grandpa had provided books about antiques, and was encouraging him to look everything up. She took them upstairs to read avidly in her bedroom.

Often, when she came home from school, she walked round the saleroom with the current catalogue, finding out what Grandpa and Rob had said about each piece. The monthly auction was the most interesting for this. She discussed many of the pieces with Rob over cups of tea.

On the days that sales were being held, she'd rush home to sit quietly at the back, listening to the auctioneer and watching what Grandpa did. He was usually here for the sales. Sometimes she helped Rob in the office afterwards, as customers came to pay for what they'd bought. It was a busy time for him. She loved every minute of it.

Patsy would have liked him to ask her out to the pictures again, but he never did. He seemed to spend most of his free time working in the paper shop. Instead, she saved up her pocket money and asked him.

'It's very kind of you.' He seemed unable to look at her. 'But I've arranged to go with Dad to the wholesaler's in Liverpool.'

There was no mistaking his embarrassment. It was that which put her off suggesting they go next week instead. Being almost grown up brought its difficulties too.

'What are you going to do when you leave school?' Grandpa wanted to know.

'Can I work here? For you?'

He'd laughed. 'Well, little one, I'll make a bargain with you. If you do a secretarial course, learn typewriting and book-keeping, I'll give you a job.'

'I'd love that.'

'You'll need a bit of practice first, but when you're good enough, I might even make you my secretary.'

'I'll be good enough,' Patsy vowed. 'I'll work at it until I am.'

'Skerries is the best secretarial school round here. You'll need to start after Christmas. Shall I apply for a place for you? You can walk up to Central Station and get the train across to Liverpool every morning.'

'Yes please,' she'd breathed.

When she'd been at the college for a month and was beginning to enjoy it, she told Rob: 'I'm learning short-hand and typing, but I like book-keeping best. I'm good at that.'

'Because you've had plenty of practice in the pub,' he laughed. 'Cassie gave you a good grounding.'

Harold Ingram was setting out his new ivory-backed hair-brushes on his tallboy. They were a gift from Mildred for his sixty-fourth birthday.

He peered into his mirror. His hair was reduced to a silver edging round the back of his head; a shiny dome rose above it. He was hardly in need of brushes now. He tried one out and finished up grooming his moustache. Even that was turning silver.

Sixty-four! Until now, he'd tried not to notice the passing years, but he was feeling the odd twinge in his joints. He had less energy and less enthusiasm for change than he'd once had. At his age, he should be thinking of retirement. Doing less, enjoying what he had, not think-ing, as he always was, of how to expand his little empire and make more money. Perhaps he should sell the busi-ness and do just that.

He'd never be able to spend the money he'd already accumulated. Mildred wanted for nothing and there'd be plenty left to divide between the twins. He couldn't go on like this for ever. It wasn't as though he had a son to whom he could pass it on.

But perhaps he'd be bored with nothing to do? As he went slowly downstairs to tea, Harold felt the need for something else in his life.

He'd heard Patsy and John arrive. Mildred always arranged a family celebration for his birthday. At the end of the meal, there would be a glass of sweet sherry, with a slice of iced fruit cake. These days, Mildred didn't put candles on it.

'You've been a long time, dear,' she said.

It wasn't easy to come to terms with one's own ageing, but he should have noticed how the years were changing Mildred. Her face was drawn and her figure stringy; her memory was none too reliable either.

'Happy birthday, Grandpa.' Patsy jumped up to kiss him and give him a small packet. 'From me and Dadda.'

It was the anticipation in her dancing blue eyes that made him open it immediately. Lucy had told him that Patsy was knitting him a pair of socks and that Mildred had had to pick up the stitches she'd dropped and help her turn the heels. He would say something nice about them even if he couldn't wear them.

There was a pair of pigskin gloves in the parcel as well. Soft and expensive. He reproached himself.

'Just what I need. A very generous gift, John.' He pulled them on. They were an excellent fit.

'You lost a glove in the saleroom.' Patsy was smiling at him. 'We never did find it.'

'How thoughtful. And socks too!'

'I knitted those.'

He could see nothing wrong with them, no obvious flaws. 'I won't try these on now, but they look just the thing. Thank you both, very much.' He kissed her. 'I feel very much indulged.'

Patsy was cheering him out of the doldrums. She enjoyed birthday treats and her bubbling mood was infectious. Harold decided he would sell up. It would give him more time to spend with her.

'I've finished my secretarial course,' Patsy told them over tea. 'I came top of the class in my final book-keeping exam.'

193

Harold saw Lucy wrinkle her pretty nose at that. She didn't like to think that Patsy was coming top of her classes. Theirs was an odd relationship, not close at all. He blamed the fact that they'd been parted at birth.

He looked from one to the other and thought that they were growing more alike, though neither was particularly like Elsa. All the same, the family resemblance was stronger than it used to be. They certainly looked like sisters.

Now almost fully grown, they were both slight and dainty. Both wore a hairband, one scarlet and one dark blue. Both had shoulder-length hair but Lucy's was brighter blonde and had more curl.

Even Harold found his eyes attracted to the perfection of her face. Kitten-like, with eyes of violet with long lashes, and a delicate nose, Lucy had the sort of looks that drew every eye.

There was a refinement about Lucy that Patsy didn't have, in accent and manners. A sophistication, too. Lucy knew exactly which clothes and colours flattered her. She was an overindulged little puss, but he couldn't say no to her. He didn't think anyone else could either.

Of the two, Patsy had grown a trifle the taller, and when Lucy was not beside her to compare, she seemed pretty too. Patsy's attraction for him was the way her face mirrored her emotions: eagerness, anticipation, enthusiasm and, most of all, the fondness she felt for him.

'You'll be thinking about a job now, Patsy?'

'Yes please. You said you'd give me one.'

'Did I?'

'You know you did,' she laughed, knowing he was teasing her.

'Will you be ready to start tomorrow?'

Her face was flushed and eager. 'Yes. What exactly will I be doing?'

He hadn't got round to giving that much thought. 'I've two lady typists, but I suppose a third?'

'I can type but I like book-keeping better.'

'There's plenty you could do in that line. Help the accountant?'

'Yes please.'

It was her shining eyes and show of enthusiasm that made him say: 'To start with, you can come round with me and see the different enterprises. Find out more about the business. It'll help you to understand the trade.'

'I know a bit about your auction rooms already. I've had the chance to see what goes on there.'

He said, to warn her: 'You'll still have a lot to pick up, I'm afraid.'

'I know, there's so much to learn about antiques. But I have been trying.'

He teased her again. 'Tomorrow I'll take you to the factory and give you a little test. See what you do know.'

'Right,' she laughed. 'I hope I pass.'

To Patsy it didn't seem like work. To sit beside Grandpa and be driven in his car was sheer bliss. His factory on Laird Street was a revelation. She'd heard about it but never seen it until now.

As he drove round the back into the yard she saw tree trunks waiting on one side, and piles of planks on the other. The doors stood open because it was a warm day. As soon as Grandpa turned off the engine, she could hear the whine of mechanical saws.

'It's like a sawmill,' she said.

He laughed. 'That's exactly what it is. We call this end the mill. I'd have liked to buy the timber ready-cut, but we use exotic wood here. I couldn't get exactly what I wanted and I couldn't be sure it was seasoned properly, so I decided this was the best way.'

Grandpa ran his hand down a plank. 'What sort of wood? Bear in mind that this is its natural state. You'll only have seen it polished.'

Patsy started to shake her head. 'It's such a dark colour, could it be mahogany?'

'You're right. And look at the beautiful grain on this. It's yew.'

As she followed him inside she put her hands over her ears. The screech of the saws went through her. She was walking ankle-deep in wood shavings, but the smell of new wood was sweet and fresh.

Grandpa lifted her hand from her ear and said: 'This is one of the most skilled jobs.'

In front of a power saw, in a maelstrom of noise and swirling sawdust, a man was transferring measurements from a drawing directly on to the wood.

'He's marking out where the cuts are to be made. The separate pieces are all cut and shaped by machine.'

He walked her further across the work floor. 'This machine is making ornamental banding, and this one turning chair legs.'

Grandpa nudged her again. 'Here's your father.' Patsy had already seen him sweeping up the sawdust and shavings. 'We use the debris to fire the kilns. To season the wood before it's made into furniture.'

Patsy was surprised to see John engaged in such a menial task, though she'd heard him ask Grandpa for unskilled work. She was sure he was capable of more. She stumbled on after her grandfather.

'This is the joinery shop, where the pieces are put together by hand and the furniture made. All our joints are dovetailed. I insist on strict attention to detail. We make a high-quality product.'

It was the other end of the same building. Even here sawdust seemed to spin like motes in the air. Grandpa greeted his employees by name, examined the pieces they were working on, congratulated them on their workmanship. They were treating him with considerable respect. He took her to where the finished pieces of furniture were waiting to be French-polished.

'These are replicas of the most popular antiques. The originals are worth a lot of money nowadays. Some things, like this sideboard, we scale down in size to fit the smaller rooms of this century. Could you date the style? Any ideas?'

Patsy studied the sideboard's slim and elegant lines. 'George the Third?'

'Yes, good girl. How would you describe it in a catalogue?'

'It's mahogany. Breakfront.'

'Where did you learn all this?'

'Rob Parry – you put some books in his office, to guide him.'

'Yes, for reference.'

'I took them upstairs to look at in bed.'

'You've done more than look at them.'

'I usually walk round the auction room the night before your monthly sale. Take a catalogue and see how the pieces are described. Find out afterwards how much they go for. Sometimes I try and guess what they'll fetch. It's a sort of game.'

'Do you get it right?'

'Not often.'

'You will, if you keep trying.'

Over the following months, Harold was surprised at the lively interest Patsy showed in everything to do with his business. In a very short time, she knew more about it than Mildred. He was enjoying having her with him, asking questions and lapping up information.

'I shall make you my personal assistant,' he told her.

Once, he'd had his office in the building where the restoration work was done. When the lease ran out on that, he'd moved everything to his new factory. Now he put a desk for Patsy in a corner of his room. He started giving her jobs to do, things that previously he'd done himself.

She was good at book-keeping. It took less energy to check her figures than it did to do the work himself. Soon she was relieving him of all the jobs he thought of as routine. He liked that. It gave him time to think of overall strategy and reorganise his accounting system to make it more efficient.

Harold decided that the factory accounts could be looked after by his factory manager, Dick Longworth, in the same way that Robert Parry looked after those of the auction room. He had a manager in each shop. He and Patsy would check their figures and collate the totals into an overall record.

He liked taking Patsy with him when he went to buy. He introduced her to the dealers who sold directly to the trade. Took her to some of the country house sales.

Before Patsy had started working with him, he'd almost decided to sell up. Now, he was looking at things differently and felt more optimistic about the future.

He knew he was pushing her for all he was worth. But if he didn't keep giving her books to study, she'd ask for them. He started talking over business problems with her. It cleared his head, and sometimes she helped with suggestions.

Harold wasn't sure whether any woman would have the staying power to run his business if he gave up. If Patsy didn't want marriage and a family, he hoped perhaps she could.

He could go on longer now that she'd taken some of the workload off his shoulders. It gave him more time. He wasn't finished yet, he still had plenty of mileage under his belt. Patsy had brought the change he needed in his life, and there was Lucy still to come. He wondered if she would be as good as Patsy. After her better education, she should be.

When Lucy was sixteen and had sat her school certificate exam, she declared that she wanted to leave school.

'I don't want to slog on to my higher,' she told him, looking up through her lashes. 'I'm sick of studying.'

'It seems a shame to give up now,' he told her, 'when you're doing well.'

She'd grumbled: 'You let Patsy go out to work.'

'You think she's having a better time? Not working so hard?'

'I'd like to work for you too, Grandpa.'

He never had been able to resist Lucy's smiles. 'Secretarial school first, then,' he agreed. 'Skerries did very well for Patsy. You can go there too.'

He was beginning to believe that between them, the twins would eventually run his business.

Vereena felt she'd spent long enough trying to get over her mother's death, and she had to accept that she'd been cheated out of the life assurance money. What little she'd received for her mother's goods and chattels hadn't gone far. And her high hopes for the Dixie Minstrels were coming to nothing. The band was splitting in two, and she blamed Polly Jones.

She and Polly had been the only two girls in the troupe. It was true that Polly had set up a few bookings for them, but that was no reason why she should push herself forward the way she did, wanting to sing solos and choose the numbers they played.

Vereena reckoned she'd done her best for Polly. She'd even taken Polly's brother into the band when she'd asked, and Martin wasn't much good. It didn't help that Polly was a pretty blonde and about fifteen years Vereena's junior, or that she was popular with the men in the band. Vereena thought her cheeky. Every time she spoke to her she answered 'yes, ma'am' and 'no, ma'am', trying to rub salt into the age gap.

Who did Polly think she was? She'd been working in Woolworth's when Vereena had taken her on. They'd had a row about a solo she wanted to sing. Vereena had refused to let her and told her to go if she didn't like it. Polly had gone and taken her brother with her.

It really stuck in Vereena's gullet when she heard they'd set up as a variety act, dubbing themselves Hank Hodges and Dixie Belle. Then two or three of her best musicians, Polly's cronies, of course, drifted away to play in other bands. And those that remained were playing like zombies; all their enthusiasm and bounce had faded.

Bookings had been falling off for some time, and yesterday, when she'd been to see their agent, he'd washed his hands of them. Told her they were playing like a bunch of amateurs, and that after one engagement, nobody ever booked them again.

All this year, the band had been grumbling that Vereena wasn't doing enough for them, while they sat back and did nothing. Bernie was the worst for that. It needed an explosion to get him up off his bottom. He was always good-tempered and pleasant enough, but totally useless. He needed a nursemaid to tell him where to find his socks every morning. She was losing patience with him.

He'd had to go back, cap in hand, to the Railway Hotel and ask for work. The new manager was making him work evenings, and particularly weekends, when they were busy. Bernie hated it and never managed to do a full week, which meant they were always short of money.

Vereena knew she'd have to do something. If there was one thing she couldn't stand, it was being hard up. Perhaps she should try and get a job, something to pay the bills and allow her to dress decently, but it wasn't easy in the current depression.

'Easier for a woman,' Bernie had retorted when she'd complained about his earnings.

Vereena wanted more than a nose-to-the-grindstone job, and it occurred to her that Harold Ingram was a well-heeled family connection. She admired men who could get up and do things for themselves. There was a growing confidence about him, he looked successful, and he employed quite a labour force these days. The sensible thing for her to do would be to ask him for work.

She took to visiting his auction room in Cambridge Place on sale days and chatting him up. But she knew many of the people there, it was a very public place. Vereena wanted to be discreet. She didn't tell Bernie of her intention, and she didn't want the rest of the family to know, particularly if her efforts failed. She had to avoid Rob Parry, who was closely involved with Patsy.

Although John Gripper worked at the furniture factory, she decided it was the best place to go, because Harold had his office there.

Vereena had heard, from a member of the band who had a brother working there, that Harold was a creature of habit. That he came to the factory two or three afternoons each week, and that he often stayed on after closing time, saying it was easier to think when the place was quiet. She decided that late afternoon would be the best time to try.

She dressed herself in her most becoming dress, of red crêpe. It was cut on the bias so that the longer skirt swirled about her legs. She had a pillbox hat with veiling to go with it.

As she rode up Laird Street on the tram, she could see the workmen surging out through the doors. She got off, hoping to avoid John Gripper. Harold's car was still parked outside. She went boldly in through the open door.

A grey-haired woman who was coming out asked: 'Can I help you?'

'I'm looking for Mr Ingram. I'd like a word.'

'Ye-es.' She could see the woman was about to ask her business. 'I'm family, really.' Vereena gave her a smile.

'Do you know where to find him?'

'Er . . . no.'

'This way.' The woman was leading her across the work floor. Opening a door and putting her head in.

'Somebody to see you, Mr Ingram,' Vereena heard her say. She put on a seductive smile and sailed in.

Harold was stung with surprise. It made him feel clumsy. He was slow getting to his feet.

'Hello, Vereena. You wanted to see me? Come and sit down.'

She settled herself slowly, crossing one leg over the other, swinging an elegant shoe. Something in her manner was alerting him, putting him on his toes.

'Sorry I can't offer you a cup of tea. Everybody's gone home. Just about to shut up shop.'

'I've not chosen an inconvenient time, I hope?'

'No, of course not. What can I do for you?'

Dark, intense eyes searched his, making it hard for him to break eye contact. He saw the blatant invitation there; impossible to miss it. He felt a stirring of interest. It was years since any woman had looked at him like this.

She wasn't skinny like Mildred. Vereena had rather a buxom figure, well fleshed out but with plenty of curve to it. Plump breasts rose invitingly into the low neckline of her dress. Not too much showing. Discreet, classy, but sensual.

She gave him another smile. 'I need a job. It's not easy – for a woman of my age.'

'You needn't worry about your age, Vereena,' he laughed. 'Not yet.' It wasn't like him to be jocular. 'You're still a good-looking woman.'

Even less like him to respond with a compliment like that. But it was genuine enough. He could feel himself tingling.

202

'I was wondering if you'd be kind enough to help.' Her lashes swept downwards. Then the dark eyes were searching into his again, making him burn.

'If I can. What sort of a job are you looking for?'

'Anything.' The legs uncrossed and recrossed under a fluttering skirt. She had splendid legs in silk stockings. 'Anything at all.' The breasts rose and fell as she sighed.

The implication was obvious. Harold could feel his heart beating faster.

'I think of myself as a relative of yours.' The skirt fluttered once more.

'Hardly that.'

'A relative by marriage.' Again the seductive smile.

'I'd rather think of you as a friend.'

Even so, Vereena was too closely connected for this. Only with one woman had he ever been unfaithful to Mildred. Norah Wells had been a sales assistant at his Liverpool shop. It had been a long liaison, lasting nearly twelve years. His conscience had given him a bad time for much longer than that.

He swallowed. 'Can you use a typewriter?'

'I'm afraid not.' Her lips quivered. He could see she was afraid he'd make no real offer. That spurred him on.

'There's not much else, except sales.'

Suddenly her smile was radiant. 'I'd like that. Yours are such lovely shops.'

What was he doing? 'Do you know anything about antiques? You'd need some knowledge. Customers ask—'

'I'll learn. I know I'll find antiques very interesting. I'd be thrilled if you'd let me try.'

She'd come at the right time. One of his sales assistants was leaving next week, to marry a man from Manchester.

'The West Kirkby shop? Would that suit you?'

Her face lit up, and she leapt up and came round the desk to him. 'Thank you. Yes, except . . .'

He was trying to get to his feet too. Her first kiss landed

203

on his cheek. It could have been a kiss of gratitude.

'Except I was hoping for something where I'd see more of you.'

Harold felt his cheeks flame.

'I want to be more – than just a shop assistant. I will be if you let me.'

She put her soft lips up to his in a lingering lover's kiss. He felt as though he was drowning. This was seduction, not gratitude. He couldn't believe it.

'You will let me, Harold?' Her breath was warm against his cheek. Her tongue crept between his lips.

He felt lifted on a tide of euphoria. His arms tightened round her shoulders.

'You're very kind.' Her voice was breathy. 'You won't be sorry you gave me this chance.' Her arms were under his jacket, pulling his body against her yielding breasts. He couldn't breathe.

She was undoing his tie. 'It's a good job everybody's gone home.'

Harold felt that things were moving at a tremendous pace. At his age, he'd thought all that was gone for good. He felt young again. He loosened her arms from around him, put her gently away, then picked up his heavy bunch of keys and went to lock all the doors. He didn't want anybody coming in now.

Until now, the only upholstery he'd done was on chair seats, but he was toying with the idea of expanding in that direction. He'd picked up a very pleasing Victorian *chaise-longue* and had it in his office to measure up.

An hour later, Vereena giggled up at him: 'A bit hard by today's standards. They'll never sell if you stuff them with horsehair like this.'

CHAPTER THIRTEEN

Patsy reached home before Dadda and started to cook sausages, mash and peas for their supper. He came upstairs ten minutes later, putting his head round the kitchen door to tell her he was home.

When she dished up and took their plates into the living room, she found a big sponge cake taking pride of place in the centre of the table.

She smiled. 'Where did that come from, Dadda? Very nice. It's home-made, isn't it?'

She thought he looked somewhat flushed. 'It was made by somebody I know at work.'

Patsy sat down. She had the feeling he was trying to tell her something important.

'She makes the tea at dinnertime. Mid-morning and afternoon too, of course.' He seemed to be concentrating on cutting into his sausage. 'Cleans Harold's office too.'

'Mrs Murray?'

'Yes, Alma.' Dadda was eating busily. 'She's a widow.'

'It was kind of her to make us such a big cake.'

'Strawberry jam sponge,' he mumbled.

Patsy could see he was embarrassed, and decided he'd be best left to tell her in his own way. She started to eat. She was hungry.

'I've asked her out on Saturday night.' He couldn't look at her.

Patsy felt a stab of disappointment. She and Dadda went to the pictures on Saturday nights. It meant that this week she'd have to stay home alone. Perhaps every week from now on. He'd know how she'd feel about that. No wonder he looked so guilty.

It was followed by another more painful stab of anguish. She remembered, a couple of years ago, Gran telling Dadda he should marry again. Of course he should, it would be better for him. But it left her feeling cold and insecure. Was she no longer coming first in his affections?

She choked: 'Serious, is it?'

'It might be.'

That sounded as though it was all in the future. Not something to get upset about now. But what would happen to her if Dadda married again? To think of it made her feel lost.

Robert Parry yawned as he turned over the sign to read 'Open' and slid back the bolts on the shop door. It was still dark outside. Cambridge Place looked bleak at six in the morning.

He swung the bundles of newspapers from the step to the counter two at a time. He'd heard them being slung out of the wholesaler's van as he was dressing. With the harsh shop lights on, and the paraffin heater behind the counter lit, he started making up the paper rounds.

His father had said he could manage, but Rob knew he was fully stretched trying to cope with his mother and the demands of the shop. So he continued to open up for him. Now Rob was working in the auction rooms he could at least get to bed early on the nights he didn't go to his evening classes.

They had both thought Gladys would eventually put the public airing of her affair with Albert Gripper out of her mind, and get on with life. It was all so long ago that few remembered him. With Cassie gone too, and the pub under new management, she'd seemed to improve a little. She'd started cooking meals and cleaning the house again.

Then they heard that Dilys was very ill with pneumonia, and it precipitated another family crisis. Harold Ingram had given Rob time off so that he could look after the shop while his parents went to see her.

He went across to Liverpool himself to sit by her bed one evening, but she was very poorly and hardly seemed to notice he was there. He covered the white hand on the counterpane with his own and tried to feel a spark of love for her. She was his half-sister but she was almost a stranger, only ever seen on short Sunday-afternoon visits.

He came home late one Friday, after the special monthly auction, to find they'd received a telegram to say that Dilys had passed away peacefully.

His mother had gone to lie down without making their evening meal. Rob was hungry; he got out the frying pan. His father had closed the shop half an hour early. He seemed to be on an emotional knife edge.

'Poor Dilys, she didn't have much in her life,' he said. 'It's probably for the best.'

Rob thought that for his mother, it was definitely for the best. The last link with that traumatic episode of her past had gone. She was free of it. Free of those visits that had to be made one Sunday afternoon each month. When they all tried to show concern and love for Dilys and received so pathetically small a response in return. Gladys could put it all behind her now. For his father, too, it meant that the burden of providing fees for her was gone.

But it wasn't that simple. Rob told himself he'd been foolish not to foresee the resurgence of grief and guilt his mother would feel. The sad little funeral in the rain brought the agony of those times into focus for her once more. She took to her bed and would have stayed there for a month this time if he had not gone home in his lunch hour to get a meal for them all and insist on her getting up and dressed.

She seemed to be on the verge of a nervous breakdown.

207

At times she talked wildly of her hate of the Gripper family. Even his father seemed to distrust them.

Rob knew their fears were unfounded and tried to explain how much he owed them, and how generous they'd been to him. Rob saw the Grippers as getting much more from life than his own family did. Cassie had always been in the thick of it, both feet firmly on the ground, sane and level-headed, enjoying all she could. While the Parrys feared and agonised about what others thought, not realising that people had their own problems.

'Give her time,' he told his father. 'She'll pick up again.' And eventually, she did.

She began by washing up the dishes after lunch, and went on to cook a meal for them when the shop closed. Gradually she took over the lighting of fires and the washing of clothes.

She agreed to go to chapel on Sundays, but rarely spoke to anyone there, striding home with her head down as soon as the service finished.

It took Rob a little time to realise that Donovan's were delivering the groceries and that he and Dad did the other shopping between them. His mother never went out into the street where she might come face to face with someone she knew. In moments when work was not pressing, he tried to figure out some way of helping her.

'The most helpful thing you can do is to have less to do with Patsy Gripper,' his mother told him angrily. 'That's just rubbing it all in. Leave her alone.'

'I don't see as much of her now, Mam. I've usually locked up and come home before she gets back from work. Anyway, she's just a friend.'

'You shouldn't encourage her. She's too young for friends like you.'

Rob knew she was right about that. For some time now, when he was with Patsy he'd felt an urge to run his fingers through her fair hair, to hold her tight, even kiss her. He knew he could very easily forget that she was still a child. Only fifteen.

'You can get into a lot of trouble with someone as young as that,' his mother said severely.

'Look at this,' his father added, pushing a newspaper in front of him. He was pointing to a report under the heading 'Jail Bait' about a man being sent to prison, convicted of leading an underage girl astray.

'Give her a chance to grow up in peace. You need a girl nearer your own age.'

Rob thought that perhaps he ought to cool what was happening between him and Patsy. She felt the same about him, he was sure. He could see it in her eyes. But she couldn't be ready for what he wanted, not for a long time, and his friendship with her was making his mother worse.

The following day, Patsy was looking over a collection of Victorian jewellery that her grandfather had brought into the auction room.

'Nothing very valuable,' he told her. 'Semi-precious stones, but some pretty pieces. This garnet bracelet should fetch a bit, it's fourteen-carat. Describe it as nineteenth-century, Robert.'

Rob was making notes for the sale catalogue. 'Green Bakelite bird brooch, metal pin. Cameo brooch, mounted on eighteen-carat. Is this modern?'

'Yes. Pick out the better pieces first,' Harold told him. 'The Bakelite bird and such can go in a job lot.'

Patsy picked up an amber necklace. 'Gran had some beads like these. I wonder if her things are worth anything?'

'Do you want to sell them?'

'No, but I'd like to know. Can I fetch them down to show you?'

She ran upstairs to find the cardboard box in which

Cassie had kept her jewellery. Just to hold it in her hands made Patsy think of the old days at the pub. She could see Cassie sitting on her bed, shaking the contents of her box before deciding what to wear on her black dress. Suddenly, it seemed as if Cassie was here with them.

'She used to wear this a lot.' Rob picked out a pearl brooch.

'Imitation.' Grandpa's eyes were soft with sympathy. 'Cameo brooch, poor workmanship, mounted on yellow metal. Yellow metal chains, this one's rolled gold and this silver. Silver and enamel earrings, pretty but not worth a lot.' He was shaking his head.

'Poor Gran,' Patsy said, feeling the sting of tears. 'She didn't have much. I can't get over what happened to her.'

Grandpa's voice was gentle. 'I know what she meant to you, but she could have died at any time, Patsy. You have to accept that.'

'She could have lived longer. Could have been alive today, if . . . I think about it often.'

'At times I find myself thinking about her too,' Rob put in. 'She was very kind to me.'

Patsy had difficulty keeping the tremor out of her voice. 'I feel she died under a cloud. I'd give a lot to know what really happened.'

'We'll never know now.' Grandpa was patting her arm.

'I wish there was some way of clearing her name. I'm sure Vereena was telling lies, causing trouble for her and Freda.'

'Why should she?' Grandpa asked more sharply. 'Freda was her mother. She must have been as upset as you were.'

'What upset Vereena was that her mother took her own life.'

'Well, of course, wouldn't that make it harder to bear?'

Patsy had thought about it a good deal. She couldn't rid herself of the feeling that Vereena might go on to do more harm to people she loved.

'Because her life policy wouldn't pay out, I mean. I'm sure that was it. She interfered with—'

'Don't be silly,' Grandpa snapped as he turned away. 'You must be careful what you say, Patsy. You're not being fair to Vereena.'

She was left with Rob, his brown eyes showing sympathy. Both he and Dadda had told her to keep quiet about her suspicions, and it seemed they were right. Nobody would believe ill of Vereena. And the last thing she wanted was to get on the wrong side of Grandpa.

'Take it easy, little one,' Rob said gently.

Patsy was indignant. 'I don't like you calling me that. You've picked it up from Grandpa. I'm only five years younger than you are.'

But she knew what he was getting at. There was a big gap between being fifteen and being twenty.

'Five and a half to be exact,' he smiled. 'Sorry, I won't do it again.'

Patsy shivered as she watched him turn to a customer. Nobody seemed as friendly as they used to be, not even Rob. They didn't understand. For her, the fact that Cassie had died in such circumstances was a black cloud that wouldn't go away.

During the following afternoon, a girl who'd bought some bedroom furniture in the auction came to Robert Parry's desk to pay for it. The sale was still in full swing, but at that moment he wasn't busy.

'I've bought lot number fifty-six.'

He looked up to see dancing green eyes and cheeks flushed with excitement under a very sophisticated hat.

'I'm afraid I'll have to keep you waiting a moment or two, until the auctioneer has finished with the sheet.'

'I managed to get what I wanted. I'm so pleased. Such a good price.' Her words came bubbling out.

Rob started to fill in his register. 'Name?'

'Miss Mackay – Josie. I'm not sure how I'm going to get it all home. There's a wardrobe, a dressing table . . .'

'Where do you live?'

'Grange Road. The milliner's, do you know it?'

'Mackay's?' Rob smiled, understanding now why her hat was so fashionable. 'I've passed it many times, but I'm not one of your customers.'

She was hooting with laughter. 'We only do ladies' hats.'

'I can arrange for your goods to be delivered, but there'll be a charge.'

Josie Mackay stayed much longer than was necessary, standing back from the counter while he dealt with other customers.

She hardly stopped talking, telling him that her sister was getting married and moving out and at last she would have a bedroom to herself. He felt he had something in common with her because her family were shopkeepers too. He was taken with her; she was a pretty girl and definitely nearer his own age than Patsy.

On the spur of the moment, he asked her if she would go to the pictures with him that same evening.

Later on, Patsy was helping Rob finish off the paperwork after the sale. They were still working at the counter, half an hour after they'd usually closed for the night.

'I wish I was better at book-keeping,' he said. 'I can't get this to add up right.'

'Was it a big sale? Here, let me do it for you.'

'Biggest I can remember. Well, more items, not more money than we take at the monthly. My brain's addled tonight, just when I wanted it clear, I'm going out.'

'Somewhere nice?'

'The pictures.'

Patsy's eyes jerked up from the ledger. She wanted very badly to go with him because Dadda was taking Alma Murray out.

'I've got myself a girlfriend,' he told her. 'She's been in here today. Josie Mackay, do you know her?'

That turned her to stone. Patsy had thought she was Rob's girlfriend. Why did he want somebody else? She knew it took her a long time to choke out, 'No.'

'From the milliner's in Grange Road.'

'Oh!' She was pushing the ledger back at him. 'Here, this is right now. I've got Dad's supper to get.'

His gentle brown eyes fastened on hers as though he was going to say something else. She had to get away from him.

'Have a nice time,' she managed, before stumbling upstairs. She felt upset and hot with jealousy for the girl she didn't know. She'd have loved to go to the pictures with Rob again.

She needed him. She hated the thought of somebody else coming between them. Apart from Dadda, Rob was the most important person in her life, but it seemed he didn't think of her in that way. She wanted to cry, but she mustn't. She wasn't a child any longer.

It was a late summer Sunday afternoon. Patsy was waiting for her father to wake up from his after-dinner nap.

Now that she had lunch with her grandparents every working day, they didn't ask her and Dadda to tea on Sundays. Nowadays, they usually met Alma Murray for a walk in the park, or as a special treat they'd go on the bus to New Brighton for a walk along the prom. Then back to Alma's house for tea.

Patsy found Alma friendly; she and Dadda were doing their best to include her in everything they did. They often took her with them to the pictures or the variety theatre on Saturday nights. Even so, she felt the odd one out.

She'd been sewing, letting down the hem on a dress of green cotton she'd inherited from Lucy. It fitted her only because it was a loose style with no waist. Now she'd grown as big as her twin, much of Lucy's wardrobe was of no use to her.

She was trying on the dress in front of her bedroom mirror, deciding she was pleased with the result and would wear it, when she heard a man's laugh below her in the street.

It made her straighten up against the glass. She'd know that laugh anywhere. She crept closer to her open window. She was looking down on a very smart leghorn straw hat with a wide brim wreathed in pink roses. Bending towards it was Robert Parry's handsome russet head. It made her jerk back out of sight.

As they crossed the road to the paper shop they came into view again. It was no good pretending that seeing Rob with Josie Mackay on his arm did not upset her.

He'd told her he was taking Josie home to have tea with his parents for a second time. It was an indication that she must give up hoping he'd grow tired of Josie.

Patsy thought she knew why her own friendship with Rob had gone no further. His family didn't approve of hers; there'd been this affair they couldn't forgive between Gladys and Cassie's husband. But it had nothing to do with her and Rob.

'Josie's a bit scatty, thinks of nothing but hats, but you'd like her, Patsy,' Rob told her quite openly. As if he didn't know she'd feel this surge of jealousy.

'She's nineteen and apprenticed to a milliner in Bold Street in Liverpool,' he'd said, his eyes shining. 'She's learning the top end of the trade. Then, when she returns to work in their own business, she'll be able to bring more style to Birkenhead.'

Rob acted as though Josie made no difference to them. He pretended to be just as friendly, pointing out pieces of particular interest as they came into the saleroom. But things couldn't be the same.

Patsy felt a great wall building up between them. She

had to hide how she felt about him and that made her stiff and self-conscious. She'd thought she could depend on Rob Parry but it seemed he was fickle. She felt he'd let her down.

Last night, she'd gone with Dadda and Alma to see Rudolph Valentino in *The Son of the Sheik*. She could see the attraction of celluloid heroes now.

Patsy told herself she had to keep her mind on what was going well for her. She felt very settled in her job. She loved the antiques trade.

She also loved working closely with her grandfather. They were on better terms than they'd been during her childhood. He was full of praise for everything she did. She didn't want anything to come between them.

She hadn't realised before that he enjoyed a joke and a laugh. He seemed much happier and more energetic, and was always making changes and improvements to his businesses.

'I've decided to do more work at home in future,' he told Patsy. 'We have two spare bedrooms here that are never used. I've told your nanna I'm taking them over as offices.'

Patsy was given one of them, overlooking the garden and Caerns Road. It became her base. She loved the elegant plasterwork on the ceiling and the view through the upper branches of the monkey puzzle tree. She saw more of Nanna and Lucy.

'I won't learn much about the day-to-day running of the factory from here,' she told Harold, who was moving his things into the room next door.

'More important for you to have peace and quiet to get on with the books,' he told her. 'It's more convenient for me, and more private too. No other employee needs to know what goes on here.'

But Patsy knew that he still kept his office at the factory and spent a fair amount of time there. Nanna said he often stayed late in the evenings to get his work finished.

What she enjoyed most was going with her grandfather to sales held at private houses. She'd thought the Caerns Road house magnificent, until she saw the fading grandeur of the mansions that had once belonged to Liverpool's merchant princes.

The years were passing. In 1929 the stock market collapsed and the depression grew steadily worse. As Grandpa pointed out, it caused families that had grown rich on trade in the good old days to sell up.

Almost every month, the contents of some old house came on to the market due to a death in the family or the foundering of a once-prosperous business. Antiques were flooding on to the market.

Grandpa always explained to her which lots he was interested in, and why.

'My profit is the difference between what I pay for an article and what I can sell it for. It doesn't matter to me whether it's a fine piece or not. It's the estimated margin between the two prices that counts.'

'Better if it isn't too expensive to buy, then? Easier to sell and ties up less capital.'

'Exactly, Patsy, and don't forget, that margin has to cover all my overheads as well as being my profit.' He bought a good deal of his stock at sales like these. 'Come on, I want you to try your hand at buying. It's an essential skill for an antique dealer.'

Patsy stuck to furniture at first, because she thought she knew more about that.

'You've made a good start,' her grandfather told her. 'I agree, at the price they went for, those tables should produce a reasonable profit margin. But you must buy in quantity, and you must buy a wide choice of articles, or you won't end up with a properly stocked business.'

'I couldn't make up my mind about the silver candlesticks,' Patsy mourned.

'You could have had them at a good price. Too late now.'

'I don't know enough about silver.'

'Then I must teach you what I know.' Harold smiled at her. 'You're doing well, love.'

Patsy also learned to pick out other dealers from the general public. Some of them Grandpa knew and introduced to her. They met time and time again, as they mostly attended the same sales.

'Another thing, Patsy, now you're seventeen you ought to learn to drive.'

If they were going far, they usually travelled with the van and a driver, so they could bring back what they bought. She knew that Grandpa didn't care for driving long distances, particularly if it was a place he hadn't been to before. It also meant they had to wait about until the sale finished and the goods could be loaded.

'We'd all be more flexible if you could get about on your own. And I wouldn't have to pay the driver to sit around for hours doing nothing when there's work he could do in Birkenhead.'

She felt a surge of pleasure. 'I'd love to learn to drive.'

'I'll find somebody to teach you.'

In a few more months, she was driving his car and loving the freedom it gave her. And all the time, against the trend, she knew that his business was growing more prosperous.

Patsy wasn't happy with the gossip she heard along Cambridge Place. It was being said that Robert Parry and Josie Mackay would soon announce their engagement.

She couldn't accept that he would, and she couldn't bring herself to ask him if it was true. He didn't mention it, so it lay between them, driving a deeper wedge.

Rob was just as friendly on the surface. He bubbled with congratulations when he saw her draw Grandpa's car alongside the kerb outside the saleroom.

'You've learned to drive before I have,' he laughed. 'I'm going to have to catch up.'

She was quick to offer: 'If you like, I'll show you how.'

She wanted to stay on good terms with Rob. She wanted his friendship if that was all he'd give. And she couldn't see that Josie Mackay was right for him. When he realised that, she wanted him to see that she'd grown up and was plenty old enough now. Very adult, in fact. She could take what had happened in her stride.

Rob's smile slid away. 'In the boss's car, you mean? Patsy, he mightn't like it. To him, I'm just another employee.'

She made herself say: 'To me you're a . . . a friend.'

He said awkwardly: 'I was thinking of asking Josie's brother.'

To Patsy, it felt like rejection. She'd have asked Grandpa first and she didn't think he'd refuse. She knew he'd ordered a new car for himself so they wouldn't be sharing this one much longer.

Patsy knew she had mixed feelings about Lucy. She still felt very drawn to her. When she was in the same room she couldn't keep her eyes away from her face. Lucy had real beauty; she wished many times she was more like her.

But at the same time, she was afraid that once Lucy came to work in the business, she'd come between her and Grandpa, in the way that Josie Mackay had come between her and Rob, and Alma Murray between her and Dadda.

It didn't help when Grandpa smiled and said to her: 'I'm looking forward to having Lucy in the business with us.'

But Lucy had to stay on at college for an extra term, because she hadn't achieved working speeds in her typing and shorthand. When she was finally ready to start work, Grandpa arranged for another desk and typewriter to be installed in Patsy's office. She told herself she must be welcoming, that this was her chance to get to know Lucy better. Twins should be close. If they sat together all day and every day, they soon would be.

When Grandpa brought Lucy in to see her new desk, she giggled. 'This isn't like a job at all. My bedroom's just across the landing.'

'We'll find plenty for you to do,' Harold told her. To Patsy, when they were alone, he said: 'I don't think Lucy's ready for management, but she can type. She can help you. Try to interest her in the accounts. Keep her busy, if you can.'

Patsy found her presence in the office a distraction. Lucy chatted away the whole time. She was up and down from her desk, making cups of tea, combing her hair and going downstairs to talk to Mildred. When Grandpa was elsewhere, she often went out shopping.

Within a week, she was complaining about having to type columns of figures for Patsy. She wrinkled her nose and said: 'I don't like typing numbers. It's not nearly so easy as typing letters.'

'Somebody has to do them,' Patsy told her. 'This is nineteen thirty. In this day and age, we can't send hand-written accounts to the auditors.'

'I'm not very good at figures. Can't you give the job to somebody else?'

'No, these are the final accounts for the year. The overall accounts for the business. Grandpa wouldn't want anybody else to see them. If you won't type them, I shall have to.'

'You'll make a better job of it, Patsy, and you're a glutton for work.' Lucy laughed. 'And anyway, you enjoy figures.'

Patsy knew that Grandpa had entrusted many important jobs to her, and because she'd been doing them for some time, she had a good grip on the work and understood how the business functioned.

She'd started by trying to impart some of her knowledge to Lucy. She'd expected her to learn quickly and want to take over a share of the work. But Lucy was showing no interest.

'Don't you want to learn how to run this business?' she asked. 'It's what Grandpa wants. He says one day it will be ours; he wants us to run it between us.'

Lucy flopped back in her chair, pouting prettily. 'It's an awful bore. I can't see myself spending my life doing this, can you?'

Patsy couldn't believe what she was hearing. 'Yes, of course. I think antiques are exciting. I want to be able to run it as well as Grandpa. He's getting on, won't always be able to work, you know.'

Lucy sighed heavily.

'What do you want to do then?'

'I want somebody to fall in love with me. I want somebody rich and handsome and suave to come and sweep me off my feet. I want to get married.'

For the first time, Patsy felt they shared a common goal. 'We all want to be loved, Lucy.'

'But I want to be loved by a man who'll work for me. I want a lovely home. I'll look after that side. Keep it all perfect.'

'With the help of someone like Mrs Judd, I suppose?' Patsy couldn't help the dry note in her voice.

'Of course. I'd like children of my own, and we'll all live happily ever after.'

'You're asking a lot.'

'Well, I haven't got it, have I? That's why I'm here typing for Gramps. But I'll never meet anyone here. I feel shut away from the world.'

Patsy felt a twinge of jealousy when she heard Lucy say: 'Gramps, I'd like to learn to drive. Then I can take you to all these sales.'

She watched him smile fondly at Lucy, but it warmed

her to hear him say: 'Patsy likes driving me round. She likes going to sales too.'

Lucy wheedled: 'Do let me try. Patsy loves working here, but she's got an awful lot to do. If I did the driving it would give her more time.'

'All right,' he agreed. 'Williams can show you how.'

Patsy found she was swallowing back feelings of resentment. She was afraid that Lucy might take over the most enjoyable part of her job.

CHAPTER FOURTEEN

As time went on, Lucy Ingram wasn't at all sure that she liked working. Spending all day alone with Patsy made her feel like a prisoner. Patsy took it all so seriously, a real eager beaver. This morning, Gramps had come into their office with a whole pile of letters and documents.

'Can you type these for me, Lucy?' he'd said, dumping them on her desk. 'I'm going to Cambridge Place now, to see how the auction's going.'

'I'll come with you,' she'd offered. 'I'm sure I can learn a lot there.'

'Better if you stay here and get my letters done,' he'd said, sounding grumpy.

She'd seen Patsy's head lift from her ledgers and smile at that.

She'd had to start on the mound of typing. It had been hard going but she'd stuck at it for an hour. Then she'd just had to have a break; she'd gone downstairs for a cup of tea with Nanna. She found her frowning over a grey cardigan she was knitting for Gramps.

'I hope I'm going to have enough wool to finish it,' she worried. 'I seem to be using it up very quickly.'

Lucy had seen her opportunity. 'Can I go out and get you some more?' A trip to the shops in Grange Road seemed very tempting, a much more pleasant way of spending the morning.

'Would you, dear? That's very kind.'

Lucy had run upstairs with a cup of tea for Patsy and

told her that Nanna was sending her out on an errand. She got herself ready and sauntered down to the tram stop on Shrewsbury Road. Recognising an old school friend waiting there, she ran the last few yards screaming with delight.

'Wonderful to see you.' Once, she and Madge Kerr had spent a lot of time together. Madge bubbled with good humour, telling of the parties she'd been to and the boyfriends she had. Lucy knew now that in leaving school she'd made the wrong choice.

'I wish I'd stayed on. It was a mistake to go to that commercial college. I hate having to type all day, and I've missed you all. You seem to be having a much better time.'

'I'm due to sit my higher soon. At least you haven't got that hanging over you.'

'What'll you do after that?'

'Get a job if I can.'

'Put that off as long as possible,' Lucy advised. 'I hate work. I hardly get out these days.'

Madge had a pert, attractive face and did all she could to enhance it with cosmetics. Nanna didn't approve.

'Too much paint,' she sniffed. 'Makes her look fast. Not nice on a young girl.'

'We're going over to Liverpool next Wednesday to the ballet,' Madge told Lucy now. 'All the old crowd. Why don't you come too? Lunch followed by a matinée at the Royal Court.'

'I'd love to,' Lucy breathed.

'But of course, you're working.'

'For my grandfather. He'll let me off for something like that.'

Lucy enjoyed her morning, matching Nanna's wool and looking through the best dress shops. She timed her return well; she was back before Gramps came home for lunch.

Only Patsy looked disapproving. 'Didn't Grandpa say that he wanted those letters to go in the afternoon post?'

'Yes. I'll have plenty of time this afternoon.'

'He usually goes back to Cambridge Place when there's a sale on. He'll need to sign them first.'

They heard Harold come upstairs to his office. 'If I were you, I'd get him to sign the ones that are ready.'

Lucy picked up the three letters she'd typed and did as Patsy suggested. She wanted to catch him alone. She told him about meeting Madge and being asked to go with a group of her old school friends to the ballet.

'Is it all right if I take time off next Wednesday? It should be good.'

He looked up, frowning, from the letters she'd put in front of him. 'No, Lucy. A job is a job. You can't go jaunting off just when you feel like it.'

'Just this once, please, Gramps.'

'Where are the other letters?'

'I'll do them this afternoon, really I will. My best typing, I promise.'

He sighed. 'I wanted them to catch this afternoon's post.'

'But can I . . .?'

'No.'

Lucy straightened up in disbelief. 'You always let Patsy do what she wants.'

That dispelled his frown. 'What Patsy wants is usually what's best for the business.'

That was hurtful. Once, Gramps had loved her more than Patsy. He'd have let her do anything she wanted. She didn't like Patsy spending so much time with him. And he let her drive his car whenever she wanted. He wasn't being fair.

Lucy wasn't finding driving easy. Gramps said she needed more practice and she could have that with Williams, not with him. He valued his life.

She was afraid that Patsy had wormed her way into what had been her territory. But once she could drive properly, she'd take him everywhere. He said his eyesight

225

wasn't as good as it had been and he didn't care to drive much now. Being his chauffeur had to be more interesting than pounding away at a typewriter all day.

Another couple of years slid by. Harold Ingram looked round with satisfaction at his comfortably furnished office in Caerns Road. He was feeling in his prime again.

Patsy was taking much of the work of running the business off his shoulders. He had time to enjoy what he did again, time to sit back and consider where he could improve his margins. And he could discuss things with her, because she understood how he worked.

He also had Vereena. She was rejuvenating him, giving him a good time. He felt he was getting everything a man could ask from life. That he was well organised and fully in control of his destiny.

He could hear Lucy laughing in the next office. It sounded a good joke. He picked up the letter she'd just typed for him and went to see what the hilarity was about.

Lucy's laugh subsided. 'I've lost that catalogue you asked for, Gramps. I know I filed it properly when it came, but I can't find it now.'

'The Friday sale at Highfield House,' Patsy added. He could see she was exasperated, though half laughing with Lucy. Nobody could be angry with Lucy for long. She charmed them all out of expecting her to be responsible for anything.

'We'll have another look for it later,' Patsy said. 'It must be here somewhere.'

Harold had been thinking for some time that he must do something about Lucy. The moment had come. He couldn't let her play about like this.

Half jokingly, he asked: 'How do you like working here, Lucy?'

She giggled. 'It doesn't seem like a real job.'

'It isn't. Not the way you do it.' He saw Patsy's eyes come up from her work, her eyebrows raised in surprise.

'Do you know, Lucy, having you here is like having a playful kitten about the place?' That only made her smile wider.

'Can I come out with you then? Drive you down to the factory?'

'Not the factory.'

Definitely not the factory. Vereena was working there. She hadn't got as far as the West Kirkby shop. He didn't want either of the girls to find out what her duties were. That was the main reason for having an office here at home.

'I've been thinking, would you like to work in the Dale Street shop instead? Would that seem a proper job to you?'

Lucy was wrinkling her pretty nose suspiciously. 'What would I be doing there?'

'They have the odd letter to type. And you could help serve in the shop.'

'Yes.' Lucy was all smiles. 'I wouldn't mind trying that.'

'Go and get yourself ready then. I'll take you over and introduce you to the staff. You can see how you get on.'

Lucy went scampering across the landing to her room, still smiling. Patsy pulled her ledgers closer and picked up her pen.

'I want you to come too, Patsy. We'll take a taxi out to that sale in Aigberth. We can come back in the van.'

After a moment's silence, he added: 'I'm a bit disappointed in Lucy. I expect you are too. Can't even turn out a decent letter. Look at the way she's scrubbed out her mistakes here. Almost a hole in the paper. I can't send out a letter like that.'

'I'll do it over,' Patsy said, 'when I come back.'

'She's not like you, doesn't have much motivation when it comes to work. More interested in parties and pretty clothes.'

227

He stroked his silvery moustache and gave her a half-smile. 'Can't expect much help from Lucy when it comes to running this business I'm afraid. It's going to be just you and me.'

Patsy didn't answer but he didn't miss her little smile of triumph.

It was a wet morning but Lucy didn't mind. It pleased her to be going out.

Gramps didn't usually go to Liverpool on wet days, because they had to park the car and cross the river by train. It was possible to take the car over on the luggage boat or to drive round via Runcorn, but usually it wasn't worth the trouble. Dale Street was a short walk from James Street station.

On the walk from the station, Lucy put her arm through Gramps's and shared the shelter of his big umbrella. Patsy followed behind.

When they reached the shop, Gramps paused to assess the window display. 'What do you think of it, Lucy?'

'There's not a lot in it.' Just a chest of drawers with some bric-à-brac on top, set against a background of swathed red velvet.

'You'll need to learn a bit about antiques.' She heard the anxiety in his voice. 'These are prime pieces. I explained last week about chests; how did I describe this sort?'

She couldn't remember. A chest was to put clothes in, wasn't it? What did the rest matter?

'Serpentine front; you can't miss that, surely? It's George the Third, mahogany with satinwood banding.'

'I know that's a lacquered box on top,' she smiled.

'A very fine one.' He swept her round to a second window. There were more smaller pieces here.

'Clock sets,' she said. And totally hideous they were.

'Describe this one for me.'

'French.'

'Yes.'

'Porcelain and ormolu, with a matched pair of porcelain urns.'

'Good girl. And the date?'

Lucy shook her head.

'Nineteenth century. You didn't do badly. You'll learn.'

She couldn't suppress a giggle. 'There's a set like this in the dining room at home, Gramps.'

'Almost. How about this then?'

She laughed. 'Twice the size and twice as hideous. Must be Victorian. The clock's mounted in black and grey marble, surmounted by a figure of Britannia. Two matching marble urns, they look like funeral urns. More suited to the graveyard than the sideboard.'

'They were designed for a mantelpiece, my dear.'

'Mantelpiece? It would have to be huge to support those things.'

She'd cheered them all up. Even Gramps was laughing. The door pinged as they went in. Lucy's heels sank into the carpet. She looked round appreciatively. The shop had an exclusive air about it.

Gramps introduced her to Mr Cook, the manager, who looked stiff and formal and a little bit dour. He was leading them towards an office at the back. It was so small they couldn't shut the door when they all crowded in.

The assistants looked old and staid. Lucy didn't think it was going to be a laugh a minute here either. But she'd be able to get out at lunchtime and go round the big department stores.

A customer was coming in, a tall, handsome man. He had the swaggering gait of an actor. He wore a loud check jacket over a yellow waistcoat and had a habit of waving his arms with tremendous enthusiasm and energy.

'Wesley Spiers,' Patsy said at her elbow. 'What's he come here for?'

Lucy felt curious. 'Who is he?'

'A dealer,' Grandpa told her. 'He won't make much on what he buys here.'

She followed his movements, but she knew that Patsy and Gramps were doing the same. There was a quality about Wesley Spiers that drew attention. His voice was over-loud and had a good carrying ring to it.

'He's interested in that clock set in the window,' Gramps said. 'Britannia and the urns. Probably buying on commission. He'll have a customer lined up for it.'

Lucy felt an urge to know Wesley Spiers better. 'Shall I go and talk to him?' She pushed her handbag and gloves at Patsy. 'I'm going to serve here, aren't I? Might as well start straight away.'

Gramps's voice followed her. 'He'll be wanting to talk about trade discount, love. I'd better come too.'

Lucy put on her most fetching smile as she approached the man. 'Can I help you?'

Large eyes of tawny gold swept down to meet hers, holding her gaze. He had plenty of thick brown hair, just greying at the temples.

'I'd very much like to have a closer look at the clock set in the window.' There was something magnetic about him. It surprised her because he wasn't young. She couldn't drag her eyes away.

For a brief moment he glanced at Gramps. 'Hello, Harold, how lucky to find you here. You don't come often, these days.'

'I've brought my granddaughter, Lucy, across. She's going to work here.'

'Really?' His eyes met hers again, his smile seemed intimate, just for her. 'I'm sorry ... I didn't recognise you.'

'You're thinking of Patsy,' Gramps told him. 'You've seen her with me at house sales.'

His eyes slid briefly to Patsy, who was talking to the

manager. 'Yes. I didn't know you had two grand-daughters.'

'Twins.'

'Really?' Wesley's tawny eyes came back to Lucy's. She warmed towards him, feeling her blood coursing through her veins. She'd never met anybody quite like him before.

Wesley had collected an entourage. One of the assistants slid back the velvet curtain, revealing the window display. The funeral-like urns were being lifted out. Then the huge, hideous clock.

Harold said: 'Bell-striking movement. Painted dial, Roman numerals. Signed "Willm Wavell, Liverpool".'

'Just what I'm looking for. For a client, of course.'

Though they were surrounded by people, Lucy felt he was speaking only to her. He seemed to have a vast knowledge of clocks and knew exactly the worth of what he was buying. He was bargaining with Gramps. She listened, fascinated, unable to tear her attention away from this man. She watched him write out a cheque.

'You'll want them delivered?' Lucy could see they were too heavy for him to carry. The matching urns were two feet high and must weigh a ton.

He looked up, smiled at her as he thought about it. 'I'll come back with my car and collect them. Tomorrow.'

Her heart seemed to miss a beat. She hoped very much she'd see him again when he did. Before leaving, he thanked Gramps for the discount he'd been given, and shook hands all round. There seemed to be a special smile for her.

Lucy's head was spinning. Never before had anyone had this effect on her. She felt suddenly alive, on top of the world. On the brink of something exciting and wonderful.

She was burning with curiosity about him. For her, she was quite sure it was love at first sight.

* * *

231

Lucy watched Patsy and Gramps leave the shop, her mind in a whirl.

'Miss Simpson will look after you.' Mr Cook didn't look over-pleased to have her services. 'She'll show you where things are, and how we approach customers. She's our senior assistant.'

Lucy thought Miss Simpson's tall, gaunt figure rather forbidding. Her greying hair was drawn back severely into a bun; her voice droned on about the behaviour required of assistants, about their duties and the stock they had to sell.

Lucy switched her mind away. She was walking on air. The timbre of Wesley Spiers's voice was still ringing in her ears. When she closed her eyes, he was before her again in his yellow waistcoat with gilt buttons, and his eyes were playing games with hers. She wanted to know more about him.

'Mr Spiers? Yes, he comes in from time to time,' Miss Simpson told her. 'He's in the business. I believe he has a shop in Southport.'

She knew no more, so Lucy had to wait until she could ask Gramps over supper that evening. She was careful to hide the interest she felt. She didn't think her grandparents would approve.

'Wesley Spiers? Strange fellow, larger than life, or acts as though he is. I don't know anything about him except that he's in the trade.'

'Do you see a lot of him?'

'He's often at house sales. Buying like I am. Often bids against me. He likes clocks. Buys a lot of them.'

The next morning, Lucy went eagerly back to the shop. She checked that the marble clock set was still in the storeroom. The thought of seeing him again made her tingle all over.

The women employed in the shop all wore white blouses with black skirts. 'It might be more appropriate if you did the same,' Miss Simpson advised.

Lucy had chosen to wear her most becoming floral summer dress with the latest cape sleeves. She wanted to look her best for Wesley.

'I don't care for black.' She caught sight of herself in a Georgian mirror and preened. 'Makes me feel dowdy.'

'Oh! Will you be with us for long?' Miss Simpson asked shortly.

'Permanently.'

'Really? I assumed you'd stay for only a few weeks – to gain experience.'

'It depends on whether I like working here or not.'

The morning dragged for Lucy. Every time the shop door pinged she turned to see if it was Wesley Spiers. At last she looked up to see his flamboyant figure striding across the carpet towards her. He was wearing a scarlet waistcoat today.

'Hello, it's Miss Ingram, isn't it?' He clasped both her hands in his. 'I hoped I'd see you again.'

Lucy felt weak at the knees as his eyes smiled into hers. Such unusual eyes, of tawny brown, golden with darker flecks in them. She guessed he'd deliberately arranged this second visit to the shop to see her. She was very conscious of Miss Simpson's presence close beside her.

'You've come for your clock?' Lucy asked.

'Yes, my car's outside.'

'We'll have somebody carry it out for you,' Lucy said, with the air of the proprietor. 'Could you arrange that, Miss Simpson?'

Miss Simpson was disconcerted. 'Yes, of course.' She sounded irritable, and left Lucy's side for the first time that morning.

Wesley Spiers continued to hold Lucy's hands. 'I was wondering if you would come out to lunch with me? I'd be very honoured if you would.'

She felt fluttery with pleasure. The magnetism she'd felt

233

yesterday was stronger than ever. She'd not been mistaken about Wesley. 'I'd like that very much.'

'I know it's naughty of me to ask, when you hardly know me, but if I don't ...' His eyes seemed to search into her soul and told her he was as smitten with her as she was with him.

'If I don't, I never will know you better. And I'd very much like to.'

Sitting beside him in his car a few minutes later, Lucy felt very daring. Mildred would be furious if she knew, she'd think Lucy ought to have a chaperone, but that made it all the more exciting.

She couldn't remember what she ate. All she could recall was twisting the starched tablecloth between her fingers below his line of vision, and marvelling that this handsome man should attach himself to her.

'I haven't been able to get you out of my mind,' he told her. 'You're the most beautiful girl I've ever seen.'

Lucy felt on fire.

'Silly for a man of my age, to go overboard like this. I should have more sense.'

'It makes sense to me,' Lucy laughed. She could see tiny lines fanning out from the corners of his eyes, and he had the broad shoulders of a man in his middle years. It made him more attractive, not less.

'I'm a lot older than you are, and ... I'm a bit worried that ...'

Lucy giggled. 'If you're trying to ask politely how old I am, I'll be twenty at Christmas.'

'Twenty? That's not too bad. I was afraid ...' He laughed and kissed her hand. To Lucy, it all seemed very romantic.

When he dropped her outside the antique shop some two hours later, she'd already agreed to meet him again the next day.

* * *

234

As the days went on, Lucy didn't care very much for working in the shop. Miss Simpson was always two feet behind her, reciting, in the way Gramps did, endless information about the age and style and value of the goods that were for sale.

She showed her the catalogues and manuals on antiques they kept in the office. Advised her to study them in her free moments. She didn't allow Lucy to approach customers on her own, telling her she was here to be taught the correct way. Lucy had regarded the office at Caerns Road as a prison, but here she felt she had a jailer.

The best thing about working in the shop was that she could meet Wesley. She'd been having lunch with him every day for a fortnight. On Wednesday, which was early-closing day in Liverpool, they planned to spend more time together. It was a sunny but blustery afternoon.

'How about a trip on the river?' he'd suggested as they finished eating.

'Sounds wonderful.' Lucy swung on his arm as they walked down to the pierhead.

They boarded the *Royal Iris* and climbed to the top deck. All the way down to New Brighton at the mouth of the river, Lucy leaned against the rail. Wesley put an arm round her waist; his body sheltered her from the brisk breeze. She watched other vessels creaming through the choppy water as Wesley told her about himself.

'Valerie, my wife, was drowned in a sailing accident about three years ago. I've a son called Rodney. He's nearly eighteen, just two or three years younger than you are. That's why I'm a bit sensitive about your age.'

Lucy snuggled closer to him. He sounded sad. It made her want to take care of him. For the first time, Wesley bent to kiss her on the lips.

235

That made her feel exhilarated, almost possessed by him. She could think of nothing else but the way his tawny eyes burned into hers. She was bursting to tell somebody about him.

The following Wednesday, an important sale was being held in Freshfield. Wesley wanted to spend the whole day there.

When the shop closed at lunchtime, Lucy went home. The savoury scent of beef casserole was still heavy in the hall, but the meal had been eaten and the table cleared. Mrs Judd had saved some for her and she ate it quickly at the kitchen table.

Gramps was out and Nanna had gone shopping. She found Patsy working in the office upstairs and couldn't keep quiet any longer.

'Wesley Spiers?' Patsy sounded surprised. 'But he's old! What do you see in him? He looks as old as Dadda.'

'Of course he isn't,' Lucy retorted hotly.

'How old is he then?'

'Forty-four.'

'That's what I mean, as old as Dadda.'

'He's two years younger.'

'Lucy, what's two years?' She could see that Patsy was aghast. 'Anyway, I don't like him. He's too full of himself.'

It made her sneer. 'I suppose you're interested in some callow youth? Not still that Rob Parry?' Patsy was staring at her balefully.

'It's better to have a husband who is much older. He'll be able to look after me better.'

'You mean he's asked you to marry him?' Patsy's blue eyes were wide with shock. 'Already?'

'Yes. I told you, we're in love.'

Patsy sounded breathless. 'Have you told Grandpa?'

'Not yet.'

'Nothing at all? Not about meeting him?'

Lucy shook her head.

'I would if I were you. But on second thoughts . . . Lucy, he won't allow it. Not Wesley Spiers.'

CHAPTER FIFTEEN

Harold Ingram was finding he couldn't get enough of Vereena's company. The high spot of the day for him was the hour they spent together in his office after the factory had closed. The days when he wasn't able to fit it in seemed very empty indeed.

Officially, Vereena was working as a clerk in the factory office. Their affair was working out well; she was discreet in what she said and did. Nobody seemed any the wiser.

He liked her sense of humour and found her entertaining, but he was afraid that she, too, might no longer be satisfied with just that hour. He'd been planning a day out with her for some weeks and the sale in Freshfield seemed the ideal opportunity.

Harold had already arranged to send his van to Preston to call on a dealer there who regularly bought china for him. The dealer had telephoned to say he'd accumulated quite a collection, including some Liverpool jugs and some rare teabowls and saucers. On its return journey, the van could come to Freshfield to collect anything he bought there.

He'd drive up with Vereena. To any acquaintance he met, he could introduce her as an assistant who, for once, had come in Patsy's stead. He felt a little guilty about leaving Patsy in the office without explanation. He knew she'd have loved to come with him as usual.

It was a lovely summer's day and he had his new car. Nothing fancy; he'd chosen another Morris saloon.

Vereena looked delicious in a dress with floating panels and a blue straw hat.

Harold enjoyed the drive up. Vereena's dark, intense eyes excited him, but she wasn't as good at reading maps and street guides as Patsy, and the journey took longer than he'd expected.

The house where the sale was being held had once belonged to a Liverpool ship owner. He'd amassed a wonderful collection of marine paintings. Harold meant to buy several.

As he parked outside, he looked over the cars already there. The only one he recognised was the yellow Cadillac belonging to Wesley Spiers. It was flash, like everything else about him.

The sale was due to start, and he wanted to take a close look at the items he'd ticked in the catalogue before they came up. He set off briskly, with Vereena making notes for him. His method was to decide beforehand the price he was prepared to pay for each lot, and then not bid above it. He was concentrating for the moment on his business.

There were a number of lots he was interested in, and as yet there didn't seem to be many dealers here. Harold felt optimistic that it was going to be a good day. With luck, prices should not go too high.

The auctioneer banged his gavel for attention, and the sale was barely underway when Harold had a mahogany side table knocked down to him cheaply. He was not interested in the two lots that followed and had moved on to a pair of whatnots when he saw Wesley Spiers heading towards him.

'I was wondering, Mr Ingram, if I might have a word.'

'Of course.' Harold smoothed out his catalogue, expecting to be asked his opinion on some item in it.

'It's of a personal nature.' Wesley looked uneasily towards Vereena. The two men moved a few steps away. 'About your granddaughter, Lucy.'

'What about her?' He knew he'd barked. He'd been taken unawares.

'I'd like your permission to see her.'

'What d'you mean, see her?'

Wesley's fingers were fiddling with the bottom button on his yellow waistcoat. He looked discomforted.

'I'm very taken with her.' He seemed tongue-tied. 'I'm afraid I took the liberty of asking her out to lunch. I'd like very much to do it again. I'd like your permission.'

'Good Lord! Lucy's young enough to be your daughter! She won't look at you.'

'I assure you she will. She wants it too.'

'Good God!' Harold was shocked. Vereena was nudging his arm.

'The pair of whatnots, coming up now.'

Harold couldn't concentrate. They were knocked down to somebody else very cheaply. He was cross with himself for missing them, and angry with Wesley. He could think only of Lucy. Mildred would be upset. Only the other day she'd said:

'Lucy's like a pretty butterfly, made for the social scene. Work doesn't suit her. She doesn't seem to settle to it.'

He, too, thought marriage would be the best way to ensure that Lucy had a happy and fulfilled life. With her beauty and her share of the business behind her, there was no reason to think she wouldn't find a very satisfactory husband.

Mildred had started giving little parties for Lucy, but thought her young for her age. She was still wrapped up in her girlfriends.

Her grandmother had said: 'Not ready to settle yet.' He'd thought her wise to come to that conclusion. 'Not ready for marriage. No reason to rush her into it.'

He'd been very careful to make it clear to Patsy that the parties were for her too, but she was very different. He was encouraging her to see her future in the business. He really believed that with more experience she'd be capable of getting as much out of it as he did.

Mildred thought that for Patsy, marriage would be an unnecessary complication. A husband and children as well as the business might prove more than she could manage. Better if Patsy didn't marry at all. They were not going to steer her towards it.

Harold knew that for himself, as well as Mildred, Wesley Spiers would be a great disappointment. Here in the sale there was no avoiding him. His loud voice was rarely silent. Everywhere Harold looked, Wesley Spiers was there, waving his arms about, holding centre stage. And worst of all, he overbid him on two longcase clocks.

Harold blamed Wesley for the fact that the sale didn't prove as profitable as he'd hoped, and for ruining his day out with Vereena. Feeling out of sorts, he set off for home early. Towards the end of the journey Vereena's company began to soothe him. He was feeling a little better by the time he was driving off the luggage boat.

'I'll drop you off at Central Station, shall I?' He'd picked her up there that morning. It was a short walk from her home in Thomas Street, yet far enough away that nosy neighbours wouldn't see her getting out of his car. Both he and Vereena had to be careful, but the secrecy gave an added fillip to their relationship.

There was a lot of traffic, and crowds were thronging outside the station, some waiting in line for the many buses that passed through to the suburbs. It was the evening rush hour; shops and factories had just closed. Harold pulled his car into the kerb.

'Sorry, Vereena. Not a good day out after all. I've not been good company.' He knew he'd been holding forth about Wesley Spiers.

She patted his knee. 'Not to worry. Nothing's changed between us.'

That was what he liked about Vereena. She could take

242

upsets like this in her stride. He leaned across and released the car door for her.

'Goodbye.' He kissed her mouth with tender affection. 'See you tomorrow.'

Passengers were streaming off the bus in front of him. He watched her get out and almost walk into John Gripper's arms.

Harold froze in horror as John's shocked eyes swung to meet his through the windscreen. He knew he must have seen him kiss Vereena. This was what he'd hoped to avoid at all costs. The crowd engulfed Vereena and John, and he could see them no more, but he couldn't move.

What had he been thinking of? This business with Wesley Spiers had upset him more than he realised. Would John suspect that Vereena was his mistress? He felt cold at all that implied. He'd known from the start that she was too closely connected, but he'd put that out of his mind. It had been Vereena he'd wanted, and up until now he'd been able to tell himself that their secret was safe.

It took him a few moments to pull himself together sufficiently to drive on. He felt sick. His mind was filled now with his own predicament.

He was home before he felt ready to face Mildred. He ran his car into the garage and was surprised to find the old bull-nose still in front of the house. It meant that Patsy hadn't gone home. It was long after her usual time and he wondered what was keeping her. He didn't want to face her either. As he let himself into the hall, he could hear their voices from the sitting room.

'Is that you, Harold?' He caught the note of anxiety in Mildred's voice and wondered what other calamity could have befallen them. Patsy and Lucy were sitting side by side on the sofa. It was unusual to see them together like this.

'What's the matter?' he asked.

243

Mildred was beside herself. 'Lucy's got herself involved with a man. She's been going to lunch with some dealer. Out with him almost every day. It seems you introduced them.'

'I've seen him today,' he said. 'He told me.'

'Told you what?' Mildred demanded.

'Asked my permission to see Lucy. To take her out.'

'I hope you refused? What did you say?'

Harold could no longer remember.

'At least he's done the decent thing,' Patsy spoke up. 'He's asked your permission, Grandpa. He isn't going behind your back. He's told you how things stand.'

Harold understood then why Patsy had stayed. She was supporting Lucy.

'Who is this man?' Mildred was playing with her beads, always a sign that she was worried. 'You say he's a dealer, but is he dealing on his own account?'

'I believe so. Has a big opinion of himself.'

'He has a shop of his own, in Southport,' Lucy said. 'Miss Simpson told me.'

'Is he in a position to support a wife? Did you ask him what he earns?'

'Well, no. How could I do that in the middle of a sale? He didn't mention marriage. I didn't realise it had gone that far.'

'Well, it has.' Lucy pouted. 'And he seems to be free with his money. I don't think there can be problems there. He's very generous.'

'You've only known the man for two weeks,' Mildred stormed. 'This is nonsense. Harold, I want you to put a stop to it.'

'No,' Lucy wailed. 'He's a lovely person.'

'He's far too old for you. Ridiculous, I call it. You could do much better for yourself, Lucy.'

'Don't say I can't see him. We're in love, Gramps. We want to be married.'

'Married? You're much too young.'

'I'm not. I'll be twenty at Christmas. My mother was exactly my age when she was married.'

How many countless times had he wished he'd withheld his permission for that? 'I certainly won't give you permission to marry Wesley Spiers, so don't ask for it.'

'Gramps, I want to marry him, and I don't want to wait. He loves me, he truly does.'

'No, Lucy. Whether you want to wait or not, you'll have to. I won't be able to stop you once you're twenty-one, but you certainly won't be marrying him until you are.'

'Help me persuade them, Patsy.' Lucy was cross. 'You said you would.'

'I don't think Grandpa is being unreasonable.' Patsy's eyes met his. 'He hasn't forbidden you to see him. That's what you were afraid of.'

'How could I enforce that?' Harold asked wearily. 'By locking you up?' Lucy had had too much of her own way in the past. She only did what she wanted to do.

'Stop her working at the shop,' Mildred said. 'Patsy and I will keep an eye on her here.'

Harold felt bone-weary. He had no heart for the argument now.

'Patsy has better things to do with her time. Lucy, we don't approve of Wesley Spiers. He's flash and he's too old for you. You'd be wise to stop seeing him.'

'No, Gramps, I can't!' she cried. 'I love him.' He could see tears glistening on her lashes. He understood what a driving force love could be.

'Then have it your way. You need to get to know him better and we need to find out more about him. To wait seems fair enough. You'll be of age in eighteen months.'

'Let's hope you see sense before then,' Mildred snapped.

Harold dropped his head in his hands. He was more worried about what John Gripper was going to do. His own troubles seemed more immediate than Lucy's.

* * *

'Vereena?'

John Gripper held on to his sister-in-law's arm in bewilderment. He felt weak with shock. He wouldn't have believed his own eyes, except that Harold Ingram was sitting in his car, transfixed, staring at him, the picture of guilt.

Vereena was shaking him off, moving away. He followed. 'Have you been out with Harold Ingram?'

'You can see I have. To a sale, doing your Patsy's job today.'

He was finding it difficult to keep up with her as she threaded her way through the crowd. 'He kissed you, I saw him.'

'No,' she said over her shoulder. 'No!'

'I saw him! And he's always coming to see you at the factory. I was wondering, even before.'

'Shut up, can't you?'

'You're all dressed up in your best. That's your new hat. You've had a day out together.'

They were going down Hind Street and had left the crowds behind. Vereena turned on him.

'So what is it to you, John Gripper? It's none of your business.'

'If you're carrying on with Harold Ingram it is my business. I mean, you're family, and so is he.'

She pounced on him angrily, her red fingernails digging into his wrist as she pulled him closer. 'You owe Harold a good deal. He's been very generous to you and Patsy.'

'What if he has? That doesn't give him the right to . . . Are you his mistress?'

'I work for Harold, that's all.'

'So do I . . .'

'And so does your Patsy, and he's given you both a home. You owe him loyalty at the very least.' He'd never seen Vereena's dark eyes flash with such fury. Her nails bit deeper.

246

'You breathe a word of this to anyone and Harold won't be pleased. He'll sack you both and put you out on the street. I'll ask him to, and he always does what I want.'

'Not to our Patsy; he's very fond of her.'

'He'll want revenge, John, if you spread the word about what you saw. You try to ruin his reputation or mine and I'll wreck things for you. Keep your mouth shut. D'you understand?'

'I understand when I'm being threatened.' John felt frustrated with anger. 'I didn't ask to see him kissing you; it sickened me. Mam always said you were a fast one. How long's this been going on?'

'If I hear one word being bandied about the factory or the pub or anywhere I'll know it's you.' Vereena's face was vicious. 'I'll make sure plenty of trouble comes your way in return.'

'Does our Bernie know about this? You're his wife, for goodness' sake.'

'You stay away from Bernie. Remember, one word to anybody and I'll let all hell loose on you.'

He watched her turn up Thomas Street, striding furiously, her long, elegant skirts swinging about her legs.

John could feel himself shaking. He still couldn't believe it. He'd always looked up to Harold Ingram, thought of him as a benefactor. Damn it, he'd been fond of him. And he was nothing but a libertine.

Vereena felt fraught as she let herself into her house. An overpowering aroma of bacon and eggs was coming from the scullery. She kicked off her high heels and padded through. Bernie was stripped to the waist at the sink, having a wash.

'Are you going out?' He was soaping his ears, washing the back of his neck; she knew he must be. His dirty plates and the remnants of his meal were still on the table. Left for her to clear up.

247

Vereena felt the teapot; decided it was hot enough and poured a cup for herself. She took it back to the living room, easing off her straw hat and hanging it on a nail that already supported a print of the Liverpool waterfront.

She collapsed on an armchair, feeling drained. She didn't think John would say anything about that kiss, but it took away her sense of security. After all Harold had said about being careful, he had to kiss her like that in a public place. Men, even the best of them, could be such fools.

Bernie came to the door, rubbing the towel under his arms. 'You look tired.'

'Exhausted. Had a hard day. Some of us have to work.' It was her usual way of reminding him that she earned more than her share of the household expenses.

He was grinning at her. 'I've got a job too.' He sounded buoyant and keen.

'Not the Railway Hotel?'

'I'm playing the Empire for the rest of this week. Morecambe next week, and Scarborough the week after that. What do you say to that?'

Vereena felt a pang of envy. She was the one with ambition and drive, the one who had tried so hard to carve out a stage career. For her, it had come to naught.

'How d'you manage that?'

'Polly Jones has asked me.'

'Not her?' Vereena felt a flush of frustration. 'Not the Dixie Belle act?'

'Hank Hodges and Dixie Belle. I've been practising my American accent. I could be on to a winner here.'

'You can't work with her!' She was angry with him.

'Why not? Much easier than the band. Only ten or fifteen minutes on stage, and easier to get bookings too. Variety shows are popular and they're always looking for something new.'

'Bernie! You know why not. She broke up our band. She hates me.'

'No. Polly doesn't give a damn about you. She reckons that band could never earn us much. Too many in it. We had to play the whole show to put anything worthwhile in our pockets, and it's harder to get bookings for that.'

'Polly Jones was always big-headed. Thought she knew better than any of us.' Vereena felt sick with envy. Polly was the last person she wanted to be successful. 'What about her brother? I thought he was partnering her.'

'He's in hospital with appendicitis, but she says I'm better. She isn't having him back. I don't think he was ever very keen.'

Vereena was overcome with fury. 'Why d'you think she's asked you? She could have chosen anyone in the band. She was very friendly with Steve Marshall.'

'She reckons I look the part and that there's none better on the banjo. I'm doing "Campdown Races" as a solo.' Bernie was beaming, looking pleased with himself. 'We used to practise together quite a bit.'

'She only wants you because you're my husband. She's trying to get back at me.'

'Don't be daft, Polly isn't like that. She never mentions you. I don't believe she ever thinks about you. Too busy with other things.'

'It's spite. I suppose she sings?'

Bernie sighed happily. 'Doing what you wouldn't let her do. I sing with her.'

'You haven't much of a voice.' She thought angrily of Polly's soaring soprano. 'I bet she carries you.'

'I can sing back-up. She says I sound great behind her.'

Bernie's heavy steps pounded upstairs. Vereena could hear him opening drawers and knew he'd leave his things strewn round the bedroom for her to clear away. He came down smelling of brilliantine. 'You must come over and see us.'

'Not tonight,' she said firmly, closing her eyes. Not any night, if she could avoid it. She felt consumed with

249

jealousy, burning up with it. She wanted to scream with frustration.

'Tomorrow, perhaps?' Bernie asked good-naturedly before he left.

Vereena had to swallow back the bile in her throat. She couldn't cope with this after the shock of meeting John.

Vereena didn't sleep well that night. She tossed and turned and woke again after a nightmare. When it was time to get up for work, she felt achy with weariness. She left Bernie sleeping peacefully.

At the factory, she had to force herself to hold her head high as she met John's knowing eyes. She could feel them on her back every time she crossed the factory floor, following her about, watching everything she did. She felt safe in the office until he came in there.

He looked as though he was trying to make up his mind what he should do. For once, there was something calculating in his mild eyes.

When Harold came late in the afternoon, he looked pale and worried. Older too; his bald head had lost its shine, his silver moustache seemed thinner and drooped more. He slumped on to the chair behind his desk, looking as though he'd had the stuffing knocked out of him.

She said with as much confidence as she could: 'You can forget what John saw. There won't be a peep out of him.'

'How can you be sure?'

'I laid it on the line to him. He must keep his mouth shut or he'll be sorry. He owes everything he has to you.'

'Did he say he'd keep quiet?'

'He will, Harold. I know the Gripper men, no backbone, any of them.'

He gave a gusty sigh. 'You're stronger than any of us, Vereena.'

'Not strong enough to face John every day. He's giving

me the creeps. Eyeing me up and down as though he can't believe what he saw.'

'You could spend a little time at the West Kirkby shop.'

'I think I'd like that. Get him off my back.'

'In any case, we can't go on meeting here as we have been.'

Harold looked so anxious, she was afraid he was going to suggest they stop seeing each other. She didn't want that. He was very generous, buying her clothes and little pieces of jewellery, and taking her over to Liverpool for expensive meals.

'Bernie's going to Morecambe next week. He's going to be away a good deal.' She told him about his new act with Polly Jones, unable to hide the bitterness she felt about that. 'With him out of the way, you could come and see me at home. It'll be much safer than here.'

He shook his head. 'Leave my car outside? What'll your neighbours think?'

'You could leave it outside your auction room and walk up. It's only a few hundred yards.'

'What if some problem cropped up? Robert Parry would start looking round for me. Or even Patsy.' He gasped with the horror of that. 'They'd know I couldn't be far away.'

Vereena felt a quiver of impatience. 'Leave it in Grange Road then. You could be in any of the shops and it's not much further to walk.'

'Oh God, Vee, what a mess I've got us in.'

She put a comforting arm across his shoulders. 'Don't worry. With average luck we'll still be all right.'

On Saturday night, Vereena allowed herself to be persuaded to go to the Empire to see Bernie on stage. Curiosity drove her there, and a terrible need to take her mind off the worry about John.

Polly Jones was vivacious and had a powerful voice that rang round the theatre. Their turn was slicker than she'd expected. Bernie looked a wonderful hunk of manhood on stage, broad-shouldered, handsome and sexy. It didn't please her to hear the tumultuous applause they received. She was overcome with resentment that it had happened to them and not to her. She couldn't enjoy the Egyptian sand dancers that followed.

Bernie had asked her to come backstage in the intermission, but when the lights went on, she saw John and Alma getting to their feet a few rows in front of her.

It made her catch her breath. To see him here was the last straw. Ever since he'd glimpsed that kiss, whenever she looked up John Gripper was close at hand. There seemed to be no escape from him.

She had a splitting headache and felt dog-tired. She decided not to wait for the second half of the show. She caught the underground home and went to bed.

Hours later, she was woken from a deep sleep when Bernie came in. She thought he'd let the front door slam accidentally. It was only as he was coming upstairs that she realised he was deliberately making as much noise as he could. The bedroom door crashed back, the newly installed electric light flashed on. She was blinking in the sudden brilliance.

'Bernie, put it off!' she protested.

He was pushing his face close to hers. It was ugly with anger. 'Is it true what John says?' he snarled. 'That you're Harold Ingram's mistress? That you've been carrying on with him for years?'

Vereena curled up in a rush of panic. She couldn't breathe. This was what she'd dreaded. John had snitched after all. 'He'd no business . . .'

'He said he thought I should know what you're up to.'

'The dirty liar. It isn't true.' Vereena was shaking with terror. She didn't know how to handle this. She could see an almighty row. There'd be bad feeling and bitterness all round. The good things she received from Harold would be gone and she'd be back in the hungry times she knew so well.

'Often you come home late from work.' Bernie was frowning, perplexed. 'John says that's—'

'No!' she screamed. 'He's a bloody liar.'

'He says Harold Ingram takes you out in his car, that he saw him kissing you. Why should he say that if it isn't true?'

Vereena's heart was hammering away. This was awful. Just like that other time when her mother died and all her carefully organised plans collapsed.

'You know our John knows all about it. You threatened him. Told him not to utter one word. Told him to keep his mouth shut.'

But he hadn't! Vereena felt maddened with rage.

'It's true, isn't it?' Bernie screamed, his grey eyes fiercer than she'd ever seen them before, all his easy-going good nature stripped from him.

She felt exhausted, unable to cope with this. She couldn't deny it any longer.

'Yes.' Anyway, what did it matter? She was fed up to the back teeth with Bernie.

'What?' He gripped her arms. His fingers were biting into her flesh. For the first time, she felt scared of him.

'Yes, I said. Yes.'

'You two-timing trollop.' He flung her back against the pillows.

Vereena struggled back to a sitting position, beside herself with rage. 'I had to do something. You won't lift a finger to help. You wait for me to provide the rent and the food. What else could I do?'

'Not this. I loved you.'

Vereena felt damp with sweat. Her nightdress was sticking to her back. 'I've been keeping you on what Harold gives me. You've enjoyed the benefits too.'

Bernie's face was like thunder. 'John said Harold Ingram was not the first, that you're little better than a whore. And everybody knows but me.'

'It's a man's responsibility to provide. But you don't. If I left it to you, we'd both starve. Is that what you want?'

'Yes, you're my wife. I'm not going to share you with every Tom, Dick and Harry.'

'Get out then. Don't share me. I've had more than enough of your lazy ways.'

Vereena bounced off the bed in fury. She heaved a suitcase down from the top of the wardrobe, and started to throw his shirts into it.

'You're no better than a prostitute,' Bernie flared.

Vereena's temper was up. She leaned across her dressing table and snatched at the handle of her hairbrush. She laid into him with the back of it.

'Go away and stay away. Go with that Polly Jones and make your fortune on the stage.' The brush caught him across the side of his face.

'Ouch, that hurt.'

She was swiping at him again and caught him across his wrist. Vereena felt herself being crushed, her arms pinned behind her and the brush being tugged from her hand. He flung it under the bed, out of her reach.

'You bitch! I'll do just that. Go with Polly Jones.'

'Good riddance,' she said. 'I've heard it all before.'

'I'm going for good in the morning.' He dragged the eiderdown from the bed, took the pillows from his side, and clumped into their spare room. She wished him joy of that; there was no proper bed there.

She threw his suitcase out on the landing and fell back on the bed, doubling over what was left of the bedclothes. But sleep was now far away. She was shaking with the horror of it, afraid she was going to vomit.

If John had told Bernie, there was no guarantee he wouldn't tell Mildred too. Harold would be in terrible trouble if he did. Mildred might even throw him out.

Vereena tried to think about the likely outcome of that.

The future looked dire for her. She tossed and turned for hours, falling at last into an exhausted sleep at five in the morning.

CHAPTER SIXTEEN

John Gripper decided it felt good to have Alma Murray hanging on his arm like this. He'd never expected to find anyone to take Elsa's place, and still felt surprised that another woman was willing to marry such an out-and-out failure as he was.

He looked down at her fondly. Alma wasn't the sort to turn heads. She was middle-aged, grey-haired and plump, with more than a suggestion of a double chin. But she was kindly and good company.

He wasn't one to rush into things but he'd delayed long enough. He didn't want to miss his chance. 'You've been very patient with me, Alma.'

'You had to think of your lass.' He'd been worried about how Patsy would take it.

'She was very clingy after her gran died. We had so many changes then.'

He sighed. Truly, he couldn't have coped with any more changes then himself. He'd been thinking of proposing to Alma for eighteen months, and hadn't quite found the courage to face all the complications it would bring, when she'd put it to him, fair and square. It took his breath away that she'd had the nerve to ask him.

He'd accepted, of course; it was what he wanted. Alma was a good woman. But even then he'd dragged out the time before doing anything more.

Alma had been kind enough to say that they could afford to be patient. Marriage was for companionship this time, not romantic passion.

He squeezed her arm. 'It's been hard to decide on . . . you know, all the practical things. Where we would live.'

'I know, I shouldn't have pressed you to come to live in my place.' Alma had a home of her own, but it was rented and no bigger or better than the flat over the saleroom.

'You said I could bring Patsy. You were generous about that.'

'She was only fifteen then. I couldn't expect you to abandon her.'

'Her grandfather offered her a home with him again when I told him.'

'I would have thought she'd have jumped at that. Posh house like they have.'

He hadn't had the heart to put it to Patsy. He was afraid she'd think he wanted her out of the flat. At fifteen she'd needed his love and affection. There was the loyalty he felt for her, too. She'd turned Harold's first offer down in order to stay with him. That had comforted him at the time. He didn't want Patsy to think he loved her any less because he was marrying Alma. He'd delayed his marriage further.

Now, at nineteen, with all sorts of responsibilities he couldn't begin to understand, Patsy reckoned she was old enough to stay where she was, whether he moved out or not. She'd told Alma she'd be quite happy if she decided to move in with them.

Eventually, Alma and Patsy between them had made the arrangements for tomorrow afternoon. A no-fuss wedding in a register office, with just the family. Mildred was giving them a fancy tea at Caerns Road, and he would be bringing Alma back to share his room in the flat over the auction room.

Patsy felt that Dadda's wedding had been hanging over her for ages. She knew he wasn't one to press for what he

258

wanted, and for him to put off marriage at his age was ridiculous She didn't feel any better about it because she knew he'd postponed it for her sake.

The day had come at last. Dadda looked tense, wearing the best suit he kept for weddings and funerals. He was fidgeting with his bowler. She drove him round to pick up the bride. She liked Alma as well as she'd like anyone Dadda wanted to marry. She had rosy cheeks and a sunny smile and was really quite jolly.

Alma was wearing a new fawn suit that strained a little on the buttons. Her iron-grey hair had been newly marcelled into head-hugging waves, under a flat brown hat.

Waiting at the register office were Harold, Mildred, Lucy and Vereena. Alma's relatives were there too. She introduced her father, who was old and frail, and her brother and sister-in-law. They were all a little stiff with the solemnity of the occasion. All except Vereena.

'Bernie's very disappointed he can't be with you,' she told Alma. 'Hates to miss your wedding. He's in Morecambe. On the stage. The show must go on, you know.'

Patsy watched the short ceremony, feeling a little numb. Afterwards, when she kissed the bride, Alma's mounds of flesh shook with laughter as she said: 'I want you to know you'll be gaining a mother, not losing a father. And you won't have so much housework to do from now on.'

At Caerns Road, it was the sort of tea Mildred put on to celebrate Grandpa's birthday. There was the same kind of iced fruit cake but decorated with wedding bells this time. Grandpa seemed very tense as he poured sweet sherry to go with it at the end of the meal.

Vereena was full of herself, more smartly dressed than the bride and laughing loudly. Patsy avoided speaking directly to her and tried not to notice her. But every so often she caught Vereena looking at her with dark, vitriolic eyes. She knew that Vereena hated her as much as she'd hated Gran.

Even now, Patsy couldn't stop the niggles of fear when she was near her. She still half expected Vereena to cause another catastrophe to blow up in her face.

She was being silly, she knew. She needed to face reality where Vereena was concerned. Reality as far as Alma was concerned, too. She must accept her and make her feel welcome, for Dadda's sake.

Lucy knew she spent more time than the other shop girls preening in front of the mirror in the cramped cloakroom. She combed out her shoulder-length blonde hair and refashioned it into the French pleat which Wesley admired so much.

'It's not fashionable,' she'd complained.

'It makes you look sophisticated and suits you so well. I love your hair like that.'

She added the merest touch of colour to her cheeks and a generous dab of Chanel perfume. Wesley was coming to take her out to lunch again. She had to look her best for him.

He'd changed her life. Lucy felt she'd been in a ferment since the day she'd first met him. He was never out of her mind. She had only to close her eyes to see him before her, his magnetic tawny eyes gazing into hers with all the longing she felt for him. She slipped her arms into her new edge-to-edge coat and headed for the stairs.

Miss Simpson was coming up. 'The shop doesn't close for lunch for another fifteen minutes,' she said, her horse-like face stern and disapproving.

'Mr Spiers is usually early,' Lucy smiled. She didn't care for working here, though she'd discovered that as Harold Ingram's granddaughter she could get away with most things. And it did provide money to spend on clothes.

Wesley was in the shop, looking at some new clocks that had come in during the morning. He saw her straight away and came over to take her arm.

'You look lovely, darling.' His smile was intimate, telling everybody how much he loved her.

Lucy didn't think she could bear to wait to marry him through all the months that stretched ahead. She'd been so angry and frustrated at her grandfather's decision. She couldn't stop railing against it. Only this morning, at breakfast, she'd had another go at him.

'I can't see what you've got against Wesley.' She'd felt tears of disappointment and frustration prickling her eyes. 'He's such a gentleman.' She loved the way he had of lifting her hand to his lips and kissing it. 'Such lovely manners.'

Grandpa snorted. 'Bit of a buck, I'd say. And a fop in those fancy waistcoats.'

'He likes to be stylish, cut a bit of a dash. What's wrong with that?'

'Gentlemen don't.'

'You're biased and old fashioned,' Lucy retorted, 'and so is Nanna.'

They were her grandparents after all. They were too old to remember what love was. She was convinced that if she'd been brought up by her parents, things would be different.

Grandpa had said: 'Forget him. You can do better. Put him out of your mind.'

As if she could! And Nanna, as usual was backing Gramps up. She was acting like a guard dog, always wanting to know where Lucy was going.

'We must have Colin round from next door. Far more suitable,' she said in her bracing way. 'More your own age.'

The problem was that loving Wesley made younger men seem raw youths. She'd been forced to sit and talk to Colin Courtney and his parents when Nanna invited them to supper. Colin was all right but a bit boring. She knew there'd be a return invitation and she'd have to go through it all again.

261

At the restaurant, they were shown to the table Wesley had booked. 'You mustn't take on so about your grandfather,' he whispered, stroking her arm. 'He's doing what he thinks is best for you.'

'But he's wrong!'

'The time will pass. It's only fifteen months.'

'That's an eternity to me.'

'I hate it as much as you do, love. We must be patient.'

'Patient!' Lucy felt overcome with urgency. She wanted to feel Wesley's arms round her. They loved each other so much that every moment they spent apart seemed a moment wasted.

Even when they were together, there were frustrations. Here they had to sit with the table between them, very conscious of other people near at hand.

'It's impossible to talk about things that really matter. Even outside, there's no privacy.'

'Not in broad daylight. I wish we could be alone,' he told her. 'Somewhere away from prying eyes. I want you all to myself. Couldn't you come out one night?'

Nanna had put her foot down. 'You're not going out on your own. To meet this man after dark? I won't allow it.'

Lucy managed it the following week, but it took deceit and preparation. She'd had to ask Nanna's permission first and return home after the shop closed. She arranged that Madge Kerr would call round on the pretext of going to the cinema with her. Madge was willing because she too had a man friend of whom her parents did not approve. They provided each other with an alibi.

She and Wesley didn't even go to the pictures. He brought his car over on the luggage boat and they drove out to New Brighton. The promenade was deserted on that cold autumn night, but he'd brought two car rugs to keep them warm.

'I've a little present for you.' He took a gift-wrapped box from the glove compartment and put it in her hand.

'What is it?' Lucy was smiling with delight as she untied the ribbons. 'A ring! An engagement ring?'

'Let's call it a love token.'

'It's too dark. I can't see it properly.'

Wesley leaned across to the glove box again and brought out a small torch. The rays flashed on a pretty red stone surrounded with brilliants.

'It's lovely. A ruby?' She tried it on the third finger of her left hand.

'Garnet, I'm afraid. It's quite old. I like to think of it being given and worn by an earlier generation of lovers.'

'But I can't wear it ... Nanna would confiscate it if she knew.'

'I've bought you a gold chain, so you can wear it round your neck. Nobody need see it there.'

'You think of everything, Wesley.'

'Your grandparents won't agree to our engagement, but that doesn't stop us having a private agreement, does it?'

Wesley threaded the ring on to the chain. Then his warm fingers undid her coat and the top buttons of the dress she wore beneath it. He was fastening the chain carefully round her neck.

'It will comfort me to think of you wearing it here.' His fingers etched a line above her breasts. 'I feel better about things now. More certain that you'll be my wife one day. You're promised to me now.'

'Of course I am,' Lucy said. 'Nothing will stop us getting married.'

Several weeks later, Wesley said: 'I wish we could do more together. I want to be with you morning, noon and night.'

Lucy giggled. 'Being taken out to lunch every day is lovely.' She dabbed her mouth with her table napkin and sat back with a smile of satisfaction. 'You always bring me to the best places.'

Around her in the dining room of the Exchange Hotel,

she could hear subdued murmurs from the other customers. It was a dark day and the light from the chandeliers sparkled on the glass and cutlery.

'Hardly the best. Just a Victorian railway hotel providing mainline station comfort for first-class travellers. A bit old-fashioned now, don't you think?'

'It's rather grand.'

It was Wesley's way to decry the hotels and restaurants they ate in. Lucy thought these elegant surroundings suited him, though he stood out from the rest of the clientele even here. He was easily the most distinguished-looking man present, with his hair just greying at the temples.

He scraped the last of the cream from his pudding plate and pushed it away from him. 'What would you like to do this afternoon?'

It was Wednesday, and the shop had closed for the day, but a gale could be heard rattling at the window panes.

His eyes smiled into hers. 'I'd like to take you to my home. Show you where I live.'

Lucy felt her heart jerk with pleasure. She'd spent many hours imagining his home. The prospect delighted her.

He said slowly, 'There isn't much else I can suggest. It's raining hard out there.'

She giggled. 'You don't have to persuade me.'

He said slowly: 'Do you feel adult enough?'

Lucy caught her breath. The word 'adult' conjured up such images. 'You know I do. We'd have been married by now if I'd had my way.'

'Good. Then let's not stay for coffee. I'll make some when we get home.'

He signalled to the waiter to bring the bill. His hand came back to cover hers where it rested on the cloth. 'I feel honoured that you trust me enough.' He lifted her hand to his lips.

'Of course I trust you.'

264

Lucy's insides were twisting with desire. She felt very daring and knew Nanna would have a fit if she ever heard about this.

'You won't tell anybody?' Wesley asked. 'Not even your twin.'

'Oh no! Patsy might tell on me.'

'Better if it's our secret.'

As he drove along bleak wet streets, she said, 'Did you say you lived in Calderstones?'

'Yes, do you know it?'

'Never been before.'

'Not far now. This is the park.'

Lucy thought it a very pleasant house, though not as large as the one she lived in. In the hall he helped her out of her coat. His fingers lingered about her neck, sending spirals of anticipation through her. She took off her hat and he laid it reverently on the hall stand.

She was alone with him at last. She giggled with pleasure and reaching up on tiptoe, kissed him full on his lips. She'd spun away before he could stop her. 'I must see round your house. It seems very smart.'

His arms closed round her in a doorway to give her a kiss such as she'd never received before. She reached up and nuzzled him.

'I do love you, Wesley. Gramps is very cruel to us, not letting us marry.'

'We will, darling, just as soon as we can.' She broke free from his arms again and went into the room.

'It's fitted out in great style.'

There was a glittering chandelier in the drawing room. He called it the drawing room, not the sitting room as Nanna did. He was pointing out the treasures in his display cabinet. The room was full of wonderful antiques, the sort Gramps would love.

'I've seen you here in my mind's eye many times,' he told her. 'You bring the place to life.'

She followed him to the kitchen where he went to make coffee. It contained every new gadget she'd ever heard of.

'I want to see all of your house. I just can't wait.'

She looked in the dining room – rather heavy dark furniture. Then, with thudding heart, headed for the stairs. Wesley was following.

'That's Rodney's room,' he said, as she pushed open the first door on the landing.

It wasn't very tidy. There was a clock with its working parts spread out on the top of the tallboy. There was a photograph on the bedside cabinet. Lucy picked it up.

'His mother,' Wesley murmured.

She was looking at a woman whose good looks were fading. She seemed quite old.

'You must have loved her. How do I compare?'

Wesley laughed, took the frame from her hand and replaced it.

'You needn't worry about what's gone before. You're young and beautiful, my love. Just to think about you lifts me to fever pitch. We're on the brink of something thrilling, not yet tasted. I love you very much.'

Wesley had the gift of lifting her too, of wiping away all her worries. But she still hesitated.

'Will Rodney live with us when we're married?'

'Absolutely not. We won't want him around. Couldn't do this if he were watching.'

Lucy melted into his arms as they wrapped round her again.

'I want to see your room,' she whispered. He drew her gently, still within his arms, to the doorway. She saw a plain dark counterpane on the double bed. A large seascape in oils on the wall facing it.

'Very masculine,' she smiled. 'Rather stark.'

'You can add the frills ... just as soon as ...' She could hear his breathing becoming heavier. 'Just as soon as we're married.'

266

His fingers were fumbling with the buttons on her dress. Lucy thrilled to his touch and felt terribly daring.

'You are sure, darling?' Wesley's breath was hot on her cheek.

Her heart was pounding. 'Of course. I do love you.' This was a point of no return. She was about to flout society's strongest rule. It was absolutely forbidden. 'But what if . . .?'

He was pushing her blouse off her shoulders. It dropped to the floor. 'What if I have a baby?'

'Your grandfather would want us to marry straight away, wouldn't he?'

She laughed recklessly. 'Then I hope I do.'

'You're delicious, Lucy,' Wesley breathed. 'I adore you.'

As usual, Robert Parry carefully locked up the saleroom for the night. He was pushing the keys into his pocket when he saw the well-polished 1924 bull-nose Morris with sparkling wire wheels come round the corner and pull to a halt.

Patsy had seen him and lifted her hand in greeting. Before going over to speak to her, he checked his mother's bedroom window, to make sure she wasn't watching.

'Hello. Haven't seen you for a long time.' Patsy was coming home later these days; he'd even wondered if it was to avoid him.

She was smiling as she opened the door and put one foot out on the running board. 'How are you, Rob?'

'Fine.'

He couldn't take his eyes off her. She seemed suddenly different. The costume of soft blue wool was more sophisticated than anything he'd seen her in before.

'You've done pretty well for yourself. Who would have thought that Cassie's little waif would be driving herself round like this?'

Nobody else around here was able to afford a car. His dad's generation were all envious. 'Harold Ingram's money, of course,' they agreed. He'd heard them rib Patsy's father. 'When you getting your Rolls, John?'

'Have you learned to drive yet?' Her blue eyes were full of self-confidence now.

'No, haven't had time.'

'That's a well-worn excuse.' She was laughing at him.

Rob felt that between his full-time job, helping in the shop and evening classes, he was justified in claiming lack of time. 'I'll do it next summer, once the exams are over.'

'My offer still stands. I'll teach you if you like. Grandpa's given this car to me.'

'I may take you up on that,' he said as he watched her put her own keys into the door and go inside.

As he went across to the shop he thought how wrong his mother was about Patsy. She was level-headed, just as Cassie had been, and going full speed ahead in pursuit of her own goals.

He'd deliberately backed away from her, more fool him. He'd told himself she was just a kid, that to take her to the pictures was rubbing his mother up the wrong way and making matters worse at home.

He'd hurt Patsy's feelings, he knew, and it had bothered his conscience. She'd been just a kid at the time but she'd thought enough of him to recommend him for two jobs.

He'd tried to pretend whenever they came face to face that nothing had changed between them, but inevitably Patsy had stood back from him as if to say, if you don't want to be friends, I won't foist myself on you. What else could he expect when he'd told her that Josie Mackay was his girlfriend? He was glad she wasn't showing any offence now.

His father was behind the counter, weary after working in the shop all day. His mother was in the living room, out of sight but monitoring everything that was being said in the shop. Expecting to hear some comment about her past.

Rob felt depressed. There seemed to be no end to it. Nobody bore his mother any ill will, it was all in her mind, a form of self-torture. All his life he'd felt her tension. She'd made things difficult when they didn't have to be. She was continuing to ruin her own life and his father's.

And, damn it, what about his life? He'd never felt for Josie Mackay one half of what he felt for Patsy. And he should never have brought Josie to meet his family.

His mother had been over the moon, making much of Josie, inviting her round to meals without first asking him if that was what he wanted. Even Dad had shown too much approval. Rob understood. They preferred him to take up with anyone rather than Patsy Gripper.

He knew he'd let it drag on far too long. For him, any joy in the relationship had gone. He was beginning to find Josie heavy going, and furthermore she was pressing him to make some commitment. Josie had a powerful way of hinting. She kept pulling him to a halt outside jewellers' shop windows and pointing out the engagement ring of her choice.

He'd known for a long time that Josie wanted to get married. All her sisters had tied the knot and were very happy. Rob felt he was being rushed to the altar, and he didn't think that Josie was the right girl for him. He'd been screwing himself up to tell her this for some time.

It wasn't easy to deliver such a hurt. She wouldn't be expecting it, but he must make his feelings clear.

He'd worked himself into an awkward corner trying to please his mother, and if he wasn't careful he'd end up by pleasing nobody. Least of all himself.

On Saturday afternoon, Rob went down to the market to buy their weekend joint. He was now doing the family shopping every week, because his mother wouldn't leave the house.

He'd just bought some potatoes and sprouts from a stall and put them in his bag. When he looked up he saw Josie and her mother coming towards him, both wearing very elegant hats.

'Hello.'

He felt uncomfortable, because he'd been going over in his mind what he'd have to say to Josie tonight. He'd come to the conclusion that however he phrased it, the message was going to be hurtful.

He'd decided not to take her to the pictures. He didn't want any distractions. He'd suggest a trip on the ferry, perhaps down to New Brighton.

'Here's Robert.' Mrs Mackay was a buxom woman. She was pushing Josie forward. 'Go on, tell him now.'

Josie wouldn't look at him. She seemed fluttery, embarrassed, even. Tongue-tied.

He said: 'I'll be seeing you tonight, won't I? I'll call round about seven.'

Her mother stepped forward impatiently. 'She's got another boyfriend. Eric works in a bank. She doesn't know how to tell you.'

Rob opened his mouth in surprise. Blinked from one to the other. He couldn't believe his luck.

'She's sick of waiting for you to make a move. You're the sort who takes up a girl's time and then can't make up his mind to do anything. She's been walking out with you for five years, and she's not getting any younger.'

Rob felt the fire run up his cheeks. 'That's all right, Josie.'

'I'm sick of having you hang round me,' she said with more venom than he'd ever heard from her before.

Rob felt as though a great weight was lifting from his shoulders. He wanted to tell her it was a mutual decision, and there were no hard feelings. But the two women were already being swallowed up in the crowd. He wanted to shout for joy.

Patsy was a lot more fun than Josie. For him, she'd always been special. He should have followed his own instincts when he had the chance, and stayed as close as he could.

Patsy had blossomed over the years, in both self-confidence and looks. She was a very attractive girl, and his boss's granddaughter. Likely to be his boss in the years to come. She was unlikely to look upon him seriously as a boyfriend now. Her horizons had expanded. He was afraid he'd thrown away his chances with Patsy.

CHAPTER SEVENTEEN

The next morning, as Rob crossed the street to open up the saleroom, a young girl pushed a note into his hand. It told him that Mr Powell, the auctioneer, had been taken ill in the night and would not be coming to work.

It was the day of the special sale, not just of household bric-à-brac, and it was due to start in a couple of hours. He went to the phone to let Harold Ingram know.

'This isn't the first time.' Ingram sounded impatient. 'I'll act as auctioneer today. Always did in the old days. But I think you should learn. Easier if you can slip into the breach when this happens.

'You can be with me. Watch what I do and then have a go yourself. I'll bring Patsy back with me after lunch to run the office.'

The auction was in full swing. Rob felt in the thick of things instead of being banished to the office. He was standing by the dais listening to Harold describing in glowing terms a Victorian cut-glass and silver inkstand when the answer to his mother's difficulties came to him.

The saleroom was crowded; he recognised many of the faces. Half the population living between the railway tracks was here, just for the fun of it.

What he must do was persuade his mother to come too. He'd ask those he knew well to greet her in a friendly fashion, to seem pleased that she was out and about again. Then, surely, she'd get over her fear and not hide herself away from them?

It seemed so obvious, he didn't know why he hadn't thought of it months ago. He made up his mind that on the next big sale he'd do it. He talked to his father about it. They both started persuading Gladys.

'You'd like that, wouldn't you, Mam? You must be the only person in Cambridge Place who hasn't been inside the auction room.'

He could see she was tempted. 'I'll come over one evening, when everybody's gone home.'

'No, Mam, come and see me auctioning the stuff off.'

She said at first that she couldn't. 'You know what I'm like in a crowd. I can't breathe properly. My chest . . .'

'Just for a few minutes,' Rob said. 'Dad'll bring you over.' He'd already persuaded him that it was worth closing the shop for an hour, if that was the only way to get her across.

'I would like to see you, but no . . . If there was a crush of people, I'd have one of my turns.'

'Then just come to the door for five minutes,' he said.

The next time Harold Ingram came in, Rob explained about his mother and asked him if he'd go out of his way to be pleasant to her, to give her confidence. Harold knew why, of course. Everybody knew why.

He went down to Donovan's shop and sat in the battered chair by the counter to have a word with Sara. Then he called on Alice Smedley, the other matriarch of Cambridge Place. Everybody agreed to help; they were a good-natured lot.

Rob had been acting as auctioneer for a few hours at each of the weekly sales that had been held since. He was beginning to feel more at ease doing it. Powell was back at work, teaching him the finer points of the trade. When the afternoon of the next big sale came round he was half afraid his mother would refuse to come across.

'Don't let her get cold feet,' he whispered to his father. 'You've got to bring her over.'

Rob felt tense as he reopened the sale at two o'clock. He'd been on the dais for half an hour and was beginning to get a bit anxious.

He saw them at last, his mother with her head low and clinging like a limpet to his father's arm. He had to give his attention to selling a set of six dining chairs, and next time he looked, Harold Ingram was with them and his mother's head was a little higher.

He sold a desk and then a set of bedroom furniture. His boss's bald dome had moved up the room but Alice Smedley was talking to his mother. It pleased him that he could no longer see his father.

The Regency library table he was selling went for a much higher price than they'd expected to get, and then Powell was at his elbow. 'The boss says it's time for me to take over.'

Rob went to find his mother. When he saw she was with a woman from Hind Street who was a regular customer at the paper shop, he felt satisfied that things had gone according to plan.

His mother had never been an outgoing person, but for once she had a smile for him: 'I'm proud of you, Robert. You did very well.'

Why should she go on hiding from the neighbours, trembling that they might show censure about something she'd done donkey's years ago, when they'd all come up and been pleasant to her? Rob felt it had to work.

As the months rolled by, Lucy felt her life was taking on new impetus. She hadn't expected her love for Wesley to grow, but she was beginning to feel obsessed by passion.

Every Wednesday afternoon now, and on many lunchtimes too, Wesley took her to his home. He provided sandwiches and wine instead of taking her to a restaurant, and they spent the time in his bed making love.

From the time she said goodbye to him on one day to

the moment they met on the next, she found herself looking forward to it. She couldn't get enough of him.

'I want to know everything about you,' she told him. 'Tell me about your son.'

'Rodney's been a bit mixed up, lost even, since his mother's death. It was so sudden. He was doing well at school up till then. I'm afraid he went to pieces, but he's pulling himself together again now.

'I remind him not to rush home from school on Wednesdays. To give us time. It's you I want.'

'Surely, if I'm to be your wife, Rodney and I ought to meet?'

'If that's what you want. I'll tell him to come home early next week.'

When she arrived the following Wednesday, she saw in the kitchen a trolley already set with Wesley's silver tea service and best china. He always used them, as well as expensive glasses to serve wine. At home, Nanna only brought hers out for special occasions.

'All occasions are special if you're here,' Wesley smiled when she told him.

Later that afternoon, Lucy hurried through her bath. As she went downstairs, she could hear the kettle beginning to whistle in the kitchen. She looked in the drawing room.

Rodney hastily cast aside a magazine and got to his feet. He was gangly, tall and reed-thin, his school uniform hanging about him. She wished Wesley were here and not in the kitchen.

'Hello,' she said. 'I'm Lucy. I expect you've heard about me.' Should she kiss him? Instead, she put out her hand.

He had a tendency to acne. An inkstained paw was put into hers. He seemed woefully ill at ease.

She thought Rodney would never have his father's good looks. His features were plain and his brown hair straight, but he had the same tawny gold eyes. She was relieved to see Wesley bringing in the tea trolley. There was a large selection of cream cakes on it now.

Rodney was on his best behaviour, clumsily handing round plates and cups, but with little to say. He made her feel grown up, though he was only two or three years her junior. Lucy found it an uncomfortable occasion for them all. She didn't ask Wesley to repeat it.

When Christmas came, she sighed: 'Another whole year to wait. Do you know what I'd like to do? I'd like us to run away to Gretna Green and get married now.'

'No, Lucy.' He kissed her gently. 'Your grandparents would never forgive me. It's only twelve more months. They'll pass.'

Lucy thought the Christmas celebrations fell a little flat that year. How could it be otherwise when she couldn't be with Wesley?

In the new year, when she went back to his house in Calderstones, he'd hung a calendar in his bedroom. She crossed the days off every time she went there. It seemed that pregnancy was not going to shorten the waiting time.

Slowly, the months went past. As the year wore on to autumn she tackled her grandfather again one suppertime.

'I haven't changed my mind about marrying Wesley. I knew I wouldn't. Only three more months and I'll be of age. I want to be married in St Saviour's church.' Their pursed lips told her what they thought of that.

'You and Nanna are against him,' she burst out. 'But he doesn't want to upset you. He doesn't want me to go against your wishes. He's a lovely person. You don't know him, Gramps.'

'I suppose we can remedy that,' he'd said gruffly. 'You can bring him here to meet us all.'

'Ask him to supper,' Nanna said. 'I'll invite your father and Patsy. Doesn't he have a son? We'd better have a look at him at the same time.'

* * *

277

Rodney Spiers was afraid that supper at Lucy's home would be an ordeal. 'Do I have to go?'

'Yes, you've been invited. Don't drink too much and keep a watch on your tongue,' his father told him sharply. 'Don't say much either, but be pleasant and polite when spoken to.'

One good thing about it was that his father had bought him an expensive grey suit. 'You must look respectable,' he'd told him. 'Isn't there anything you can do about those spots?'

'Does it matter how I look?' Rodney felt cross. If he could get rid of his acne, he'd have done it long ago. It wasn't for want of trying. Anyway, nobody seemed to see him. He could be the invisible man when Dad was about. Dad drew everybody's attention.

'Seems you're aiming to make a good impression,' Rodney said, watching the champagne, flowers and chocolates being loaded into the yellow Cadillac before they set out.

'Of course I am. You know the plan.' Dad was short, clearly a bit tense himself.

Rodney did know the plan. Backwards. Dad had talked him through it ten times already. He knew what was required of him; he'd been his back-up since he was ten. Dad thought he could con anybody, and Rodney had seen him do it over and over. But in his opinion, the present scheme was not going to work.

The aim of Dad's plans was always the same. First and foremost he wanted to live the rich life and have plenty of money. Rodney couldn't argue with that. It was what most people wanted; he did himself. But Dad craved money. He never had enough.

Secondly, he liked young women. He went through them like lightning, and they seemed to be getting younger. Lucy was the youngest yet. She was actually six months younger than Rodney, and the very first he could fancy for himself. Not that he stood a chance. Not yet, anyway.

Dad's present plan was to combine his two passions. He was going to marry Lucy, and her money was going to provide the good life he craved.

Sometimes Rodney felt older than his father. In one way Dad was like a child, wanting everything now. He couldn't wait. Rodney reckoned he had more patience and more foresight.

Marriage had never been part of Dad's earlier plans, and this was the most long drawn out. It was taking a lot of money to carry it through, but Dad was putting his heart and soul into it.

'If you really want to be helpful, try and make a friend of the twin sister. Get her on your side.'

The thought of the twin sister was another good reason to go. If she looked like Lucy he'd be going overboard for her.

'Posh house,' he said as Dad pulled up on the drive.

Their own house was good. Dad liked luxury. 'Have to have it, to make the right impression. I don't want to seem poor, do I?'

Lucy opened the door to them looking a dream in a pretty blue dress. All Rodney's instincts were to protect her, not allow her to be exploited like this. Her cheeks were pink with excitement. How had Dad managed to make her feel like that? Apparently she'd even suggested a quick trip to Gretna Green, but that wasn't part of the plan. Might upset her family. They had to see Dad as whiter than white. He wasn't sure about the twin sister. She wasn't like Lucy.

In accordance with his instructions, Rodney presented the three boxes of chocolates his father had provided. One to Lucy, one to her twin sister and the biggest to her grandmother. He understood that it was important to get Granny on their side too. She was peering at him

279

through thick glasses; he didn't think she liked what she saw.

By some ghastly mismanagement on his part, he found himself sitting next to her in the sitting room. She asked him about his mother. He knew better than to mention that she'd been a foul-mouthed alcoholic who had fallen under the wheels of a bus whilst in her cups. The drowning story had stood them in good stead for years. Much more respectable.

She was giving him the quiz about what he wanted to do when he left school. He did his best without letting on that he'd left school years ago. In deference to Lucy's youth, Dad had insisted he knock a couple of years off his own age and appear more juvenile.

'Shouldn't be too hard for you,' he'd said. 'And whatever you do, don't tell them you've been a barman and a bus conductor and failed to stick at anything.'

When Granny got up to see to something, Rodney took the opportunity to move nearer to Patsy. He tried to draw her out.

'Did you see the show at the Argyle last week? Harry Lauder was wonderful.'

She hadn't been, of course. Seemed she hadn't been anywhere. He suggested they go together next week.

The bright-blue eyes seemed to look through him. 'It's kind of you to ask, but no thank you.'

Rodney's first feeling was of relief. She wasn't his sort and she'd have been hard going. He'd done what Dad had asked him to do but she hadn't risen to the bait. He had the feeling she didn't believe half of what his father said.

Dad needn't have warned him to go easy on the drink; no way would his tongue be loosened on what was offered. Dad could teach them a thing or two about good living. The family didn't look all that rich, but Dad had appraised their business and said it was rock solid. Rodney hoped he knew what he was doing.

* * *

Next morning at breakfast, Lucy knew that Wesley hadn't made the good impression she'd hoped for, though he'd put himself out to be friendly to everybody.

'You asked him so many questions,' she complained. 'You didn't give him a chance to—'

Grandpa was bristling. 'I felt the need to enquire into his circumstances, and it's raised more doubts. I feel I was misled into believing Wesley owned his own shop.'

'In Southport,' Lucy agreed. 'Miss Simpson told me.'

'It was only when pressed that he admitted that wasn't so.' Nanna was indignant. 'He used to be employed there, that's all.'

'He earns his living by dealing in antiques on his own account and selling them on in the trade.' Grandpa drove his spoon angrily into his boiled egg.

'Living on his wits.' Mildred sounded horrified. 'Absolutely no security.'

'He admitted his income varies greatly from one month to the next, and I'm afraid that what he has, he spends too freely.'

'I don't care for him.' Nanna shuddered.

'Nothing you say can stop us now,' Lucy told them equally angry.

Lucy expected Wesley to be angry too when she told him. He held her close, with her cheek against his hairy jacket, and tried to explain.

'I'm taking their favourite granddaughter from them. A prince would have to prove himself before they thought him good enough for you.'

'I'm going to book the church. Put our wedding plans in hand,' she said.

'We should be putting plans for our married life in hand too,' he told her seriously. 'Even more important.'

'What d'you mean?'

His tawny eyes looked into hers. 'Will you ask your grandfather to give me a job?'

'But I don't want to change anything. If you're happy as you are . . .'

'They want you to have a husband with a regular income. That way, I'll be more acceptable.'

'But from Calderstones? It's too far to come.'

'That's the other thing I want to do. Move house. I think we should look for something nearer. Not too close to Caerns Road, of course.'

'But I love this house. I could be very happy here.'

'But your family wouldn't be able to see much of you, and you'd miss them.'

Lucy screwed up her nose. 'I don't know about that. They're being very difficult.'

Wesley was serious. He took both her hands in his. 'Darling, I don't want to take you out of their circle. They're getting older. I think it would be better all round if you were nearer.'

'You're far too generous to them. Especially since they aren't kind to you. I think we should let things stay as they are. I'm sure I shall be very happy on what you earn.'

'I don't want to upset your family. They love you too, Lucy. Let's start house-hunting on your side of the water.'

Lucy let him have his way. He seemed so caring and thoughtful for the well-being of her family. She enjoyed all the preparations and the house-hunting. They chose a place in Templemore Road. She helped Wesley re-arrange all the lovely pieces of furniture he brought from Calderstones.

'Not quite so fine a place as your old home,' Wesley smiled.

'It's lovely,' Lucy protested.

'Let's ask your family round. I want to show them I'm not totally uncivilised.'

'You're far more civilised than they are really.'

As Christmas drew close once again, Lucy knew she was pregnant. By now her wedding plans were well advanced; the date was set for a few days after Christmas.

She felt excited and so very happy that she was going to have her way at last. All she'd ever wanted was to be Wesley's wife.

Harold had always thought of the twins' birthday party as the first of the Christmas festivities. It wasn't easy to feel cheerful on the anniversary of Elsa's death, but over the years he'd done his best. For the girls' sake, he'd had to.

It seemed no time since they were babies, but the days when he'd booked magicians and conjurors to amuse them were long gone. Today, the twins came of age. Their poor mother, bless her, never had.

Harold put on his jacket and went downstairs. He admired the paper lanterns, the holly and streamers the girls had used to decorate the hall. They'd taken up the rugs from the parquet floor so they could dance.

Lucy had been excited all day. She'd gone rushing out to buy more gramophone records to dance to. 'We must have Henry Hall, Gramps. He's the tops.'

'Harry Roy too,' Patsy had called from her desk.

He'd had to persuade Mildred that giving Patsy a car for her twenty-first birthday was a good idea.

'We give Lucy everything,' he'd explained. 'Yet Patsy does so much more for the business. Lucy will have a husband to drive her round, but Patsy will have to look after herself.'

Her eyes had lit up like beacons when she saw the car. It was nothing fancy. A small Cowley saloon; he'd found Morris cars dependable in the past. In no time at all, she'd had the bonnet up, sat in the driver's seat, and taken Mildred for a little spin in it. He knew he'd done the right thing. He'd sent her off early to collect her father and Alma, so she could show it to them and get changed for the party without too much rush.

'They're off our hands now,' Mildred said, fussing over the huge birthday cake the twins were to share. It was the centrepiece on the supper table.

He wasn't sure Lucy would be off his hands. He didn't trust Wesley Spiers. Their wedding was only five days off and he couldn't stop it now. She was insisting on it, and she was of age.

'I think we can congratulate ourselves that we've done well by them.' Mildred was trying to fix the twenty-one candles on the cake.

'We've done our best,' he agreed. But he wasn't sure it was good enough. He was afraid there'd be trouble up ahead for Lucy.

Patsy let herself in with her key. She was wearing a velvet party frock in midnight blue. She'd brought Alma and John with her, and, for the first time, Robert Parry.

Harold had invited Robert himself; he hoped Patsy wasn't cross about it. He was tired of telling her to invite her own friends, that it was her party too.

He gave Rob a warm welcome. He'd known him since he was knee-high, but the lad had never been here before. He looked ill at ease in his new suit. He was staying close to Patsy but his eyes were taking everything in. A good lad. A good worker.

The doorbell rang, and Lucy rushed to get to the door first. He'd allowed her to invite Wesley and his son Rodney; no point in forbidding that now. But it was Colin Courtney from next door. Nobody could fail to notice how Lucy's face fell with disappointment.

Harold sighed. He and Mildred had discussed Colin many times. They both wished Lucy had taken up with him, a nice, steady lad from a solid professional background, and just about a year older. He had a good education behind him, and was at Liverpool University now. He'd be articled to an accountant when he finished, and follow in his father's footsteps. Not a fly-by-night like Wesley Spiers.

Colin would be able to earn a decent living. Lucy would know where she was with him. Patsy thought he was quite keen on Lucy, but she wasn't interested in him. Harold knew who he'd sooner trust.

Again the doorbell, and again Lucy rushed to the door. It was that girl Madge. She'd been coming for years, but he'd never taken to her either. This year she had a husband in tow who was even older than Wesley. He looked like a staid old bachelor, with moth-eaten greying hair. He couldn't understand the young girls of today.

He took a turn round the floor with Lucy, partly to still the impatience he could see she was feeling. At the first peal of the bell she shot from his arms. Wesley and his son had arrived at last. Lucy was transformed, beaming at everybody, hanging on to Wesley's arm as she brought him in and led him round to be introduced.

Wesley waited until every eye was on him before slipping a magnificent sapphire surrounded with diamonds on the third finger of Lucy's left hand. He kissed her very publicly too.

'I've been waiting to do this for ages,' he said with theatrical gusto. 'And we don't need the mistletoe.'

Lucy, her face pink with excitement, was running round showing her ring to everybody and being kissed and congratulated.

Then the gramophone was rewound and Wesley was holding Lucy close as they edged round the hall. Much too close. She had eyes for nobody else. Harold wasn't sure he approved of this modern dancing. He led Mildred out on to the floor; she was flinching at the volume of noise the party was already putting up.

Patsy was sitting talking to Colin and Robert. She'd taken Rodney into the circle and they were all discussing something with deep concentration. Patsy had few friends of her own age. She looked so serious, but she'd inherited Cassie's high cheekbones and was growing more attractive as she got older. Her eyes seemed a more vivid blue now. Alert eyes that missed nothing of what went on round her. There was an air of energy about Patsy. She was much more astute than Lucy.

Lucy was the real head-turner. There was a sensuality about her that Patsy didn't have. She laughed more, took life easier. Was less able to look after herself. The one most likely to be hurt.

Harold loved them both very much. But while he put himself out to help Lucy, he received help from Patsy. Considering they were twins, they were a very strange pair.

Patsy got up to change the record. This year, the party was going with a real swing. Even Dadda and Alma were trying to join in and dance.

When the music stopped, she couldn't help but see that Wesley didn't allow Lucy to escape from him. They stood in the centre of the hall with their arms wrapped round each other. Nanna only allowed that because they were going to be married within the next few days. Her face said she didn't approve of it, even so.

To Patsy, it seemed that her sister was going to have exactly what she wanted from life: a husband who loved her more than anybody else in the world. She felt a touch envious of that.

Rob brought her another glass of the fruit cup and put it in her hand. He seemed to be more friendly of late, but she couldn't say where she stood exactly with him. Not these days.

She smiled at Colin. He couldn't take his eyes off Lucy. 'That's him? He's old enough to be her father!'

Patsy didn't understand how Lucy managed such an age

difference. The five years between her and Rob had proved a huge stumbling block.

'Lucy's dazzled by him.' They watched Wesley bend to whisper something meant only for her ears. Lucy smiled up at him in response.

Patsy had known Colin for years. He was rather shy, and his straight brown hair and owlish glasses gave him a studious air. He always came to their parties.

'Such a nice friend,' Nanna said. She was friendly with his parents.

Patsy had heard Lucy say to Madge: 'Colin isn't much fun. Rather a dull old stick really.'

She hadn't found him dull when he'd taken her to the music hall one time. He'd seemed lively and intelligent. It was just that he talked of Lucy the whole time.

Patsy reckoned he'd invited her because Nanna was always getting them together at little suppers and Lucy was ignoring his advances. He wasn't interested in Patsy at all; she was just as near as he could get to Lucy.

Rodney too seemed very taken with Lucy. 'Your sister's a real smasher,' he told her, and went on the say the same thing in a slightly different way at least three more times.

Lucy drew Patsy's eyes too. She'd always watched her, wanting to have more in common, to be closer. It was what everybody wanted. Everybody seemed to love Lucy.

Rodney could see that his father was pleased.

'Almost there, Rodders,' he said on the way home. Dad was letting him drive his car these days. 'You didn't think I'd manage it, did you?'

Rodney hadn't thought his father would have enough patience. Courting Lucy was expensive; only the best was good enough for her. The sapphire ring he'd managed to nick from a shop in Preston, but he'd had to splash a lot of money around on everything else.

That came easily to Wesley. The problem was, he

couldn't control his urge to spend. Money ran through his hands like water, and gave him the bigger problem of continually having to find more.

They'd only survived this far because Dad had managed to raise some money courtesy of Aunt Ida. She was ninety and no longer able to keep track of her possessions.

Uncle Clarence, her husband, was dead now. He'd been a clockmaker and taught Dad all there was to know about clocks. There'd been a lot of clocks about her house.

'She won't miss them now,' Dad had said. 'Can't see well enough to tell the time, and anyway, it means nothing to her any more.'

Aunt Ida was a poor old sod really. Hardly knew where she was. Rodney didn't like to see his father take advantage of her. He ought to feel some loyalty and affection because Ida had brought him up.

Rodney knew he'd think more highly of himself if he'd stopped Dad doing it. He should have really. Aunt Ida had always welcomed him, given him a home when he needed it, when life with his father had broken down. It had had a habit of doing that. Like when Dad had been sent to prison, and that other time when he'd abandoned Rodney and his drunkard of a mother.

His father had taken some fine old clocks from Ida's house. He'd found a lot more up in Ida's attic and had worked hard restoring them. He was clever at that sort of thing, Rodney had to give him that. He'd made enough to augment his income over the expensive time of moving house and making wedding arrangements.

But Rodney didn't think Wesley would be able to run the Ingram business if he got it. Making money wasn't one of his strengths. Dad thought it was, of course, that all he needed was a chance.

Book Four
1933–1935

CHAPTER EIGHTEEN

Christmas 1933

Harold Ingram shifted his weight restlessly from one foot to the other. Waiting in the porch while the notes of the organ rang through the church added to his unease.

This would be the second time he'd led a bride to the altar. He hoped Lucy was going to be luckier than her mother. He pushed the door open and peeped down the aisle. He could see Wesley Spiers's back in a hired grey morning suit.

'Doesn't the church look beautiful?' Patsy was beside him in billowing skirts of lavender silk.

Harold had thought four o'clock on a December afternoon a strange time to choose for the wedding, but now he could see the charm. In the blue winter dusk, the candles and lamps sparkling amongst the Christmas evergreens provided a warm glow. The church seemed enchanting.

'Relax, Gramps.' He could feel Lucy's hand on his arm, as light as a feather. 'I'm the one who's supposed to be nervous, not you.'

'I'm not nervous.'

'Neither am I, because I want this so much.' She was smiling and serene.

In her bridal finery, she was shimmeringly beautiful, and she knew it, the little minx. Lucy twisted them all round her little finger. She was having her own way and marrying Spiers against Harold's better judgement. She'd never stopped wheedling and coaxing him to allow it. Both he and Mildred had prayed she'd get over her infatuation.

He'd tried to reason with her, pointing out that Wesley was middle-aged and should have established himself in life by now, if he ever was going to by his own efforts.

'And you're used to a comfortable standard of living. You couldn't cope if you were short of money.'

'I won't be. You've seen his house. I love it.'

Harold had ascertained that Wesley's pleasant house was rented. Further, he was afraid that Lucy had seen much more of it than he had. Mildred thought it very wrong for Wesley to allow her to go there unchaperoned, and was almost certain he'd taken advantage of her.

He had to agree. Seeing them together, they looked like lovers. Lucy couldn't be prised from his side; couldn't stop herself stroking his arm, or reaching out for his hand.

'I shall marry Wesley as soon as I'm of age,' she'd told him through clenched teeth. 'With or without your approval. In the register office, if I have to.'

'I can't understand what she sees in him,' Patsy had said. 'Such a dandy, and a terrible show-off. He acts like a man half his age. But you'll have to accept him, Grandpa. Otherwise you'll open up a rift between Lucy and the rest of us.'

Mildred had frowned. 'That would cut her off. Make it harder for her if things went wrong.'

'They seem very happy together,' Patsy said. 'Nothing may go wrong.'

He'd sighed. 'You're right, Patsy, of course. I may not like it, but I'll have to give my blessing.'

'You could give Wesley a job, if that's all you've got against him.' She'd smiled at him. 'That would provide them with a steady income.'

He was always being surprised by Patsy. She had a way of thinking things through. 'Why can't she be more like you? You've got all the sense.'

'I always wanted to be like her,' she'd laughed.

Mildred had sighed and pushed her thick spectacles up her nose. 'Perhaps Lucy will be happier running a home. She certainly doesn't like going to work. Will you take him into the business?'

'I suppose I must. Once they're married.'

'Wesley's very knowledgeable about antiques. He'll carry on with what you're building up for Lucy. And with what we're giving her, she'll have a comfortable and settled life.'

He hoped Mildred was right, but he still had his doubts about Wesley. He'd had a marriage settlement drawn up for Lucy, to provide a small income for her that Wesley couldn't get his hands on. Just in case.

He'd done the same for Patsy, feeling that he couldn't leave her out; and to reward her for all she was doing for him, he'd bought her the new car.

The Bach fugue came to an end, and after a moment's silence the organ struck up a lively voluntary. 'This is it.' Lucy was urging him through the door. 'Come on.'

Heads turned to see her come in in her froth of white lace and satin. He even heard gasps of admiration. Lucy's kitten-like beauty drew every eye.

They reached the altar and he handed her over to her groom. There was no mistaking the adoration in her eyes as she looked up at Wesley. Harold hoped she'd be happy with her choice.

Wesley's son, Rodney, was acting as best man, and Harold wasn't sure he approved of that either. He asked himself if he'd have felt better if Lucy was marrying the son. But he wasn't sure he liked him any better.

'Dearly beloved, we are gathered together . . .'

Behind him Vereena cleared her throat. A sound so easily recognisable it sent a shiver down his spine. He'd had nightmares after John Gripper had seen him kiss her. He'd been so afraid he'd tell Mildred or Patsy and blow his life apart. Both he and Vereena had been much more careful since then.

Today, they would come face to face in front of the entire family again. On John's wedding day he'd been stiff with apprehension, but John had had other things on his mind then.

He was afraid that John might let some hint drop without realising what he was doing. It was impossible to keep the family apart at weddings. Harold admitted to himself that he'd been in a sweat about John since that awful day, half afraid he might offend him or get his back up and thereby give him a reason to retaliate by telling what he knew. He'd treated him with kid gloves ever since, even given him a pay rise.

He'd suggested John should give his daughter away, but he hadn't wanted to do it. John never wanted to put himself forward to do anything.

Again he heard Vereena clear her throat. She'd been wonderfully calm and supportive of him, and she'd kept her head, though it was on her that all the problems had fallen.

John had told Bernie, and Bernie had abandoned her and gone off with another woman. Vereena had been furious, but not, he thought, too upset about losing him. In the long run it had been all to the good.

He'd helped her find a better house, one with a proper bathroom, and away from Cambridge Place and that triangle of streets between the railway lines. He'd found her some decent furniture and he'd been able to make the place comfortable for them both.

He felt safer going to Clifton Park. Her new neighbours were less interested because they didn't know her, and she was further away from Patsy and John.

There was the added advantage that he didn't have to stop Patsy coming to the factory. He ought to start taking her there so she'd know what was going on and could help more with that side of the business.

'Secondly, it was ordained for a remedy against sin and to avoid fornication . . .'

Harold swallowed hard. Marriage had not provided that remedy for him.

Mildred must never know. She was his wife and he owed her a good deal. Rather prim and proper, she still wore her hair twisted into old-fashioned earphones. She'd settled into old age now and was a little dull, but they'd been married a long time, and he didn't want anything to change. He wished his conscience wouldn't bother him so much.

'Wilt though have this woman to thy wedded wife . . .'

Wesley spoke up firmly. Harold hoped he'd keep his vows. It would break Lucy's heart if he didn't.

It was a bright Saturday afternoon in January, and Patsy was washing her new Cowley in the street outside the auction room. She was taking a delight in removing every mud splash and didn't see Robert Parry coming over.

'Smashing car you've got there, Patsy,' he said, making her jump. 'Lovely square lines. Gleaming. Very smart.'

Usually some inbuilt antennae warned her of his approach. He had a way of smiling down, his dark eyes searching out hers.

'I'm thrilled with it.'

'What happened to the old bull-nosed Morris?'

'It's still round at Caerns Road.'

'What's the boss going to do with it?'

Patsy laughed. 'He offered it to Lucy. She said it was too old and asked him to buy her a new one.'

'Lucky her, having a grandfather who can.'

'He refused. Said he didn't want to upstage her husband by giving her a car, and that he'd already given her what she asked for, a big wedding.'

'But he's given you one.'

'Exactly what Lucy said. Grandpa told her he had to

make it up to me. A car was the only thing he could think of.'

'Is the old Morris all right? I mean, were you having any trouble with it?'

'No, nothing much. Very draughty compared with this.'

'You've got a saloon now; the old bull-nose had a canvas top. Would he sell it to me, do you think?'

'Why don't you ask him?'

'I think I will. I'd love a car of my own.'

'How's your mother?' she asked.

'Much better. I can't tell you what a relief it is. I haven't said thank you for all your help. Dad told me that you were very kind to her.'

'I've seen her helping in your shop again.'

'Yes, that makes all the difference. Dad's able to have a rest in the afternoon when trade's slack. He's feeling better and so am I. I don't have to open up the shop for him three mornings a week. Wonderful, not having to get out of bed at half five in the morning.'

A few days later, Patsy was working in her office when Grandpa said:

'Your friend Robert Parry is interested in the old Morris.'

'So I believe.'

'I've told him he can have it.'

'As a gift, you mean?'

'As a bonus. He's done very well for the business, and so has the car. It's over ten years old.'

Rob was waiting for her when she went home that evening. She could see he was excited about it.

'Will you help me bring it home, Patsy?'

'Yes, of course.'

'Show me how to drive it?'

She didn't know what made her deliver such a dig: 'Josie Mackay's brother doesn't have the time after all?'

She felt him draw back. 'It's all off between me and Josie. You haven't heard the gossip then?'

Patsy shook her head. She didn't spend as much time in Cambridge Place as she used to.

'I've been trying to tell you for the last few weeks. I mean . . .' He looked uncomfortable.

Patsy was getting the impression that now Josie was gone, he wanted to spend more time with her again. She wasn't going to let pride stand in her way; she jumped at the chance.

'Grandpa will be here tomorrow afternoon for the sale. If I come home before he leaves, he can take us both back to Caerns Road to pick up the old bull-nose. How about that?'

'Great. About showing me how to drive . . .'

She smiled. 'I offered a long time ago, didn't I? We could have a go on Saturday afternoon.'

Rob looked overcome. She said: 'I've a book upstairs on how to drive. Do you want to borrow it?'

'Love to. Thanks, Patsy.'

'The sooner you learn, the better. I hear they'll be bringing in driving tests soon.'

On Saturday, Patsy watched Rob's capable hands on the steering wheel. To sit beside him like this brought her little eddies of pleasure. She thought he had more aptitude for driving than she'd had when she started. He was learning fast.

It was getting dark when they returned to Cambridge Place. He stopped the car outside the paper shop but made no move to get out. 'You're a good teacher.'

Her heart lurched. She had the feeling he was going to invite her to go to the pictures with him. It was seven years since he'd taken her to see Rudolph Valentino, and she'd be equally thrilled to go with him again.

Instead, he put a paper bag in her hand. It was very heavy. 'Just a token to say thank you,' he was saying.

She was disappointed, but was trying not to show it. 'You don't have to, Rob.' She slid a paperweight into the palm of her hand. 'It's beautiful,' she breathed. It really was. There was a rose in the centre with overlapping pink petals.

'Mid-nineteenth century. I hoped you'd like it.'

'I love it, thank you very much.'

It seemed Rob didn't want to get too close to her after all, even if Josie wasn't on the scene. Somehow they couldn't bridge all those years.

He didn't understand that for her the old attraction had never gone away. All afternoon, sitting beside him, she'd been feeling the tug. Perhaps this way was better. It would only reopen old wounds if she were to take up with him again. Her future was in the business; she must apply herself to that. She could manage very well on her own.

Ever since Patsy had come to work at Caerns Road she'd eaten lunch with her grandparents. It was always a substantial affair because they liked to eat their main meal in the middle of the day.

Today she was hungry. She heard her grandfather's heavy steps going downstairs and ran after him. The dining room door was open, a joint of roast beef waited on the table to be carved. She sniffed appreciatively at the scent.

But Grandpa had gone to the sitting room and it surprised her to hear voices coming from there. She went to the door.

'Hello, Gramps.' Lucy was getting up from the settee to kiss him. 'Hello, Patsy.'

'Lucy's staying for lunch with us,' Nanna told them. 'There'll be plenty.'

'It's on the table,' Mrs Judd said from the hall as she took in vegetable dishes. 'Don't let it get cold.'

As they sat down, Lucy said: 'I've a favour to ask, Gramps.'

'Oh yes?' His tone was dry. 'I wondered what had brought you round. We don't see much of you these days.'

Patsy thought she looked uncomfortable.

'I'm so busy, cooking and cleaning.'

'You have a woman to help?'

'Yes, but just a daily, not like Mrs Judd. Gramps, could you find Rodney a job too?'

Patsy caught her breath. Grandpa had given Wesley the title of undermanager in the factory, and told him to help Dick Longworth, who'd be retiring in a few months.

'He has to have a half-decent job,' he'd said to Patsy. 'He's family now, whether we like it or not. If he's any good, I'll offer him Dick's job.'

Now he said drily: 'Not another Spiers in need of support?'

Lucy pouted prettily. 'He's left school and he can't find anything.'

'I'm not surprised. There's three million others out of work.'

'Yes, but Rodney's at home with me all the time. If he could get a job, he could pay for lodgings somewhere else.'

'He's getting under your feet, is he?'

'We'd like to be on our own. We're newlyweds and all that.'

Patsy knew that her grandfather could never say no to anything Lucy wanted.

'I'll think about it,' he said gruffly. 'What does he want to do?'

'A clerk, something like that. Please, please, Gramps.'

'You'd better tell him to come down to the factory and I'll talk to him. See what I can do.'

'Thank you.' Lucy was all smiles.

'How's married life?' Patsy asked.

'Absolute heaven.'

'You're looking very well,' Nanna agreed. 'It seems to suit you. You're even putting on a little weight.'

'I always knew it would.'

'You're settling down now,' Nanna said complacently, but Patsy could sense Lucy's tension.

'There's something else . . .' Lucy swallowed hard. 'I'm going to have a baby.'

There was a second's surprised silence. Nanna said nervously: 'Well . . . that's good news, isn't it, Harold? Yes, we should be pleased. I must start knitting for you, a matinée jacket to begin with.'

Patsy counted up that Lucy had been married for less than five weeks. 'You've not wasted much time,' she told her.

They all saw the pink flush run up Lucy's cheeks. 'None at all,' she said lightly. 'It'll be born in June.'

Patsy's fork stopped halfway to her mouth. She watched both her grandparents freeze with horror. Nanna said: 'But that's only . . .'

Lucy was on the defensive. 'We wanted to be married much sooner. Would have done if you hadn't made us wait.'

Grandpa recovered first. 'I don't know what to say. Your reputation! Had Wesley no thought . . .?'

'It's not Wesley's fault. You made us wait. It's no good blaming anyone but yourselves.'

'I'm shocked!' Nanna was dabbing her handkerchief at her eyes. 'Oh Lucy, you shouldn't have had a big white wedding! All those people there. You're a very wilful girl!'

Patsy could see her sister's composure crumbling. She pushed her chair back and went to put a comforting arm round her shoulders.

'As long as it's what you want, Lucy. Really want.'

'It is, and it's what Wesley wants too.'

'Then all will be well. You'll be happy.'

Harold Ingram felt thoroughly churned up. Lucy couldn't get out of the house quickly enough once she'd dropped her bombshell. Mildred had gone to lie down on her bed, worried stiff about what their friends were going to say.

He couldn't stop striding up and down Patsy's office. 'The little minx. I might have known she'd be up to no good. She's a fool. That husband of hers ... Dick Longworth doesn't think much of him either.'

Patsy had her ledgers open in front of her. 'Lucy loves him.'

'Besotted with him, I'd say.' He knew he was stopping Patsy working, but he couldn't even sit down, let alone think of work.

'He tried to deceive us, you know. About his financial position. Making out he had his own shop. I don't like that sort of thing.'

'They're married, Grandpa. Off your hands. If this is the way Lucy wants it, does it matter?'

It did, for two reasons. He couldn't explain the first to Patsy, but it was on his conscience. He was afraid that Lucy had inherited from him too great an interest in the opposite sex.

After the first years of marriage, Mildred had not satisfied him; he didn't think one woman could. He was always craving more love, seeking more. He was ashamed of his appetite for sex and it was going on unabated into old age. He didn't want his granddaughter to be saddled with the same urgent need. It had brought such complexities to his life.

The other reason was no less painful. Lucy was stirring up terrible memories for him and Mildred. 'Her mother ... your mother ... Well, you know what happened to her.' Harold paused in front of Patsy's desk.

'We thought she was in too much of a hurry. To start a

family, I mean. Not that she did what Lucy's done. Your parents were married for eleven months. A pitifully short time really, poor Elsa. I'm filled with dread when I think of going through it again.'

Patsy came and put her arms round him.

'There's no reason to suppose that will happen to Lucy. Things are different nowadays. When the time comes, you can get her into a nursing home where a strict eye can be kept on her.'

'I'm frightened for her, all the same.'

'You can't protect Lucy, not from everything in life.'

He sighed. 'I wish she was more like you. You do all the work and she gets all the fussing.'

'I'm quite happy, Grandpa.'

'I don't do enough for you. Never have.'

'You do plenty. You've given me a wonderful car.'

'Would you like to move away from Cambridge Place? Have a flat of your own in a better area?'

'No, Grandpa, thank you. I'm happy enough there with Dadda and Alma.'

'Lucy would have jumped at an offer like that. You're not at all like twins.'

A couple of weeks went by. Patsy knew that her grandparents were worrying about Lucy. They hadn't seen her since the débâcle of that lunch.

'Shall I go and visit her?' Patsy offered. 'Ask her to come round?'

'We would like her to, of course,' Nanna said. 'Easier for you to do it.' Patsy went when she knew Wesley would be at the factory.

She'd seen the house before; Wesley had invited the whole family round for a meal shortly after he'd moved in. The consensus of opinion after that was that he'd organised himself very efficiently. He'd hired a woman to clean and cook, and the meal had been served very elegantly on

Royal Doulton china, with an impressive George III condiment set.

Now, as Patsy drew up in Templemore Road, she saw another car outside and knew her sister wasn't alone. Lucy came to the door before she knocked, wearing an attractive peach-coloured dress and smiling a welcome. She looked pregnant. Patsy knew she couldn't have hidden it much longer than she had.

'Lovely to see you.' Lucy was bubbling. 'Madge is here too.'

Patsy had never taken to Madge. She couldn't forget the childish jealousy she'd felt because she'd been closer to Lucy. It seemed she still was.

'Madge has only been married a few months. Isn't it nice that we still have so much in common? She's helping me get the house fixed up.'

'I thought you had everything settled.' Patsy had been impressed by its décor.

'Oh no!' Madge laughed. 'Lucy had just set out the things Wesley brought over from his other house.'

'Madge has ambitions to be an interior designer,' Lucy giggled. 'She's helped us do some wonderful things. Come in and see our sitting room.'

Patsy stood in the doorway and marvelled. The room with its plain walls and cream Indian carpet set off the fine Georgian furniture to perfection.

'It's better, isn't it?'

'It's perfection now. Restful and comfortable and—'

'Elegant?' Lucy suggested.

Patsy had been about to say 'expensive-looking'.

'We're trying to focus attention on the lovely old furniture that Wesley's choosing,' Madge explained.

'Grandpa would love this,' Patsy said. 'Exactly to his taste.' She knew he'd think it very extravagant for somebody in Wesley's position.

'Exactly to Wesley's taste too,' Lucy smiled. 'Let me

show you the rest of my house.'

'She's fine,' Patsy was able to report. 'Looks very well and seems happy. She's fixing up a nursery, all gossamer frills and furbelows.

'She knew she'd upset you, Nanna. The good news is that Wesley's saying they mustn't cut themselves off from you.'

'I'm glad about that.'

'She'll drop in for coffee tomorrow morning, and she's going to ask you over for lunch on Sunday. A family do. Dad and Alma and me, too. How's that?'

'I'm very pleased.'

'Didn't think Wesley had that much sense,' Grandpa said when she told him.

CHAPTER NINETEEN

At coffee time a couple of days later, Patsy found that her grandparents were still discussing Lucy.

'Don't worry,' Patsy told them. 'She's happy and she's keeping well. They both seem to be looking forward to the baby.'

'Ridiculously extravagant, what he's done to that house,' Grandpa grunted. 'If he's got that sort of money to spend, he'd have been wiser to buy it.'

'He can always sell the furniture again if he's hard up,' Patsy pointed out. 'He's in a good position to do that.'

When Dick Longworth retired, Harold promoted Wesley to be factory manager.

'I hope I've done the right thing,' he said to Patsy. 'Wesley has big ideas but I'm not sure how practical they are.'

Six months into the marriage, baby Fay was born, with very little trouble. Wesley had taken Lucy to the nursing home only four hours earlier. When Patsy drove her grandparents to see her that same afternoon, Lucy was all smiles, sitting up in a pretty lace nightgown nursing her new baby.

'Let me hold her,' Patsy begged. She took her infant niece over to the window, marvelling at what Lucy had achieved. Fay was a beautiful baby with a downy blonde head and her mother's even features.

Wesley was dancing attendance, reaching out to touch his new daughter and then feeling for Lucy's hand. Lucy's violet eyes were full of adoration for both. Patsy felt envious of the happiness that Lucy was showing. Even her grandparents seemed reassured.

In the months that followed, Lucy found a nursemaid to take the hard work out of looking after Fay. She invited the family round to little dinner parties, and talked of outings and tennis games and visits from her friend Madge.

'She's settled down now,' Nanna said. 'She's content with married life.'

'Certainly seems to suit her better than working,' Grandpa agreed.

Patsy felt that Lucy led a gilded life, with her luxurious home and her attentive husband. Now that she had a baby daughter to complete her circle, she thought her sister could ask no more of life. Particularly since her only responsibility was to keep them all well and happy.

Within a few short months, Lucy announced that she was expecting another baby, and seemed delighted at the prospect.

Patsy felt that her grandfather was relying on her more and more. Suddenly he seemed frail; there were tortuous purple veins showing at his temples now and his eyesight was bothering him. His doctor had told him he had glaucoma and must give up driving.

He was driving less, but he hadn't given it up. Quite often, late in the afternoons, she saw him slip off by himself without telling anybody where he was going.

'You're not supposed to drive,' Patsy said with mock severity.

'I'm not totally blind yet,' he'd barked back.

'Why don't you let me drive you round?'

'Come on then. We'll go to the factory. I've a lot to show you there.'

'In the factory?' Since he'd moved her base to Caerns

Road she'd had the feeling he didn't want her to go anywhere near the place. 'A change of policy?'

She saw him wince and look at her strangely, but he said: 'If you're going to run this business you must be familiar with every part of it. Making replicas is the most successful part. The most profitable.'

'I know that, I do your books.'

'You won't know the place.' He smiled. 'I'm expanding it fast.'

It seemed a long time since she'd been inside. The factory seemed bigger than she remembered, and much busier. Noisier, too, and the workforce had grown. Great stacks of new wood waited outside to be used, and there were more machines. She could see side tables and dining chairs taking shape.

Everywhere were the piles of sweet-smelling wood shavings she remembered so well. Grandpa stopped to speak to many of his workmen, introducing them by name and telling her what their duties were.

They were moving slowly round the main work floor when Wesley Spiers came to meet them, hand outstretched. He was wearing a purple tweed jacket, so hairy that sawdust adhered to it.

'My dear sister-in-law,' he gushed, grasping Patsy's hand. She hoped he wasn't going to raise it to his lips. 'Lovely to welcome you here. I wish I could persuade Lucy to come and look round.'

His eyes smiled with a feigned intimacy into hers. There was sawdust on his elegantly cut brown hair too, held there in the brilliantine.

Harold sounded grumpy: 'Patsy's interest is professional. She'll be running the business one day.'

Wesley's lips tightened at that. She saw he didn't care much for the idea. 'Let me show you round,' he said stiffly.

'Patsy's not like Lucy at all,' Grandpa told him. 'Got

her head screwed on the right way, this one.' He stopped to run his hand over the smooth top of a chest.

'You're making davenports now?' Patsy could see a whole row of them, in a half-finished state.

'They're very pretty when they're finished,' Wesley said. 'A George the Third replica.'

Patsy smiled at her grandfather. She recognised them immediately. 'George the Fourth actually.'

Wesley looked somewhat deflated. Until that moment, everything about him had been saying, watch me, aren't I a splendid fellow? Aren't I clever?

Patsy tried not to smile too widely: 'Mahogany. Four drawers down one side. When it's finished, dummy drawer handles will be fitted on the other. A hinged writing slope which will eventually be leather lined.'

She opened one of them up. 'It'll have a fitted interior. Four little drawers here, with pigeonholes and stationery slides.' She was laughing at their astonishment.

'I remember the original. It has a secret compartment.' Her fingers explored the beading.

'No secret compartments in these,' Harold told her.

'This is a copy of the one Auntie Freda had, isn't it? There was one in hers.'

'I didn't know that.'

'There was. You bought it, didn't you, Grandpa?' It was bringing back memories Patsy didn't want. That had been a terrible time for her, Cassie's death, and Freda's too.

She heard him sigh. 'I liked the davenport too well to part with it. It stands in an alcove in my dressing room.'

'You still have it?' Patsy gave a little shudder. 'Yes, you must have.'

'Clocks are my speciality,' Wesley said coldly. 'Particularly longcase.'

'Too complicated to reproduce,' her grandfather grunted. 'The dials, for instance. We'd have to order them and the movements from a specialist manufacturer.'

'It could be done,' Wesley insisted. 'I know a firm—'

'Too many originals still about. Made by country crafts-men everywhere, and they're not expensive. I think we should leave it to the clock manufacturers. They're making new ones in the traditional style. Not really our field, Wesley.'

Patsy was dropping in to see her sister more often. At Christmas, Lucy announced that the baby she was expect-ing was in fact twins, and she seemed content to have it so. Lucy's life was so different from Patsy's own, it fascinated her. She would sit nursing her infant niece and watch Lucy ordering fine wine and out-of-season delicacies for Wes-ley's dinner.

Lucy's main preoccupation seemed to be her clothes and her hairdressing. There were always fresh flowers in the house.

Patsy thought that by comparison, her life over the auction room was austere. The meals she ate with Dadda and Alma were not very different from those Cassie had taught her to cook. Alma was a thrifty housekeeper too.

She loved her job and would hate to be without that. The last thing she wanted was to replace it with Lucy's round of trivial pleasures. It wasn't Lucy's ever-open purse she envied – she had money enough – but it did seem that she did all the work while Lucy enjoyed the results of it.

Everybody seemed to love Lucy, she was the pivot of a happy family; while in her home, Patsy felt the odd one out.

She knew that Alma and Dadda did their best to make her feel included. They insisted on taking her with them to the pictures on Saturday nights. She spent most of her other evenings reading or listening to the wireless at home, sometimes alone. Patsy felt she was settling into spinsterhood. Nanna, particularly, seemed to expect that for her.

'You wouldn't have the time and energy for family life,' she assured her. 'To make a success of running the business you'll have to give it your full attention. Harold always has, and he's had me to support him. I think for a girl you're doing wonderfully well, but you'll have to manage without the back-up he's had.'

Patsy could see no difficulty; she felt she could cope with both job and family. Nanna didn't know what she was talking about. She forced herself not to think of Robert Parry, except in connection with the work he did. She didn't allow herself to stop and chat with him in the way she once had. She was friendly but cool, because that was how he was treating her.

She knew it was an act she was putting on. There was something about Rob Parry that made her burn with interest as soon as he came near. He'd only to smile at her and she was catching her breath. But he'd let her know by his actions that she could expect nothing from him. Diplomatically, of course, but he was holding back, she could feel it.

Working in Caerns Road, she occasionally saw Colin Courtney. He was now articled to a firm of accountants and hoped to qualify soon. Occasionally, she was invited with her grandparents to supper at his house. He was quiet and diffident and she rather liked him, except that he was always seeking news of Lucy.

Rodney Spiers was now working in the factory and had asked her out again. She'd turned him down without a second thought. She wanted nothing to do with him. Other men she knew in the company were either married or not in her age group.

Patsy knew that she wanted what every woman was supposed to want, a husband and family of her own, but she could see no way of achieving it. She was beginning to think she would have to find her fulfilment in the business after all.

* * *

As summer came round again, Harold Ingram knew he had reason to be worried. Wesley had been running the factory for almost a year and he was finding it increasingly difficult to get any figures from him. He had to ask for them several times. Last month, he'd laid the law down.

'It has always been my rule that each manager sends me the monthly trading figures on the first of the following month. I get them from the shops and the auction room. I must have them from the factory too.'

Patsy collated them into an overall account that told him how his business was faring.

'The factory figures are more complicated,' Wesley had excused himself.

'They represent the greater part of my business, so they're more important to me.'

'There's a lot of work . . .'

'Isn't Rodney helping you? If Dick Longworth could produce them on time, I see no reason why you can't. It's important to me to keep a check on what the factory's producing and what its costs are.'

This month, again, he'd had to ask Wesley for them; he knew Patsy had asked too. For Harold they were particularly important because this month would complete the financial year for his business. He very much wanted to know what his annual profit was.

It was now the sixth of the month and his patience was exhausted. Harold made up his mind to tell Wesley that if they were not ready now, he was going to leave Patsy in his office until they were. Patsy would help him get his work up to date.

'I'm not prepared to accept such tardiness,' he told Patsy. 'I'm going to change the system, perhaps put somebody else in the factory to oversee all the accounts.'

'Me?'

'No, I don't want you to have too much routine work. We'll get a proper accountant. He'll report direct to us.

We've got to know exactly what's happening there.'

Wesley had promised definitely that Rodney would bring the figures to Caerns Road this morning. When they hadn't arrived by early afternoon, Harold asked Patsy to drive him down to the factory. Rodney Spiers met them on the factory floor as they walked through. Absurd to think of Lucy being stepmother to this great gangling fellow. He seemed anxious.

'Dad's had to rush off. He's taking Lucy to the nursing home. She's just rung to say she thinks the twins are coming.'

Harold hadn't been expecting anything to happen just yet; none of them had, though Mildred had said that twins were inclined to come early. She'd be nervous too, now that the birth was imminent.

'Have you heard how she is?'

Patsy went to the phone without being asked. There was no news from the nursing home except that Lucy had arrived. Harold felt uneasy. Patsy understood, and took over.

'Your father promised to have the monthly figures ready,' she told Rodney. 'He promised to bring them in, but since he hasn't, we've come to collect them.'

'Oh yes, Dad said to tell you they're on his desk.'

That surprised Harold; he'd expected to have to do battle about them. 'They're ready?'

He strode to Wesley's office, where two pages of typed figures were waiting for him. He glanced at the totals and was stung with disappointment. Money coming in from sales had been drifting lower over the last few months. It was down again. Much lower this month. Annual profit wouldn't be as high as he'd been hoping.

He handed them over to Patsy. Now the birth of the twins was upon them he had other things on his mind. 'Back to Caerns Road, I think.'

He could see her frowning at the figures, her fair head

bent deep in thought. She looked up and caught his eye.

'We'll take the books with us too, Rodney.'

'What books?'

'The ledgers from which these figures have been extracted.'

'Oh!'

'You help with the accounts, don't you?'

'Sometimes.'

'I'll take all the supporting documents as well,' Patsy told him.

'What documents?'

'Invoices, bank statements, credit notes, delivery notes.' Patsy's voice was growing more brisk. 'Where do you keep those?'

'I don't know. Dad locks them away.'

'Grandpa?'

'In the filing cabinets. This one, I think.' Harold took out his personal set of duplicate keys and unlocked it. That Patsy seemed dissatisfied with the figures made him more uneasy. He'd never completely trusted Wesley.

'We'll need them for the auditors,' Patsy was saying. 'Help us carry these files out to the car, Rodney, will you?'

It was late afternoon when they arrived back in Caerns Road. Harold shared a pot of tea with Patsy and Mildred and then rang the nursing home again. There was still no news and they told him they didn't expect any for some time.

Harold felt restless, more so because Patsy had settled down at her desk and was checking invoices and bank statements against Wesley's totals. Mildred wanted to go down to Templemore Road. She felt that in Lucy's absence, she had a duty to see that the nursemaid looked after little Fay properly. She was now thirteen months old.

'I'll run you down there,' he told her. After that he'd go down to see Vereena. He couldn't stand the waiting around, the suspense and the worry. Vereena would take his mind off all that.

Vereena was in fine form and gave him the lift he needed. When he went home, in time for dinner, he found Patsy still at her desk.

'The figures don't add up, Grandpa.' Her face was anxious. 'There's something strange going on down there. Take davenports, for instance. How many have you made?'

'I tried fifty to start with. Then orders started coming in for more.' Harold opened up his desk and took out his own records. 'A hundred and ten up till now.'

'That's what the books say. We've been paid for ninety-five. The physical inventory says eight in the store, but that leaves a discrepancy of seven.'

Harold's stomach lurched. Also on Wesley's desk had been an order for a library table from a furniture shop in Grange Road. He'd gone to the storeroom to see if there was one there.

'There are no davenports in the store. I distinctly noticed. Not much of anything there.'

Patsy's vivid blue eyes stared up into his, aghast. 'And it's not just the number of davenports. The library tables aren't all accounted for. Nor the Pembroke tables.'

All his suspicions of Wesley were flooding back. He should have expected something like this. Wesley's standard of living was sky-high. Surely he couldn't achieve that on the salary Harold was paying him?

Months ago, he'd said something in that vein to Wesley after he'd drunk a couple of glasses of his whisky. They'd both been in a jocular mood.

Wesley had explained that he still did a bit of dealing on his own account. Harold had wanted to believe him, even though it meant he was dealing when he should have been working in the factory.

'My head's spinning,' Patsy said, 'but I think I'm right. By the way, no news about Lucy yet.'

'Go home, Patsy, you've stuck at it too long. I'll look

through the figures tonight. Won't be able to do anything until tomorrow anyway.'

Harold felt anxious all evening. He could see that Mildred was very much on edge too.

'Lucy's taking too long.' She'd just put down the phone after enquiring yet again. 'I do hope she's all right.'

'Nothing's going wrong, is it?'

'They say all is well, but I can't help thinking of Elsa.'

Harold couldn't either. If Elsa hadn't had twins, she might have been with them now.

Mildred went up to bed, and he decided to go too. He took the factory accounts with him and spent hours poring over them. By midnight he knew that Patsy was right, and that Wesley Spiers was defrauding him.

He felt a *frisson* of worry run down his spine. Wesley had openly said that he was dealing on his own account. If, instead of selling his clients antiques, he was selling them replica furniture made in the factory, that would explain why sales through the books were falling. Wesley was diverting them to his private account. It would be simple enough for him to do.

It might just be that Wesley was making genuine mistakes. Omitting items. He hoped that it was so. He'd rather have a grandson-in-law who was incompetent than one who was a thief. Either way, Wesley had a lot of explaining to do.

Harold knew he'd disturbed Mildred. She was tossing and turning. 'Please phone again,' she urged. 'There might be news now.'

But he got the usual response. They told him that all was progressing normally. He put out the lights and tried to sleep, but had a rotten night. Before he was properly awake, he could hear Mildred telephoning again.

She was shaking him then, eyes bright with pleasure behind her thick spectacles, hardly able to contain herself.

'Twin boys, not identical. Mother and babies all doing well. Oh, Harold, I'm so relieved! Lucy's fine.'

He punched his pillows up. That was one worry fewer. But he couldn't unload his suspicions about Wesley on Mildred. Not now, when she was bubbling with joy.

'Five pounds five ounces, and five pounds one. Good weights, they said, for twins. I've spoken to Wesley too; he says both he and Lucy are over the moon.'

Immediately after breakfast, Mildred wanted to go to see the new additions to the family. He drove her to the nursing home. Lucy's room was full of red roses.

'Lovely to have so many visitors.' Lucy was all smiles. 'Patsy brought Dadda and Alma, on the way to work. Alma knitted these bootees for the babies. The shawls are from Dadda and the nightgowns from Patsy. And Wesley's given me these beautiful diamond earrings to mark the event.'

'Twin sons are very special.' Wesley smirked at Harold. 'I wanted to show my pleasure.'

'And the red roses,' she added.

Wesley was sitting by her bedside, nursing one of the babies, a model husband; Lucy hugged the other. They seemed a happy family.

Harold couldn't meet Wesley's gaze. He knew he'd shatter Lucy's peace of mind when he voiced his concerns about the factory accounts. He felt his stomach lurch at the thought. Not today, he told himself, he couldn't possibly do it today. Let them have their day of joy and triumph. He'd talk this out with Wesley tomorrow.

When he and Mildred got back to Caerns Road, Patsy's car was in the drive. He knew he should move the office to the factory, where they could keep a closer eye on what was going on. If it hadn't been for his affair with Vereena, it would always have been there. He had himself to blame for making things easier for Wesley to fiddle than they needed to be.

He slumped down in a chair in Patsy's office. She asked: 'Did you look at the accounts? What d'you think?' Her eyes were worried.

'I think you're right.'

'Should we go through his figures again? My head's clearer this morning. Could we be mistaken?'

Harold shook his head. 'It sickens me to think of it. Can't trust him. Don't want him in that factory at all. What am I to do about him, Patsy?'

He couldn't let Wesley stay where he was. He'd given him too much power.

'Trouble is, in charge of a shop . . . he could still fiddle.'

'The auction room?'

'Easier still. The turnover is faster. Harder for us to keep an eye on it. I don't want him anywhere near our money after this.'

'Lucy will have to know what's happening.'

Harold pulled himself wearily to his feet and went to get the factory accounts and files. He'd left them in his dressing room. He'd made a few notes while he'd been waiting for breakfast this morning. They were on top of his davenport. He used it often for jotting down things that came to him out of office hours, a habit set up when his office had been at the factory.

There was another note about something else he'd meant to follow up. An advert he'd seen in a newspaper a day or two ago. A timber merchant was shipping hard woods from the Gold Coast.

He lifted the writing slope to find it, and while shuffling through his papers, remembered what Patsy had told him about the davenport. That it had a secret compartment.

It didn't seem likely, there hardly seemed room for it, but he pressed and pulled at the beading as he'd seen Patsy do on the replica. It surprised him when a flap dropped down, revealing a false bottom to the drawer over the stationery compartment.

317

Inside, he could see a piece of crumpled notepaper. He smoothed it out and found that there were a few lines of shaky writing on it. It was very difficult to decipher. Harold switched on his lamp and held it directly underneath.

As he read the first line, he could feel himself stiffening with horror. He knew what it was.

I can't go on any longer. I can't bear the awful pain, or the loneliness, or knowing it will get worse.

There's nothing more the doctor can do for me. I know it's wrong to end my life, but I'm a burden to everyone and have been for years.

I haven't the strength to struggle on. I'd rather die.

Winifred Mary Tarrant

'Oh God!' Harold felt for a chair and sat down. It was Freda Tarrant's suicide note! But how had it come to be hidden inside the secret compartment?

He could see Freda now, as she'd been on the day he'd bought the davenport. Ill and drained, no longer very interested in selling it. No longer very interested in life.

The circumstances of her death were coming back to him. There'd been doubt as to how she had died. It had taken an autopsy to find the pills in her stomach. That was how the coroner had arrived at his verdict of suicide. He remembered quite clearly that in court it was said that Freda hadn't left a note.

Harold tried to swallow the lump in his throat. Freda had written this.

'Harold? Coffee's ready,' he heard Mildred call from the hall below. Patsy's footsteps were going down. He went slowly after her, holding the note between finger and thumb, trying to think.

On that awful day, Patsy had been white and tearful in the coroner's court, lost because Cassie was dead and very upset by the rumours that she had killed her friend.

318

'What's that you've found?' Mildred wanted to know. He passed it to her silently, still wondering how it had come to be hidden inside the davenport.

'Freda wouldn't have put it there.' Mildred was frowning. 'She wrote it to explain what she was doing. She'd want it to be found.'

Patsy was on her feet, reading it over Mildred's shoulder. Her anguished eyes fastened on Harold's.

'Poor, poor Gran . . . She kept saying Freda had committed suicide. This is evidence that she was right.' Harold thought she looked thoroughly shaken up.

Patsy went on slowly: 'Vereena must . . . She accused Gran of poisoning her mother.'

Harold felt cold fingers clutching his entrails. He knew Vereena was involved. She had to have been.

'She was there when I picked the davenport up from Freda's that day. She told me her mother was better . . .'

'But Freda had already written that note, must have done.' Mildred's face was full of horror.

'It was already hidden, too.' His mouth felt dry.

'Only Vereena could have put it there.'

Harold felt sick. 'No, Vereena wouldn't . . .'

But all the years Vereena had been growing up, the davenport had been in her home. She'd have known all about the secret compartment.

He could see Patsy making the same equation. Her face cleared.

'I tried to tell you, Grandpa. I thought it must be something like this.'

Harold remembered how he'd bitten her head off when she'd suggested it. He hadn't wanted to hear anything against Vereena, fool that he was.

'She did it for the life insurance. She didn't want her mother's death to be suicide. Don't you see? If her mother had died of natural causes, or even if . . .' He could see the colour draining from Patsy's face. 'Even if Gran was found to have . . .'

Mildred said: 'How awful. Surely no one would . . .?'

Patsy went on: 'Vereena was always asking her mother for money. She'll do anything for it. She's like that.'

Harold felt the fire rush up his cheeks. Was Vereena doing what she did for him for the money he gave her? He was afraid she could be. She had a way of leading him on to buy things for her.

He leapt to his feet, strode to the window and back, rattling the coins in his pocket. He made himself sit down. He mustn't let his agitation show.

Patsy's voice was choked. 'I'm glad she didn't gain anything. The policy didn't pay out.'

'I never cared much for Vereena.' Mildred was wrinkling her nose.

Harold had liked her too well. He was very fond of her. Loved her.

Patsy looked close to tears. 'I'm glad it's come to light. I'm glad to know for certain Gran didn't harm Freda. In a way, it's set my mind at rest. I never doubted what Gran was saying, but all the same . . .'

'Your father too,' Mildred added. 'He was upset about the way his mother died. He'll be pleased.'

'Poor Gran, what a shock it must have been to be accused of killing Freda. No wonder she had a heart attack. I blame Vereena.'

Harold felt suffused with guilt. He didn't know where to look, couldn't even swallow his coffee.

It had to be Vereena. Whichever way he looked at it, it was Vereena who had hidden the suicide note. What she'd done to Cassie, she'd done for financial gain. That stuck in his craw. He was seeing a side of her she'd kept hidden. He felt completely turned off.

'It's all long since over.' Mildred suddenly lost interest. 'There's nothing you can do about it now. Forget it.'

He knew that finding the note had brought back feelings of loss and grief for Patsy, but he could feel uncontrollable anger welling up inside him. He was on his feet again, hot with rage and self-loathing. He had to get away from them. He took the stairs at the double and shut himself in his office.

He was tasting gall. He went up and down the room like a caged lion until he wondered if he could be heard on the floor below. He flung himself in his chair.

Church and society laid down strict rules of conduct that he'd only pretended to follow. In reality he'd flouted them. He'd committed adultery. Not once, but many times. He'd cheated on Mildred, tried to cover up from Patsy what he was doing.

He felt heavy with guilt and revulsion and totally put off Vereena. He felt she'd manipulated him, and he was an old fool to have let her. What he'd found out tarnished everything.

Damn it, he felt hurt too. He'd loved her, thought her a very different person.

And if Mildred ever found out about her, the quiet comfort of his own home would be shattered. He stood it until lunchtime. Made some effort to eat the fried cod, though he could see his fork shaking as he lifted it to his mouth.

He made up his mind to go and see Vereena straight away. He wanted to settle the score with her once and for all.

'I'm just going down to the factory,' he announced as calmly as he could when they got up from the table.

'Shall I drive you, Grandpa?' Patsy offered.

'No.' He was unusually brusque. 'I want you to work on the accounts today.'

'Wait a moment, you can drop me off at the nursing home.' Mildred was heading upstairs. Harold hung back, wanting to be alone. His mind was going round in circles. He ought to be happy for Lucy; instead, he was fearful that what Wesley had done would harm her.

321

'I promised to drop a book off for Lucy. She's nothing to read. Then I'll walk round to Templemore Road to see little Fay.'

He'd have to take her. He was brushing impatiently at his bowler when Mildred came down again. 'Are you ready?'

'I know it's out of your way, but it'll only take you a few minutes.'

It wasn't out of his way at all, not if he was going to see Vereena.

'What is the matter with you, Harold? You're like a cat on hot bricks.'

'It's upset me, finding that note. Bringing it all back. Poor Cassie.'

'Oh, for heaven's sake!'

He started the car with such a jerk he sprayed gravel from the drive on to the lawn. He could hear Mildred clucking with disapproval.

'Slow down,' she said, as he swung out of Caerns Road into Alton.

'You could easily have walked,' he grumbled. It wasn't far, just down Shrewsbury Road. He could see the place now.

'There's Wesley.' Mildred was pointing. He could see him standing on the pavement, waving his hands about, showing off as usual.

'Who's that with him?'

The woman had her back to them. She was smiling up at Wesley, hand on hip, in the same provocative pose Vereena used on him. She moved, turning slightly. He recognised the hat he'd bought her last month.

'It's Vereena.' He was choking. It infuriated him further to see her. Could it be he was not the only man she'd taken up with?

He heard Mildred say: 'The hussy. I hope Wesley's got the sense to stay clear of the likes of her.'

Wesley had seen them coming. Harold saw his expression turning to one of shocked horror. It was Mildred's strangled scream that made him look back to the road.

He rammed on the brakes, swung on the steering wheel in a desperate attempt to avoid the van. He knew he didn't stand a chance. Pain seared through him as his head slammed against the steering wheel in the sudden juddering crash. Greater pain as his head whipped backwards. Above the frenzy of tearing metal and splintering glass, he could hear Mildred screaming.

CHAPTER TWENTY

6 July 1935

Once she'd heard Grandpa's car drive off, it seemed to Patsy that an ominous silence settled on the house. She sat at her desk, opened the factory files and stared at Wesley's figures. There seemed little point in inserting them into the annual accounts until the problem had been sorted out. The true picture needed to be established first.

She would have preferred to go out. She felt oppressed by events. Finding Freda's suicide note like that had given them all an emotionally charged morning. For once, she felt too keyed up to work.

She pushed the files to the back of her desk and tried to get on with something else. She knew she was making little progress. The problem Wesley had created was weighing on her mind. She was thinking of Lucy and how best to break it to her. It was going to cause difficulties. If they were not careful, it could even cause the family split that had threatened earlier.

The front doorbell broke the brooding silence, ringing through the house.

Surely Wesley must realise that he couldn't hide what he was doing, and that Grandpa wouldn't allow him to continue. She'd almost convinced herself she was wrong. It was a simple error on Wesley's part, they were too suspicious, reading too much into it.

Below her, the doorbell rang more urgently. Patsy

straightened up. Perhaps Mrs Judd had also gone out? She went running down to answer it.

She opened the door to find Wesley on the doorstep. It left her gasping and somewhat disconcerted. Her first thought was that he'd discovered his error and come round to apologise.

'Grandpa's not here,' she said.

'I know.'

Wesley looked different, not his usual bombastic self. He seemed upset, shocked even. It made her shiver.

'Lucy? She is all right?'

'Lucy's fine. Can I come in? Something terrible's happened.'

Patsy backed up the hall and watched him close the door. She noticed his hand was shaking. He said: 'Perhaps you'd better sit down.'

'What's happened?' She was swallowing back the feeling of fear rising in her throat. 'For God's sake! What is it?'

'Your grandfather . . . He's crashed his car.' His eyes burned down at her. 'I'm sorry.'

Patsy's stomach turned over with dread. 'Badly? Is he hurt?'

'Worse than that, I'm afraid.'

She felt sick. 'You mean . . .?'

'He ran into a parked van. Drove it over the pavement and against the wall. Such a tangle of twisted metal. It killed him!'

She felt stunned. 'Nanna? What about Nanna?'

Wesley was shaking his head. 'She's badly hurt. Very badly. Unconscious.'

'Oh my God!' Patsy's gut was wrenching.

'We saw it happen, right before our eyes. Outside the nursing home. You know that high wall that runs round it? I'd been to see Lucy . . .'

'Rodney was with you? You said "we".'

'No, Vereena. I met her outside. She'd come to see the twins, but it upset her so much she couldn't go in.'

Patsy could feel the blood surging to her head. This was too awful to take in.

'I ran back inside, got them to call an ambulance. A doctor came back with me . . . I'm so sorry.'

'Grandpa's eyes – he couldn't see properly. I didn't like him driving.'

'A cup of tea? Can somebody make you one?'

'No.'

Tea wouldn't help. Grandpa dead? Impossible to believe when only an hour or so ago . . . If only she could put the clock back. Make him see sense about giving up driving.

They were in the kitchen. Wesley was filling the kettle. He looked uncomfortable.

'I'm not very good at breaking news like this . . . Haven't done it very well, have I? I'm sorry.'

'There's no good way.' She could feel the tears coming now. Her face was wet.

The air was fragrant with the scent of baking. A cake had been left on a rack to cool. It was Nanna's favourite seed cake. She wouldn't be back to eat it. Would she ever come back?

'Where is she? Nanna, I mean.'

'They took her to the General Hospital.'

'Would you phone? Ask how she is?'

As she made a pot of tea, Patsy could hear him speaking in the hall. Monosyllables mostly. She held her breath, straining to listen. She knew before he came back to the door.

'I don't know how to say this. Your grandmother died before she reached hospital. Lucy's going to be devastated.'

He was pouring a cup of tea for her. Patsy sank slowly on to the rocking chair and wept.

327

It made it worse to hear that Vereena had been there. She was always on hand when something terrible happened. Patsy couldn't stamp back the feeling that it was all Vereena's fault.

Both Rob and Dadda had told her that Vereena couldn't do any more harm, but they were wrong. Look what had happened now. Could it be Vereena's fault that Grandpa and Nanna had died? Vereena didn't seem to care what she did to them all.

Patsy felt the double disaster had come out of the blue. Wesley left her almost immediately to break the news to Lucy. She knew she'd have to tell everybody else. It took her an hour to pull herself together before she could face it.

She went to the bathroom and splashed cold water on her face before going to the factory. She drove her car slowly and with extreme caution, afraid that she too might have an accident.

As she went inside, craftsmen paused in their work to greet her. 'I want my father,' was all she could say as she walked on.

Through a blur of unshed tears, she found her way to the corner partitioned off as an office. Hilda Cropper, the middle-aged woman who did the secretarial work, looked up from her desk. Rodney Spiers was the only other person there.

Patsy said: 'Would you find my father for me, Rodney? And Alma. Ask them to come here.'

As soon as he'd gone she told Hilda Cropper of the accident. Miss Cropper slumped on her desk, her face ghostly grey. 'He was a good man,' she whispered. 'A good boss. None better.'

When Miss Cropper looked up, Patsy could see tears in her eyes. She found it hard not to break down again herself.

'Will you let everybody know,' she choked. 'I'd be grateful if you'd ring round the shops and the auction room.'

She didn't feel up to doing that. She couldn't take their shock or their sympathy. Her father's bewildered face appeared at the door. Alma was looking over his shoulder.

'I want you both to come home,' Patsy said. 'I've got my car outside.'

Dadda was looking past Miss Cropper to the office clock. 'We can't come yet, Patsy. It's not time.'

'Come on,' she said, with such authority that he fell into step beside her. Once outside in the fresh air, she told them the awful news.

'You poor thing.' It was Alma who gave her a comforting hug and ushered them both into the car. 'Such a shock for you.'

Patsy realised she was doing most of the weeping; she'd had longer for the horror of it to sink in. She drove straight back to Cambridge Place, though she felt there was much she should be looking at in the factory.

'Poor Mildred.' Dadda was beside her in the front seat. She could see a tear rolling down his cheek. 'To die just when Lucy's twins are born. She was so thrilled with them when I saw her this morning.'

It seemed another life since she'd taken Dadda and Alma to see Lucy in the nursing home this morning. They'd stayed on a few minutes after her, timing their departure to catch the bus to the factory.

'Grandpa too. Poor Grandpa.'

'He did very well for himself. Always has. Lived life to the full.'

Alma stirred on the back seat. 'A good man.' It sounded almost a refrain as she said it. 'Everybody admired him.'

As soon as they were home, Alma put the kettle on to

329

make tea. They received a visit from the police but they learned nothing new from them. It left them all restless and on edge; they had endless discussions about trivialities.

Alma cooked a meal though none of them were hungry. As they sat down to eat it, Patsy told them how Grandpa had found Freda's suicide note before setting out on his last fateful journey. About how they'd talked over what must have happened and come to the conclusion that only Vereena could have hidden it in the davenport.

'That upset Grandpa. Even Nanna noticed and told him he was like a cat on hot bricks. I'm sure he wouldn't have been able to concentrate on driving. Not in the mood he was in.'

She glanced up from her plate to find Dadda's mild eyes on her.

'Did you know Vereena was his mistress? Had been for years.'

That gave her a nasty jolt. 'Dadda! Are you sure?'

'Vereena used to work at the factory. He'd come just on closing time to see her. They stayed on after he'd locked up. That was why you were moved to Caerns Road.'

It brought a nasty taste to Patsy's mouth. She found it hard to equate that with her perception of Grandpa. But he had been terribly upset this morning when he'd found Freda's suicide note. He hadn't liked hearing her blame Vereena for hiding it.

'One day I saw him drop her off from his car. He kissed her. Vereena admitted it to me. That was why Bernie left her,' said Dadda.

'What?' She could feel the blood pounding through her head. 'Why didn't you tell me?'

'You were too young to understand.'

'Did Nanna know?'

'I don't think so. Hardly anybody did. He fixed Vereena up with a place in Clifton Park after that.'

Patsy stiffened. So that was why Grandpa went on driving. There were places he wanted to go that nobody else must know about.

'Vereena and Wesley saw the crash,' she said, appalled at the thought. 'They were standing on the pavement.'

Was that what had deflected Harold's attention? Seeing Vereena with Wesley?

'I don't suppose it matters to Harold who knows now,' John said, putting down his knife and fork.

'It does, of course it does. His reputation.'

'I wouldn't say anything outside the family. Not to the neighbours and certainly not at work. The place won't be the same without him.'

'No.' Patsy sat hunched over the table. She was sure now that Vereena was to blame for her grandparents' death. Very definitely to blame. The thought left her gasping.

Afterwards, when the meal was cleared away, Dadda didn't know what to do with himself. He was staring out of the window like a lost soul.

Patsy put her arms round him. The sweet scent of raw wood was on his rough flannel shirt. She could feel hot tears prickling her eyes, all at once they came flooding out.

'I told you Vereena was evil,' she sobbed. 'Years ago. You wouldn't listen to me. I tried to tell you she'd do it again. Harm people we love. You wouldn't listen, Dadda. Well, she has done it again.

'If only I'd opened my mouth then. Let everyone know what she was like. Perhaps Grandpa wouldn't have been taken in. Perhaps this wouldn't have happened.'

'Patsy, you were only a child.'

She could see she was upsetting him. 'Thirteen.'

'Too young . . .'

'I was right.'

'You couldn't have accused her.'

331

'But *you* could have.'

As she watched his gentle face crumple, Patsy knew that was a cruel stab. Dadda had never been fond of Vereena but he couldn't have denounced her. He wasn't the sort to denounce anyone.

He said slowly: 'We didn't know about Freda's suicide note then. There was no proof.'

It didn't stop Patsy feeling a heartburning resentment against Vereena. She might have prevented this new catastrophe if she'd pressed hard enough all those years ago. It made her feel sick to think of it. She'd failed her family, failed to stop Grandpa and Nanna dying.

She blamed herself. She should have screamed it from the rooftops. In future she must follow her own gut feeling.

She was almost overcome then, by the terrible urge to seek revenge. She felt maddened by it. It was white hot and searing; she had to make Vereena pay for what she'd done. Nothing was too bad for Vereena. She wanted to make her suffer.

Patsy knew revenge was something she had to put out of her mind, at least for the time being. She had other, more urgent problems to deal with, another catastrophe was blowing up in her face.

All the difficult decisions Grandpa had been worried about would now have to be taken by her. He would have been tough with Wesley. She'd have to be now. She hoped she'd be able to cope.

Patsy knew exactly what the legal position would be. Both Grandpa and Nanna had drawn up new wills quite recently. They'd shown them to her. They were very simple and very clear. Apart from one small legacy, everything was to be divided equally between her and Lucy.

'Running the business will be down to you,' Grandpa

had told her. 'You won't find Lucy much help.'

He hadn't known then that Lucy would have given birth to twins the very same morning. How could she be expected to help in any way? What Patsy felt she needed was support and advice, but it was not forthcoming from her father.

'I know you were very close to Grandpa.' Dadda's eyes were glazed with sympathy. 'He was a good businessman. Knew the antiques trade inside out. I don't know how you're going to manage.' His worried eyes met hers. 'It's such a big concern now. But at least you've got Wesley to help you. I'm glad about that.'

Patsy froze in horror. She tried haltingly to explain about the problems Wesley was causing. Dadda hardly seemed to believe her, he could offer no suggestions about the business, no concrete help. Patsy knew she couldn't expect that; it was beyond Dadda's capabilities. But it left her feeling overwhelmed by loss and grief and duty.

Later that evening, Robert Parry came to knock on their door. 'Patsy, I'm so sorry.' The kiss he put on her cheek was a peck of sympathy, but it made the heat run up her neck.

'I hope I haven't come too soon? I don't want to intrude. Not at a time like this.'

'No, Rob. Come in.'

She was relieved to see him. She needed somebody to talk to, somebody who would understand and who could help.

'We're all terribly churned up about it,' Rob said. 'We were very fond of him.'

She wasn't going to blame Rob as she had Dadda, though he too had advised her not to make trouble for Vereena all those years ago. She couldn't do anything about Vereena. Not yet. It was how she'd cope with Wesley in the days ahead that was bothering her. She didn't want to fail again. Let her family down.

Patsy felt caged in in the small flat. She wanted to get away from Dadda and Alma. They were kind, trying to share her trouble, but they didn't understand.

'Could we go for a walk?'

It was drizzling, an overcast evening, but Rob showed no surprise. 'Yes, if you'd like to.'

She put on her coat. 'I need some air.'

When the door closed behind them, Rob said: 'How can I help, Patsy? You must be feeling awful, having to pick up all his responsibilities at a moment's notice.' There was a gentleness about him.

Patsy clung to his arm and stepped out briskly. The cold drizzle was blowing in her face. She felt stripped to the bone. She no longer cared that he'd once preferred Josie Mackay. Her pride had gone. She wanted Rob now, had to have his help. Tears were stinging her eyes again, and she was blinking them back.

The rain began to fall more heavily. They'd reached Central Station.

'Where shall we go?' he asked, drawing her inside the booking office and putting his arms round her. Patsy put her face against his neck. His collar was damp against her chin. She clung to him as the early-evening crowds swirled past on their way to and from the trains. She could feel the heat of his body through the layers of their clothes.

'Come on.' With his arm round her waist he drew her to the ticket window and then down the steps to the trains. 'Too wet to walk about,' he said.

Patsy felt the empty ache inside her as she told him of the part Vereena had played in her grandparents' deaths. The proof they'd found that her meddling had caused Cassie's death too.

'I could throttle Vereena with my bare hands,' she exploded. 'I feel so full of hate. So bitter about what she's done. I want to make her pay, to suffer as she made Gran suffer.'

She felt Rob's arms pulling her closer. 'No, Patsy,' he said softly. 'Don't let your mind fill with malice. Don't try to retaliate.'

'Why?' she demanded hotly. 'She deserves a flogging, nothing is too bad for . . .'

He put a gentle finger against her lips. 'I'm sure you're right about that, but if you let yourself be vindictive, if you fill your mind with virulent loathing, it'll poison you.'

A train drew in to the platform, and as the crowd rushed to get on, he turned her away to an empty bench. They sat close together, his arm still round her waist.

'You know about the trouble between our families,' he said in a low whisper. 'You were there the night our shop window was booted in and my mother and Cassie had a go at each other.'

Patsy swallowed hard. 'A public slanging match.' Impossible to forget the things they'd said.

'My mother kept the hate and the guilt she felt fermenting inside her for years. It turned her in on herself, made her a nervous wreck. She was always worried about what Cassie would do or say. You know my mother was filled with the most venomous hate.'

'For me too, I could feel it.' Patsy shivered. 'The blame for what happened lay between her and my . . . Alfred Gripper.'

'But it spilled out into hate for all his family. Even you. She feared you. You knew too much. To do that makes no sense.'

'I know, but . . .'

'What you probably don't know is that Mam's state of mind was contagious. At home, Dad and I could always feel her anxiety. Even when she was having a good day, there was this feeling that it would all crumble in an instant if something went wrong. Dad did his best to support her . . .'

'You did too.'

'Not always. I took the job you persuaded Cassie to offer me, against Mam's wishes. She hated me working in the pub, hated me being anywhere near you. She wasn't too bad until I did that. I hadn't realised then that I would make her worse. Make things worse for Dad and myself too.'

'You were very understanding. You did your best for her.'

'She thought you and I were too close. I was fool enough to take up with Josie Mackay because I knew she'd approve of her. I thought she'd get better again if I did what she wanted.'

'You mean you didn't like Josie?' Patsy felt overcome.

'If I'm to be honest, yes, I liked her. She's a chatty sort of person, good company and at times good fun. I didn't love her. I had no deep feelings for her in the way I have for you.

'I thought they might come with time. That's being cruelly honest, isn't it? But they didn't. I know now I was stupid even to think they would.'

For Patsy, the agonies she'd felt over Josie Mackay were quickly vanishing.

'I didn't think things through. Didn't stop to think about how it would affect you and me. Didn't consider your feelings. I'm sorry. I didn't realise that what I did would build a barrier between us. Turn you off. And I couldn't straighten things out between us after Josie got fed up with me.'

'Is that what happened?'

'She took up with a man who works in the bank.'

'I couldn't forget her,' Patsy said. 'I thought you wanted her, not me.'

'That shows how the human mind works. What I did didn't please anybody. Not even my mother.'

'She's better now?'

'Yes, thank goodness. For her, the answer was much simpler.'

Patsy shivered again, but it was partly a shiver of relief.

'Are you cold? It hardly seems like summer.' Rob was urging her to her feet. The station was above ground. The roof over the platform sheltered them from the rain but not from the gusting wind.

'We'll get on the next train. I wanted you to know why I did those things. I wanted you to understand that my mother poisoned her mind with hate. Poisoned her own life, and my father's, and by turning to Josie Mackay, I almost helped her poison yours and mine.' He kissed her cheek. 'I'm sorry.'

'Your mother suffered more than Gran.'

'That's why I don't want you to brood about what Vereena's done to your family. If you thirst for vengeance, you might end up like my mother. Your family always seemed so normal compared with mine. Not neurotic and twisted.

'Cassie was the one who was wronged, but she kept her feet flat on the ground. She was practical, knowing exactly where she was heading and why. She continued to enjoy her life. You're like that and I don't want you to change. Forget Vereena, don't let her poison your life. Hope that if she has enough rope, sooner or later she'll hang herself.'

The train stopped against the platform. It was warm inside. Patsy snuggled against him. He was right: she must forget Vereena. But it took her a long time to calm down.

'You've lots of other worries, I'm sure.' Rob had a lopsided smile. 'Worries we can do something about.'

Patsy started then to tell him about Wesley, and soon her troubles were pouring out.

'I didn't know.' Rob was shocked. 'And here I've been going on about—'

'It's a hundred times worse because he's Lucy's husband.'

'I didn't realise you had anything like this to cope with.'

'I can't think ... First, I must find out whether he's made a genuine mistake.' She sighed. 'But I don't think so. There'd have to be many mistakes to show up in the figures like this.'

Beside her, Rob said thoughtfully, 'You must establish exactly what's missing. A physical inventory of what's in the storerooms.'

'Rodney's just done one, so that these figures could be drawn up.'

'Then he could be the one making the mistakes.'

'I think the discrepancies were there before. Grandpa didn't trust either of them. He was talking of moving Wesley. Demoting him.'

'I doubt if Lucy would let you get away with that.'

'But if I don't . . . How can I trust any figures they provide after this?'

'Put somebody else in.'

'Grandpa thought of doing that too!'

'Somebody to act as accountant, who'll report direct to you.'

'They're always late producing any figures, and Wesley said he needed more help.' Patsy sighed again. 'But who? I'd have to be sure Wesley didn't influence him.'

She could see Rob giving it a lot of thought. 'Kenny Hewitt, my clerk?'

In recent months, Rob had been acting regularly as auctioneer. Grandpa had said to her: 'Turnover is growing, we'll give up hiring an auctioneer by the session and take on another full-time assistant. Both he and Rob Parry can switch about, learn to do all the different jobs there. It'll make it easier to run if they're more flexible.' It had worked very well.

Now Rob said: 'Kenny's honest, I can vouch for that. And careful with figures.'

Patsy tried to think. 'Will you have Rodney Spiers? I want to separate father and son. No, on second thoughts, I don't want to saddle you with him.'

Rob pulled a face. 'I'd rather choose another assistant for myself.'

338

'I'll talk to Kenny Hewitt before I leave in the morning. He can come to the factory with me and make another inventory. Shouldn't take him long; Grandpa said there weren't many finished pieces there. Mostly we make to order now.'

The rain had eased off when they got out in Liverpool. Rob's arm was round her waist again as they walked down towards the river. They had a cup of tea from a stall at the pierhead, and then caught the ferry back. By then it was raining again, but they huddled together on the lower deck in the lee of the wind. Patsy was beginning to feel better, more confident that she'd be able to cope with Wesley.

At Woodside, they caught a bus. 'Will you leave the funeral arrangements to your father?'

'No, Rob. You know what Dadda's like. He hates ... Besides, I'd rather see to it myself. I want to get started on what has to be done.'

'Tomorrow morning then, I'll make an appointment for you. The undertakers are relatives of mine, remember. Do you want me to come with you?'

'Yes please.'

Rob turned and kissed her cheek, then put his lips against hers.

She felt closer to him than she'd been for years. 'You were a great comfort when Gran died. I don't know what I'd have done without you then. I always seem to turn to you when I'm troubled.'

He kissed her again, more passionately this time. 'I hope you always will,' he said.

CHAPTER TWENTY-ONE

July 1935

For Patsy, the following day seemed as long as a week and passed in a blur of grief and worry.

She went to Grandpa's office in Caerns Road, meaning to sort and pack up his files. Everything in the house reminded her poignantly of her grandparents. She drove back to the auction room, unable to finish what she'd meant to do.

'Perhaps we should sell his house,' she said to Rob.

'Why don't you and your family live there? Isn't it a bit cramped upstairs for three?'

'Yes, but . . .' She did feel on top of Dadda and Alma. They could do with more space.

'Surely no one would choose to live in Cambridge Place if they didn't have to?'

Patsy thought of the lights that never went out, the awful smells that came from the gasworks, and the frequent trains that thundered through.

'Don't tell me you'd miss the place?' He was teasing her.

'I'd miss the people.'

They were looking out of the auction room window. Several ragged children were going past pushing home-made carts, wooden crates mounted on old pram wheels, on their way to fetch coke from the gasworks because it was cheaper than having it delivered.

'You'd miss the drunks being thrown out of the Railway Hotel after you've gone to bed at night?' His brown eyes were smiling down at her.

'I meant the Donovans from the shop,' she said. They'd gone out of their way to be kind. 'And Alice Smedley. Anyway, Dad won't want to leave.'

'Ask him.'

That evening she did. John said slowly, 'Caerns Road is a lovely house, but not for me and Alma. What about you?'

Alma's plump face turned to her, her double chins quivering. 'Don't take this the wrong way, Patsy. I'd be sorry to see you go, but wouldn't you like a place of your own?'

Patsy sighed. In a way she would, but she couldn't live there. There was too much to remind her.

'It's such a big house for one. The sensible thing would be to sell it. Use the money to expand the business.'

She felt she was making no progress. She was letting herself drift.

'Nonsense,' Rob told her sternly. 'Give yourself a little time.'

Patsy knew that for her, the only way was to make decisions and get on with what faced her. The most important thing she had to do was also the hardest. She'd had to put that off until Kenneth Hewitt brought her the new inventory.

When she compared it with that of the week before, she knew she'd be a fool to put it off any longer. She steeled herself to tackle Wesley. She'd have to appear strong, even though she felt events had knocked her sideways. She went down to the factory without giving him prior warning.

It didn't please her to find he'd already moved into the office Grandpa had kept for his own use. He'd moved Grandpa's things out and furnished it with a Victorian

342

partner's desk and a comfortable carpet. The scent of his cigars was already heavy in the air.

'I was planning to use this office myself,' she said coldly. 'I'd be glad if you'd move back to your old one.'

Wesley was scowling with ill-humour. All the other offices were partitioned off from the factory floor with six-foot-high walls. There was no way of shutting out the noise or the sawdust.

'I've decided I need to spend more time here. Keep a closer eye on what's going on.'

'That won't be necessary, surely?' He looked disconcerted.

'I've arranged for my filing cabinets to come from Caerns Road this afternoon. Please put Grandpa's desk back for me.'

'Patsy, I can run the company for you. There's no need to worry your pretty head about it.' There was an uneasy look in his handsome eyes.

'Grandpa was grooming me to take over. It's come sooner than any of us expected, but I want to do it.'

'Patsy, there's no hurry. You've had a shock.'

'What's that got to do with it?'

He laughed. 'It's not as easy as all that.' His attitude said: the little woman won't understand.

'What's so difficult? Perhaps you'd enlighten me.'

He was wearing a dark suit with a black tie. Dressed for effect, Patsy thought, as she spread out her documents on the desk in front of him.

'Now then, how do you explain the discrepancies in these two inventories?'

'Goods are leaving the factory every day.'

'I know that.'

'Even a few days can make a big difference to the stocks held here.'

'Then show me the purchase orders and van delivery notes. Kenny Hewitt found only these three for that

343

period, and they don't account for the difference. Surely you don't allow goods to leave the factory without any paperwork?'

'Of course not, but sometimes mistakes are made.'

'It's Rodney's job, isn't it, to make them out?'

'Rodney's upset. We're all very upset.'

'But he'd no reason to be upset before Grandpa's accident, and that's when the problems arose.'

'If he's made a mistake, we'll put it right.'

'The van delivery notes for last week,' Patsy said, trying to be patient. 'If there are more, let's get them here now.'

'Wouldn't it be better to leave it? At a time like this, we're all torn in two. Lucy is absolutely pulverised. It's hard for any of us to concentrate on matters like these.'

Wesley's eyes wouldn't meet hers. For the first time since she'd known him, he didn't want to hold centre stage. Rather he looked as though he'd like to melt into the background. She thought of him as an actor, but he wasn't giving a convincing performance of a man who had nothing to hide.

'The books have to be correct, Wesley. This is unforgivable. Can we get Rodney in? I'd like a word with him.'

'He's not here at the moment.'

'Where's he gone?'

'I've sent him out on an errand.'

Patsy felt anger spiral through her. 'To buy flowers for Lucy, I suppose? Or something equally important? It's not good enough.'

She was fulminating. 'I want Kenneth Hewitt to keep the books here in future. He'll be directly responsible to me.'

'What about Rodney? That's his job.' Wesley was affronted.

'He doesn't appear capable of doing it. How do I know how the business is doing if I can't get accurate figures? I'll give him a week's wages in lieu of notice. I don't want him to come back in here.'

'You can't possibly do that, Patsy! I won't stand for it. Lucy will be furious.'

'You don't understand, Wesley. *I'm* furious. In your position, you should have checked these figures. You should have prevented this. What were you thinking of?'

'You don't realise how much I have to do. I'm kept very busy.'

'It's too much for you? Well, I've already eased your burden. In future, Kenneth Hewitt will keep the books and make sure everything's accounted for.'

'But you're undermining my authority as manager. I won't have it.' Wesley was blustering now, throwing his arms about.

'As *factory* manager, Wesley. I'm in overall charge.'

'You're taking too much on yourself.' His handsome face had flushed brick-red.

'This is what my grandfather would be doing if he was still alive. We discussed it before—'

'Your grandfather owned this business, Patsy. You're forgetting that you own only half. Lucy is entitled to an equal say in this.' Wesley was glowering at her from the other side of the desk.

'Lucy's never taken any interest . . .'

'She will in future, I promise you.'

'It would be unreasonable to object to a full enquiry. We need to find out exactly where all this furniture has gone. It represents a goodly part of our profit for last year. I want you to start on that immediately.'

'I've already told you, if there's a mistake, it can be sorted, it won't take long. There's no need to take it all to heart like this.'

'I'll be in tomorrow. I'll be delighted if you can explain it to me then.'

Patsy collected all the files and stalked out. In future there would be no pretence of friendship between her and Wesley.

* * *

Patsy sat outside in her car for five minutes, feeling thoroughly churned up, afraid she hadn't got the better of Wesley. She wasn't looking forward to working with him every day, but she'd have to if she was to control what was going on in the factory.

She was facing another difficult task now. She needed to tell Lucy about it before Wesley did. After all, Lucy owned the other half of the business. Patsy drove slowly down to the nursing home. Lucy was lying back against the pillows, her bright blonde hair glinting in the sunlight that streamed into her room. There was no sign of the twins.

Patsy tried to appear calmer than she was. 'How are you all?'

There was a note of complaint in Lucy's voice. 'Had a wakeful night with the babies. They've taken them away so I can rest now.'

'Couldn't they have taken them away in the night?'

'They do every night, but I can hear mine in the nursery. I know their cries already.' Lucy gave her a wan smile.

'Such a terrible thing. Poor Nanna and Gramps being killed like that. I can't help thinking of them. Takes away all the joy of having the twins.'

Patsy nodded. 'Look, there are things we need to talk about . . .'

'Yes.' Lucy pulled herself lazily up the bed, revealing more of her lacy nightgown. 'The house in Caerns Road – who owns that now?'

'Both wills are quite straightforward. When they're proved, we'll own everything between us. Straight down the middle.'

'So half that house will be mine?'

'Yes.'

'Then I'd like to live there, Patsy.'

Patsy felt taken aback. 'But you have a lovely house in Templemore Road. You've just refurbished it in grand style. I didn't think you'd want to move.'

'Wesley thinks Caerns Road would suit us better. It's larger and our family's growing, after all. Then there's Mrs Judd. I'll need more help in the house; twins bring a lot of work.'

Patsy took a deep breath and told herself to stay calm. Wesley wanted the best of everything for himself.

'But you've spent so much on Templemore Road. You've made it luxurious.'

'We can take the furniture, and it would save us paying rent.'

'It wouldn't, Lucy. The Caerns Road house is a business asset. You'd be charged the market rent in the way Dad and I are on the Cambridge Place flat.'

She laughed. 'You know I don't understand all the ins and outs of business. You wouldn't want the house. Dadda and Alma wouldn't fit in with the neighbours.'

'I was thinking of selling it, and using the capital in the business.'

'I grew up there, Patsy. I think of it as home. You do understand?'

Patsy met her sister's imploring gaze. Lucy had as much right to decide what happened to the house as she had, and she was well practised at getting what she wanted.

'Wesley and I can move in, then?'

'I suppose so, if you're that keen.'

'I know you're happy in Cambridge Place, otherwise I wouldn't ask. Wesley thinks you'd find it more convenient if you moved your office there too. I never could see the point of having offices in Caerns Road.'

'I'm planning to move that to the factory. Use Grandpa's old office there.'

'Oh?' Her sister's violet eyes surveyed her seriously. 'I'm not sure that Wesley would think that a good idea.'

'He doesn't. I've already told him. We had a row.'

'With Wesley? I hope you haven't upset him.'

'I have. I've sacked Rodney. Given him a week's wages in lieu of notice.'

'Patsy, you can't do that! I won't have it. He'll want to come back and live with us.' Lucy's beautiful face was taut with anger.

'Things have gone missing from the factory.' Patsy explained what had been happening. 'Grandpa was very upset.'

'But sack Rodney! No . . .'

'If it had been anybody but relatives of yours . . .'

'You're not saying . . .? That Wesley and Rodney . . .? Don't be silly!'

'I haven't put it like that to Wesley. He's calling it a simple mistake.'

'I should think so.'

'Grandpa thought it was fraud. Did it never occur to you that Wesley was spending more than his salary? On your house in Templemore Road, for instance?'

'And that's enough to convict him?' Lucy's violet eyes were blazing now. 'If you must know, his Aunt Ida died and left him a legacy.'

That jolted Patsy's confidence. 'He told you that?'

'Yes. You've no right to accuse him of theft!'

'I haven't. There are discrepancies in the books that I've asked him to explain. I've told him I want a full enquiry. Our profit for last year is much reduced. As co-owner you need to know these things.'

'There'll be some simple explanation. Wesley would never do anything wrong, I know he wouldn't.'

'I hope you're right.'

Lucy was blinking away her tears. 'I don't know how you can think such a thing of Wesley. He's such a lovely person.'

Patsy was straining her ears. Could she hear his voice down the corridor? A moment later, Wesley appeared in the doorway with another bunch of roses. The smile on his face slipped when he saw her.

Patsy got to her feet. 'I came to tell Lucy what had happened,' she said.

'Trying to get your story in first.' It was almost a snarl. He was pulling a chair close to Lucy's bed. Kissing her hand, running his fingers up her arm.

'Lucy, darling, when it comes to the business, your say in how it's run is exactly equal to Patsy's. I'm sure you don't want Rodney sacked. I think you ought to make a stand on that.'

'I already have.' She put up her face to be kissed. 'I've told Patsy that Rodney must stay. After all, it's a family business, Patsy.'

Patsy stumbled out to her car, aware that for her, running the business was going to be a lot more difficult than it had been for Harold. Neither she nor Grandpa had foreseen that Wesley might use Lucy in this way.

To be sure of getting her own way, Patsy knew she needed fifty-one per cent of the business against Lucy's forty-nine. And there was no way she could have that now.

The double funeral had loomed over Patsy for days. She found it more painful than she'd expected. The church had been packed. Harold Ingram had been popular with his employees and many had come to pay their last respects. Patsy found them hard to recognise in their best suits and hard bowler hats.

She shivered now, as she walked out to the grave with her father on one side and Robert Parry on the other, each offering sympathy and support. Despite their presence, she felt very much alone and on her own, knowing that the livelihoods of all these people depended on her. She would have to run Grandpa's company from now on. No longer Grandpa's – hers and Lucy's.

The sky was heavy with cloud. Crows cawed mournfully from the surrounding trees. Wesley Spiers stood facing her on the other side of the grave, carefully averting his gaze from hers. He looked every inch a family mourner, with his funereal tie and his black trilby clasped piously across his chest.

The awful, awful moment came. She had to watch first Grandpa's coffin and then Nanna's being lowered into the gaping hole.

If he could, Grandpa would be saying: 'Come on, you know you can cope. Haven't I taught you everything I know?'

And Gran, if she was up there watching, would add: 'You'll manage fine, Patsy. The women of our family always do.' It didn't stop Patsy feeling she still needed their help.

Lucy was still in the nursing home, and could not come. Patsy had been in to see her this morning and she'd cried into a lacy handkerchief. Her friend Madge was expected to keep her company on this sad afternoon.

Patsy used the company van to take all the filing cabinets from Caerns Road to the factory. Dadda had told her that Wesley had moved his own things out of Grandpa's office with very bad grace.

When she asked Wesley about the missing furniture, he said he was still looking into the problem. She was growing more certain that he was defrauding the company.

'Such a lot has disappeared,' she said to Dadda and Alma over supper. 'In the last month, the figures for Regency dining chairs leaving the factory are twelve short of the number made.'

'Two sets of six?'

'And two large dining tables to go with them. We're missing Pembroke tables, desks and davenports. It's blatant. Nobody could expect all that to go unnoticed. The materials have been bought and paid for. The man hours have been worked . . .'

If Wesley hadn't sold them for the benefit of his private account, she didn't know what had happened to them.

'Will you keep watch for me? You're around the factory all the time.'

'We'll keep a running count on finished pieces, won't we, John?' Alma said. 'I'll keep a pad in my apron pocket and count them when I take the tea round.'

'Those taken to the storeroom particularly,' Patsy said.

'It's kept locked.'

'I'll get you a key. Just don't let Wesley see you use it.'

She was afraid more things would go. 'He thought an old man wouldn't notice,' she said bitterly. 'And he expects me to be as easy to fool as Lucy.'

Wesley quibbled about the rent she wanted to charge for the Caerns Road house, but eventually they agreed a compromise.

'I suppose you'll want to sell the furniture that's there?' he asked. 'Lucy would like to have a few things.'

'Mementoes,' Lucy added. 'We must keep a few things. Both of us.'

Patsy arranged to meet them at the house one afternoon. It seemed empty without her grandparents, though Mrs Judd provided them with tea and cake.

'I'd like the six still-life paintings that hang on the stairs,' Lucy decided, 'and Nanna's diamond ring.'

'And the antique rugs,' Wesley said. 'I love the Kazak, don't you?'

'Hideous,' Lucy giggled. 'But expensive.'

Patsy chose to keep the davenport for herself. She'd always admired its pretty lines. It was only when she saw it in her bedroom at Cambridge Place that she realised it was a memento of Freda; of Vereena's scheming ways and Gran's sudden end. Things she didn't want to be reminded of. She moved it out to the living room, and went back to choose again. She picked out Mildred's triple row of pearls. She'd seldom seen her without them embellishing the neckline of her dress.

'Cultured,' Lucy said drily when she told her. 'You'd be better keeping the sapphire earrings, they're more valuable.'

'She seldom wore them. Less of a memento.'

Patsy asked Robert to bring the delivery van and help her sort out what was left in the house. They disposed of it between the shops and the auction room.

The next time she went to see Lucy in Templemore Road, she had books of wallpaper patterns and samples of curtain material spread across her dining table.

'What do you think of this for the nursery? We're working out colour schemes for the Caerns Road house.'

'You'll have it looking grander than it's ever been.'

'Wesley's arranging for the painters and decorators to go in next week,' Lucy said contentedly.

The problem of the factory accounts dragged on. When Patsy told Wesley that she meant to hand them over to the auditors, he asked for a little more time to sort them out. She was very much afraid he wouldn't in the end, and she'd have to write the loss off.

As the weeks passed, Patsy wondered whether Wesley's show of love for Lucy was an act he put on to achieve his own ends. It seemed too theatrical. But Lucy seemed as much in love with him as ever, and very happy with her home and family.

Patsy was finding him impossible to work with. He was too ready to spend money, with no clear idea about getting a return on it. She was careful to give him no grounds to complain about the way she treated him. She discussed with him what they should make in the factory over the next six months.

She wanted to add a music canterbury to their list, and had asked the draughtsman to work on the design. Apart from that she thought they should stay with the designs that had proved popular in the past.

It was Wesley's job to work out the materials needed, and to order them. She asked to see the orders before they went out and did her own sums as a check that he was right.

Wesley tried to bypass her and send them out without her seeing them. Miss Cropper, who did most of the office work, took them out of the mail to show her. She was furious when she found Wesley was ordering more wood than was needed. It caused them to have another confrontation.

Then her father told her that Wesley had cancelled the work the draughtsman was doing on the canterbury and asked him to concentrate instead on a design for a long-case clock.

Patsy shot to his office, infuriated. He was about to leave but she waved him back to his desk.

'I'm making the decisions about what we'll make now, not you. Grandpa didn't think it a good idea to make longcase clocks, and neither do I.'

'Don't shout.' Wesley was peevish. 'Half the workforce can hear you here.'

'Come to my office then.' She shut the door quietly behind them and waved him to a seat.

He turned on her. 'As the manager, surely I have some say in what's made?'

'Of course. If you have suggestions, by all means make them, but you're not to go ahead like this without even mentioning it to me.'

'Lucy thinks a clock would be an excellent thing to make. Everybody likes grandfather clocks.'

'Lucy's opinion would be better confined to her hats and her babies.'

'Now hang on—'

'Lucy will back you up whatever it is you want. We're in

353

this to make money, Wesley. That's what business is about. Not indulging our own interests.

'The only way we'll be making clock cases is to a specific order from a clock manufacturer. You can give up the idea of designing one yourself.'

'You don't allow me to do anything.' She could see that Wesley's dander was up now. 'I'm supposed to be the manager, but I can't even reorder toilet paper without referring it to you.'

'That's right, I want to see all the orders going out. You wouldn't dare to act in this high-handed manner if Grandpa were here.'

She was trembling when he left her. In Grandpa's time, there had been a pleasant working atmosphere. What Wesley was doing was turning her into a sharp-tongued shrew.

Two days later, she was crossing the factory floor when she received another shock. Vereena, looking older and much plumper in a green blouse and skirt, went into Wesley's office with some files on her arm.

Patsy followed, and found that a table had recently been moved in. Vereena was pulling up a chair to sit down.

'What are you doing here?' Patsy was so enraged she could hardly get her words out.

'I've been given my old job back,' she said, her eyes challenging Patsy. 'Accounts clerk.'

'Who says so?' Patsy demanded. The need she'd felt for revenge against Vereena was white-hot again.

'Wesley – Mr Spiers – said the job was mine if I wanted it.'

'I'm afraid not. Somebody else is doing that job already.'

Patsy could feel her hackles rising further. She'd brought Kenny Hewitt here to do it, and she wasn't going to let Wesley push him out. She had to have a workforce she could trust, and she couldn't trust Vereena.

'I just have to have a job.' Vereena's lip was quivering. 'I need the money.'

'I'm sorry, Vereena. There's no job for you in Mersey Antiques. There never will be.'

'But Wesley said there was.' Vereena was indignant.

Patsy almost let fly. She had to keep a tight hold on her tongue. 'Please don't argue. Wesley has no right to hire staff without my knowledge. When did you start?'

'This morning.'

'Get your coat and come with me. Mr Hewitt can pay you for your morning's work. Then I want you to leave.'

Patsy left her with Kenny and went back to her office, knowing that this would cause another argument with Wesley. He was deliberately seeking ways to rile her.

She sat waiting, filled with dread, wondering if she'd manage to find the strength to stand up to him. She heard his footsteps, rapid and heavy, coming to her door. She took a deep breath and steeled herself to face him. When she saw Vereena following him in, Patsy knew it was going to be two against one.

'Patsy, do try to be reasonable. We want to expand the business, don't we?'

'Yes.'

'We need another clerk here. We're all pressurised now.'

'No, Wesley. Kenny Hewitt is doing all the accounting work now. I'll decide when he needs help.'

He flushed with indignation. 'Only last week you told me to hire new staff.'

'An extra cabinet-maker is what I said, as you very well know. There's no job for Vereena.'

Wesley was blustering, waving his arms about. 'She's done the job before. She worked for your grandfather. I know her—'

'So do I, Wesley, and a good deal better than you do.'
She hadn't asked either of them to sit, and Vereena's dark
eyes, full of the bitter intensity she remembered so well,
were burning down at her.

'I asked you to leave, Vereena, but since you haven't,
I'll tell you why I don't want you working here.'

Her heart was pounding, and she took another deep
breath. 'I know all about your liaison with my grandfather. I know how you hid your mother's suicide note in
the davenport in an attempt to collect her insurance
money. I know you accused my grandmother of murder,
causing her to have a heart attack.'

Vereena's mouth fell open. She choked: 'I don't know
what you're talking about.'

Patsy didn't stop. 'I know too much, Vereena. I won't
have you anywhere near me, or this business. Not ever.'

She thought for an awful moment that Vereena was
raising her hand to clout her in the way she used to when
she was tiny and in her care.

Hate flashed from Vereena's eyes. 'You're getting too
big for your boots, miss.'

'Much too big. I can't even hire a clerk for the office
now,' Wesley griped. 'I don't know why you need a
manager.'

'To be frank, I don't. If you went too, I'd be delighted. I
own half this business and I'm not happy with what you're
trying to do to it.'

She could see Wesley quivering with rage. 'Yes, but as
you say, only half. Lucy—'

'Lucy's never taken the slightest interest in what goes
on here, and you know it. All she wants is the money it
makes. Unless you stop interfering, Wesley, it won't make
money. I want you to understand, once and for all, that
I'm running this business. Now go, both of you, and let me
get on with it.'

But it wasn't that simple. When they'd gone, Patsy put

356

her head in her hands. She felt like crying. She hated these rows, hated having to stand up to Wesley, but if she didn't, he'd be taking over. She'd be working here with as much say in management as the average accounts clerk. This wasn't how Grandpa had meant it to be.

It was a long time before she felt calm again.

CHAPTER TWENTY-TWO

Vereena slammed the factory door and went slowly out into the rain-swept street. It was one of those dull, dark days before Christmas. No one else was waiting at the bus stop, which must mean she'd just missed one.

She was boiling with rage. How dare Patsy pull the rug from under her just when she'd thought she'd found a job? She felt like crying. It was a huge disappointment. She had to have a job. She was feeling desperate about money.

She'd thought her future was secure with Harold. He was a silly old man who liked to think he was the world's greatest lover, a bit of a bore really, but he'd paid all her living expenses and been reasonably generous with gifts and money for clothes.

She'd grown used to the comfort of the house he'd found for her in Clifton Road. It was large and gracious, and Harold had furnished it lavishly. But now she was months behind with the rent.

A hundred years ago, Clifton Road had been a fashionable address. It had been built for the upper middle classes, but once the gasworks had been built in Argyle Street South they brought noise and nuisance and nose-holding odours to the area. The well-to-do had moved west into Oxton, leaving a few gracious houses in a central position, where Harold needn't worry about meeting people who knew him.

If only he hadn't died! The income she'd come to rely

on was gone. She hadn't received a penny since his death except what she'd been able to raise by her own efforts.

She'd been hoping for a legacy in his will. She surely deserved that. She'd devoted years of her life to giving him a good time, and he'd had so much that the twins would hardly notice a few thousand. But she'd heard from Wesley that his estate had been settled; that there had been only one small bequest, to Mrs Judd.

She'd found it hard to accept that Harold had given no thought to her needs. She'd expected better than that from him. She felt he'd let her down.

She huddled back against the wall to wait, buttoning up her coat. It strained uncomfortably across her abdomen, although she'd already moved the buttons nearer the edge. She was forty-six; it was impossible not to put on weight at her age. Her face had grown flabby, she was losing her looks, and her clothes were no longer smart.

She tried to snuggle down into the huge collar of beige beaver fur standing up around her shoulders, but it was damp against her cheek. She could see moisture beading on it.

Her tiny pillbox hat offered no protection against the rain. It was covered with veiling that was tearing into holes. Her outfit had once been high fashion; now everything she had looked worn and dated.

Was this her bus coming out of the depot? She peered up to see the number, and cold rain blew into her face. She was shivering as she found a seat. It was damp from a previous passenger. What was she going to do now?

This morning she'd been down to her last half a crown, but she thought she'd be all right. Wesley had promised her her old job back at Mersey Antiques. But now Patsy Gripper had shown her the door, and been none too polite either, the little upstart. Vereena didn't know where she found the nerve to say such things to her.

And now, although she'd given her a ten-shilling note,

that and her half a crown were all she had between her and starvation. Vereena was feeling obsessed about her lack of money.

When she'd heard about Harold's death, her first idea had been to take in lodgers. She had a large and pleasant house with six bedrooms. Eight if she counted those in the attics meant for servants. The problem was that only the two biggest bedrooms had been furnished.

She'd advertised in the *Birkenhead News* for a professional man, hoping he'd prove to be more than a lodger once he'd got to know her.

She chose carefully, vetting those who came to see the room. After Harold, she wanted someone she could really care about. She chose George Chesters, a handsome widower the same age as herself. He told her he worked in the office at Cammell Laird, giving the impression he was in a position of importance there.

It didn't take her long to find out that he drank. She approved at first; she liked a man who knew how to enjoy himself. But George turned out to be an alcoholic and was frequently in a state that prevented him working at all. When his rent was due he never had money to pay. When she realised he was battening on her, she'd thrown him out.

By then, she'd already asked Robert Parry to put a pretty antique sewing table that Harold had given her into one of his monthly auctions. She didn't sew so she wouldn't miss it. With the money, she was able to bid for plain beds and wardrobes to furnish three more of her bedrooms.

With four lodgers, Vereena thought she might be able to survive, but there'd been an argument about meals they thought she'd agreed to provide.

One man had gone for her with a knife and she'd had to send for the police. They'd advised her to take in only women lodgers, but by then she'd gone off the idea altogether.

And all the time, she'd had to keep going back to Robert Parry to sell off her good furniture, bit by bit. He must know about her problem but he pretended otherwise, always joking about something else. Not that it mattered now. She wouldn't need to see him again; she'd nothing much left that was worth selling.

The trouble was, she couldn't afford the rent on the house Harold had found for her. It was too big and too expensive. She had to get money from somewhere. Wesley had money and threw it around, but not in her direction. He was rather mean when it came to that.

She had to have a job. And not just any job. She'd found work in Woolworth's, but it hadn't paid enough for her needs. Hadn't lasted long, either; they'd given her her cards, just because she'd taken a few chocolates. It wasn't as though anything cost more than sixpence there.

The bus was nearing Argyle Street and would turn towards Woodside. She got off. There was no sign of a bus coming the other way. She decided to walk instead of waiting. If only she could get back into teaching, but too long had elapsed since she'd trained, and the schools were staffed by old maids.

Vereena felt at the end of her tether. Everything looked black. What sort of a Christmas was she going to have this year, alone and without money? For the first time she thought of her mother and understood what might have driven her to commit suicide. Now it seemed a reasonable way out.

Patsy knew she'd delivered a blow to Vereena's hopes but it gave her no satisfaction. When she felt more in control of herself, she went to Caerns Road to see Lucy. She wanted, above everything else, to bring this war with Wesley to an end. She felt she couldn't stand it any longer. It was wearing her out.

362

The house had been repainted on the outside, and there was fresh white gravel on the path and a lot of new shrubs in the front garden. The old monkey puzzle tree had grown larger over the years. It really looked majestic now.

Mrs Judd opened the door looking unfamiliar in a smart striped uniform with an organdie cap. In Nanna's day she'd always worn a white apron over her own dresses.

Looking up the hall, Patsy hardly recognised the house. It had been transformed, with lighter wallpaper and a new pale-beige carpet that spread everywhere. The antique rugs she remembered had been laid on top. Her sister was in the sitting room, lying on a *chaise-longue*.

'Lovely to see you.' Lucy put aside the magazine she'd been reading and swung her feet to the carpet. 'I've just finished decorating the tree in the nursery. Fay is thrilled, it looks lovely. Come up and see it.'

'Not just now, Lucy. I—'

'I thought I'd have a little rest before I started putting up the holly and mistletoe.' Lucy's giggle came bubbling out. Patsy marvelled at the comfortable life she led.

'I love this old house and everything in it. To me, coming back here is like coming home. I never want to live anywhere else. I'm dying to show you what we've done. Doesn't it look wonderful? We've put it back into period. All eighteen sixty or earlier.'

'The carpets look very modern to me. Fitted carpets were not—'

'We have to have some modern comfort.'

Patsy flung herself into a Georgian armchair, unable to contain her worries any longer.

'Lucy, you've got to listen to me first. I can't run the business this way. Wesley's going out of his way to make things ten times harder than they need be.'

She heard Lucy's gasp of surprise. 'Of course he isn't . . .'

'He ignores my decisions, he goes behind my back to set up systems of his own.'

363

'He's only trying to help . . .'

'I ask the staff to do one thing, and he tells them to do something quite different.'

'Wesley wants to expand the business. He thinks it has potential.'

'All my energy is spent on fighting him instead of getting on with the work.'

'Then don't fight him.' Lucy's eyes were sparking anger. Patsy knew she'd ruffled her twin now.

'Grandpa taught me to run the business his way, you know that. If you want it to go on earning money you've got to stop backing Wesley's judgement against mine. He's not going about things the right way.'

'Wesley wants to make money too. He wants what you want. He's on your side.'

'No, Lucy, on your side, perhaps, but not mine. He doesn't like me.'

Lucy clucked with impatience. 'Oh, he does. He was saying only the other day how much he admires the way you work, day in and day out.'

'I'm not surprised at that, because he's off out all the time. Never tells me where he's going. He might do better if he spent more time at his desk.'

'Wesley does a little dealing on his own account, you've always known that. He needs to, Patsy, to earn sufficient income for us.'

Patsy could feel her exasperation mounting. The last thing she wanted was to have another row with her sister. She burst out: 'If he did that full-time, it would suit me very well.'

'You're being nasty now.'

'I mean it. He's interfering in a thousand ways. I have to watch him like a hawk, otherwise he does things he knows I don't want. He spends company money unnecessarily, and when I object he says it's what you want and you have an equal right. You know that isn't what Grandpa intended.'

'Patsy! Why can't you get on with him? My two nearest and dearest, and you fight like cat and dog.'

'We can't, things are going from bad to worse. You've got to tell Wesley to stand back. I have to have full control of the factory. Grandpa would never have allowed him to countermand my decisions.'

'I'm sure he doesn't. You're wrong about him. Wesley wouldn't do anything to harm our interests. After all, they're his interests too.'

Patsy was afraid it was no good appealing to Lucy, but she tried once more.

'Lucy, you and I have got to pull together. It's our business. He's trying to drive a wedge between us.'

'Don't be silly, Patsy,' she laughed. 'I don't believe you.'

Mrs Judd came to the door. 'Will Patsy be staying for lunch? It's the fish pie you like so much and it'll be ready in ten minutes. There'll be plenty.'

Lucy asked, 'Will you?'

'Will Wesley be coming home?'

'No.'

That surprised Patsy because Wesley was often missing from the factory over lunchtime.

'You'll stay then?' There was no welcome on Lucy's face.

'No thank you. Another time.'

Lucy faced her defiantly. 'Wesley thinks it might be better if we split the business. I thought he was going a bit over the top, but clearly . . .' She shook her head numbly.

'What do you mean?'

'You keep the shops and the auction room. I have the factory – and this house.'

Patsy felt the blood drain from her face. It was a moment before she could speak.

'Wesley's put you up to this. It's his idea. This way he'll be able to run the factory.' She felt eaten up with bitterness.

365

'He asked you to put it to me, didn't he?'

'What if he did? If you can't get on, it's a way out. What do you say?'

Patsy turned on her heel and strode out of the house without another word.

Patsy headed home. She needed peace to think this out. Her flat over the old shop could only be reached by going through what was now the reception office for the auction room. Rob was there alone.

On the spur of the moment she said: 'Can you come upstairs? I've got to talk to somebody.'

His eyes met hers. 'I thought it strange, you coming home at this time. I'll call one of the men to mind the shop.'

She sat by the window in the living room, resting her throbbing head against the glass. Life was going on below her in Cambridge Place. Ordinary life, where people were content to get on with each other.

'More trouble at the factory?' Rob asked quietly from behind her.

'Yes, and trouble with Lucy too. D'you know what she's just suggested? That we split the business! She wants the factory and Grandpa's house; I'm to have this place and the two shops. I can't believe it's come to this.'

Rob was frowning, thinking it out. 'Lucy'll be taking the lion's share.'

'I know that. It's Wesley's idea, of course. And it would get him off my back once and for all. I can't go on like this, full of suspicion, poking round the factory, searching for ways to stop him cheating us.'

'If you have proof you should go to the police.'

'And what would Lucy say to that? It's put me in a terrible position.'

'You don't want to split it?'

'I'm beginning to hate the place, but I think it would be better – and fairer – to keep the business together.'

In a gesture of desperation, Patsy pushed her blonde hair off her forehead. 'But it isn't making money. I could understand him wanting it if it was. Month by month the figures are worse than they were last year. We're heading for a loss on the factory. So in that way, it makes sense to agree and get him off my back. But it sticks in my gullet to give Wesley what he wants.'

'Then you've got to fight back.'

'I'm fighting like an alley cat, Rob. But he's getting away with it. I'm not stopping him. Each month the figures are down, so whatever he's doing, it's still going on. I feel desperate.'

She felt his arms go round her and pull her close. She wished she could forget the outside world, give herself up to this comfort.

She felt his lips on hers. 'Patsy, I know this isn't the best time to tell you, but I want you to know I love you.'

It brought tears rushing to her eyes.

'Hey,' he whispered. 'I thought you'd like that. I hoped it would comfort you.'

'It does, Rob. It does. It's just that . . .'

'You're too fraught with problems to think of anything else?'

'Something like that.' She blew her nose. 'I'm sorry. You know how I feel about you. Always have, but right now . . .'

She laughed, looking up at him through a blur of tears. 'Not very romantic, am I? Oh, Rob, you and me. It's what I always wanted. Really it is.'

'Isn't the business what you wanted?'

She nodded slowly. 'Of course, but I need you too. The business by itself . . . Well, people are more important. You're more important to me.'

She'd longed all these years to hear him say he loved her. She should be feeling flurries of excitement running up and down her spine. Instead she felt numb.

He gave her another hug. 'We ought to get married, have a place of our own. If we were together, I'd be able to help you more. You'd be able to relax.'

Patsy laid her cheek against his neck and clung tightly to him. 'You're not proposing?'

'Course I am. But you're too fraught to think about it properly. You need to settle other things first.'

'What am I going to do, Rob?' She blew her nose again.

'I hate to see you like this. I wish there was more I could do. You need to get away from it. Have a break. It's driving you into the ground.'

'I'm almost afraid to turn my back, never mind take a break.'

'You'll be a nervous wreck if you go on like this. Let me take you out tonight.'

'Lucy won't listen to me. She thinks the sun shines out of him. If I agree to this split, I think the way things are going, Wesley could lose all Lucy's money for her.'

She felt another hot flush of anger. 'I don't think Wesley knows what he's doing. You should have seen how they did up the house in Templemore Road. It was rented on a month-to-month basis, but they turned it into a palace. Then they ditched that to start over again on Caerns Road.'

He kissed her again. 'Come on, Patsy. What about the pictures tonight? Take your mind off all this.'

That pulled her up. 'Thanks, I'd like that. What's on?'

'Gary Cooper.'

'Should be good.'

But Patsy couldn't lose herself in the story. Even Gary Cooper couldn't take her mind away from her troubles.

The evening left her feeling closer to Rob, and warmed by his love. She wasn't alone any longer, but the problems caused by Wesley wouldn't go away.

Rodney Spiers was disgruntled; he felt generally uneasy about the way things were going. He was sitting in his father's office, keeping his voice low because they didn't want to be overheard.

'I don't like that Vereena woman. What made you ask her round for lunch at your place last Sunday?'

'She's Lucy's aunt. She wants to see the babies.'

'The only thing she wants is a free hand-out. She's nothing but a hanger-on.'

Wesley laughed. 'No, Vereena's all right.'

Rodney had seen her preening at his father. 'She fancies you. You don't want Lucy to notice, do you?'

Vereena wouldn't get him, of course. Dad liked them young and she was a raddled old hag. She couldn't measure up against Lucy, for goodness' sake. Why would Dad want her? 'She'll cause trouble.'

'I rather like her.'

'You never will see sense. Another thing, I'm sick of this job.'

Rodney felt that the net was tightening round them. He didn't think they'd survive Patsy's scrutiny for much longer. He was afraid the whole thing was about to blow up in his face.

'I've got to have you here,' Wesley told him crossly. 'Somebody has to watch my back.'

Rodney sniffed. It was almost as though he expected Patsy to shove a knife in it. She was making them both nervous.

'She's like a bloodhound, sniffing round all the time.'

He knew his dad was impatient to get his hands on more money, and Patsy was slowing him down. Threatening to upset the whole applecart.

'I think we should back out, Dad,' he'd told him. 'Let Patsy run the place.'

'What? After old Harold died like that? Such a stroke of luck for me. I'm in a much stronger position now.'

'I know your plan was to have control of the company, but you'll never get the shops or the auction room.'

'I've got Patsy fighting tooth and nail to kick me out of the factory.'

'You aren't making the place pay. That's the crux of it. Better if you let Patsy make the money. She'll give Lucy her share. All above board then. It can run for ever. We can do our own thing.'

Dad couldn't see it. 'Nonsense! If that girl can make it pay, so can I. Probably better.'

Rodney sighed. Poor Dad, he had too high an opinion of himself. He couldn't see his own limitations, couldn't understand that running the company was beyond his capabilities. He was unable to control money. He had to spend and spend and was always in urgent need of more. He was taking too much profit out. Left to his dad, Rodney was sure the whole thing would go down the pan. And fast.

For his own part, he was much more careful. His father was paying for his help and he was putting the money in the bank. He kept a suitcase at the ready, so he could do a quick flit if he had to. He couldn't see how this could drag on much longer. A few more months at the most.

Book Five
Christmas 1935

CHAPTER TWENTY-THREE

Vereena felt more and more restless as Christmas approached. She couldn't keep away from the shops on her doorstep though she had no money to spend. Turkeys and geese hung in their feathers outside butchers' shops. Her mouth watered just to see the delicacies in the grocers, and the streets rang with Christmas music.

She knew that the following day, Robert Parry would be holding his last auction before Christmas. She was down to her last two pounds and would have to have money from somewhere to survive over the holiday.

She looked round her home. She'd already sold everything she knew to be of value. The silver had gone and the antique furniture, but there must be something else on which she could raise a few shillings.

The fire irons? Big and heavy and old, but made of steel. She lifted the poker. Very heavy. Perhaps the jug and plate were worth more? She didn't much care for them, but Harold had brought them and set them out on her mantelpiece, so they might be worth something. She wrapped them carefully in newspaper and took them round to Mersey Antiques.

'Liverpool pottery,' Robert Parry told her.

'Are they worth anything?'

'Yes, highly sought after.'

Vereena felt relief. 'Really?'

He was smiling at her. 'Yes, really.'

Previously when she'd entered articles in an auction,

she hadn't come to see them sold. Patsy Gripper was usually here on sale days and she didn't want to come face to face with her. Other people she knew came just to pass an hour or so. Nosy-parkers looking to see what people were buying and selling.

This time Vereena couldn't keep away. She had nothing else to do and a lot depended on what her jug and plate made. She found them in the catalogue listed as a Liverpool creamware jug, *circa* 1800. Transfer-printed in black with a three-masted ship enhanced with yellow enamel. And a Liverpool plate, *circa* 1790 decorated with flowering branches. They were much older than she'd thought.

She sat quietly at the back, listening to the bidding going up, fizzing with excitement and hardly able to believe that the man a few rows in front of her was willing to part with thirty pounds for them.

Her luck had changed. She'd buy a few comforts for Christmas. She felt more on top of things and could look to the future again. The money she had now would buy time to sort herself out.

She knew she'd have to wait until tomorrow to collect her money from Robert Parry, but now she could spend what she had left on provisions. She ordered more coal and felt that at last she was thinking clearly again.

She was very fond of the house, it was easily the most comfortable she'd ever lived in. But she hadn't been able to pay the rent since Harold had died, and now she owed so much that the rent man was turning nasty.

He'd warned her at the end of last month that she'd have to pay a full month's rent as well as some of her arrears this time, or the bailiffs would be sent in. The agent had followed that up with a letter setting out what she owed. Her heart turned over every time she thought of it.

The rent was twenty-two shillings and sixpence a week, and she owed so much that it would take almost all she'd get from the jug and plate. She couldn't possibly pay.

She'd have to pack her things and leave one night without telling anybody. If she didn't, she'd be thrown out and the bailiffs would sell off the rest of her stuff. Even though she'd auctioned the best, what remained was worth something. The carpet in the sitting room was a good one. Better to get another place organised. Take her things and go in her own time.

She'd start looking for somewhere cheaper. Perhaps rooms, or if she moved back to the streets between the railway lines, where property was old and cheap, she could afford a whole house. With her own things, she could make herself comfortable.

The following day, as she collected her cheque from Mersey Antiques and then headed towards the bank to cash it, she looked round to see if there were any 'to let' signs.

She paused at the bottom of Jackson Street, looking up to the house where once she'd lived with Bernie. The front door was open, there was a woman on the step. Talking to . . . Surely it couldn't be . . .?

When the man turned and started to walk towards her, she knew it was Bernie. Older and a little stouter. Affluent-looking in a belted camel overcoat and smart trilby. Bernie, her husband, had always had a wonderful smile. It was lighting up his face now. He'd recognised her and was hurrying towards her.

'Vee? I can't believe it's you!' She felt his arms go round her in an affectionate hug.

'I've just been to our old house to ask about you. They'd never heard of you. Said they'd been living there for years. I thought it was hopeless, then I turn round and see you.'

'It's me all right.' Vereena hadn't realised until now how lonely she'd felt these last few months.

'Come and have a drink at the Railway, I'm dying to hear all the news.' He took her arm, hurried her back the way she'd come.

'You've made it on the stage, Bernie. Done well.'

'Done wonderfully well.'

They went into the private bar, and she asked for gin and orange. Alice Smedley was there, drinking in the middle of the day, looking a real slut now. But she greeted them like long-lost friends.

'You're quite famous now, Bernie. Read about you in the papers sometimes. How about buying me a drink?'

'I'll get her one to shut her up,' he'd whispered to Vereena as he got up.

When he came back, Vereena said: 'I've read reviews of your show too. In the *Echo*, not so long ago. They said you and Polly were another Anne Zeigler and Webster Booth.'

'Last month at the Empire. Yes, somebody up there's looking after me.'

Vereena didn't tell him that that was the last thing she could say. She couldn't take her eyes off him. He'd filled out with good living. It suited him. She thought perhaps this was her second stroke of luck and saw him as a future meal ticket. Perhaps it wouldn't be necessary to move house after all.

'So where are you living now?'

'Clifton Road.'

His eyebrows went up in appreciation. 'You haven't done too badly yourself.'

'I've missed you, though.' She blessed the fact that she'd been able to buy groceries yesterday. He needn't know how close to starvation she'd been, nor just how desperate to find a man who could keep her.

'Come on, come and see for yourself. I'll do you an omelette for lunch. How about it?'

Really, she'd always been very fond of Bernie. It was just that he'd never earned a decent wage. Things would be very different now.

Bernie's grin had the power to move her as it had

decades ago. 'That's nice of you.' Before leaving the pub he bought a bottle of gin for her. She saw the notes in his wallet. There were a lot of them.

She took him via the bank. She let him see her stuffing the thick bundle of notes into her purse. She wanted him to believe it was love that was driving her back to his arms, not economic need. Bernie was the answer to her prayers.

He said: 'I've missed you. Been a bit lonely on my own. To tell the truth, that's why I came looking for you.'

'Christmas is better with a bit of company. Will you be able to stay?'

'Yes, if you'll have me.'

Vereena smiled. Things were going her way. 'Course I'll have you. What's Polly Jones doing then?'

'Going home to her family,' he said lightly. 'Like me.' They reached her house. It was handsome, in white-painted stone.

'You have come up in the world, Vee.' His eyes were out on sticks.

'Had to get a bathroom,' she said, letting him in. 'We couldn't run to that in the old days, could we?'

'We'll have the best Christmas ever,' he murmured, taking her into his arms and kissing her. 'Better than the old days, you'll see.'

Vereena breathed a sigh of relief. It had been a desperate plan to do a moonlight flit to some hovel between the railway lines. Thank goodness Bernie had turned up in time to prevent her doing that.

Rodney reckoned he'd be a nervous wreck if he had to stay and watch his father at work for much longer.

Christmas ought to be fun, and in his opinion, spending it with his father's new family fell short of that. He'd have to watch Lucy and his father making cow's eyes at each other.

Dad certainly knew how to hook the girls, he had to

give him that. He said he loved Lucy, but Rodney had his doubts. His dad was inclined to change his mind about girls. Lucy's feelings were genuine enough, though. There was love and longing in her eyes. He wished he could make her look at him like that.

He didn't know what to make of her father and step-mother, but Patsy's eyes, full of suspicion, would follow him round. Patsy had him running scared.

'Christmas will be very expensive,' his father said one morning. 'I'll have to have more money to pay the bills when they come in afterwards. Another load.'

The thought of going through that again put Rodney even more on edge. 'No, Dad.'

'Just this one last time. I've fixed it up with Peckham and White.'

'Dad! Grow up! You can't keep doing it.' There were times when Rodney felt his father was foolhardy. 'Patsy is suspicious. You don't want to give her proof.'

'You don't realise how much things cost. I've got to have more.'

'But—'

'Lucy's got expensive tastes too, you know, the nanny and all that.'

Everything Dad had said he wanted and had worked for, he'd achieved, but he wasn't managing. The salary he'd expected to provide the good life didn't stretch. It was generous enough, but if it were three times bigger he still wouldn't manage. The signs were there to see. Dad had no grasp on money.

'You're bleeding the business dry, and then what will Lucy do? You ought to think of that.'

Dad rolled his eyes upwards, as well he might. They'd covered this ground many times before. Dad was getting restive. Fed up. Seeing now that his grand plan wasn't working out. He even seemed to be losing patience with Lucy. Rodney had heard him snap at her the last time he'd

378

gone to their house. It made him wonder if Wesley was going off her.

'I've the staff to pay, I have to do it.'

'No . . .'

His father looked quite savage. 'Look, it's set up and I need your help. You aren't going to leave me high and dry, are you?'

Put like that, what could he do? 'This has got to be the last time.'

Wesley relaxed now he'd got his way. 'Wednesday night then, Rodders.'

It left him shivering at the thought. Patsy was making them both nervous. She left her office door open these days and sat facing it. Every time he went past, her eyes came up from her files. She was watching them. It was giving him the creeps.

'Definitely the last time.' He'd heard that before too. 'Same plan as before.'

Dad hired a plain van, and after the factory had closed for the night, they went back and loaded up. Then he made Rodney park it in the street outside his lodgings. In the morning, he drove it up to Southport and delivered the stuff.

Rodney thought the worst part was loading the van, creeping about and heaving heavy desks across the factory in semi-darkness. It wasn't quite like thieving, because his father had a full set of keys to get in.

'The twenty-eighth then, Rodders. Keep it free.'

As Christmas drew nearer, Patsy felt her nerves winding tighter. The arguments with Wesley were getting her down. She had the awful feeling that things were coming to a head.

Lucy seemed happier than ever. 'Come round and see me,' she told Patsy on the telephone. 'We're going to have a real family Christmas. I must tell you about the parties I'm arranging.'

Patsy slipped round when she saw that Wesley was sitting at his desk. Lucy's face was alight with excitement.

'This time of the year means a lot to Wesley and me.' Patsy didn't have to be told that Wesley's appetite for parties and celebrations more than matched Lucy's. 'In the old days, Gramps and Nanna always gave us a lovely time.'

'Starting on Christmas Eve to celebrate our birthday.'

Lucy nodded. 'Wesley thinks I should give the birthday party this year. And of course, you must all come for Christmas dinner.'

Patsy didn't feel much like celebrating. She seemed to have a lot weighing her down. But she made the effort, bought herself a new red dress and asked Rob to come to the birthday party with her.

Lucy kept up all the family traditions, inviting Dadda and Alma, and Colin Courtney from next door. Her friend Madge brought her husband Vic, who seemed even older than Wesley. He sat in a corner all night, talking to Dadda, while Madge danced every dance. She seemed to have no shortage of partners.

Patsy watched her circle the floor in Colin's arms. Once she'd seen Madge as a rival for Lucy's affections, and even now she felt a twinge of envy that Madge was still her best friend. She and Lucy were growing further and further apart. Wesley was doing his best to widen the gap, and that upset Patsy as much as what he was doing to their business. It suited Wesley's plans that they should quarrel.

'This is for you,' he said, presenting her with a silver thimble. 'We can't avoid the giving and receiving of gifts at this time of the year.'

Apart from that, he was careful to stay well away from her, but she caught his gaze smouldering across the room at her every time she looked up.

Mrs Judd baked the usual birthday cake, and together they blew out the candles. The supper was more luxurious than anything Nanna had provided, but served buffet-style because there were many more guests. There was even champagne.

Patsy felt that the party was not a complete success. She was afraid it had rather an atmosphere, because she and Wesley were barely hiding their dislike of each other.

Lucy had asked her with Dadda and Alma for Christmas dinner the following day. Dadda had been afraid Lucy would find she'd taken on too much entertaining. Patsy didn't want to go through it again and was glad the invitation had been declined.

Alma said she'd cook a special dinner for them at home.

'Ought we to ask Lucy?' Dadda worried. 'After all, she's close family.'

'We can't cope with three young children as well,' Patsy pointed out, 'not in this small room. And she'll probably want to bring her nanny.'

As a compromise, it was decided that they would eat dinner in the evening and invite Lucy and Wesley to come alone. Patsy was quite pleased when they refused.

'We'll go round to Caerns Road in the morning and take them their presents,' Dadda said.

Patsy spent the time there playing with Fay, Lucy's little girl. She'd bought her a teddy bear, with fluffy toys for the babies.

There was a time when she'd have hunted high and low to find Lucy exactly the right present. She'd always wanted to give her what she liked best.

'You'll never manage it,' Cassie had told her. 'Lucy's always given so many lovely things.' It had taken her years to accept the truth of that.

She'd seen a pair of cut-glass candlesticks in the West Kirkby shop that she liked, and hoped Lucy would too. She avoided having to buy a gift for Wesley by presenting them as a joint gift. She didn't want to ruin Lucy's Christmas by showing any ill-will towards Wesley.

On Boxing Day, Rob suggested they go out for a trip in

his car. It was a cold day, but bright with sun. The old bull-nose rattled more than she remembered but Patsy was happy to be away from the factory and bowling through open countryside with him.

He stopped the car overlooking the Dee Estuary, and talked again about marriage.

Patsy knew she ought to feel elated. At last she had what she'd always wanted; Rob was showing how much he loved her. Somehow she couldn't relax, couldn't enjoy anything. She was tense and aching with indecision.

Vereena woke up to find Bernie standing by her bed offering her a cup of morning tea.

'It's late,' he said. 'Thought we ought to make a move.'

Vereena pulled herself up the bed. 'Lovely to be woken this way. Not that I've had much sleep.'

Bernie's smile dazzled her as he climbed in beside her. He was wearing expensive blue silk pyjamas. 'You're complaining?'

She laughed. 'What do you think?' Bernie had always been a good lover, it was one reason they'd stayed together so long. It was five months since Harold had died and she'd had no one since.

Balancing his tea in one hand, he reached across to kiss her. Vereena felt a surge of happiness. No need to be on her best behaviour with Bernie. Getting back with him was as easy as slipping on a pair of comfortable old shoes. Better not put it like that to him, though.

'Having you back after all this time, it's like having a new man.' She kissed the tip of his nose in return. The fight they'd had before he left no longer rankled. He was her husband of twenty-three years.

'We'll do our Christmas shopping today,' she said, and felt pleasure that it was possible.

'And I must get my luggage from the station if I'm to stay a few days.'

'Stay as long as possible. I want you to, you know that. Where are you booked to play next?'

'Er – Bristol, but I've got a couple of weeks off. It's pantomime everywhere at this time of the year.'

'You've got to have a break sometime.'

'I needed one.'

'I hope you'll come back here. Every time you have a break in future.'

'I will that. Now I know you'll have me.'

'Course I'll have you, Bernie. I've missed you.'

It was a cold, crisp day, and the streets were thronged with Christmas shoppers. There were carollers on every corner. There was a clatter of coins from Bernie every time he passed a collecting tin. It was lovely to see him in the money at last. He'd always been generous.

Bernie chose a goose large enough for a family, as well as a piece of ham.

'There'll be just the two of us,' she giggled as he insisted on paying for them.

'Like another honeymoon,' Bernie murmured. He made her feel a girl again. All her worries had gone. He'd come like a miracle in the nick of time to save her.

The Salvation Army brass band was playing carols in Grange Road. Vereena felt uplifted by the spirit of Christmas.

Bernie bought wine and chocolates and tangerines and nuts. When they'd carried all that home, he said: 'We'll go out and have a slap-up lunch, and then I must buy you your Christmas present. No need to ask what you'd like, I suppose?'

'What d'you mean?'

'Clothes are always what you want.'

'Perhaps a new dress,' she smiled.

He took her into Robb's department store. They passed the queue of children waiting to see Father Christmas and went to the ladies' fashion department.

Vereena was in her element. This was what she'd missed so much. She tried on several dresses and settled for one in red wool. He insisted on getting her a new coat to go with it.

'And something for both of us to enjoy. I'll get a few records and we'll dance on Christmas night.'

'I haven't got a gramophone,' she laughed. So he bought one of those too. Bernie was being very generous.

Vereena bought him a navy silk dressing gown. It went well with his silk pyjamas. Made him look as rich and sophisticated as Noel Coward.

When Bernie unpacked his cases, he brought out a record. He wound up the new gramophone and set it to play. 'Recognise this?'

Vereena listened, enthralled. There was no mistaking Bernie's banjo-playing, nor his voice in her favourite 'Swanee River'. Polly Jones's voice led his and was stronger, but she could put up with that.

Vereena couldn't remember when she'd been this happy. It was like coming in out of the cold. Bernie wore his silk dressing gown half the morning and half the evening. They had a blissful Christmas and went on celebrating right through to the New Year.

Back in the factory after the holiday, everything seemed quiet. Nobody seemed to want to buckle down to work again. It was the day before Lucy's wedding anniversary. Patsy bought them a card and a gift. She knew Lucy was planning yet another celebration.

'I'm glad they haven't asked us,' she was saying to Alma, who'd brought a cup of tea to her office, when Wesley put his head round the door.

'Can I have a word, Patsy?'

He looked cock-a-hoop, as though about to deliver a blow he knew would maim. He was waiting for Alma to go. Patsy felt herself tense. She was afraid something bad was coming.

384

'Something for you to sign.'

He pushed what appeared to be a legal document across her desk to her. She opened it up, her heart thudding.

'It's about splitting the business between you and Lucy.' There was a triumphant smile on his lips.

Her heart skipped a couple of beats. 'What's the hurry? I haven't said I would.'

'But it's a good idea, isn't it?'

'Who for, you? You've had this drawn up by a solicitor? You should have waited.'

'I don't see any point in waiting. We aren't able to get on. Your ideas are very different from mine. This way we'll solve the difficulty.'

'What if I decide against it? You'll have wasted your solicitor's fee.'

'I think you'll sign. Neither Lucy nor I can see any other way.' He looked smug, self-satisfied, quite sure he was going to have his own way.

'I'll leave it with you. Don't forget, you'll have to have your signature witnessed for it to be legal.'

Patsy slumped across her desk when he'd gone. She was feeling desperate. She was going to lose part of the business Grandpa had entrusted to her care, and it was all happening so fast.

She started to read the document before her. Lucy was to have full ownership of the freehold of the factory in Laird Street, and the two businesses carried on at the premises, namely, the restoration of antique furniture and the manufacture of replica antiques. In addition, she was to have full ownership of the freehold of the house in Caerns Road.

Patsy made up her mind in a hurry. She wouldn't agree to this. She strode to Wesley's office, meaning to throw his document on his desk and tell him so. His room was empty.

'He's gone out,' one of the French-polishers told her. 'Just saw him drive off.'

She was shaking with frustration and anger. She mustn't let him get the better of her. Grandpa would expect her to look after Lucy's inheritance too. She didn't think it would be safe in Wesley's hands.

She was going back to her own office when she saw Alma beckoning her into the kitchen. She closed the door carefully behind them.

'There's something funny going on here. Mr Spiers gave this to the new foreman.' Alma put a work order into Patsy's hand.

'Alf Swann?' Wesley had hired him a few weeks previously.

'Yes.'

Patsy studied it. The work order was for ten davenports. 'This is right.' She knew that one of their wholesalers had reordered them.

'Come and talk to him. Written orders is one thing, verbal orders something else.'

Alma led her across the floor to Alf Swann. His face sagged in plump wrinkles like a bulldog's. He'd come with good references to take the place of a man who'd retired suddenly because of ill-health.

'Ten davenports ordered,' Patsy said. 'Nothing the matter with that.'

'Mr Spiers just said to me, "Make it twelve while you're at it."'

'What?' She took them both across to the bench that served as Swann's desk.

'I tried to give this back to him to alter the figure, but he said, "I'll make out a new order later."'

Patsy felt her heart thudding. She had to raise her voice above the noise of sawing from the mill. 'Has this happened before?'

'Yes, several times.'

386

'You're making furniture without a work order?'

The man nodded. 'He says it's all right. He's the boss, isn't he?'

'What about materials? This way, you won't be issued with enough wood.'

'He brings what's needed himself.'

'Or asks your dadda to fetch it over,' Alma told her.

'What else has he asked you to make that you haven't had work orders for?'

'Three roll-top desks, I remember that. Card tables, a lot of those.'

'How many's a lot? Can you remember exactly?'

'Well, two here, an odd one there. That sort of thing.' The old man scratched his head. 'And those yew chests . . .'

'Thank you,' Patsy said, fighting her anger at what Wesley was doing. But she felt a moment of triumph too. At last she knew how he was doing it.

'Thanks, Alma.' She squeezed her stepmother's arm. She'd grown fond of her over the years; she'd been good for Dadda too. Patsy felt that with solid knowledge like Alma had given her, she could perhaps trap Wesley. Certainly it ought to convince Lucy.

Patsy was spending more time with Rob. Even if they didn't go out, he came back to the auction room almost every evening. Sometimes he joined her upstairs to sit with Alma and Dadda, but more often they stayed in the old shop or walked round the saleroom, where they could be alone.

That evening, she told him she'd found how Wesley was defrauding the company.

'Nothing could be simpler. The factory's making furniture specifically for Wesley. He tells the foreman to make a few extra chests here and a couple of davenports there, tacking what he wants on the end of a bona fida order.

387

'Then he orders Dadda to carry over the extra wood, or does it himself. It's all word of mouth and no supporting paperwork. Once the piece of furniture has left the factory, there's no proof that it was ever made.'

'But I thought you said a steady number of desks and things were going missing?'

'This is as well as, Rob.'

'A new way? Because he knows you're keeping watch on his figures?'

'I don't know. Maybe he's always done it this way too. This is how he reduces our profit. We're paying to have the pieces made, paying for materials, and he's spiriting them away for his own gain. What can I do about it, Rob?'

He was very serious. 'It's a police matter.'

Patsy shivered. 'I dread to think how Lucy will take that.'

Rob thought some more. 'If you signed the agreement to split the business, it would be Lucy's problem not yours.'

'She couldn't handle it. She wouldn't want the police brought in. He's her husband and she's happy to let him do anything he pleases. If I sign the agreement, then Wesley will get what he wants. I won't let him have it.'

'Police, then?'

'I think it'll have to come to it,' she said grimly. 'But should I tell Lucy first? What is the best way to handle this?'

'Settle it once and for all. Just call in the police.'

Patsy was afraid there was no other way, but she still hesitated.

'You're worried stiff.' Rob put his arms round her. 'How can I help? Can I take you to the pictures? Come on, it'll get your mind off all this.'

The picture houses were within easy walking distance, but Rob insisted on taking her there by car. Patsy sat in the passenger seat of the old bull-nose Morris and closed her eyes.

388

She found it soothing to be driven. Soothing to sit in the old car she knew so well. She wished she could put the clock back to the days when it had been hers and she'd had no worries.

Once in the dark cinema, she tried to concentrate on the film, but she'd had a strange feeling in the pit of her stomach all day. She knew there was a lot of furniture ready to leave the factory. Two loads had gone out during the afternoon, another two were planned for tomorrow. Logic told her this was a good time for Wesley to take more.

In the anticlimax that followed Christmas, she couldn't help but notice that most of the workers had less energy than usual. Only Wesley, and perhaps Rodney, seemed alert, as though poised to take action.

When they came out at the end of the show, she said: 'Let's take a look round the factory, Rob.'

'Now?'

'If Wesley's taking furniture without anybody seeing him, he must be doing it at night.'

CHAPTER TWENTY-FOUR

28 December 1935

Rodney had been on tenterhooks all day.

'Let's load the van early,' his father said. 'It'll be dark anyway. If we meet at half eight, I'll have time to play with the children and have supper. Lucy asks questions if I'm out late.'

'It's Christmas, there'll be more people about. Going to parties and that.' Rodney felt safer when everybody had gone to bed.

After work, when he went back to his lodgings, he felt too nervous to eat much, even though it was the first day they were given a hot meal instead of cold turkey.

When he walked up to the corner at half past eight, the van was already parked in front of Dad's car. It was a bright moonlit night. Neither of them had given any thought to that.

The factory was lit up like a Christmas tree by a row of outside lights. As his father swung the van round to drive round the back, they both caught sight of the policeman striding along the pavement towards them.

'Should have waited,' Wesley gasped. 'I'd started to turn before I saw him.'

Rodney froze in his seat. They were in the big yard where raw timber and planks were stacked up. The building had several double doors on this side, with a concrete loading platform in front of them.

'Get out,' his father hissed. 'Do what you usually do. Look as though you've every right to be here.'

Rodney's legs felt weak as he opened the rear van doors. As his father backed up against the platform – which was level with the floor of the van, making it easier to load – he knew the police officer had followed them.

Wesley jumped out, rattling his keys. He leapt up on the platform and swaggered over to one of the sets of double doors, unlocking them and swinging them open. Rodney could feel his scalp crawling. He was afraid they looked like thieves.

'Nice night, officer.' His father was switching on lights along the platform that normally he wouldn't have dared touch. 'Just our luck to get a rush job now.'

Rodney had to tell himself that Dad could handle this sort of situation better than anybody. But he was having to say he was the manager here and show identification. This was a disaster. If Patsy missed the stuff they were about to take, how could they deny being here now?

'Just checking, sir,' the policeman said.

'Thank you, officer. It's good to know you keep an eye on our property.'

'It's patrolled regularly. It's on my beat. Good night, sir.'

Rodney felt in a cold sweat as they watched him go. He whispered, because he could still hear the crunch of his boots, 'That's done it. We'll have to call it off now.'

'I've hired the van. Fixed up with Peckham's to take the stuff.'

'We'll never get away with it.'

'We will.' Dad was whistling to show he didn't care.

It was an eerie place at night. Without the screaming whine from the electric saws and the shouts of the operators, the silence seemed heavy. The place was still and empty when Rodney was used to seeing it buzzing with activity.

His heart was still thumping. 'What about these lights?'

'I'd have liked to ask him how much time we had before he came round again. Thought it might sound suspicious.' Slowly Wesley reached up and put out the platform lights. 'Don't want to attract any more attention.'

Rodney followed him inside and quietly pulled the door to behind him. In the beam of his torch, sawdust was still spinning in the air and the smell of new wood was as overpowering as ever.

The bright moonlight shone in, making it more ghostly. 'Won't need the lights here,' Dad whispered.

In the semi-darkness his father was a deeper shadow. Rodney followed him, feeling an urge to move on tiptoe, but their footsteps were muffled by the carpet of sawdust and shavings. In the storeroom, they were both blinking in the bright light. Here the windows were kept shuttered for security reasons and they needn't worry about it being seen. It seemed crowded with furniture.

Dad did things properly. He'd made up a fake order with what he knew was available. Now they had to carry the furniture out to the van and load it.

'Better put this in the van first,' Wesley was whispering. The Regency dining table seemed vast. It was a long, slow process, backwards and forwards through the factory. With sawdust on the floor, it was like walking on sand, and they had to tie everything down in the van.

'This part isn't easy in the dark,' Rodney complained.

'You should be used to it. You've done it often enough.'

Rodney knew if he did it a thousand times he'd still have cramps in his stomach. And it was hard manual work – he certainly wasn't used to that.

The roll-top desk was heavy. They were both sweating before one half of the stuff was in, but there could be no let-up now. It was grit-the-teeth time. Rodney grazed his knuckles against a door frame. He felt exhausted. They were both getting short-tempered.

393

His father was made even more cross because the van wasn't big enough to take all he'd written on the order. It was almost filled now, and they'd gone back to the store-room to get four last dining chairs when the lights of a car raked through the windows as it turned. It sounded as though it was pulling up in front of the building.

Rodney felt as though his throat had blocked. His heart was racing. His dad's finger was against his lips; he didn't need to be urged to hurry. He was running with a chair on each arm, and his legs felt as though they were made of rubber. They were fighting the seconds to get outside and shut the door behind them.

The sound of the key turning in the front door was unmistakable. Rodney was being pushed out on the platform and Dad was closing the door as the front one opened. He kept his eye to the crack.

'It's Patsy,' he whispered, aghast.

'The police! He must have rung her.'

Rodney was fighting the urge to run. If Patsy found them now she'd know exactly what they were doing. They rammed the chairs into the van.

'Quietly,' his father breathed. 'We don't want to get caught in the act.' The lights were all on inside.

'What's she doing?'

'I didn't lock the storeroom door.' His father's breath was warm against his neck.

'What about the light? Did we leave that on?'

'No.'

'But she'll see the stuff's gone if she goes there.'

'She'll go to her office.'

'She only needs to look out of a window on this side and she'll see us. It's like broad daylight here.'

'No, the glass is covered with sawdust.'

'Not in the kitchen.'

His father was easing off the handbrake. 'Help me push.' They moved the van forward a few feet so they could close the doors at the back.

Rodney was making for the driver's seat. 'What if she hears us go?'

His father was up on the platform again, trying to see inside. He came back to whisper: 'I could stand back against this wall. If she comes . . . if she opens this door, I'll give her a push and send her flying off the platform. She'll break an ankle at the very least. She never sleeps, damn her.'

'Come on,' Rodney urged, backing towards the van. 'Let's get away from here.'

His father got in quietly. He hadn't closed the door when Rodney put a hand on his arm. He was tense with terrible anxiety again.

'Can we get out past her car?'

He knew it wouldn't be difficult to block their exit. Then they'd be caught like rats in a trap. If she'd done that, he was going to get out and run for it.

The roadway into the yard ran down the side of the building and was just wide enough for a pantechnicon to manoeuvre through. He'd heard Patsy talk of making another way in from the back. Often cars had to back up if they met a vehicle in the narrow bottleneck.

'I'll go and see.' His father slid out again and went quietly to the corner of the building. In the bright moonlight, how could Patsy fail to see him?

Rodney listened. He could hear nothing but the occasional car out on the road. He kept his eye on the double door. If she came out to the back, he'd start the engine and get going just as fast as he could.

Patsy must know they were doing this. She had that look on her face every time she saw him. There were more lights going on inside. He hoped she wouldn't go to the kitchen.

Dad was at his best bluffing his way out of tight corners, spinning believable tales. But there was no possible tale he could spin to explain away what they were doing here now.

Wesley was coming back more swiftly. 'It's the old bull-nose. Robert Parry must be here too, but there's just about enough room to get past. They didn't think of blocking us in.'

'I can't stand any more of this.'

'Come on then. Start the engine and don't hang about. No lights till we're out on the road.'

'They won't recognise the van even if they see it.'

'She could ring Lucy and ask if I'm at home.'

'I told you we shouldn't do it.'

The engine juddered to life, making an horrendous noise. Rodney got the van rolling slowly across the yard, heading for the dark corner.

'She can't help but hear this.'

There was room for cars to park at the front, but usually they didn't. Tonight the old Morris had been left close to the front door.

'I think I can see her coming to the door.' His father's voice was agonised. 'Hurry up, Rodders.'

He was out on the road and accelerating to get round the corner. She wouldn't be able to see them now.

'Lights on,' his father reminded.

'This is the last time.' Rodney's mouth was dry. 'Never, ever again, so don't ask me. You're on your own from now on.' He felt thoroughly shaken up. 'You've got a stronger stomach for this sort of thing than I have.'

'I wouldn't say that.' His father was slumped in the seat, his face grey. He looked a lot older. 'Perhaps you're right, Rodders. We've pushed this as far as we can.'

'I'm not having this parked outside my place all night. I wouldn't be able to sleep.'

'Patsy couldn't have recognised us.'

'She must have seen the van drive off. She suspects us. Why wouldn't she phone the police?'

'Because Lucy—'

'She won't go on thinking of Lucy's feelings. Not for ever. She'd know you wouldn't take it to Caerns Road. My place would be the first she'd think of.'

'You're making too much fuss.'

'Patsy's quick on the uptake. Dad, I've had enough. I want out of this.'

'You'll take it to Southport tomorrow?'

'No, I—'

'You've got to. You can't let me down. Peckham's are expecting it. Come on, don't louse it up now. Not when we've got this far. They'll pay you, cash in hand. You aren't going to turn that down?'

'All right,' Rodney said grudgingly. He shivered, finding it impossible to throw off the feeling of impending disaster.

'Here's my car.'

Rodney drew in behind it. 'There's some wasteland half a mile down here. I'll leave the van there, just in case, and I'll have it on its way to Southport before daylight. Follow me, I'll need a lift back to my lodgings.'

'The sooner I get home the better,' Wesley worried. 'What if she does phone the police?'

Rodney was indignant. 'It'll only take five more minutes.'

He knew they'd both got the wind up. 'I'm going back to pack my things. I'm getting out while the going's good.'

'What d'you mean, getting out?'

'Right out. Away. Before this breaks. I've had a basinful.'

'What'll you do?'

'I wouldn't mind going to London. On my own. I need a new start.' He'd been thinking of it for some time. 'I'll lie low at Auntie Ida's for a few days.'

'I'll come and see you.'

'I'll bet. You'll want your money for this load. Collect my week's wages for me. I won't be sorry not to see the inside of that factory again, I can tell you.'

* * *

As Rob drove up Laird Street, Patsy was reassured to find the factory looking as it always did after dark, lit up by the row of lights along the front.

'I'm a fool,' she said. 'Bringing you here at this time of night. It's all in my mind. I'm going nuts.'

'Patsy, you're the sanest person I know.'

'I suppose we might as well check inside now we're here.' She got out, unlocked the front door and went in.

The place was quite creepy at night. Her heart was thumping. She had the most awful feeling that she was being watched and was glad she'd asked Rob to come with her.

She clutched his arm. 'What was that noise?'

'All buildings make odd noises. In the day, you can't hear anything but the machines.'

Patsy felt she ought to keep a tighter rein on her nerves; they were running away with her. There was a sense of brooding about the place. She felt she'd interrupted something.

She turned on every light she came to, drawing Rob with her. She checked the row of davenports that the French-polishers were working on. None had gone from there. She went up to the stockroom, put her key in the lock. Her fingers were suddenly shaking. Had she left it unlocked? She pushed the door open, put on the light, trying to think back.

She froze in horror. 'Things have gone! There was much more than this.' Rob was crowding in beside her to look. 'No, wait a minute. Two loads went out.'

That was it. She mustn't jump to the wrong conclusion. She turned on her heel and ran back to her office. She'd kept a careful record of what should be here. She left the lights burning everywhere, to stop the dreadful feeling that somebody was watching her from the shadows.

She gave the list to Rob. 'A dining table has gone.' He was counting. 'A roll-top desk.'

'I'm right then.' Patsy felt sick. It was hopeless. However hard she tried, the stuff was being spirited away from under her very nose.

She felt a surge of anger, wanting to thump her fist and stamp her feet with frustration. 'How am I going to stop this? It must be Wesley. It must be.'

At that moment she heard an engine jerking to life. She knew from Rob's face that he'd heard it too. He was running towards the doors at the back. Patsy paused at a window, brushed the sawdust from the glass in time to see something move.

'We interrupted them,' Rob was gasping, his eyes wide with shock. 'They were here all the time.'

Patsy could feel her scalp crawl. No wonder she'd had the feeling she was being watched. She shot across to the other side of the building and wrenched open the front door. A green van came round the corner of the building and shot into the road.

She clung to the door, feeling as if her knees could no longer support the weight of her body.

'They were here all the time,' Rob repeated. 'I'm a fool! Why didn't I think to leave my car where it would block the exit? No forethought.'

Patsy was even more angry now. Angry with herself as well as Wesley. Here she was, suspicious of what might be happening, and she'd not been able to stop him.

'Call the police,' Rob advised. 'A theft has very definitely taken place.'

Feeling dithery, she went back to her office and sat down in front of the phone.

'No, let's go round to Caerns Road. Find out if Wesley's there or not.'

'What good will that do?'

'If he's been home all evening, then it isn't him and I can involve the police without worrying about Lucy.'

'And if he's out?'

'Then it's a family matter and probably better kept to ourselves. But I'll be able to prove to Lucy that he's up to no good.'

It came then like a shaft of light. Patsy felt heartened. 'Do you know, I think we'll be able to pin Wesley down.'

She heard Rob laugh. 'You're going to bargain with him. Wesley gets out and stays away from the business in future, or you go to the police.'

'Exactly.' Patsy felt better than she had for ages. At last she could see a way out of the impasse.

Patsy felt a stab of disappointment when she saw Wesley's yellow Cadillac parked in his drive.

Rob pulled in behind it. As they walked towards the front door, he put his hand on the bonnet. 'Engine's still warm. He's just come in.'

That gave them both a lift. Lucy opened the door herself. She looked surprised to see them. Patsy had made a point of not calling in the evenings or at weekends unless she'd received a specific invitation.

'Hello, can we come in?'

'Is something the matter?' Lucy was heading back to her sitting room.

'Yes.'

Wesley was coming downstairs, whistling softly under his breath. He carried a twin son in the crook of each arm. His jacket was off and his slippers on. He looked as though he'd spent the evening here with his family.

'Aren't they lovely when they're just bathed?' He was offering an infant to her.

Patsy hardened her heart. She knew this was Wesley's way of deflecting her attention. Lucy took baby Oliver and put him over her shoulder.

'What's the matter, Patsy?'

'Have you been down to the factory this evening, Wesley, since it closed, I mean?'

She didn't miss the glance he shot in Lucy's direction. 'No,' he said.

'I thought you said that's where you were going.' Lucy was frowning. 'A job you hadn't finished.'

'No,' he said again. 'Actually I went to see Rodney. He's not well.'

Patsy kept her eyes on her sister's face. Lucy was asking: 'But why did you say . . .?'

'You know how you worry, darling. You're always afraid I'm going to bring home germs to the children. Rodney was taken ill at work, a high fever. I was concerned. He was worse tonight, I've asked the doctor to visit.'

His tawny eyes met Patsy's. 'He won't be at work for some time, I'm afraid. Quite poorly. I do hope he hasn't given it to everybody else.'

Patsy thought he sounded sincere. She could almost believe him.

'I hope it isn't catching,' Lucy said, patting her infant fondly on the back. The nanny came to the door.

'Mr Spiers, you didn't lift them from their cots? Not after I'd got them both settled for the night?'

'They weren't asleep when I looked in,' he said easily.

'Let me take them, now you've shown them off.' She was clucking with disapproval. Patsy exchanged glances with Rob. His face said: Wesley wanted them as props.

'There's been another theft of furniture from the factory,' Patsy announced.

'What?' A flush was creeping up Lucy's cheeks.

'Are you sure?' Wesley still seemed cool. 'Two loads were dispatched this afternoon, you know.'

'And one more tonight, after we closed,' Patsy added. 'We saw the van drive off, didn't we, Rob? I'll have to tell the police.'

'Yes,' Lucy agreed. 'Yes, you must, this has to be stopped.'

Patsy said carefully: 'We can ring from here, now. You're all agreed I should do that?'

Wesley stirred himself. 'I do just wonder if you're making a mistake. Tomorrow we'll check what's in the storeroom.'

'Rob and I have done that. We know exactly what's missing.'

Wesley frowned and looked as though he was trying to be reasonable. 'Patsy, you can't know exactly. A lot of stuff was shipped out this afternoon and more is being moved in as it's finished. We'll sort it out tomorrow, all right? There's probably some explanation.'

'Perhaps you had better make sure first.' Lucy took her lead from her husband.

'Wesley can bluff his way out of anything,' Rob said dourly as they got back into the old bull-nose. 'You can ring from the auction room. Or we can go straight to the police station now. I think we should.'

'It's very late.' Patsy felt exhausted. 'And it'll mean hours down there, making statements. Even if we do report it now, are the police likely to do anything before tomorrow?'

'You can't keep putting it off.'

'No, you're right. Let's go to the station then.'

It was almost three o'clock when Patsy got to bed. She was wide awake by then, the events of the evening going round and round in her mind. It took her a long time to get to sleep.

It seemed no time at all before Alma was waking her for breakfast. 'You were very late coming home last night.'

Patsy, feeling fuddled and dazed, started to tell her about going to the factory and calling in the police. Alma called Dadda in to hear the news.

'You've done the right thing,' he told her. 'You've got to stop the thieving.'

'You stay where you are for a bit,' Alma advised. 'Have your sleep out. I'll bring you a cup of tea. You can't work day and night.'

Patsy decided to take her advice. When she next woke up it was broad daylight. It was sale day and she could hear a crowd gathering in the auction room below. The cup by her bed was full of cold tea. She knew that Dadda and Alma had long since gone to work.

She dressed slowly, still feeling light-headed. She was worried about Lucy, afraid it would come as a big shock when she found that Wesley hadn't been telling the truth.

She made herself tea and toast before going downstairs. Rob had hired a new man to run the reception office. She stayed with him for a short time but he seemed on top of the job.

The sale had started and the room was crowded. Rob was acting as auctioneer. His late night didn't seem to have affected him. Everything was functioning normally here.

Patsy knew she was trying to put off going to the factory. She was nervous about coming face to face with Wesley again. He'd been trying to persuade her to put off going to the police last night. Now he'd have to talk to them.

At first glance, the factory seemed to be running normally. Everybody was working, the saws were whining, the place humming with noise. She thought Dadda must have been watching for her. She beckoned him to her office. 'Have the police been?'

'Yes, they were here for ages, questioning everybody. I showed them the figures I'd kept. Alma did too.'

'How's Wesley taking it?'

'He isn't here.'

'What?'

'He was here early on, I saw him. But he went without saying anything before the police came. Rodney didn't turn in this morning.'

'Wesley says he isn't well, but I don't know.'

403

'The police spent a lot of time talking to Kenny Hewitt. He had to show them the records of what had been made and all that.'

Dadda had barely closed her door behind him when there was a tap on it and Kenny Hewitt put his head round.

'Something else has come up, Patsy.'

'Come and sit down, Kenny. I want to know what's been happening.'

'More than I first thought.'

'You heard about last night?'

He nodded, looking frightened. His face was white. 'Things are worse than you think. My desk's been broken into, so's the safe.'

She couldn't take it in. He was pushing two chequebooks and a sheet of paper in front of her. 'There's quite a few cheques missing. These are the numbers.'

She swallowed hard. 'Cheques stolen, you mean?'

'I made one out yesterday for the week's wages, ready for you to sign this morning. It's gone. So have others. There's no-record anywhere about the amounts or what they were for . . .'

Patsy felt her heart turn over. She was appalled. 'Since yesterday, you mean?'

'Yes, I locked them all in the safe last night.'

'Nobody else is entitled to sign . . .'

'Mr Spiers is,' Kenny reminded her.

He was; her grandfather had allowed him to sign cheques for small amounts, but certainly not for large sums like the week's wages.

'I rang the bank as soon as I noticed. The manager told me they'd cashed five separate cheques on company accounts soon after they opened this morning.'

Cold fingers were wringing her entrails. 'Who signed them?' she choked.

'The bank thought you had. Your name was on them. All of them.'

The office was spinning round her. Miss Cropper's typewriter began to clack in the next office.

'Forged,' she whispered, aghast. It took a moment for the significance to sink in. She licked her lips. 'How much is left in those accounts?'

It was a moment before he could bring himself to answer. Now he was whispering too.

'Virtually nothing. We keep running totals. He knew exactly how much was there.'

She stared at him. 'I'd better let the police know.' Her mouth was dry. Things were going from bad to worse.

'I told them; they were here when I realised . . .'

'Thank you, Kenny.' She felt near tears.

'It's a more serious offence than they first thought. They're sending a senior officer back to talk to you. That's what I came to tell you.'

CHAPTER TWENTY-FIVE

29 December 1935

The phone was ringing, shattering the peace of the silent house. Lucy rushed to pick it up before it woke her babies from their pre-lunch nap. 'Hello?'

'Mrs Spiers? Is your husband there?'

'No.' She knew Hilda Cropper's voice. Wesley referred to her as his secretary.

'Can I have a quick word with him?'

'He's not here, Miss Cropper. Did you think he would be? He doesn't come home for lunch. He sends you out to buy a sandwich for him, doesn't he?'

'Sometimes.' She seemed guarded. 'I just thought . . . it being your wedding anniversary . . . He said he was taking you out. To have lunch and choose a new watch for you.'

'No.' Her reflection bounced back at her from the Georgian giltwood mirror behind the phone. She looked mystified. Wesley had made no such suggestions to her.

More than once he'd told her: 'Now I've got a responsible job, I don't like taking a long break at lunchtime. It's easier to keep my mind on things if I don't. Now we're married, and I can have dinner with you every night. It suits me better.'

But she'd suggested they go out for a meal this evening, just the two of them. After all, a wedding anniversary was a personal celebration. But he'd brushed the idea aside.

'We can do that any time,' he'd said. 'Let's have our friends in to dinner here.'

Lucy gave little dinner parties often. He loved to play host to their friends, sitting at the head of the table. But they'd done a good deal of entertaining over Christmas, and she'd have liked a change. Lucy smiled again. Wesley could always persuade her to do what he wanted.

'Must have a very special dinner and lots of champagne.' His face had been pink with enthusiasm, his smile wide.

'If your husband comes in,' Miss Cropper was always formal, 'ask him to give me a call, will you?'

'Yes, but you'll see him first, I'm sure.'

Lucy put the phone down and listened. All remained quiet upstairs. Hilda Cropper had it wrong about lunch, but perhaps Wesley had gone out to buy her a watch? She smiled to herself. A coincidence if he had. She'd bought him a Rolex.

Wesley liked to have all the obvious signs of wealth. He wanted to show everyone that he was making a success of the business. That meant a lot to him.

She'd wanted him to take another day off after Christmas. He was working very hard, coming home later and later in the evenings.

'I'm not seeing as much of you as I used to, not as much as I'd like. My life is all babies and housekeeping now. Couldn't you get more help at work?'

After all, if the business was doing as well as he said it was, there was no reason not to make their own lives easier.

'I can't take any more time off.' He'd kissed her. 'Or I'll have Patsy on my back for not working hard enough.' They'd laughed, because Patsy could think of nothing but work. She had nothing else in her life.

Lucy went to the dining room to survey the mahogany dining table now extended to its full twelve feet. She'd set it for eight. A shaft of wintry sunlight shone in to sparkle on the silver and cut glass. Outside, ground frost still showed white under the monkey puzzle tree although it was lunchtime.

She picked up the last of the starched napkins, folding and refolding it into the shape of a water lily. Wesley liked the formality of folded napkins.

She hurried down the passage to the kitchen that she and Wesley had fitted up with the latest equipment. Mrs Judd was just coming in with a laden shopping basket.

'The rolls were warm when I got them. The sole didn't look too good, so I bought smoked salmon instead, like you said.'

'That's fine.' Lucy smiled with satisfaction. Mrs Judd's preparations for the dinner were spreading everywhere. A large fruit cake stood ready to be iced on the table.

'I'll pipe "Happy Anniversary" on it, shall I?' she asked.

'Yes.' Lucy giggled to herself because she knew Wesley would probably prefer 'Two glorious years' or something like that.

Nanny came in through the back door with Fay. They usually went for a walk at this time. The child ran to Lucy's arms.

Fay had white-blonde hair and was small and slight for her age. Rather like a piece of fragile china. As Lucy hugged her tiny body closer, delighting in her little daughter, she could hear the first whimpers from above.

'The boys have heard me come in.' Nanny grinned, casting her eyes towards the ceiling.

'They might settle again.' They usually slept longer than this.

The phone started to shrill again. Unusual at this time of day. Lucy hurled herself across the hall to still it.

'It's Kenneth Hewitt from the factory, Mrs Spiers. Is your husband there? I've somebody with me who'd like a word with him.'

'He isn't, no.' She didn't know who she was talking to, but he sounded nervous.

409

'Do you know where he's gone?'

'I don't think . . . No.'

'Tell him I want an urgent word if he does come home. There's something we need to sort out straight away.'

'Right, I'll tell him.'

Lucy put the phone down, wondering why everybody seemed suddenly to want Wesley.

There was another cry from upstairs. Michael was usually the first to wake up. Already Lucy could hear Oliver too.

'Time to get them up.' She was heading towards the stairs when the front door bell rang.

'I'll see to the boys,' Nanny said behind her. 'That's bound to be for you.'

Lucy changed direction and opened the door. Fay was clinging to her dress.

'Mrs Spiers?' A young lad was holding out a large box to her. 'For you.'

Lucy took it, wondering what it was. An anniversary gift, but certainly not the watch Hilda Cropper had said Wesley meant to get her. She took it to the sitting room, turned it over. There was something familiar about the box. The name of a dress shop was printed on the lid. There was no indication on the outside as to who had sent it.

'What is it, Mummy?' Fay piped.

She cut the strings and opened it. The evening dress inside was her own. She lifted the folds of crimson silk and wondered. Her friend Madge had borrowed it from her to wear at a dance that was being held on New Year's Eve.

Lucy frowned. Why return it before she'd used it? There was a card.

'Forgive me' was all it said. Madge had signed it.

She held up the dress. Had Madge torn it? Damaged it in some way? There wasn't a mark on it. And why go to the trouble of sending it round? Madge had been here yesterday and would be here again tonight for dinner.

410

Lucy was mystified. What was there to forgive Madge for? Was it just that she'd bought herself another dress and decided not to wear this?

Nanny's heavy step sounded on the stairs. She was carrying a baby on each arm. She asked: 'Has something happened?'

'Yes. Keep your eye on Fay for a minute.'

She went to the phone to talk to Madge. It rang for a long time. She was about to give up when she heard it being picked up. Nobody spoke, but she heard what sounded like a stifled gasp. Or was it a sob?

The voice when it came was so tense it shocked her. 'Is that you, Madge? Where are you?' She knew it was Madge's husband.

'No. It's Lucy Spiers. I wanted to talk to Madge.'

'She isn't here.' There was a catch in Victor Walker's voice that warned Lucy it was no ordinary absence. It gave her a sinking feeling in the pit of her stomach. Something was very wrong.

'What's happened, Vic?'

He was a bank manager, staid, with a dour, strait-laced face. Lucy thought him rather dull. According to Madge he was suspicious of her friends, though she said he approved of Lucy.

His voice was indistinct, a little confused. She caught the words 'Terrible shock. Can't believe . . .'

'I don't understand. Is Madge all right?'

He was very agitated but tried to tell her again. 'Came home at lunchtime to see her. Discovered this morning she'd drained our joint account. All our funds. Lucy, she's taken all her clothes.'

'Where's she gone?' Lucy was aghast.

'Don't you know?' There was an edge of anger in his voice now.

'No.'

'She's always over at your house. Almost every day.

411

She's been hanging round that husband of yours.'

'What? Of course she hasn't. She's my friend.'

'Some friend. She's run off with your husband.'

Lucy thought her heart had stopped. She couldn't breathe, couldn't say a word.

'Are you still there?'

She had to choke the word out. 'Yes.' Her cheeks felt on fire.

'You must have known about them?'

'No!' It had never occurred to her. Madge and Wesley? 'No! Not Wesley.'

'He's still there with you, then? Is he?'

Lucy swallowed, her mouth suddenly dry as bone.

His voice was a hoarse whisper. 'Madge – she's left a note. She says she's gone with Wesley. There's no doubt.' His voice gathered strength. 'It's been going on for ages, I've known . . .'

Lucy felt weak at the knees. In the hall mirror she could see her face twist with anguish. She turned round and slumped against the table. She'd had a message from Madge too: 'Forgive me'. It took on a whole new meaning now.

Vic asked: 'Hasn't Wesley left you a note?'

'No.'

But had she looked? She'd eaten breakfast in bed this morning, then had a bath and dressed. She'd noticed no note. Wesley wouldn't just go off and leave her like this. Leave her and the children! He doted on the twins. But he wasn't at the factory. Nobody seemed to know where he'd gone. She felt sick.

'Goodbye,' she said hurriedly, and crashed the phone down to race upstairs.

She closed her bedroom door behind her, leaned against it and looked round slowly, her heart racing. There was no note. Not on his bedside table. She went to the door of his dressing room. Nothing on his tallboy.

412

Nothing propped up against his photograph of her and the children.

Perhaps he'd left it out of sight? He wouldn't want Mrs Judd to see it. Lucy tugged the top drawer of his tallboy open and froze. Usually it was stuffed with his socks and pocket handkerchiefs. Most of them had gone. Her heart missed a beat. His silver alarm clock had gone too.

She opened his wardrobe then. More of his clothes were missing. So was the matching luggage he'd given her as a gift on Christmas Day. He'd taken that! Lucy collapsed on the double bed they'd shared for the last two years and let the tears run down her face.

She couldn't believe that Wesley would go without a word of explanation or even goodbye. It hurt, it hurt like hell. She wanted him back with all her heart. She needed him. The children did too.

Wesley loved her. He'd told her so only last night. He'd given no sign of this. Or had he? She'd thought him distraught over Christmas, but had put it down to the trouble with Patsy. She thought he needed a rest, a good holiday.

Now she felt betrayed. The thought of him being with Madge made it worse. Made her burn with jealousy. Madge of all people! The two people she'd loved best preferred each other to her.

She'd relied on Wesley for so much. How was she going to manage without him? She caught her breath. Life as she knew it was collapsing before her eyes.

She sank down on the bed again in another wild fit of weeping.

Lucy heard the knock on her bedroom door. She sat up slowly, tasting the salt of her tears.

'What is it?'

'Lunch is ready, Mrs Spiers,' Nanny called. On days when a dinner party was being arranged, they usually ate a nursery lunch with Fay.

Lucy was shocked when she caught sight of herself in the cheval looking-glass. Her eyes were red and swollen; she looked terrible.

'I don't want any,' she called back. She felt as though her world had come to an end.

'I'll look after you all, my darlings,' Wesley had told her many times, trying to make his arms stretch round all four of them.

She'd thought they were happy together. Wasn't he always beaming at her and saying: 'We have the perfect marriage, Lucy, my love.'

And now he'd deserted her. She found it hard to believe. It had destroyed her pride and her self-esteem.

She felt frightened at the prospect of bringing up her babies by herself. How was she to manage? Where had she gone wrong? What was the matter with her?

The knock on her door came again. 'I said I don't want any lunch,' she flashed out in anger. All she wanted was to be left alone.

'I know.' It was Nanny again. 'There's a policeman here. An officer by the name of Byers.'

'What does he want?' It was an effort to keep her voice steady.

'He asked for Mr Spiers but I told him he wasn't here. He wants to talk to you.'

'Get rid of him. I can't possibly talk to anyone now,' she said, turning her face to the wall again. 'I don't feel well.'

Lucy stayed hunched up on the bed, crying, for what seemed like hours. It made her feel worse. She wanted Wesley back. Nothing else would ease the ache she felt.

She knew it must be almost teatime. She was feeling empty; she needed somebody to talk to, somebody who would help. She made up her mind to phone Patsy. She went to the bathroom, splashed cold water on her burning face, soaked a face flannel and held it against her eyes.

As she went downstairs, she could hear Nanny playing

the old upright piano in the playroom, and Fay jumping up and down to the music. Dancing, she called it.

Before she reached the phone, she caught sight of the dining table, set magnificently for dinner tonight. She jerked to a stop, sagging against the dining-room door. She couldn't cope with guests!

Wesley had deliberately pushed her into arranging this dinner party tonight, knowing that he and Madge wouldn't be here. She found that callous, unnecessarily cruel. He knew she'd be thinking of menus and table settings; that she'd be less likely to notice he was packing four suitcases with his clothes and belongings and taking them out to his car. That was why he'd done it.

She felt a rush of anger. And Madge? When she'd invited her and Vic, she'd said: 'Oh goody, you always put on a lovely meal.' It stabbed at her that Madge and Wesley must have planned this together. That it was her wedding anniversary made it worse.

She must cancel the other guests. The thought of facing them, of sitting six round the table instead of the planned eight, appalled her.

They were Wesley's friends and she'd have to tell them. That stuck in her throat. Where to start? Paul and Davina? She didn't know their number and couldn't remember their surname. She dropped the phone directory on the floor. Perhaps it was all a mistake? She had only Vic's word for it.

Madge and Vic knew Paul and Davina better than she did. She could ask Vic for their number, he wouldn't need to be told why. Lucy steeled herself. He wouldn't come, not after . . . but she'd make sure at the same time.

'Number please,' the operator said. Lucy gave it, dithering as she waited. Surely Wesley meant to come back? 'I'm trying to connect you.'

At last, Madge's husband lifted his phone. 'It's Lucy Spiers again, Vic. I just want to tell you that the dinner party tonight is cancelled. Not that you're likely to feel like coming . . .'

'What are you talking about?' He sounded irritable, confused.

'Have you forgotten? It's our wedding anniversary. You were supposed to be coming to dinner. It was Wesley's idea, anyway. It's cancelled.'

Another long pause. 'It's the first I've heard of it,' he said at last. It was the sympathy in his voice that made the tears start to her eyes again. 'Madge said nothing about it to me.'

She was shaking all over as she slammed the phone down. This was far worse than she'd first supposed. She had to speak to Patsy. She'd know what to do.

The front door bell was ringing and ringing. She groped her way towards it. As soon as she opened it, she felt Patsy's arms come round her.

'Thank goodness you've come,' Lucy sobbed.

'I've been meaning to,' her voice sounded strange, 'since early this morning. But it's been one thing after another.'

'Wesley's left me.' Patsy's new coat was soft against her cheek.

'Come on.' She felt Patsy urging her into the sitting room, closing the door carefully, sitting close against her on the sofa. Warm hands were holding hers.

'He's gone off with Madge.'

'With Madge?' Through a blur of tears she could see Patsy's astounded face. 'You mean . . . But that's not all he's done. He hasn't just deserted you.'

'Patsy, you've got to help me. I want him back. I want you to help me get him back.'

Her twin was staring at her open-mouthed, looking dumbfounded. 'No! No, that's the last thing—'

'You don't understand, Patsy. I need him.'

Patsy was shaking her. 'It's you who doesn't understand. He's stolen company money . . . the week's wages. He forged my signature . . .'

Lucy moistened her lips. Not Wesley! She felt as though a huge hole was opening up at her feet.

'There's got to be some mistake.'

'There's no mistake about this. He broke into the safe and into Kenny Hewitt's desk. He's bled every penny he could from the factory accounts. Even the petty cash from Miss Cropper's desk.'

Patsy's eyes were cutting through her like blue steel. 'This is a disaster for us all! It'll be touch and go whether we can survive. The company, I mean.'

'Wesley wouldn't ... Anyway, one week's wages – surely that won't make much difference? Mersey Antiques makes a good profit.'

'Lucy, he's brainwashed you. How many times have I tried to tell you? The factory's made a loss this year. Wesley's been taking our furniture all the time he's been working for us. Selling it as though it was his own. Grandpa noticed, he was worried about it. It was all coming to a head when he died. I've been trying to stop him ever since.'

That made her pull away, sit up straight. She was stiff with fear. This was worse than anything she'd imagined. Patsy was afraid too.

'I couldn't make you see what he was doing; you wouldn't listen. He's taken the profit made by the shops and the auction room. I thought at least we'd have those to set against the factory loss. I've been at my wits' end since Grandpa died.'

Lucy's cheeks were on fire. Patsy had tried to tell her, but what she'd suggested had seemed so outrageous ... Wesley not honest, taking things that didn't belong to him, greedy and underhand.

To her Wesley had been generous; he couldn't give her enough. He'd laughed off what Patsy was saying. She'd believed him. Well ... there had been moments when she'd wondered. Like the times he stayed out half the night without telling her where he was going.

At first, she'd found his attitude to money hard to understand. Gramps had treated it very differently. Wesley was perennially looking for more, but it seemed to drop into his lap. And then he spent it so freely, it was as though he didn't really need it at all.

There was a numb feeling in the pit of her stomach. 'You're sure? That Wesley . . .?'

'I'm certain.'

Lucy felt cold with shock, a little bewildered. She hadn't wanted to listen to Patsy. She'd wanted to believe Wesley.

'I had no proof. I just knew he was responsible. If I could have moved him out of the factory then, before he stole money from the accounts, it would have halved our loss. Now the police are looking for him.' Her voice had become a hoarse whisper. 'Didn't they come here?'

'The police . . .?'

'There's an aunt Rodney spoke of.'

'Aunt Ida.'

'Do you know her address? The police need it.'

'I must have it somewhere.' Lucy felt quite fuddled. 'I sent her—'

'Find it, Lucy. It's urgent. Don't you understand, we could be bankrupt? We could lose everything.'

It was sinking in. Feeling stunned, Lucy went to her desk. 'It's here.' She handed her address book to Patsy.

Patsy got to her feet. 'They asked me to phone it through.' Lucy could hear her doing it.

She felt sick, the room was spinning round. The rugs were making patterns before her eyes. This was dreadful. She'd thought nothing could be worse when she'd found he'd run away with Madge. But now . . . She covered her face with her hands.

'There's something else.' Patsy had come back and closed the door again. 'I hate to say this, Lucy, but shouldn't you check your private bank accounts? Wesley might have . . .'

'No, he wouldn't do such a thing!' It was outrageous to suggest it.

'I know Grandpa opened an account for you. Is there much in it?'

'He wouldn't touch that.' But until now, she wouldn't have believed he'd take company money.

'Do you have a housekeeping account too?'

'We had a joint account. Wesley said he wanted our family accounts to be open and above board. He was very generous, Patsy. Always buying things for me.'

She saw disbelief on Patsy's face. 'Come on, look out your statements and chequebooks.'

They were usually kept in the desk drawer in the study. She couldn't find them. Patsy was tipping everything out.

'Perhaps they're upstairs. Mine might be in my handbag.' She could see Patsy's face growing more concerned. She failed to find any trace of them.

'Let's go down to the bank before it closes. You need to find out where you stand.'

'Wesley couldn't take money from my private account. He'd ask me if he wanted some.' Lucy knew she was trying to convince herself.

'Did he ask you?'

'Occasionally.'

'You need to put a stop on the account. Now, as soon as possible. Come on.'

Lucy couldn't believe what was happening. It was horrible that Patsy should even think . . .

At the bank, Patsy drew her towards the counter. 'Ask how much is in both accounts,' she directed. 'Ask to see statements.'

The wait seemed long. Lucy could hardly breathe. She left it to Patsy and went to the door for some fresh air.

A few minutes later, Patsy came over to her. 'We're too late.' Her sister's face was stiff with tension. 'I'm sorry, we're too late.'

'What do you mean?' Lucy could feel her scalp crawling with fear.

'We're going to have a word with the manager. I'll ask him to call the police.' Patsy took her arm.

He was sympathetic. He showed her the cheque by which all funds in her personal account had been withdrawn only that morning. The signature on it appeared to be hers.

'Wesley's forged it,' Patsy murmured.

Even worse, he'd arranged a massive overdraft on their joint account just before Christmas. She had no money left at all and he'd left a debt in her name. She believed what Patsy was telling her now.

Lucy felt desperate. She was aching with horror at what was happening to her. From the bank they'd gone to the police station and she'd had to make a statement. Now Patsy was driving her home. She stared mesmerised at her twin's hands on the steering wheel.

'I thought I was a good wife. I thought we were happy.'

'Don't think about it now.'

'You've got to help me. There's nobody else I can turn to.'

'Of course I'll help.' A hand left the wheel to cover hers for a moment. 'I'll do everything I can.'

'I've been such a fool. I let him twist me round his finger. I gave him everything I had, body and soul. I turned my back on my own family, allowing you to become a victim as well. I've let you down. I've let him ruin the business.'

She heard Patsy sigh. 'Perhaps we can pull it round. I need to think. See what can be done.'

Lucy felt despair. 'What am I going to do?'

'We'll talk about that tomorrow. You've had all you can take now, and there are other things I must see to.' She turned the car into the drive.

'I'm sorry, Patsy. I've landed you in it, haven't I?' Tears were running down her face as she got out. She could hear Patsy turning the car round. She let herself into the house and raced upstairs to throw herself on the bed again.

She thumped her pillows. She was sickened by the sight of Wesley's pillows on the same bed and sent them hurtling across the room. She was furious with him, and even more angry with herself for being taken in.

She heard Patsy's footsteps coming upstairs. 'I couldn't leave you like this.'

Lucy felt her perch on the edge of her bed. 'Gramps warned me about him. Nanna warned me. You warned me.' She'd listened instead to Wesley, who said he loved her. 'I thought I knew better.'

She felt rage, hot and suffocating, rising in her throat. She was burning with it. She couldn't control this fever for revenge, any more than she had been able to control the floods of tears, the desperate grief. Grief that Wesley could deliberately do this to her and his children. For over three years she'd been bewitched by him, feeling love, warmth, adoration. And all that time he'd been manipulating her to achieve exactly that response. How could she have been so blind?

'He was a con man,' Patsy said kindly. 'He was good at making you believe.'

Wesley had had no pity for her. No gratitude for what she'd given him. He'd used her for his own ends. To offer everything as she had, to be used in that way, was the greatest blow she'd ever been dealt. Wesley had married her for her share of the business. Her money. He'd set her up from the word go.

Patsy was being diplomatic, careful not to say that in so many words, but it was what she thought.

'I hate Wesley.' She wanted to make him suffer too. 'I'd like to see him thrashed to within an inch of his life.'

'No, Lucy. Don't think like that.'

'You don't understand what it's like to feel like this. You're too level-headed, too good.'

'I understand. I felt just the same about Vereena. Rob told me she wasn't worth it, and he was right.'

She listened then to Patsy's voice, low and soothing, telling her how she'd thirsted for revenge too, and all Rob had had to say about it.

'Put Wesley behind you. Forget all about him. If you let yourself seethe like this, you'll be more likely to destroy yourself than him. It's good advice, Lucy. I took it. I want you to take it too.'

'He was all I asked of life, Patsy. I loved him.'

'I know. I don't know what else to say. I don't know any other way to help you. Forget him. You still have the children . . .'

'His children.'

'Lovely children. Come on, why don't you wash your face and I'll see about a cup of tea?'

Lucy sat up.

'That's better.' Patsy was smiling encouragement.

Her tears had given her puffy, prickling eyes again and had solved nothing. It was the sound of her twin sons starting to cry in the nursery that made her realise she'd just have to pull herself together.

CHAPTER TWENTY-SIX

For Patsy, it had been a terrible day. She'd come to work this morning thinking she knew the worst and had handled it properly.

It had been another ghastly shock to find Wesley had been several jumps ahead of her. She felt dazed and exhausted by the emotional impact.

'What's going to happen to us all?' Dadda had asked. 'The men want to know when they'll be paid . . . if they'll be paid . . .'

'They will.' She was grim-faced. 'Tell them they will. There's a sale today in the auction room. That will provide enough for this week's wages.'

'Their jobs,' Dadda said. 'They fear for their jobs.'

Patsy knew she was facing some hard decisions. She had no trouble taking the first. If she could manage it, Mersey Antiques was going to survive in the form Grandpa had left it.

How this was to be achieved she didn't know. It would need some hard thinking, and she couldn't do that now. She went to Kenny Hewitt's desk.

'I need to know exactly what the financial position is. What we owe and what we can expect to come in. Will you work out some figures for me?'

She couldn't stay in the factory any longer. Every face reflected mute sympathy. She felt drained, wrung out like an old dishcloth. She went back to the auction room. She wanted to be with Rob.

The sale was finished and the crowds were gone. He and the new man he'd hired were totalling up the receipts behind the counter.

'Come up and talk to me when you're straight,' she told him.

She went upstairs, put the kettle on to make tea, and sat down to wait for Rob. He understood better than anyone else how the business ran. He came bounding up full of energy she no longer had.

'How do you feel about working in the factory?' she asked. 'I need the best brains there. To help get it back on its feet.'

He was smiling at her. 'I'd like that. Always knew promotion would be there. I'll do anything I can to help.'

'I need to cut costs.'

'You'll be saving Wesley's salary, Rodney's too.'

'Yes, but it's hard to see much else. Grandpa ran the whole thing on tight margins. Kenny Hewitt's working out exactly where we stand.'

'He's good as an accountant.'

'He's flexible and keeps his head in an emergency.'

'Can run the auction room too.'

'We'll manage between the three of us,' Patsy said. 'We need to keep expenses down.'

'And sales up.'

'Come to the factory with me tomorrow morning. We'll sit down with Kenny and work out a plan.'

Patsy slept the sleep of the truly exhausted that night and felt better in the morning. It helped to know that Wesley had gone, and that everybody would be pulling with her from now on.

When Kenny put the figures in front of her, Patsy stared at them, appalled. The outstanding bills for wood and materials and power well outstripped cash that they could expect to come in.

'In addition,' Patsy said, 'we'll have to support Lucy

and her children.' They both looked at her as though she'd gone out of her mind.

'She owns half this business and has little else now.'

Kenny said: 'You'll need to find working capital.'

She'd already faced that. 'I'll ask the bank for an overdraft.'

'Borrowing costs money. Too much now will—'

'I know. Hopefully it'll only be short-term. I'll tell Lucy we must put the Caerns Road house on the market. She's a lot of expensive things there that can go into the shops. She's been left with personal debts to pay off.'

'The auction room is doing well.' Rob was frowning.

'So are the shops,' Patsy added. 'But the profit from them will be swallowed up by the running costs at the factory. The business is sound if we can keep it going and pay off the debts we've been left with.'

'What we need is a three-year plan,' Rob said. 'With hard work, care and thrift, between us we should be able to get it all back in profit.'

Patsy scribbled down what must be achieved in the first year and what they could leave to subsequent years. It was several hours before she was satisfied.

After Rob and Kenny had gone, Patsy sat quietly for a few minutes. It was possible that the company could come out of this intact, just. Now she had to get Lucy's agreement for their plan.

As she answered the telephone, Lucy tried not to look at her reflection in the hall mirror. She felt totally different: bereft and empty on the one hand, yet fuming and furious on the other.

She found it hard to believe that such a disaster had left her looking much as she always had. Paler, perhaps, with the corners of her mouth turning down.

'I want to come round.' Patsy's voice sounded cautious. 'To tell you what we've decided about the company.'

'I'm not going anywhere.'

'I'll come now then. We need to talk about other things too.' Lucy knew that meant her affairs.

Patsy looked businesslike when she came in with her briefcase. Lucy couldn't concentrate on all the details she was reeling off about the factory, and hardly understood the sheets of figures she was shown. What she did understand was that Patsy was taking steps in the right direction. She was doing her best to limit the damage and put things right.

'What we have to decide now, Lucy, is how you're going to manage.'

Patsy obviously expected her to have plans all cut and dried, but she'd never been much good at that.

'I'm afraid we can't support you at the standard you've grown used to.'

She found her sister's alert blue eyes going round the room, pausing on the more extravagant pieces of furniture. They returned to study her face. 'You'll have to cut down on expenses. Dadda and I live very simply. You'll have to do the same.'

'I'd come to that conclusion myself.'

'Good. Where will you make a start?'

Lucy shook her head. It was all too recent to make decisions. She was still hurting. 'I've asked myself that a thousand times since yesterday.'

'You won't be able to afford help in the house.' Patsy's voice was gentle.

'What?'

'Mrs Judd and Nanny. You'll have to tell them to go. There won't be any money to pay their wages.'

Lucy felt her hackles rise. She hadn't thought it was that bad. 'I don't know if I can manage by myself. With three babies . . .'

Patsy leaned closer to her. 'I don't know if I can do one half of the things facing me now, but I have to try.' She

426

paused to let that sink in. 'A nanny was always an in-
dulgence.'

'But Mrs Judd? She's always been affordable. Been here
for years. Nanna had her all the time I was growing up.'

'Before Wesley came. Before we got into this mess.'
Patsy's mouth straightened with determination. 'This
house will have to be sold.'

Lucy pressed her knuckles against her lips. She wanted
to scream out: 'No, not this house. I've never wanted to live
anywhere else.'

She knew she mustn't object. Daren't, because they
wouldn't be in all this trouble if she'd listened sooner.

'We need the proceeds to provide working capital for the
factory.'

Lucy was torn between anger and tears again. 'I have to
have a roof over the children's heads.'

Patsy's voice was sympathetic. 'If the business goes
bankrupt you'd lose it anyway. It's not a limited company.'

She was astounded. She knew that her mouth was
hanging open. 'Could it come to that?'

'If we aren't very careful.' Patsy's warm hand took hers.
'There's the flat over the shop in West Kirkby.'

'Over the shop?' That was an awful comedown. It stuck
in her gullet.

'In the High Street. But all round it's a middle-class
residential area. You'll be better there than between the
railway lines.

'You have your marriage settlement, Wesley couldn't
touch that. You'll still have the small private income that
provides. Grandpa gave me the same.'

Lucy burst out: 'I suppose you can live in comfort on
yours?' Up until now, she'd spent hers on clothes and
things for the children.

She saw Patsy blink in dismay. She said quietly: 'I was
thinking of cutting my salary. Grandpa was very generous.
I can manage on less while things are this difficult.'

That made Lucy feel guilty. She was struggling to contain her tears again.

Patsy was going on: 'But you have three children. It won't be so easy for you.'

'No.'

'Have you ever seen the rooms over the West Kirkby shop?'

'No.'

'I'll take you this afternoon. They'll need a quick lick of paint. Nobody's lived there for a while. The manager already had a house nearby and didn't want to move, and because the only entrance is through the shop, we couldn't rent on the open market.

'There is a bathroom, but it's ancient. I'm afraid you won't like it after living here. It's an economy measure, but it may not be for long.'

'How long?'

'Two or three years, say.'

Lucy swallowed hard. It seemed a lifetime.

'All this furniture is yours, of course, and it's top-of-the-market stuff. You must decide what you want to take with you.'

Lucy looked round helplessly.

'We'll put what you don't want through the shops. It should raise more than enough to pay off the overdraft Wesley's left you. You might even have some left. Damage limitation. I'll put this house on the market tomorrow.'

Lucy blew her nose. The future sounded dire.

'About Mrs Judd and Nanny? You'll tell them now?'

Lucy quaked inwardly at the thought. Could she face them? She still felt raw inside. But if she didn't face them today, it wouldn't be any easier tomorrow.

'I'm no help to you, Patsy. I'm sorry.' She swallowed uneasily. 'Worse than no help, a liability.'

'No, not that.' Patsy was smiling. 'But it has to be done. Shall we call them in here now and get it over with?'

She had to agree. She got up and summoned Nanny, but she let Patsy explain the position to her and ask her to accept a month's notice.

Nanny was uppity. 'I was offered a job in Geneva just before Christmas. I turned it down. I didn't want to put you to any trouble.'

'Why don't you ask if the offer's still open?' Patsy suggested. Lucy was glad of her help.

'I thought I was settled here.'

'I'm sorry, but that's the way things are.'

'I'll pack my things and leave today,' she told them, before stalking out with her nose in the air.

Mrs Judd was a different matter. 'I was afraid something like this . . .' She was shaking her grizzled head. 'So much expense, so much waste . . . There was no sense. I didn't think it could last.

'Mr Ingram left me a legacy. I'll be all right. It's just that I've lived in all my life. It'll take me a bit to set up on my own.'

'You can take the furniture in your bedroom,' Lucy told her. Wesley had spent nothing on the staff quarters.

'Could I stay on with you for a month or so? Until I find the right place. Without payment, I mean.'

'The flat has three bedrooms,' Patsy said, 'but it's very small.'

'Of course.' Lucy felt a flush of relief. 'I'll be glad to have you, you know that. Stay on as long as you like.' If she had Mrs Judd, she'd be able to manage. It was being entirely alone with three tiny children that scared her.

'Your family's always been very generous.' Mrs Judd looked as upset as Lucy was herself about their changed position. 'Shall I make you a cup of tea?'

'Yes please,' Patsy said.

As she went through the door, little Fay came running in. She was in tears because Nanny was leaving. Lucy pulled her on to her knee. She had to show Patsy that she could cope. 'Instead of tea, what about a glass of champagne? Nothing like it as a pick-me-up.'

'Lucy! Champagne!' Patsy turned on her, horrified.

'There's a whole case in the pantry. Wesley ordered it for our wedding anniversary.'

'How much of it have you drunk?'

'None yet. Yesterday was the day, and—'

'Send it back.' Patsy was grim-faced. 'You can't afford champagne. Neither of us can. Debts are stacking up against you, Lucy. This is one you can avoid.'

Lucy cuddled Fay more tightly, feeling her confidence crumble.

'You're right, of course. Sorry, tea it is. Champagne is what Wesley would have suggested. I'll have to get out of the habit of thinking like him.'

'All this luxury.' Patsy was frowning. 'It's unreal. What's wrong with the world everybody else lives in?'

Lucy shivered. There hadn't been much reality about her life with Wesley.

It was early in January and Vereena was upstairs getting ready to go out to the shops when she heard Bernie answer the front door. He came running up to the bedroom they shared.

'It's the rent man.'

Vereena felt a shiver run down her spine. She'd been dreading this moment, but at least she had Bernie here by her side.

'Could you help?' She deliberately kept her tone light, as though it was of no consequence whether he did or not. Bernie was still in his dressing gown. He was slow to find his wallet.

'I'm a bit low at the moment.'

Vereena went stiff with shock. Outside in the street a car backfired. Her heart was hammering.

'Hadn't you better go down and talk to him?'

She went very slowly and carefully. The stairs seemed to swim before her eyes. The uniformed collector was already in the hall with the front door shut behind him.

'Good morning, Mrs Gripper.' He always started by being affable. 'Got your rent book handy, have you?'

He always said that too. She took it from the drawer in the hall table. Her hands were shaking with fear.

'Twenty-five weeks overdue.' He looked at her over the top of his half-moon specs. 'You'll have to pay something this month.'

They needed more food. Bernie had a big appetite. She'd planned to buy a nice piece of pork.

'I could give you two pounds,' she said, taking the notes from her purse.

He took them. 'I'll write this against your arrears, but I'm afraid it isn't enough. You got our letter? Explaining that with arrears like yours, you must pay what's due for the current month as well. Otherwise your debt is building up.'

'I'm sorry . . .'

'Another six pounds is the minimum I can accept.' His voice was loud and echoing through the house. Bernie must be able to hear what was going on but he was skulking upstairs, leaving her to deal with it. Just as he'd always left her to deal with anything unpleasant.

'I warned you last time I called, and we sent you a letter setting it all out, that if you didn't pay this month, we'd have to send in the bailiffs.' He looked severe now.

Vereena ran upstairs to Bernie. 'I've got to have more. Just another ten pounds. Help me, Bernie, please.'

He was dressed now, staring out of the bedroom window, jangling the change in his trouser pockets. 'I can't.'

'Just some of it then, so we don't get the bailiffs in. There's still stuff worth having here.'

He pulled his trouser pockets inside out. 'I'm down to my last ten bob. Sorry, Vee.'

She couldn't get her breath. Couldn't believe it had come to this. Her heart was hammering wildly. She let out a wail of protest. 'But I thought you had plenty of money.'

Bernie's voice was agonised. 'I thought you had.'

She stared at him, still unable to believe her ears. 'You said you'd gone up in the world.'

'So did you.'

Vereena's mouth was dry. She'd heard from others about what happened when the bailiffs came in. She'd hoped to avoid the experience.

'Come down and help me get rid of him,' she implored. 'Please.'

Bernie was doing it with bad grace, coming down slowly behind her, whistling tunelessly to show that the problem was none of his making.

She asked: 'When will you be getting paid again? If I promise faithfully to pay next month, he may let me off.'

The rent collector looked serious. 'You've had two warning letters. My orders are not to let it go any further. But if you promise to take six pounds down to the agent's office this afternoon, then it might be put off until next month.'

She turned back to look at Bernie. If only Harold were still here . . . 'Just six more pounds, Bernie, please. That's all it would take.' Surely he had that much?

Vereena saw that he'd gone pale. Her last hope faded. Nervously she moistened her lips.

The rent collector said: 'I'm afraid that's it, then. You had the warning.' The door slammed behind him.

Vereena sank down on the stairs, put her hands over her face and rocked in agony.

'Come on, Vee.' He was urging her to her feet. Putting an arm round her shoulders, drawing her into the sitting room. 'We had a good Christmas, didn't we?'

'Oh, for God's sake! What does Christmas matter now? I'm going to lose all this.' Fear was twisting her gut. She

432

let out another wail. 'Why didn't you tell me? I thought you had plenty of money.'

His voice was stiff. 'This isn't my problem.'

Vereena screamed at him: 'The bailiffs will take everything I have. It's all your fault.'

'Come off it. I didn't know anything about this.'

Bernie never took responsibility for anything. He hadn't changed; she'd been a fool to think he had.

'But you're going to Bristol. When did you say you opened there?'

He had the grace to look shamefaced at last. 'I'm not going anywhere, Vee. Polly Jones and me, well, we had a row. We've split up. If you must know, she's got herself another fella. He's the new Hank Hodges.'

She stared at him open-mouthed, unable to believe what she was hearing.

'You mean, she's thrown you over? But you can go solo, you've had years of experience. You know the ropes now.'

'I can't. Polly made all the bookings. She's the lead singer. Without her, I'd be no good.'

Vereena was choking with resentment. 'You can't even blow your nose without help. You never could manage anything. Always hanging about for somebody else to do things for you.'

She was at fever pitch. 'You were looking for a meal ticket all the time. You came back to sponge on me,' she accused. 'You stopped me putting my plans into action. I'd have done a moonlight flit from here by now. Taken everything worth having with me. Now I've nowhere to go and there's no time left.' What had she been thinking of?

'Vee, you're my wife. We've been married twenty-three years.'

'You great oaf. I'd never have had you back if you'd told me this.'

'That's why I didn't.'

'You let me spend good money on you. I've nothing left. What am I going to do now?'

Vereena felt rage, hot and suffocating, rising in her throat. She could feel herself burning with it. Couldn't control it.

'You're nothing but a parasite. Always have been, all your life. I don't know why I've put up with you.'

'Take it easy, Vee. Don't get scratchy. We'll be all right.' Bernie's easy-going manner inflamed her more.

She'd always had a volatile temper; now it exploded. 'I hate you. I could have avoided all this. Why did you have to turn up?' He'd lulled her into a false sense of security.

She wanted to make him suffer too. She was beside herself, in a frenzy. She snatched up the poker from the hearth. Bernie was going to pay for what he'd done to her.

'We'll find a couple of rooms. Didn't I see a board up opposite?' He was at the window, lifting the curtains.

Hardly knowing what she did, she brought the heavy steel poker down across the back of his head.

He reeled, screaming, clutching at the curtain to keep himself upright. 'Hold on . . .' She saw terror in his eyes and knew she had the upper hand. He tried to get away from her. It made her lose all reason.

'You lily-livered coward,' she screamed as she followed him up the hall. Sizzling fury was taking her over. He was trying to turn the Yale lock on the front door when she lifted the poker again and with all her strength brought it down against his head.

Bernie's screams went on and on, tearing through her, but she was determined he'd never cheat her again. He wrenched the door open and fell down the front steps as she raised the poker for yet another blow. She was going to thrash the living daylights out of him this time.

He collapsed at the feet of the milkman, who was coming with her usual two pints. She caught a glimpse of his horrified face before he dropped the bottles and ran.

Bernie lay in a heap on the frosty path, a pool of blood spreading round his head. She flung the poker down after him and strode back indoors where it was warm.

It seemed no time at all before the ambulance came and took Bernie away.

Surely she hadn't hurt him all that much? All these policemen looking at her strangely like this. Treating her like a hot potato. Wanting her to go down to the station. She knew from that and the awful ache in the pit of her stomach that she'd done a most dreadful thing.

It was Saturday. When the factory closed at midday, Patsy called into an estate agent's on the way home to put the Caerns Road house on the market.

When she reached the auction rooms, she saw her father watching for her at the window. As soon as she went upstairs she knew something else had happened. Alma was not making any effort to get a meal on the table. They both looked stunned.

'More bad news, I'm afraid,' Dadda said soberly. His face was white.

Patsy pulled up short, her coat only half off. Had Wesley come back? Another fraud come to light?

'It's Bernie. The police have been here.' The story of how Vereena had killed him came spilling out.

Patsy shivered. 'It's horrific.' She'd always been scared of Vereena, known she had a vicious temper. She shouldn't be surprised.

'When I was young, she was always belting into me.' But to beat Uncle Bernie to death with a poker? She hadn't believed her capable of that. It sickened her.

'She's in police custody,' Dadda murmured. 'Very fitting.'

'It's where she put Gran,' Patsy said slowly.

'She's done for herself this time. She deserves all she's going to get.'

Patsy warmed her hands on the cup of tea Alma poured for her. Rob had been right. She hadn't needed to seek revenge. Vereena now had her just desserts; it was better this way.

She shivered again. 'It's a macabre end.'

As the days went on, Patsy could see a change in Lucy. She had deep violet shadows under her eyes, which gave her an ethereal air and made her even more beautiful. She was beginning to make plans for herself.

She said: 'I've got to come to terms with this, haven't I?' Patsy was thankful to find her sister had resilience.

Lucy had never learned to drive properly and had been in the habit of ringing for a taxi if Wesley were not available to chauffeur her. So when Patsy was due to pay another visit to the West Kirkby shop, she asked her sister if she'd like to go with her.

They'd already gone together to measure up for curtains and carpets. The flat had been redecorated; colour-washed throughout in pale cream. That had been Lucy's decision. She'd taken out the samples of wallpaper, paint and curtaining she'd used for her last two homes and after a few moments tossed them away.

'If we take some curtains with us, I could put them up. It'll make it easier on moving day.'

'A good idea,' Patsy told her. She'd gone round the Caerns Road house to help decide which would be the best to take. But Lucy had made her own decisions.

'I took a tape measure to the carpet squares upstairs. Come and see. This one would fit the living room.' They were in a spare bedroom that had never been used. 'I'll take the curtains too.'

'Ideal,' Patsy approved. 'You chose them to complement each other. They'll all fit; the windows are smaller in the flat. What about the other rooms?'

Patsy was going out to her car with her arms full of

books and magazines when she saw Colin Courtney on the next-door drive.

He came to the wall to ask: 'Is it right, Lucy's moving out?'

'Yes.' She hesitated a moment. 'You heard what happened?'

'Awful for her. We're all shocked. When's she going?'

'Saturday afternoon. We can use the company van then. Rob's going to drive it, and Dadda's coming to help.'

Colin peered at her through his owlish glasses. 'Could she use another hand? I'd be glad to do what I can.'

'I'm sure she could. Why don't you ask her?'

As she got into her car, Patsy saw him coming round to ring Lucy's doorbell. She hoped things would work out. Colin had always had a soft spot for Lucy.

The next day, in West Kirkby, Patsy spent an hour working in the shop, checking through the books. When she went upstairs, the curtains had been put up with the help of one of the shop girls. Lucy was going from room to room, making notes of the furniture she wanted to bring with her. Patsy was relieved; in Lucy's position, this was what she'd be doing.

She said: 'You're going to be all right. The flat will look nice.'

Lucy seemed doubtful. 'Better than I first thought, but it's very small.'

It was bigger than the rooms over the auction room. Patsy had thought of moving here herself, but it would have put distance between her and Rob. She'd have seen less of him.

'Not like Caerns Road.' Lucy's mouth had tightened. 'If only Wesley hadn't—'

'You must forget what he did. Forget vengeance, Lucy.'

'Easier said than done.'

Patsy said gently, 'You know what happened to Vereena. I count that as divine justice. She's getting the treatment she meted out to Gran. Perhaps one day you'll hear of some dire misfortune overtaking Wesley, then you'll be glad you didn't poison your mind with hate.'

Lucy went to the window and looked down on the busy street below.

'Wesley was offering what I wanted. I took it with both hands. It was life through rose-tinted glasses and I never questioned how he achieved it. I should have. I knew Gramps didn't live like that, or you.'

'You'll be fine. With Mrs Judd staying for the time being, it'll help you settle in.'

'Yes. Thanks for sorting me out, Patsy. I don't know what I'd have done without you.'

'I'm your twin. Who else could you turn to?' It gave Patsy a warm feeling that she had. It was what she'd always wanted.

'I've grown up,' Lucy admitted. 'I think it's taken me longer than you.'

Patsy agreed. 'When Grandpa died, I put on a spurt. I had to manage on my own then.'

'You always managed. I envied you, so independent and capable.'

'I envied you, Lucy. You attracted love.'

'Attention, not love.'

'I always wanted to attach myself to you, share everything with you. But so did everybody else.'

'And I trusted them all.' Lucy smiled. She seemed almost her old self. 'At least I know who I can trust now. You above everyone else.'

Patsy was very touched. For the first time, she felt really close to her twin.

'We should dovetail together. Like Grandpa's furniture.'

'In future,' Lucy said, 'we will.'

* * *

Rob drove the old bull-nose Morris into the Mersey Tunnel. It had been dark outside, and Patsy was blinking in the sudden yellow glare. Now that she could see Rob, she couldn't take her eyes from him. She noticed the way his russet hair curved into his neck, and how his dark eyes concentrated on the way ahead. Noticed too that he wore the new blue tie she'd given him for Christmas.

They'd been to a house sale near Southport and she was well pleased with the things they'd bought. All the way home she'd been very conscious of his presence beside her.

They came out in the dark streets of Birkenhead. The wind was gusting against the car, flapping its canvas hood. It was a blustery evening. More than blustery, almost gale force.

'It's been a lovely afternoon out,' she said, huddling deeper into the old leather seat. 'A treat to get away from the factory.'

She saw Rob's face turn momentarily towards her, then, without a word, he changed direction. They were no longer heading home. 'Where are we going?'

She saw his lopsided smile. 'Somewhere different.' He headed out along the New Chester Road, and then cut down to the river and parked.

'There's something I want to say to you, Patsy. It can't wait any longer.'

In front of her, Patsy could see huge white-topped waves racing in to crash against the stone promontory. Years ago, New Ferry pier would have stretched out into the river here. In the blustery wind and with the high tide, water kept splattering on the windscreen.

Rob was taking her hands in his. 'It's time you thought of yourself. And perhaps time you thought of me, too.'

Patsy was contrite. 'I've not been much fun over the last few months, have I?'

'I've found pleasure in being with you. You know that.'

'I've been horribly preoccupied.'

'Not surprising, with all the problems you inherited.'

'I'm sorry.'

'You do feel better now?' His finger was lifting her chin. His breath was warm against her cheek.

'Better now Wesley's gone.'

'I meant, now you've sorted out what needs to be done for the business.'

'Much better about that too. It's a load off my mind.'

'We'll pull it round. You mustn't worry about it.' He kissed the tip of her nose.

'I don't know what I'd have done without you, Rob. You've been a rock.'

'I haven't done much.'

'You have. More than you realise.' She'd drawn strength and confidence from him.

'I've tried to put ... other things to the back of my mind, but now ...'

'I know. You keep asking me to come and choose an engagement ring, and I keep putting you off.' She laughed. 'That's no way to show ... You're right, it's high time. Tomorrow, definitely, we'll do it.'

He was gathering her into his arms. 'Let's forget about getting engaged.'

'What?' She drew back to look at his face, unable to believe he meant it. His dark eyes were full of love.

'Let's get married instead. Now, as soon as we can. Why put it off any longer?'

Patsy's heart lurched with pleasure.

'If we're to tighten our belts over the next three years we'll need some compensation.' She could see his lopsided smile getting wider.

'It's a lovely idea.' She laughed. 'Let's do it. We won't need to spend a fortune on the wedding. Dadda and Alma didn't.'

'Patsy, there's nothing the matter with my personal

440

finances. I've been saving up for ages with this in mind. We could rent a little place of our own.'

Patsy sighed happily. 'I can think of nothing I'd like better.'

'Good. I've seen just the place. Nothing grand. Ideal for the first year or so. You were so engrossed, I decided I'd better go ahead on this.'

Patsy tightened her arms round him. 'I do love you,' she whispered. 'Always have.'